Secret of *le Saint*

Secret of *le Saint*

Sarah Kneip

Secret of le Saint

Cover Design by Kathryn Massmann

First Printing: 2019

ISBN 978-0-359-52652-9

Published by Sarah Kneip
125 First Street SE
Richmond, MN 56368

Printed in the United States of America

To the Sacred Heart of Jesus

"O God, you are my God—
For you I long!
For you my body yearns;
For you my soul thirsts,
Like a land parched, lifeless,
And without water."
Psalm 63:2

Special thanks:

To Margaret Bussell: your help in editing this novel of its plot problems, narrator glitches, run-on sentences and punctuation errors is immensely appreciated. Your logical and constructive criticism was such a great help and motivation to continue to rewrite. I truly cannot thank you enough.

To my mom and dad: Dad, all your technical advice helped make my hero sound like a capable mechanic which was very important to me. Mom, this book is the fruit of all your "unclears" during high school. And thanks to both of you for patiently answering all my "way back when" questions.

And to Kathryn; your talents in both photography and design always amaze me. Thank you for sharing them with me.

Prologue: 1951

A man stood in the shadow of an awning in front of Halverson's Plumbing. He wore no overcoat but didn't feel the chill of the mid October Minnesota weather. It was late, nearly eleven at night and the air was cold; even without the cigarette he was smoking his breath would have been seen. He stood stationary, not leaning against the building; never leaning from one foot to the other; only smoking and waiting. If anyone else had been out on the street that late, his presence would not have been thought suspicious; he was the owner of Halverson's, or one half the owner. The better half, his brother always teased. But Bart Halverson didn't think so. Tonight he felt a failure.

His eyes moved back and forth, as he watched for signs of life at Davidson's Apothecary. Its structure stood just a block up and on the opposite side of the street. There was a light on somewhere towards the back, and occasionally Halverson saw the form of a man moving around inside. He waited and smoked.

Halverson had never seen his profession as anything to be ashamed of. He was proud of the Plumbing business he and his brother had built up from nothing. He was just trying to make a living, raise a family. But it was proving an impossible task. A task that he felt incapable of completing, despite the business's success. Accusations filled his head; that he wasn't good enough, that he could never be successful; he could never build a life for his family in his hometown.

But he *was* a good man, he argued back at the accusations in his head. His wife told him so often. His customers praised his work and his honesty. Honesty. He grimaced. Where was that honesty tonight? He studied the glowing end of his cigarette for a moment. But these circumstances…This wasn't what life was supposed to look like. He had come back from a War six years ago and joined his brother, and they had done well. But always there had been the strangling claws of Ricardo Balestrini. First had been the intimidation; a red line drawn on a map of the City of Gilmore with instructions that the Halversons were forbidden from servicing customers outside the territory Balestrini had assigned to them. When Halverson's brother had done so anyway, he had met with an "accident" and his arm was broken. His brother had never told Bart what had actually happened, but he insisted they follow Balestrini's rules. Bart had tried to keep up as much service as he could handle, but they lost nearly half their customers for a full two months, many who didn't come back afterward.

Next, came the required protection fee.

Protection, Balestrini's wiseguys had said. Protection from what, Halverson had had the nerve to ask. They said, you just never knew what kind of hoodlums came into a neighborhood. He had refused, despite his brother's insistence that they pay. He had taken care of his family and business thus far, he would take care of things from here on out.

Only he hadn't been able to. The day after the first offer for protection, he had found a shipment of new plumbing fixtures damaged. Damaged by strong arms, Bart's brother had insisted, that were sure to be able to damage much more than plumbing fixtures if they didn't submit. The hoodlums had even covered their tails nicely. The shipping company had a signed receipt saying he received the load undamaged…only Bart hadn't signed it. But the police said the signature looked like his signature to them, and unless he wanted to take it to court…

The Halverson brothers didn't have money to go to court. And the next time Balestrini's wiseguy came to offer protection, they did what they had to do and paid the protection fee. A protection fee—the irony being that the hoodlums that were protecting them were the hoodlums that were threatening them—and the frustrating thing about that was there was nothing he could do about it except pay the fee.

So Halverson sat in his office at his desk, month after aggravating month, and paid the fee for protection. He sat there week after week and watched those same thugs visiting the neighboring businesses, extracting the same fee for the same circular-reasoned protection. And he laid there night after night, wondering how to get out from under the thumb of the ring leader named Balestrini.

But there was no answer and there was no place to seek an answer. He needed a miracle. But he didn't believe in miracles anymore. He had spent some four years, fighting his way across Pacific Island jungles believing in miracles, only to come home and find his hometown overrun by its own dictator. He had learned that there were no such things as miracles.

Halverson's Plumbing had been doing well, supporting two families, but they couldn't make the payment anymore. His wife was sickly. Tuberculosis was running her down, and how could he pay for her to go away to a sanitarium? How could he care for the children by himself? It would be a hard job doing it without the extra cost to Balestrini; but with the cost, it was impossible. So poor Rose stayed and coughed so that it made his heart bleed as much as her lungs. Halverson had tried to see clearly through the fog of worry that made him sick to his stomach each time he tried to sleep at night. He was a responsible and honest businessman. He would even be successful if he just didn't have to make the extra payment. So he had made up his mind that *this* was the only answer. And tonight was the night. There was no delaying, no turning back.

At last Halverson saw Davidson walk out the front door of the Apothecary and head up the street in the opposite direction. Halverson crushed the feeling of being pulled in two directions; as if he were caught in an actual vise that was tearing him between saving his family and the immoral thing he was about to do. It wasn't immoral, he argued. Everyone knew Davidson was on Balestrini's payroll; why Davidson even treated Balestrini's thugs when they were sick. Halverson was simply taking back what had been taken from him. He wasn't stealing to become rich, he was stealing what was his, what he needed to survive, for his wife to survive.

Halverson threw the cigarette to the pavement and crushed it out with his heel as he stepped out from under the awning. The street was dark, only a light at the corner illumined the intersection, but he walked away from the light, and towards the Apothecary.

He drew up to the door of the building and almost as a continuous movement of his last step, he turned; and thrust an elbow through the glass of the door. His face registered no pain, though clearly from the blood on his shirt sleeve he had cut his arm. He reached inside and unlocked the door. He entered quickly and made his way around the counter, the eerie lighting from the street lamp illuminated everything in grotesque and looming shapes, but he took no note of anything. He opened the cash register and began to take out the money and stuff it into his pockets. He knew that Davidson always kept extra cash, in a zipped pouch beneath the counter, in a box marked Peppermint. He reached for it and began to empty its contents into another pocket.

"What do you think you're doing, Halverson?" a voice asked conversationally from the curtained backroom.

Halverson hesitated. He should have known that there was a reason Davidson had been so late. But he hadn't guessed it when Davidson had left alone. He looked up, and found the silhouette of a man watching him, the shape of the man's white Panama glaring in the light from the backroom. He didn't need more light to identify him, he knew the voice. He knew it from too many meetings and payments. He couldn't hesitate long. "Duncan. Busy fixing books, are you? I should have known you would be here *working* late, as they say."

"Put the money back, Halverson. I've already called the police," the man informed him, still calmly. He even leaned against the frame of the doorway.

"I can't do that. I have more need of it than you. Besides, it's probably mine anyway."

"Put it back."

"Try to stop me," Halverson threatened, and drew a .38 from the waistband of his trousers.

"I don't have to," Duncan replied coolly. "The police will. It will look so much better in the newspapers, you know?"

Halverson lowered the gun. He had no need of it. Duncan wouldn't use force; he had called for backup. Halverson hurriedly finished stuffing the money into his pockets.

He moved around the counter and Duncan did nothing to stop him, he only said, "You won't get away with it, Halverson."

"Who will stop me? The Police? Or Balestrini? But then it's all the same isn't it?" He turned and instead of going to the front door he made his way to the side door that he knew would lead to the alley.

He shouldn't have been concerned about Duncan but he was. He knew what the man was, what he was capable of. And he watched him as he went out the door instead of watching his exit.

He moved up the alley, but there was a police officer already blocking his escape. The policeman called, "Stop. Police." But Halverson knew he couldn't stop. He needed the money. His brother—their business—needed it. They didn't need a man in jail, they needed help. Halverson was supposed to have helped by doing this. He should have known better. But there was no turning back.

He started up the alley in the opposite direction when a second police officer blocked his exit. This one he recognized. Halverson knew him and he saw by the look in the cop's eyes that he recognized Halverson as well. This one was a good cop, Halverson thought. Halverson stared at him, and when the officer met his gaze there was almost a wounded expression in his eyes. His only two escape routes were blocked; there were two guns trained on Halverson and his own was still in his hand. The officer spoke, "Halverson, what are you doing?"

Halverson eyed him warily, caught between what he had to do and what he couldn't undo. He remained stationary, his mind racing but coming up with no solution.

The officer pleaded, "Don't do this, Halverson. Put down the gun."

Halverson could see real compassion in his eyes. Finally, he lifted his gun slightly, his finger off the trigger, and flipped its grip upwards, holding the gun toward the officer. He said nothing, but his eyes pleaded with the cop to take it.

The officer looked relieved and took a cautious step forward when a shot rang out. It took Halverson a moment to realize what had happened. It couldn't have been his own gun that fired and the officer in front of him looked just as surprised as he was. Then the extreme pain that he felt intensified and he felt himself falling, falling and he couldn't stop himself and he couldn't reason out what had happened.

"He was surrendering," the officer in front of Halverson yelled.

Halverson heard the other insist, "He would have shot you!"

But he couldn't think of anything. Only that Rose was at home coughing and in pain and he couldn't help her. He felt hands on his body. He wished they wouldn't touch him, his whole body was aflame. He felt so much pain as the hands rolled him over that he wanted to scream but he didn't make a sound. He opened his eyes, tried to focus on the policeman kneeling above him.

"Halverson, you'll be fine," the officer lied to him. "Look at me, you're gonna be okay. Open your eyes, man. Don't go to sleep."

Halverson did as he was commanded. He wanted to tell the policeman that he was a good man. The determination in his usually strong voice only came out in a whisper; "I didn't…I had…oh, please, don't tell Rose what I've done. If only there had been another way…it hurts so bad."

The officer leaned closer, whispering, "Why'd you do it, Halverson? Why?"

Halverson's eyes rolled back in his head, but then he focused again, "I had to. Somebody had to. Don't you know? Somebody had to do it…Rose…"

Halverson tried to finish saying what was so important but the words refused to come to his lips. He could feel his body getting heavier, feel the officer's arms straining to hold him up. But Halverson couldn't help him. He wouldn't be able to help anyone. Not his brother, not his sweet Rose, or their children, and not the officer, who held him as he lay dying. He couldn't help any of them. He had failed once again. He had failed.

Chapter I:
August 1954

Danny Navarone pulled himself out from under the Dodge pickup. He rolled off the creeper, pushed it out of his way, stood up and wiped his hands across his coveralls and grinned. Made him feel good to finish a job. He turned to face the other mechanic. “You finished?” he asked.

Greg looked up from sizing the spindle for the new kingpin he was replacing in the automobile. “Do I look done?” he growled above the whir of the Sunnen hone.

“No, I guess not,” Danny admitted. He walked over to the hoist and lowered the Dodge to the floor. “Leonard still here?” he asked above the noise of the car hoist’s hydraulics.

“Yes, I’m here!” came a loud reply through the open office door.

“I finished the Dodge,” Danny yelled back. “You can call Bender and let him know he can pick it up whenever he’s a mind to.”

A man much older than either of his mechanics came from the office. Leonard Spry had passed sixty a few years previously. Danny was a little more than half his age, and seemed to be almost twice his height. In reality, Leonard had topped off at five feet three inches, and Danny stood a full foot taller than his boss. "Christopher Columbus!" Leonard exclaimed, as the car settled on the cement floor of the garage. "How did you do that? I told Bender it wouldn't be ready until Thursday."

"I told you," Greg growled from the bench—Greg growled everything, it meant nothing as to how he felt about the information, he just growled. "You've got the two best mechanics in the world!"

Leonard glanced over at him, "Yes, I know. You've been telling me that for the last two years. I just get confused as to who you think is the other half of the two best mechanics."

"Funny man," Greg growled, and turned the spindle over before slipping it back onto the hone.

Danny unzipped his coveralls.

"I've a message for you," Leonard informed him. "Your sister called."

"Is that the message?"

Leonard made an annoyed face and continued, "She just said you should stop by the rectory after work."

Danny raised an eyebrow but didn't pause in removing his coveralls. He kept his voice neutral as he replied, "Oh? Any reason?"

Leonard shrugged, "Said something came up and she was gonna leave your kids with Father Navarone until you got off."

Danny shook his head, as he slipped into his jacket and zipped it. "At the rectory? Why didn't she leave them with my sister Sharon?" Danny muttered more to himself than to the two men present.

"Don't ask me. I just delivered the message. Well, I'll see yah in the morning."

"Don't forget to call Bender…"

Leonard shook his head, "Think I'll wait until morning. If I do it now he'll expect us to get things done that fast every time…"

Danny laughed, but just shook his head as he put his fedora on. "It's your garage." He looked back at Greg. "Don't hone your fingers off," he said by way of a salutation.

Greg growled a muffled reply and continued to move the spindle back and forth on the hone.

***

Danny slid onto the torn leather seat of his '42 pickup and slammed the door. He had to slam the door on his Chevy, otherwise it didn't latch closed…sometimes slamming it didn't even help and it would swing open on a left-hand turn. He'd have to fix that, but a mechanic's automobile was always the last to be fixed.

Danny leaned over and pulled an envelope from the glove box. It was thick but he knew it wasn't thick enough. There was only three hundred and thirty dollars in it, and Father Clancy had said he needed four hundred and fifty dollars by tonight. It would have to do. There hadn't been any opportunities to pick up the rest. He slipped the envelope into the breast pocket of his jacket and drove away from Leonard's Garage.

Despite his annoyance that his kid-sister had left his kids at the rectory instead of with their older sister Sharon, Danny had to admit it was convenient the way the situation had worked out. He had needed to stop by the Rectory anyway, and Debbie had unconsciously played right into the set up. Worked out nice.

Debbie had been nanny to his kids for the last two years; before that their sister Barbara had helped him out for the first year after his wife's death which had been just three years ago last April. Sometimes the unorganized way Debbie got things done threw his life for a loop compared to Barbara's minute by minute planning, but this time it had fit into the schedule perfectly. Not that Danny was worried about anything. That he knew of, no one was even remotely suspicious. Still it was useful when situations helped to throw off any potentiality of suspicion.

He parked his truck on Sibley Street. The entire length of the block was occupied by the buildings of St. Francis de Sales Parish. On the corner stood the two-story, Parish school built of red brick. A large open playground lay sandwiched between the School and the Church. The Church was built of fieldstone, with twin steeples. It had been built nearly sixty years previously from the generosity and labor of the area settlers, many of whose descendants still populated the pews.

Danny walked alongside the Church to the back, where the Rectory stood, a large building in its own right, but still dwarfed by the enormity of the Church. Unlike the Church, this structure was built of wood. The paint of the window frames was chipping, and Danny remembered his mother's admonition to get his brothers together and repaint them…but he only remembered when he was walking *up to* the rectory and never when he was leaving.

Today, however, he didn't notice the chipping paint or even the windows as he approached the house. He noticed instead a young woman standing under the elm tree which filled the yard between the Rectory and the Church.

She looked rather picturesque standing just beneath the branches of late-summer green leaves. They seemed to reach down to caress the small navy blue hat that nestled atop her wealth of curly blonde hair which she had attempted to pin up all around it. Her dark blue suit was tailored perfectly for her attractive figure. She wasn't looking back at Danny which was why he allowed himself to study her as he approached. She was, rather, intently watching something up in the tree. She was so intent, in fact, that she didn't even hear him approach her from behind. Before he reached her side, she even reached up toward the branch as if she would attempt to climb it; which would have been an interesting sight considering the A-line of her skirt and the two-inch heels of her pumps.

"I don't mean to intrude, but may I help you with something?" Danny asked as he drew up beside her.

She turned slightly, obviously surprised at the sound of his voice. "Oh, goodness!"

When she looked up at him, she had to tip her head almost as far back as when she had been looking in the tree, her two inch heels doing very little to decrease the distance between them. Danny felt a small smile pulling at his lips, though he stayed it, recognizing the anxiety in her face.

She recovered her surprise and gasped, "Yes, yes, please help. There's a little girl stuck in this tree. She can't get down."

The woman's eyes shown a rich brown and so large he was almost sorry to look away. But he did, even though he knew what he would see. He wasn't as worried about the girl in the tree as he was interested in the one beneath it. Yet, he looked up and saw, as he expected, his own 5 year-old daughter Janey, perched on a sprawling branch of the elm tree, her blue floral dress wrinkled and pulled up slightly, revealing a skinned knee.

The little girl, in her turn, wasn't as concerned about the skinned knee as she was about the man standing below her. She watched her father with eyes almost as wide as the woman's below, although hers were a deep blue like his. Janey smiled tentatively. "Hello, Daddy."

Danny ignored the greeting and looked back at the woman, whose anxious brown eyes met his own. "She's not stuck," he informed the woman, "she's hiding."

"Whatever from?" the woman asked, having relaxed slightly at the girl's greeting of her father.

Danny glanced back up at the little girl but continued to speak to the woman. "She's hiding because she knows she's not supposed to climb trees in her dress. Because little ladies don't climb trees in dresses, do they?"

The little girl shook her head of curly pigtails and then grimaced as they tangled in the leaves and branches about her head.

"Are you coming down?" he demanded.

Janey thought for a moment, "Maybe I should wait, Daddy. Maybe you want to say hello to Father Clancy first," she offered.

Danny folded his arms across his chest. "Let me rephrase that. Come down, Janet Marie. Or I'll come up to get you."

Janey shifted and turned her little body around to climb down, revealing to those below exactly why little girls shouldn't climb trees in dresses.

The woman beside him did her best to muffle her laugh, and murmured so only the father could hear, "Perhaps, little ladies should be made to wear bloomers." When Danny glanced at her, her eyes were laughing, although she was doing a very fine job of not smiling. "Just in case the temptation to climb a tree should come upon her without warning," she explained.

Janey had turned round once more and tucked her dress beneath her, looked at her father, and ordered, "Turn around, please, Daddy. You're a boy."

Danny, who had been well aware of this fact for some years before his daughter had arrived in the world, obliged her sudden care for propriety, shook his head and covered his face with one hand, while continuing to watch his daughter's descent between his fingers.

Janey was an expert tree-climber, thanks to the strict tutelage of her two older brothers. Descending trees, however, seemed to be her down-fall, literally. This time, Danny—though he wouldn't have said as much out loud—was proud that she almost made it down on her own. Unfortunately, as she stretched out a tentative foot for the next branch, the hem of her dress caught on a twig above, setting the poor girl off-kilter. Danny stepped in to catch her, and held onto her a moment, until Janey's own stunned grasp of his arm loosened. He set her down.

She looked down at her dress and saw the torn hem. "Oh no," she cried in devastation. "Oh, Daddy! My favorite dress is torn."

"Reason number two why you shouldn't climb trees in dresses," was his unsympathetic reply.

But the woman knelt down and expertly fingered the fabric and lace. "It's not so bad," she assured Janey. She lifted the lace. "You see? Look. The hem has just been pulled out. Why, your mother can stitch it back together in no time, I am sure."

Janey, still distraught, put two chubby hands to her cheeks. "Oh no," she cried. "I haven't got a mother," though clearly the tears were for her dress lost for want of a mother, and not the lost mother.

Danny stiffened. He hated this moment with strangers. Now would come the over-dramatized version of "*you poor darling girl, No Mother*!" He couldn't bare it. Janey had very few memories of her mother, and she never mentioned the fact for sympathy, only as a point of fact in any given conversation; yet the response they gave always made her squeamish about strangers, especially woman.

But much to Danny's surprise this woman did not respond in the way he expected.

Still fiddling with the torn lace and un-done hem, she said casually, "Well I haven't one either. So I learned to sew it myself. You must have an aunt or a grandmother who can help you sew it, haven't you?"

Janey looked up at her and nodded excitedly, "Yes, Auntie Debbie could do it."

Danny, relieved at the turn in the conversation, refrained from disillusioning his daughter with the truth that Debbie was much too flighty to sit still long enough to hem her dress. But his mother would fix it with no signs of the tear remaining.

"Well, there you see. All's not lost. It will be just as good as new." The woman smiled brilliantly to match the girl's excitement. "But you will have to be careful not to tear it further, or it shall be more difficult to fix," she admonished gently.

Janey nodded emphatically.

But the woman obviously knew children well enough to realize that the implied direction hadn't sunk in. "What I mean is, no more climbing trees," she stated bluntly. Then she stole a glance up at Danny, and whispered with a sly smile, as if Danny couldn't full well hear what she said. "At least for today."

Danny grinned. She was a rare woman, and she couldn't know how much he appreciated her not fawning over Janey. And to the surprise of both Danny and the young woman, Janey threw her arms around the latter in an impetuous hug. It unsteadied the woman's already precarious crouching position and both the girls nearly toppled over, but for Danny putting out two strong hands to steady them. He disentangled his daughter and helped the woman to her feet.

"Careful, Sunshine," Danny cautioned. He waited while Janey gave his leg an embarrassed hug, and hid her face at her suddenly uncharacteristic forwardness. He patted her back. "It's alright. Go find those two renegade brothers of yours. I'll say hello to Father Clancy and then we'll go."

Janey turned to go, then spun back. "Good bye and thank you very much." Then, with a very unladylike swoosh of her short skirt, she took off running to the other side of the rectory.

Danny realized he still held the arm of the woman and he let it go quickly, apologetically. "I am sorry. I…that is, she doesn't take to strangers at all…I don't know where that came from."

"Don't apologize. You have a very sweet daughter, even if she is a bit of a tomboy."

Danny gave a half shrug, "She loves her ruffles and lace, as you can see. But she also considers it a priority to keep up with her brothers. Which causes many interesting situations around the place." The conversation seemed to be dying off and Danny motioned toward the rectory. "Were you headed to the Rectory or the street when you were waylaid by the damsel in the tree?"

"Rectory. To see a priest."

"Good place to find one."

She laughed, "I suppose that was superfluous."

He put a guiding hand on her elbow to politely walk her to the sidewalk. “A bit, but I’ll forgive it, just to hear you say that word without stumbling over it as most of us would.”

“Sorry, I guess I ramble…”

“Dad! Dad!” excited yells interrupted the woman as they reached the top of the rectory steps.

Two boys rushed up the porch steps behind them, taking the steps two at a time, which the elder did smoothly while the younger brother made an expert job of falling *up* the steps.

Josiah, who was nine, reached his father first. “Father Larson’s dog had puppies! Can we have one?”

Toby, who was six-and three quarters years old added, “Father said we could have one! And we should do what Father says, you always say…”

Danny laughed at his son’s logic, “We’ll see,” he began but before he could continue the rectory door opened and an elderly priest came out.

“Well, well. What a prefect family we have here.”

The woman blushed, and opened her mouth to object. But the priest caught himself. “Oh Daniel!” he exclaimed. “I’m sorry. I was distracted. I didn’t think of what I was saying. And Miss Edwards, good to see you again. Well, well, come to collect your raga muffins no doubt, Daniel. But I think Mrs. Larson has some cookies in the kitchen that must be sampled before you leave. Why don’t you go and ask her politely if you may have the job of sampling them. Daniel, he’s in the study if you need to see him and Miss Edwards, why don’t you, you look flustered, why don’t you come into the sitting room and we can chat. Did you have something to see me about…”

The children hurried to the kitchen and Danny smiled as he made his way down the hall to the study. Father Larson had to be close to 70 years old and although sometimes things got mixed up coming out of his mouth, they were always perfectly orderly in his mind, such that he could organize anything and anybody in a matter of seconds, before anyone else knew what was happening.

Danny knocked on the study door and then went in as Father Larson had suggested. Father Clarence Navarone leaned over a ledger, pencil in hand, the glow of the lamp or the balancing of the books making him squint as he figured some cipher in his head.

His dark hair, a hint of grey beginning at the temples, was exactly like that of the man standing in the doorway. When Danny closed the door, the priest looked up with two blue eyes that also matched the man watching him. And the grin that spread across his face was almost a mirror reflection of his brother's grinning down at him. "Dan'l. I didn't hear you come in. When did you get here?"

"Just a bit ago. Don't worry, Father Larson has everything organized and everyone in his place."

"That's Father Larson," Clancy agreed, rising from his chair and stretching out a hand to his brother. "The ultimate organizer. A hard man to follow."

"You do alright. Sorry about Debbie unloading the kids on you. Sometimes I don't know if Debbie thinks before she rushes around and does things."

"Oh, she thought this one through alright," Clancy countered as he walked around his desk. He was just as tall as Danny, possibly a half inch taller, although that was debatable and had been debated many times in the first half of their 34 or 35 years of existence.

Danny raised an eyebrow. "She thought *what* through?" he asked a little suspiciously.

"She gave me instructions…"

"Instructions? I don't think I want to hear the rest of this."

"I don't think you do either," he smiled, "But I gave my word as your brother and a priest—apparently one or the other wasn't good enough—that I would talk to you."

"What are we supposed to talk about?"

Clancy was silent and didn't meet Danny's gaze for a moment. The mood changed and Danny felt instantly on edge.

His brother looked up finally, "Your kids need a nanny."

Danny raised one eyebrow, and asked uncertainly, "What's the matter with the one they have?"

Clancy hesitated. "Debbie wants to start nursing school…this fall."

"By this fall, you mean in a couple weeks when the program starts?"

"In just over one week, when the program starts," Clancy

corrected.

Danny frowned, "Why so suddenly?"

Father Clancy rubbed the afternoon stubble on his chin and explained softly, "It's not suddenly, Dan'l. She's waited two years, since high school, for something she's wanted for six years."

Danny didn't respond. He was thinking of other things that had happened in those years. He nodded slowly.

Father Clancy watched and waited, knowing his brother's thinking habits.

Finally, Danny raised his head, "You're right…*she's* right. She should go this fall." He said the words, knowing full well that his simple admission gave him much to think and plan and figure out. How many things would have to change in their household…but he wouldn't change his mind. He knew he had to let her go. Then his brow wrinkled. "She had to ask *you* to get *my* permission?"

Clancy gave a laugh and shrugged, happy for a lighter direction of the conversation. "Oh you know, true to the mold of the Navarone women, never go straight to the source, and always have someone else do the dirty work for you."

Danny grinned, "Seems to work for them."

"Guess that's why they keep using the tactic. One of these days the Navarone men are going to catch on."

"Yup, one of these days," Danny agreed. He reached into his coat pocket and handed his brother the envelope he had pulled from the glove box. "And one of these days the Navarone men won't be so short on cash…but today is not that day. We're short. 'Bout a hundred and twenty to be exact. And I've got nothing. Don't get paid till Friday…"

Clancy shook his head, in surprise not disgust. "I know you told me never to ask you. But just where do you get this money? And how come sometimes when I ask you, you seem to have a bottomless pit and sometimes you come up short? I'm not complaining, mind you, it just does seem like a confusing conundrum to me."

"Don't ask me, Father," Danny replied, a smile pulling at the corner of his lips.

Father Clancy smiled outright. "I know. I won't…But if you just told me something, perhaps I could help."

Danny looked at his brother knowingly. "If I told you *something*, you would probably tell me to stop doing the something and then nobody could help."

"Oh. Well then, I guess it's better the way it is."

"Yes, it is. Just trust me, Clancy."

"I do. I just also worry."

"For my soul or my body?"

Clancy furrowed his brow. "Which should I be worried about, Dan'l?"

Danny rubbed his own stubbly chin. "Probably both," he acknowledged.

"That's what I was afraid of." Clancy shrugged, "Don't worry about being short. I'll raid the rectory poor box or hock Father Larson's bicycle."

Danny laughed. "You won't get any hundred and twenty for that rusty contraption, it's older than Father Larson. I'd better give you my truck…"

Clancy raised one eyebrow, and gave his own laugh, much like his brother's. "You think you can get a hundred and twenty for that? I'd have better luck with Father Larson's bicycle."

"Hey! At least she runs."

"Yah, on a downhill slant."

Danny would have defended his Chevy, only Greg had had to give him a push to get it started just yesterday, so he really had nothing to go on.

"Well anyway, I'll see Flags on Thursday. Hopefully we'll figure something out then."

"Sure. You'll think of something," Clancy agreed, and watched as his brother turned to leave the study. "Dan'l."

"Yah?"

Clancy looked down at the desk drawer where he shoved the envelope of cash. "Just be careful, will yah? Whatever you figure out…be careful…I…"

Danny nodded. "Sure, Clancy. What's the matter?" he gave a grin. "It's just bowling," he laughed.

Clancy laughed too, then cleared his throat. "Dan'l, I'm serious.

I'm grateful for what you're doing…how you're helping…but I don't want to be grateful at your funeral. Those kids, they need you, they need you a lot."

Danny met his brother's gaze. "I know that, Clancy. I'm not going to do anything that would hurt them. But I also can't just stop what I'm doing, can I?" He wasn't really asking if he could; he wanted Clancy to admit what they both already knew.

Clancy's brow furrowed. "The first time you came to me with money three years ago, you gave it to me to give to Rose Halverson, after her husband was killed. I didn't know what we were starting. Sometimes I still don't know what we have started. But you aren't bringing me money that you were saving for a new truck anymore, Danny. And it makes me wary."

"Of me?"

"Of what I may be encouraging you to do."

"We, none of us, can stop what we started, can we? As long as what we are doing is helping…if we stop, then somebody will get hurt. And then who'll be to blame." Danny shook his head. "If there was gonna be a quittin' time it was before we started on this merry-go-round."

They were both silent.

Clancy closed the desk drawer and they both stood for several moments lost in their own thoughts. Clancy broke the silence. "Yah, but how long does it keep going, Danny? Forever?"

His brother didn't answer at first and Clancy looked up to search his face. And it was only then that Danny muttered, deep in thought, "Till we figure out how to stop the merry-go-round altogether."

For a moment they stared at each other. Both realizing the danger that that would unfold. Fear was somewhere in both their eyes, but neither acknowledged it in his brother's look.

Danny spoke first. "Until then, we just keep doing what we're doing…" his voice dropped slightly, and so did his gaze. "It's the only way to deal with what happened. Can you understand that? Tell me you understand, Clancy." He looked back up.

Clancy nodded slowly. "Sure. Sure, Dan'l, I understand. I just don't want to lose you, too. I don't want to see them lose you. So, just be careful; that's all I'm saying, lil' brother."

Danny nodded in agreement and opened the door to end the conversation.

"That and…find a nanny," Clancy continued with a grin.

Danny laughed, grateful for the lighter topic. "Find one? What do you want me to do, look in the want ads?"

"What's wrong with that? Lots of people look for work in the want ads…or an employment agency?"

"Clarence, you want me to find some stranger off the street, open my house and just leave my kids with her?"

"Yes. I do. That's how it's done, Dan'l. Not everyone is an aunt or a grandma or a third cousin once removed. Some people start out as strangers and then they become friends…or at least acquaintances."

Danny shook his head, but acknowledged, "I know. I know that. It's just hard, Clancy. You know how hard it is for Janey to warm up to someone. How am I supposed to rope someone off the streets and expect her to adjust?"

"You're not giving your children away, Dan'l. You're just getting them a nanny for after school, and to do the laundry and cook."

Danny shook his head. "You make it sound so easy. But it's not that simple."

Clancy folded his arms, "You want me to do it for you?"

"No, I don't."

"Then do it yourself, little brother…or Debbie will have *my* neck."

Father Larson stood outside the door and spoke, "Sorry to interrupt this loving parting, Father Clarence, but it seems there's been a little confusion. The lady, Miss Edwards, said she was told by a friend to see *you*. Apparently I won't do. She said a friend told her that her brother is a priest at St. Francis and he could help her."

"Well, finally one of our four sisters is trying to run your life instead of mine. Thank you for the reprieve. I'm leaving now."

"I'll see you this weekend," Clancy said as a farewell as he walked toward the sitting room.

"Of course you will," Danny agreed. "Unless you're not going to Mass on Sunday?"

"Funny man. You can see yourself out…don't forget your three packages. Our housekeeper, good woman that she is, doesn't mind feeding them cookies but she would frown upon bedding them down for the night."

Danny raised an eyebrow, "You make 'em sound like cattle."

Father Clancy ignored the last comment and walked down the hall toward the sitting room where Father Larson had left Miss Edwards. He found the young woman, whom he had never seen before, waiting patiently. "Good evening. I am sorry to have kept you waiting," he greeted.

She stood to greet him, but paused in extending her hand to him, her mouth half open with unspoken words. "Well I never!" she exclaimed in annoyance.

Father Clarence stopped abruptly at the greeting. "You never what?" he asked, when she didn't continue.

"You! It's a pretty cheap trick. And I don't think it's funny at all."

"Trick?"

But despite his confusion she walked past him to the hall.

Father Clancy followed on her heels, confused and slightly worried.

"Miss Edwards, please tell me…"

The woman had stopped dead in her tracks as she entered the hallway. Clancy saw his brother coming down the hall with his brood. Danny held Janey by one hand and had a hand on the collar of Toby's coat guiding him down the hall, with Josiah following behind, tossing his cap in the air and catching it.

Clancy gave a small laugh of relief. Conundrum solved. Once again, someone had mistaken the brothers for one another.

Miss Edwards was still figuring it out in her mind, but as soon as Clancy saw the look on her face, he knew what had been going on in her mind. Miss Edwards gasped at Danny and said unthinkingly, "You're in street clothes."

Danny could have smiled at the woman—she was easy to smile at—but instead he looked down at himself, wondering if his attire could be offensive in some way. Perhaps he had forgotten to take off his grease-covered overalls. But he was dressed in his dickies and coat, minus a tie, but he didn't think a lack of tie could be *that* offensive. "As a matter of fact, I am," he agreed. "Is there a problem with that?"

"But you," she turned back to the man who had followed her from the sitting room. She looked from one to the other, then her gaze dropped to the children surrounding Danny.

Janey smiled at her.

Miss Edwards stated lamely, "You're *not* a priest?"

"Another one of those superfluous statements?" Danny asked, before agreeing. "No, I'm not a priest."

"Oh. No, what I meant was," she looked at Father Clarence, "you *are* a priest."

"Yes, I am a priest," Father Clarence acknowledged, struggling to keep a straight face.

"Oh dear," Miss Edwards put a gloved hand to her quickly coloring face. "I've never been so embarrassed. I saw *him* outside with his kids…and then you came into the room…and I thought he…I mean you…went into the other room and just…put on a cassock?...as a joke or something...oh dear this is so embarrassing…"

"Not as embarrassed as you are going to be if you don't stop talking…" Danny murmured, a smile pulling at his lips once more.

"It's just…"

"You don't have to explain, Miss Edwards," Father Clancy assured her. "It happens quite often. I was just unprepared for it, as I had no idea you had met Dan'l earlier or I could have explained before this escalated."

"I did escalate it rather quickly," the woman admitted sheepishly. She looked again from one to the other, "I can't believe it. Are you twins?"

"No," both men said in unison. Danny continued, "Well, Irish twins, if you will."

Father Clancy laughed but answered the woman more directly. "We were born in the same year, but eleven months apart."

Miss Edwards, mortified by her earlier reaction to the priest, tried to redeem herself and demanded unreasonably, "Why do you have to look so much alike?"

Danny felt sorry for her embarrassment, though she looked pretty with her cheeks so pink. "It's not unreasonable to be confused by our looks. It actually happens quite often; sometimes even by extended family members," he assured her. When she wasn't placated, he tried to offer some consolation, "Well, I tried to rearrange his face a couple times when we were young, but it didn't work."

"Yah, because I rearranged yours right back," Father Clancy laughed, but he stopped suddenly at the astonished look on the young woman's face. "What's the matter?" he asked. "Didn't you know priests fought with their brothers too?"

"No. I mean, of course, I suppose so. But I've just never seen two people look so much alike. How, how is that even possible?"

"There's more, our brother Mark could make us a trio," Father Clancy offered.

Janey piped up, "But you can tell Uncle Mark apart because he has a funny eye."

Danny tried to shush his daughter with a free finger, but the information was out and he had to explain, a smile tugging at the corner of his mouth, "He has a glass eye."

"He lost it in the War," Toby added, determined to get his two cents into the adult's conversation if his sister had been allowed to.

"Well, we have just become a wealth of information," Danny sighed. "So I think it is time for us to leave. Say your good-byes," he ordered hoping no one would offer more information than necessary in leaving politely.

Chapter II

Debbie Navarone stirred the kettle of green beans she was preparing for supper. She was in a hurry and didn't seem to notice that the boiling water splashed over the edge of the pot. She rushed from the stove to test if the fresh bread had cooled enough to cut. At just twenty years, Debbie was a flurry of dark curls, bright skirts and excited exclamations. Danny told her she moved so fast she was never there to hear her own words after they vacated her mouth. Father Clancy told her she had better slow down, because he knew for certain her angel couldn't keep up and he, so it was said, had wings.

Debbie was significantly more scattered this evening. She had been so thrilled when Danny told her to take the opportunity to join the Nursing Program that she couldn't contain her enthusiasm. She had a million things to prepare in order to leave, and a million things to wrap up here so she could leave. And primary on her mind this night was finding a replacement for her current post as nanny to her niece and nephews.

Tonight was Thursday and Danny always went bowling on Thursdays. Which meant that she wouldn't have the entire evening, as usual, for meandering the conversation to the subject and outcome of which she wanted her brother to be convinced. Tonight, she would have to have it out and settled by six thirty, before he left at a quarter to seven, which meant suppertime was the only moment she would have to broach the conversation. Supper was hardly the time with the kiddos around to be sure her conversation would be followed through to her determined end, but it was all she had.

She pulled the bread knife from the drawer, remembered the roast in the oven and whirled around toward the oven. Danny, coming thru the door from the hall, caught her and stopped the knife from doing any serious damage; "Hoh, hoh, hold on! I said you could go to school. No need to become violent," he laughed, knowing full well, she was distracted more than ever and vaguely wondering how this temperament was going to successfully play out in the nursing profession.

"Oh good, Danny, You're home."

"Yes, I am," he agreed, taking the knife from her grasp and walking past her to cut the fresh bread.

She followed through on checking the roast. "I talked to Mother Mary Rose today."

"And she changed her mind, she can't take you into the nursing program?" Danny teased.

Debbie laughed. "No. She said everything is set. Mom and Dad will drive me up on Labor Day and I can settle in. Classes begin the day after. Oh Danny, I'm so excited. You have no idea."

"I have a slight idea, Deborah," Danny said wryly. "As the last two days, every other phrase out of your mouth is, 'I'm so excited.'"

She laughed, leaving the open oven to throw her arms around her brother. "Oh, I love you so much! I am just so excited!"

Danny laughed, "You left the oven door open."

"Oh, who cares!" she exclaimed and rushed back over, took the roast out and closed the door. "But Danny, there is something that I need to talk to you about."

"Sure." He put the cutting board full of sliced bread on the table and motioned to the roast. "Are we eating that or are you leaving it on the stove?"

"Yes, of course," she grabbed the roaster with two pot holders and Danny brought the pot of beans. "But wait, you aren't listening. About the kiddos. I had an idea. I know this girl…"

"Girl?"

"Lady, I mean. She's older than I…"

"Oh, older than you" he feigned surprise.

Debbie slapped his arm lightly. "Be serious, Daniel. She needs work and I thought she would be perfect with the kiddos…"

"So you just went ahead and hired some girl off the street?"

Debbie pursed her lips, and tilted her head, "Don't be silly, Danny, you know me better than that. She's a friend of mine, sort of…I mean I met her…"

"Ten minutes before you hired her presumably."

"I didn't hire her," she insisted. "I just asked her if she were interested in work."

"Debbie, you ask a stranger if they want a job mowing your lawn or washing a car. You don't ask them to care for your children."

"I didn't offer her the job. I asked her if she wanted an interview…besides Clancy met her too."

"That's a reference? Clancy knows her? He knows a good many people that I would not trust with my children."

"He knows the Bishop."

"He also knows several guys at the State Reformatory in St. Cloud. I don't consider knowing Clancy a very good reference point, Deborah."

"Danny, you're not being fair. Will you let me tell you about her?"

"My supper's getting cold. Were we going to eat this, or just admire it? I'll start cutting the roast. Call the kids in, will you?"

The conversation wasn't going as planned at all. If she didn't speak her peace, her brother would leave for bowling before she had even broached the subject, let alone gotten the response she wanted from him. Once the kids were present, she would have less freedom to talk. "Danny listen, first."

Danny folded his arms. Clearly, he wasn't going to get his supper until his sister had spoken her piece. "Shoot."

Debbie, surprised that he was giving her his full attention and not sidestepping the subject was-for once in her life-almost speechless and all of her plotted conversations were lost to her tongue. She grasped the most concise and straightforward point of the matter. "Don't you think Miss Edwards would make a wonderful nanny?"

Danny's brow furrowed. "Miss Edwards?"

"Yes, you know, JoAnna Edwards?"

"I don't think I do. Should I?"

"Well, yes, Danny. Didn't you meet her at the rectory the other night…"

Connecting the pieces, Danny smiled slowly at the memory of the Clancy-Danny mix up. "Oh yes, I did, sort of. Not really a formal meeting more in passing…" Another connection formed in his mind and his brow furrowed. "You mean; *the other night* when you conveniently sent me to the rectory for a meeting that you set up. Is that it?"

"Ah…what…what do you mean?" Debbie asked fidgeting with her apron.

Danny's brow furrowed deeper, and his voice gained an annoyed edge. "I mean, you didn't really need to rush off the other evening when you left the kids in a tree at Clancy's…"

"In a tree?"

"…What really happened was you found a woman who needed a job and you contrived to give her one. Did Clancy know about this plot?"

Debbie sighed. "I guess not."

"You *guess* not? What does that mean?"

Debbie took a deep breath and then in a voice of full resignation, she began. "Well, I met Miss Edwards at church after Monday morning Mass. And she mentioned that she was looking for work, so I mentioned that my brother was the parish priest. I suggested that she come around to the rectory later and speak with him. You know, that he might know of people in the parish who might be hiring…it's all true! I mean he knows lots of people and he's done it before; recommended people to look for work here or there…" She threw up her hands in exasperation. "Only I thought that if you were also there, and she mentioned needing work, and gee, I really wanted to go to school this fall. And well, I thought maybe you'd let me go easier if you had a replacement already in mind…and that Clancy would think that she would be great to watch the kiddos, and he was gonna mention my going to school to you and maybe he would also mention Miss Edwards to you and you would think that was swell and everything would work out…"

"Just the way you wanted it to," Danny finished for her.

"That's not what I was going to say,"

"But it fits the bill more or less."

Debbie shrugged. "She is very nice."

Danny glared at her, and Debbie grimaced, an attempt at a smile. "Supper's getting cold," she informed him, "I'll call the kids." She sidestepped past him and leaned out the back door, "Come and get it or I'll throw it out!" she yelled to the children.

Danny picked up the knife and took a little of the aggression he felt out on the roast.

Grace was said and the children shared their adventures as they passed the food and served themselves. Danny was lost in his own thoughts and Debbie tried not to worry what they might be as she passed the bowl of mashed potatoes to Josiah. She didn't like to anger her brothers; even though she had six of them and they were never all angry at her at once, being the youngest she didn't like it when any one was ever mad at her.

"Gary Patterson broke his leg yesterday," Josiah informed the table. "He had a big cast and it's as hard as steel. You can hit it with a stick and nothing happens."

"Josiah Michael, you did *not* hit Gary's cast with a stick, did you?" Debbie exclaimed.

Josiah's eyes widened, "No, I didn't. But Jacob did. And it didn't do a thing! Aunt Debbie will you be able to make a cast like that after you go to school?"

"I expect so," Debbie started to reply.

Toby interrupted, "You're leaving?"

"Yes, Tobias, I told you already," Debbie explained when Danny didn't stop his son from interrupting the discussion. "I'm going to go study with the Sisters to be a nurse."

"Just like Uncle Chuck," Janey exclaimed happily, through a mouthful of buttered bread.

"Uncle Chuck's not a nurse, silly," Josiah laughed. "He's a doctor."

"Yup," Janey agreed as if her brother had just confirmed her statement instead of contradicting it.

"Why can't you go to school at our school? We have Sisters

there!" Toby asked.

"Because I have to go to the Saint Cloud Hospital School of Nursing to be a nurse. Not an elementary school."

"Won't you come back?"

"Of course, silly," she assured him ruffling his already messed hair. "But it's a three year program. I'll be back for visits, but not to take care of you guys."

"Won't you miss us?" Janey asked suddenly less interested in her bread.

"Of course, I will, Janey. It will be three torturous years away from everyone…"

"You'll only be an hour away, Debbie," Danny finally stepped in, as he caught the buttered bread that Janey dropped. It landed upside down in the palm of his large hand and he had to whip butter off his hand before he handed the bread back to his daughter.

"Yes, and I can't come back every evening and fix supper if I am an hour away, can I?" Oh, her impetuous self had caught her again! Just as her mother kept warning her it would. Debbie met Danny's glare only for a moment and then distracted herself by pouring Toby a glass of milk.

"But who will be here when daddy's at work?" Janey cried to the table.

Danny smiled reassuringly, "We'll find somebody, Janey. Don't worry. Maybe Aunt Barbara will come."

Janey shook her head knowingly, "No. She can't. Grandma said, 'cause another baby is coming, that she won't be able to."

"That's what Grandma told you, huh?" Danny looked at Janey, who nodded, her eyes widening with the knowledge. Danny sighed, "Well, don't mind what Grandma or Aunt Debbie says. We'll find somebody."

"That nice lady that we met at Father Clancy's could come and take care of us," Janey suggested.

Danny's brow netted and he shot a glance at Debbie. She shook her head and lifted hands palm upward.

"She was funny!" Toby laughed. "She thought Daddy was uncle Clancy."

Josiah shrugged, "It's not that funny. Lots of people think Daddy is uncle Clancy or the other way around. Isn't that so, Daddy?"

Danny acknowledged that as an aside, but he was more interested in his little's girl's seemingly uninitiated request. "Why do you want her to come, Janey?" Danny asked slowly. "You don't even know her."

Janey looked around the table suddenly bashful as all eyes were on her. She shrank a little in her chair. "She was nice," she murmured, "And she knew how to fix my dress."

Danny could agree on both points, but she was prematurely silent and he prodded, "Anything else?"

Janey looked a little more bashful and then suddenly a spark lit her eyes and she exclaimed, "Toby said she was sure pretty and when he grows up he's gonna marry her."

"I did not!" Toby flared, when his brother burst into laughter.

Danny held back a smile, while he quieted both boys. That wasn't the information for which he had been fishing. "I meant, I think there's something else you wanted to add about Miss Edwards, not about your brothers."

Janey looked back down at her plate. "Someone else has to take care of us because Debbie is leaving."

"Yes?"

She squirmed in her seat. Finally relenting to her father's continued stare, she exclaimed with an outburst, "Well all those other ladies always act so silly and squishy and tell me I'm a poor deer because I haven't got a mother! I'm *not* a poor deer, am I Daddy? Deers have antlers!"

Danny smiled at his daughter's defiance and her misunderstanding. "No, Janey, you aren't a poor deer," he assured her.

She looked very relieved to hear it and continued a little less perturbed, "And that lady, she didn't have a mother either and she wasn't a poor deer, just like me."

He patted her cheek. "Just like you," he assured her.

Janey grinned. "So she can come instead of those other ladies, right daddy?"

He didn't answer and Debbie rushed in without thinking once again. "That would be perfect! See the kids even like her, Danny! What could be better…?"

"Deborah!" he stopped her with the word and a glare. "It isn't your place to make this decision. You're going to school. We got along here before you came…"

"Yes, but before I graduated and came, Aunt Barbara was only just married, and no babies and before that Lilian was still here."

She stopped abruptly, this time her impetuousness had caused her to flounder colossally. She hadn't meant to say it so flippantly, as if Lilian could help that she wasn't here anymore. But Danny didn't acknowledge anything; that she had spoken the last sentence or the name of his deceased wife. He focused on his supper for a time, as if the conversation were over…a little as if it had never taken place. The boys could feel the tension in the air. Their mother was talked about often in stories and happy memories, but not in heated arguments. When the adult conversation of nannies did not resume, they reverted to the one about Gary Patterson's broken leg, which was much more interesting if they did say so themselves.

Supper had been cleared away and the children were all off playing in the last few moments of daylight when Danny found his sister in the living room, leaning over the phonograph. She glanced up, "Danny, there's still something wrong with your turntable."

"Sorry," he gave a half-hearted apology. "I'm going out…"

"I know. Bowling," she interrupted, as she raised the arm of the phonograph and peered at the needle. "And you will be back late," she recited, "and I shouldn't wait up and I should make sure Janey stays in bed and doesn't fall asleep in the hallway waiting for you…I know, Danny."

He paused a little longer in the doorway. "Debbie?"

"I know," Debbie interrupted again, putting a hand to her head. "Supper's episode was my fault. I was just trying to help, but I stuck my foot in where it doesn't belong."

One eyebrow rose higher than the other, as Danny asked, "Just your foot?"

Debbie gave a smile, grateful for her brother's teasing. She placed a hand level with her hip, with a questioning look.

"Closer to it," Danny agreed. "But that wasn't what I was going to say." He looked down and didn't meet her gaze when he spoke, "I wanted to tell you that I am grateful for what you gave up these last two years. I couldn't have done this…any of this without your sacrifice and I…I appreciate all you've given up. I'm sorry you've missed your opportunity for so long, Deborah. I really am. So you…you should go to school; learn all those bones, and medicines or whatever else it is you study." He looked up and smiled at her. "Then maybe you can come back and be Chuck's nurse…annoy someone else in the family for once."

Debbie smiled at the taunt. "Oh Danny," she cried and rushed over to him and threw her arms around him.

"I know," he said. "You're so excited."

She looked up at him and shook her head, "I am but I don't want to leave you in a bind, Danny."

He nodded and hesitated, before he could get the words out. "Then I guess before you go you should see if your Miss Edwards will come for an interview."

"Really?!"

Danny shrugged, "Well, if my kid sister and my parish priest both recommend her, I can't go wrong, can I?"

She shook her head, happily.

"But it's just an interview, understand? No promises."

"I understand. But she is really nice…I met her at Church, you know…couldn't be a better reference, could there?"

Danny shook his head in resignation. He wasn't going to win the battle. He might as well retreat. "Good night, Deborah!" he exclaimed and closed the door swiftly behind him.

Chapter III

Danny parked his truck on 7th Street. There were three bowling alleys on 7th and every night of the week seemed to be bowling night on 7th. Thursday was bowling night for Danny, and Brennen's Alley was his alley of choice. His extended family had been so happy when Danny took up bowling after Lilian's death. His brother, Paul, thought at last Danny would have a social life. His sister, Sharon, thought, at least then she wouldn't have to worry he was sitting at home alone, with nothing to occupy his mind, after the children were asleep. His mother, of course, thought he would surely meet someone who knew someone whom he would pursue. Only his father, thought it was a little strange and out of character for Dan'l, whom, he said had cleaned out enough gutters when he was a child on the farm to ever want to do it as a hobby. And Clancy had only raised an eyebrow and muttered "I'll believe it when I see it."

But every Thursday night Danny left the house with his bowling bag. Truth be told, only Clancy and their father had guessed rightly. But they didn't know the whole truth…Danny hoped that no one knew the whole truth; that every Thursday, after he parked the truck, Danny walked into the front door of the bowling alley, stuffed his bag of shoes and ball into the small locker provided, pocketed the key and walked out the back door of Brennen's Bowling Alley. From there he walked across the narrow alley and through the back door of a small bar called *Arnie's.*

The back door led into a kitchen which served as the kitchen to both the bar out front and Arnie's home above the establishment. The doorway was too short for Danny's stature, but he rarely remembered to duck until he bumped his forehead on the doorframe. Every fifth bump or so he asked Arnie to raise the door-head, but Arnie, having topped off at five six some years ago, never seemed to take the request very seriously.

Tonight Danny remembered before hitting his head and reached up and smacked the doorframe with his hand instead of his forehead. Startled, Mrs. Arnie looked up from the stove, a look of pain on her face, "Dat hurt, jah?"

"That hurt, no." Danny corrected, with a smile for her. "But at least I know there would have been some sympathy for me. When is he gonna raise that doorway?"

"Raise da door. Lower mein prices!" Arnie greeted from the doorway which led from the kitchen to the bar. "Whatcha t-ink dis is? Da all request hour. I don't got no money for silly renovations. I got my place to keep up."

Danny raised an eyebrow. "You keep this place up?" he teased.

Arnie laughed good-naturedly. He was a small, middle-aged German, stout and powerfully built. Thick grey hair made a ring about the shiny bald patch atop his head. He could give as good as he could get and that went for teasing as well as threats. He didn't scare easy; fact was Danny doubted he scared at all. If anyone had gotten up the nerve to try to intimidate Arnie, they would have ended up being fairly intimidated themselves.

"Eh, Danny-Boy!" he smiled with a toothy grin. "D'is place is my home. I work hard to make it look welcome, nein?"

"That's right. Welcoming, nein," Danny replied with a laugh, as he followed Arnie into the bar, nodding a goodnight to Mrs. Arnie as he left the kitchen. The kitchen was well-kept, compliments of Arnie's wife, but the front of the establishment, looked as if nothing had changed since the place had opened. The same torn paper hung from the same smoke-stained walls. The same old light fixtures hung from the same fly-specked ceiling. If it wasn't for the fact that Danny knew Arnie's wife wouldn't have allowed it, he'd have said Arnie was wearing the same checkered shirt he had worn the last seven days. Even the same haggard crowd lined the bar and the booths. Regulars, they were called.

Danny, a regular himself, put a hand on the bar as Arnie made his way behind it to pour someone a beer. He continued speaking to Danny, in a good-natured tone, "Oh, such a gut, gut friend. What'd you come here for? T'ings are bad at work? You come here and insult me. T'ings are bad at home? You come here and insult me."

"Things are just fine all around," Danny assured him.

"Ah. So you just like to come here and insult me."

"That's about the size of it," Danny laughed,

Arnie motioned for him to follow as he made his way down the bar to mix a drink. Danny stood directly across the bar from him, as he worked.

Arnie laughed good-naturedly with the regulars until the bantering around them subsided. Then he turned toward Danny. "How are you doing?"

Arnie, for all his light-hearted joking always put so much more feeling behind those simple words than anyone else Danny knew. Sometimes it made him feel uneasy how deeply Arnie meant the words. But tonight he just smiled. "I'm doing well, Arnie. The kids are well. Josiah changed the oil on my folks' car for the first time all by himself the other night. He was pretty proud of himself."

"Ah, jah, not as proud as his old man, I t-ink," Arnie winked.

Danny smirked, "Well maybe not. But pretty darn close, I'm telling yah. Maybe he'll follow in his old man's shoes."

"Which pair?" Arnie asked, as he started mixing two new drinks.

Danny looked up and met his gaze for a moment. But he dropped his own under Arnie's inquisitive look. "Is Flags here tonight?"

"Whatdayah t'ink?" Arnie asked, not pausing in his actions. He looked up when he finished and passed both drinks to Danny. "*Arnie's* wouldn't be *Arnie's* without Flags, now would it?"

Danny gave a half smile, "I suppose not."

Arnie nodded his head past Danny's right shoulder. "He's there. In his regular booth."

Danny nodded slightly, laid a bill on the bar, took both drinks and walked to a dimly lit side booth. He stood for a full minute watching the man who sat slouched over on the table. The man didn't move. Danny shook his head as he slid onto the torn, faded red seat across from him. "Are you sleeping, Flags, or just studying the grain of the wood?"

The smaller man sat up slowly and looked across the table at his new guest. His thin tweed hair had receded much farther than most at the age of forty, and what hair was there needed to be combed. He looked as if he hadn't bathed or shaved or washed his clothes in weeks. But this, Danny knew, was only because he had probably slept the night before in those very clothes. Danny couldn't tell if his eyes were blood-shot or not, because they were only half-open as Flags studied him with a confused look.

"Danny. Danny-boy," he greeted with somewhat of a lisp. "My won'erful, buddy. If I had a dime I'd buy you a drink."

"A dime wouldn't buy you anything, Flags. But I brought you one," he pushed it across the table.

"Ah, Danny, you didn't hafta do that." He reached for the drink, missed it and knocked it over.

Danny set the glass up with a swift, frustrated movement. "Flags, what are you doing to me?" he muttered under his breathe. "I needed your help. You told me you'd be sober."

"Then why'd you bring me another drink?" Flags demanded, irritably.

Danny whipped up the spilled drink with a forgotten, dirty bar towel. "It's ginger ale. I always buy you ginger ale. If you weren't so drunk you'd remember that."

Flags covered his face with his hands as if he would give in to drunken sobs. Frustrated, Danny was about ready to leave the bar when he heard Flags mutter, "You darn fool, I'm more sober than you. Help me out to the alley. I've got the very thing you need, tonight."

Danny masked his feeling of surprise, scoffed for the benefit of anyone watching as Flags proceeded to fall to pieces in the remainder of his own glass of whiskey. Danny went through the motions of trying to calm him, but Flags was not to be consoled until Danny finally relented and swinging an arm around his neck, half-carried and half-dragged Flags out the back door and into the alley.

Frustrated, Danny propped his friend against the brick wall. Flags laughed, “Hey, I’m pretty good at that.”

“At what?” Danny snapped. The whole evening would come to naught if Flags wasn’t really sober.

Flags shoved his hands in his pockets and then looked up at Danny and grinned. “Acting drunk.”

Danny did a double take and then looked his friend up and down. He gave a quiet laugh of relief. “Yah,” he acknowledged. “It’s ’cause you get an awful lot of practice. Dagnabbit, you scared me.”

Flags grinned again. “Didn’t think anything scared you anymore, Lieut.”

“No? Then I guess I hide it well. Come on, enough of the small talk. You told me you’d have a plan by tonight.”

“Sure,” Flags turned and headed deeper into the alley. “I’ve got a place we can knock off, easy as pie. Did you bring your sidearm?”

“Never go bowling without it,” Danny muttered following his friend away from Brennen’s Bowling Alley.

Danny followed Flags down one alley after another. It began to rain and for a moment—the rain, the night and Flags’ determination on his mission—reminded Danny of Anzio and he had a sudden uneasy feeling they were heading into much more than just a night of collecting a few misappropriated funds, but for months of drudgery and warfare. The farther into the city of Gilmore they ventured the deeper the feeling sank and Danny wished he could hear bombing in the distance so that he could shake it off as an awful memory of Anzio. But there was no bombing and there was no Italian mud; only asphalt alleys and brick buildings, a little rundown in places but by no means bombed out. He shrugged off the memories but the uneasy feeling remained.

He heard Flags, several paces ahead of him, give a choked back laugh. “What’s so funny?” Danny asked suspiciously. “Flags, you sure you’re not drunk?”

“I’m not drunk…yet. But you’re gonna get a kick out of this job…I think so.” Then he gave another muffled laugh.

Danny caught up to him. “This is a humorous holdup? That’s what you went for? Instead of finding an easy one, or a less dangerous one. You went for the place that would make me laugh? And you're sure you're not drunk?"

"You need to laugh more, Lieut. So I thought I could kill two birds with one stone."

"I find it easier to laugh, when I don't have to worry about someone putting a bullet in my back. A burglary is no place to laugh, Flags."

Flags just grinned and motioned for Danny to follow. Danny did, but he really wished his uneasy feeling would leave, and he wished he had made Flags walk a straight line before he had started to follow him down the alley.

Flags stopped and put out an arm to block Danny. Danny stopped and looked at him enquiringly.

Flags stared ahead with his crazy grin and finally Danny followed his gaze. They stood in front of the warehouse; a giant brick monstrosity, much like the other dozen or more they had passed in the night. He squinted against the light mist and the dim street lights to read the old paint lettering on the side of the building. Tall white chipped paint spelled the words McGrady's Brewery. Danny turned and stared at Flags, "Really? A brewery?"

"Don't you think it's appropriate?" Flags asked. Then he laughed. "I thought it was funny."

"You would. But we don't need contraband, we need money. I don't have time to go fencing Balestrini's goods."

Flags shrugged off Danny's comments, "It'll be fine. I saw a couple guys. On Thursday evening before they close down they stop by and bring a whole lot a money."

"Money? Cash?"

"Greenback dollars. It's actually *legitimate* funds. It's the payroll for the guys who run the brewery trucks. They get paid on Friday after they make their last delivery. Or they *would* get paid. But now they won't…do you think we should feel guilty? Taking truck drivers' paychecks?" Before Danny could respond, Flags continued. "I don't. And I don't think I could work up the feeling of guilt either."

Danny was still contemplating the morality of stealing payroll money when Flags started moving ahead. "Let Balestrini pull the money from some other pot to pay his guys. He's got enough of it floating around town."

Danny followed Flags' lead. More because he couldn't let Flags go into the situation by himself than because he was completely convinced this was a good idea. But when it came right down to it, most of the things he and Flags did on these Thursday evenings weren't good ideas, they were just the only idea and they went with it. When Danny could get Flags into a serious discussion-which wasn't often-Flags always told him an evening hadn't ended poorly yet. And their luck couldn't hold forever, so they might as well take advantage of it.

If he had asked Father Clancy's opinion, he would have said it wasn't luck.

Danny was inclined to agree, so he made the sign of the cross and followed Flags.

Chapter IV

Friday evening came at last. Finally. Danny was always exhausted after Thursday evening's bowling ventures, some weeks more than others. But the really exhausting part was trying to conceal it on Fridays. From Leonard, but mostly from Greg who was working right beside him. Danny didn't like to be happy over someone else's misfortune, but when Greg called in sick with the flu he breathed a little easier. Supper that evening had been a quick affair, offering Danny further relief.

Debbie, who always went back to their folks on the weekend, had her bag packed and was ready to leave before Danny had finished the dishes. She watched her brother for several seconds before he looked up from the last pot he was scrubbing. "Is something wrong, Debbie?"

She shook her head but didn't answer.

"Then stop watching me. Go on home. Mom and Dad will be waiting for you. I'll see you on Monday."

"Well, I…I wasn't sure what you thought of interviewing Miss Edwards."

He pulled the drain and leaned on the sink, head down. He was exhausted after last night and did not want to have this conversation with Debbie. Frankly, he worried about interviewing Miss Edwards. He had liked what he had seen of Miss Edwards at the rectory, but that was simply in regards to her attractiveness as a woman. However, he wasn't at all sure how he felt about that attractive woman being in his home. But he wasn't going to let his kid-sister know that. "I asked you to ask her, didn't I?"

"Yes…but I…well I just wanted to reiterate that I really, really and truly did not prompt Janey to talk about her at supper…I had no idea that the kids even met her when you were at Father Clancy's…I…"

Danny smiled. "All the more reason that we should see if this will work out, isn't it? Stop worrying. First you worry because I don't have anyone, and now you're worrying that I might have someone. Nervous that you might be too easily replaced?" he teased as he wiped the suds off his hands and tossed the crumpled towel on the counter.

Debbie grinned. "You know I'm not. You can't replace a sister. You are stuck with me for life, whether you want me or not. You can get a new nanny, a new housekeeper or a new wife, but I will always be your sister and probably always be hangin' out here in my spare time. Get used to it, brother."

He leaned against the sink and met his sister's gaze across the kitchen. "I have," he assured her. Then he quickly added, "I'll try to have the turntable fixed when you come home on your first visit so that you *will* visit."

"Funny, aren't you? I don't come for the turntable; I come for the amazing meals in this house."

Danny groaned, "Now who's being funny."

"Hey! I have become a very good cook in the last two years."

Danny thought about this and then, with a glint in his eyes he replied, "I'll grant you that you cook much better now than when you first came…but *very good* is a relative term."

Debbie rolled her eyes and laughed. "I hope when you speak with Miss Edwards, you won't be as hard on her as you are on your kid-sister."

"Course not. I'll be a perfect gentleman."

"Okay, but…" she hesitated.

"But what?"

"Well…don't be grumpy at her," Debbie advised.

Danny raised an eyebrow. “Grumpy?”

“Well, I mean. It’s okay to smile at people. Whenever you are questioning people, your cop instincts come out and you look like you are giving them the third degree instead of just being interested in the answers to the questions you are asking…its rather intimidating.”

“Would you like to do the interview for me?” Danny asked sarcastically.

“I would but when I talked to Mom on the phone today, and told her that Miss Edwards was coming, she suddenly informed me that I should be home before dark…I think she was trying to tell me I should stop interfering in other people’s lives…”

“You mean your mother thinks you are a compulsive meddler,” Danny clarified.

Debbie made a face. “Compulsive makes it sound like I can’t stop myself.”

Danny looked at her with an unspoken question.

“I have complete control,” Debbie defended herself. “I could stop. But then where would you be?”

“Heaven only knows, I suppose.” Danny muttered. “But I will do my best to discuss the job with the lady without your supervision.”

Debbie looked dubious, but gave her brother a hug good-bye anyhow. After bidding farewell to her niece and nephews Debbie headed home.

Danny retreated to his study. With any luck, he would be able to pay a few bills before Miss Edwards arrived for the interview. He hoped it would be a short interview; either she was in or out. He didn’t want to make a government project out of the interview.

With determination, Danny opened the desk drawer, but the yelling of playful voices outside distracted him. He leaned against the window frame and observed his children in the backyard. The boys were busy building precarious additions to their treehouse. Janey stood below them, picking up dropped nails and dodging falling boards. That none of the children had ever had a broken bone was a miracle. But Danny wasn’t about to stop the ventures of childhood on the off chance that he might be preventing a broken bone either. Sometimes their undertakings made him catch his breath, but he tried not to interfere with their activities. He wondered if he would feel differently if Lilian were still here. If their mother were standing beside him as they watched the children out the window, would they be calling admonishments to *be careful—get down from there—watch out*? Or would she be okay with their antics as well?

Danny turned away from the window to distract his thoughts from her memory. But he still couldn't concentrate on the bills. He lit a cigarette and paced the perimeter of the study. Debbie was right—despite her youthful, impetuous, and somewhat conniving manner—she was right. He had to do something about the care of his kids in a week.

He had a fleeting thought that perhaps there was no need to hire anyone for the children. The kids would be starting school in a week; there would only be those short hours after school until he was off work and the Sisters had a nursey for children whose mothers had to work. He grimaced; Josiah and Toby would balk at the thought of hanging out in the nursey until he came for them. But Toby and Janey were too young to go home to an empty house even with Josiah to keep order.

A replacement for Debbie wouldn't be easy. He hadn't had to look for help outside the family since Debbie had come to live with them. However, he realized that realistically he had only postponed the inevitable. During the short interlude between Barbara and Debbie's assistance, he had gone through the motions of hiring a nanny. One of the women had been upset with the boys for climbing a tree. When Danny had tentatively asked her why she told them not to climb the tree, she had been indignant and walked out before the end of the first day. How Danny was supposed to keep his boys from climbing trees when he couldn't even keep his little girl from climbing a tree, Danny wasn't at all sure, and frankly he didn't care. He held obedience and discipline in high regard, but he preferred it to be tempered with more love than Socialism.

The pendulum could swing the other direction too, he had found. The younger women he had interviewed had made him feel as if *he* were the one being looked over instead of his children. There wasn't any discipline in their gaze, nor any love, just infatuation and Danny didn't have the time or the tact to deal with that every evening at the supper table.

On the other hand, Miss Edwards was different. She hadn't gushed over Janey being motherless. She hadn't instantly primped when he had met her in the rectory hall. She acted like a normal individual, for which he was grateful. Still, he wasn't so sure that hiring her was the obvious answer. Her large brown eyes were easy to gaze into, and her smile was contagious. But every evening at the supper table? He didn't think he wanted to see her that often. It would be too easy to get used to that smile across from him. He didn't want to let himself get used to that.

The only solution was that he had to find someone besides Miss Edwards to replace Debbie. After all, he had promised to interview Miss Edwards; he hadn't promised to hire her. This interview would simply get the ball rolling, get him on the track of finding someone else. Someone that would let the boys be boys; would mother his little tomboy-girl; and would not try to entrap him. That's why sisters made such great nannies. Too bad he had run out of them. Sharon and Barbara were both married with children of their own; Julia was in the convent and now Debbie was off to school.

Danny sighed and finally sat down at his desk. With resignation to the fate of their lives he crushed his cigarette in the ash tray. The boys seemed doomed to be tormented for climbing trees; Janey would forever be a *poor-little-girl* and he would forever have to thwart the attentions of over-bearing mother figures and love-sick girls. There seemed no happy medium…except Miss Edwards.

Danny shook his head again. He had to stop thinking about Miss Edwards. Difficult thing, considering she was coming to his house that evening. Why did he keep thinking of her? He knew why. It was her easy smile. It reminded him so of Lilian's smile.

A smile he loved so dearly. Lilian's round face with laughing blue eyes. Laughter that had caught his heart the first time he had heard it, and every time there after. A smile that was always there; sometimes even when he was angry, laughing up at him, and cajoling him into a better mood, just as Janey did when he tried to discipline her. How he longed to see that smile tonight; to hear Lilian telling him she knew he would do the right thing.

That was not a good train of thought. He hadn't let himself go down the road of opening longing for Lilian in a long time. And he wouldn't again, if he had any control of his thoughts. Danny forced his concentration back to the bills to distract himself from the longings and the hurt of his heart. Life didn't give him time for hurting. He had to keep pushing forward.

He had only made two payments when Toby poked his head in the doorway. "Daddy, can we have cookies?"

Danny glanced at the clock, it was nearly ten after seven. Miss Edwards should have been here. His brow netted. This was like prolonging purgatory. He felt frustrated at his wasting time in thought, and now the awkwardness of the interview being postponed. He rose from his chair, the nettle of his brow deepening.

"Cookie…singular," he corrected.

Toby grinned and raced ahead of his father to the kitchen, exclaiming, "He said yes!"

The cookie jar was opened and cookies dispersed. Danny filled two glasses with milk. He placed one on the table before Toby and the other he handed to Janey. She took it, but before he had replaced the milk in the refrigerator, she managed to drop it on the floor with a crash. She stared up at him, her eyes wide in surprise, but no more surprise than his own.

Before Danny had a chance to make any kind of comment, the doorbell rang.

"Doorbell!" Tobias announced from the other side of the table. There was an echo as Josiah yelled the same information from upstairs. It always amazed Danny, how children thought they were the only ones who could hear these things and had to broadcast it to the rest of civilization.

"Thanks!" he muttered with an edge of sarcasm. He scooped up the biggest pieces of Janey's broken glass, and pointed a finger at her sternly. "Don't get off that chair, young lady," he ordered and headed toward the front door.

If this was Miss Edwards, she was late. He wasn't in a mood to receive anyone at the moment, especially anyone who was late. She would have to deal with his annoyance because he wasn't going to be polite and try to hide it.

He yanked open the door. He couldn't see her face as she stood in the growing shadow of the doorway and he remembered with increasing annoyance that he still needed to replace the porch lightbulb.

Her greeting was drowned by Josiah's second announcement that someone was at the door. "Josiah!" Danny called over his shoulder. "Come down here!"

He turned back toward the door. "Won't you come in, Miss Edwards?"

"Thank you, yes," she replied and stepped forward. She was dressed again in her tailored blue suit. Her blonde hair reminded him of the color of wheat, summer wheat, just about the third, well maybe the fourth, week of July, when the yellowness began to give way to brown. Her hair looked about as difficult to control as a shock of wheat, but she had tamed it masterfully with an army of bobby pins.

Thankfully Josiah pounded down the staircase like a herd of elephants, distracting Danny from the thought.

As Danny closed the door, he turned to Josiah, who had reached the bottom of the staircase. The boy stood shamefacedly, now that he saw the company was not a relative. Danny opened his mouth to admonish him, grateful that the woman could see an unruly situation firsthand and know that his children were not angels as some young women thought. Perhaps she would be overwhelmed by the strictness of the household and leave, Danny hoped. But before he could admonish his son, Josiah spoke. "Sorry Dad, I'm sorry. That wasn't very polite."

Danny's brow wrinkled in annoyance at the polite apology. "It's alright," he said gruffly well aware that he was being completely oxymoronic in his thoughts. He turned to face the woman.

She held out her hand. "Mr. Navarone? I remember you from the other day, but it wasn't a very orderly introduction," she said with an understanding smile.

He still had broken glass in his hand and used it as a deterrent from shaking her hand. "Sorry, slight accident. Yes, I'm Daniel Navarone."

"That's alright, Mr. Navarone. I'm sorry I'm late, I had…"

"Yes, you are late," he agreed. Why did she have to be so darned pleasant? Why couldn't she be shocked at his loud son, or the broken glass in his hand? It wasn't normal to open a door with a handful of broken glass. Why couldn't she just go away, her and her wheat colored hair?

"I'm sorry," she said again, and he instantly felt like a heel for making her do it. She tried to smile again, but this time it was a little less confident. "Mr. Navarone, I realize this was probably not your idea.

Deborah is very convincing even when one doesn't want to be convinced…"

He met her gaze and wondered if she wasn't as interested in this interview as Debbie had been in making it. He gave a small laugh, though he wasn't feeling lighthearted toward anyone. "Yes, yes she can. I should probably be worried that she uses that tactic on more than older brothers."

"She's very sweet and convincing. But I, ah…I think you should know, that I have never been a nanny before."

"Don't you like kids?"

"Of course I do. I just haven't had the opportunity to be around them very much."

Danny handed Josiah the broken glass and invited Miss Edwards into the living room and offered her a chair. The more questions Danny asked and the more she replied, the more Danny was convinced she would fit very nicely into the rhythm of their lives, and the more he was convinced he did not want her for a nanny. It was so idiotic to be that afraid of the nearness of a woman he had just met. Yet, she sat before him, brown eyes wide, not batting them, not trying to please him, but attentively trying to answer his questions with honesty. And she had that easy smile that touched her eyes and made them laugh in their own right. She looked as if she were perfectly at home in that chair in his living room and in some paradoxical arrangement in his mind it was obvious to him that he had better not have her around too often.

He heard the telephone ring. "Josiah, go answer the telephone, please," he ordered, though he sorely wanted to use it as an excuse to leave the living room himself.

"How are you at canning?" he asked abruptly, unable to remember what they had been discussing. "We have a good sized garden out back. Still trying to get more tomatoes canned before it freezes…"

She looked surprised at his question. Danny wasn't sure if it was the sudden switch in the conversation or the subject that he had broached. He vaguely hoped she knew nothing about it and would run in dread at the thought of being required to learn the task. In reality, when the vegetables were ready for canning, the kids and he would pick them and haul them out to the home place for his mother and sisters to preserve. It wasn't really necessary for the nanny to do it, but if it would make his rejection of her application easier, he would use it to the full extent.

"Yes. I used to help my grandmother. I haven't done it for a while, but I'm sure I could relearn it."

"Dad, telephone's for you," Josiah said, leaning around the doorway into the living room.

Danny stood up quickly. Then remembered himself. "Would you excuse me for a moment, Miss Edwards? Josiah, sit with Miss Edwards." He started to walk out and muttered to his son, "Be polite." He turned away without a backwards glance.

Opening the kitchen door, Danny found Toby with a dustpan dumping the glass into the trash. "Thanks, sport," he smiled, pleased that Toby had been responsible enough to do it without being told.

He picked up the receiver to discover Arnie on the other end. He was upset and sputtered a few times before Danny told him to calm down. "Its Flags," he finally got out clearly.

Danny paused. "Just a second," he murmured. He turned to Janey and Toby, "Toby, Janey, go upstairs and play," he ordered and they immediately left the kitchen. "What about Flags?" he murmured into the phone.

"He's drunk."

"You're calling me because Flags is drunk?"

"No, I'm calling you because he was spouting off in da bar. Said some things, I don't really know what he was talkin' about. But he mentioned da McGrady Brewery…"

Danny caught his breath. "And?"

"And nothing. I couldn't make head or tail out of what he was talking about, but that doesn't mean somebody else didn't…I just thought you should know."

Danny wanted to thank him, but he wasn't feeling thankful at the moment. He was uneasy. "Where's Flags now?"

"When he started going off, I got a couple of da guys to help me take him out da back way…after d'ey left him being sick in the alley…the Mrs. and I brought him upstairs and put him to bed. Once he sleeps it off he'll be better…he'll be sorry, Danny…I just thought you should know…"

"What else happened?"

Arnie went on to describe the various patrons' responses—the ones who ignored him as they always did and the ones who took note of his behavior or his words. But nothing seemed worrisome to Danny. Except that it could be a very worrisome situation. Arnie assured him that Flags never said Danny's name; the only specific item he had heard was the mention of McGrady's Brewery.

Danny hung the receiver back on the phone. His hand rested on it for a moment, thoughts racing and wondering. If anyone suspected Flags had anything to do with the McGrady payroll raid they could tie it back to Danny. And if they tied it to Danny, they would find out soon enough where he lived. And if they knew where he lived…he flinched at the thought. He was getting ahead of himself. Nothing incriminating had been said. No one knew anything. It had just been a slip of the tongue and no one attributed anything to it. Why shouldn't a drunk talk about a brewery? It was perfectly logical. It was as reasonable as a baker talking about an oven, or a fisherman his bait. Nothing more. Still Father Clancy's words wove their way into his thoughts. *I don't want to be grateful at your funeral.*

Danny shook off the thought. He was blowing this situation out of proportion. He had to remember the facts and stop imaging further than that. But instead of remembering the facts of the evening, he remembered the young woman he had left—how long ago?—sitting in the living room. He groaned. Half because he had left her so long and half because he had to go back. There was something about the woman he had left that made him not want to rejoin her. The phone call made him even more certain he wouldn't let her come back. His first duty was to his children; he couldn't make himself responsible for another life by bringing a woman in and potentially endangering her as well. She would have to go, he had his hands full enough without creating more potential casualties.

He pushed open the swinging kitchen door and walked down the hall. But the living room was empty. Even the light was off. He opened the door to his study and found Josiah bent over a book; "Where is she?" he asked without preamble.

Josiah shrugged, "I donno…I think Toby took her doll again. She's probably looking for it."

"Not Janey. Miss Edwards."

Josiah was still engrossed in his book. "Oh, her. She left a while ago."

"Josiah, look at me when I'm speaking to you."

Obediently, Josiah put the book down and looked at his father.

"Did she say anything?"

"At first she was talking to Toby and Janey. Then when you didn't come back she said she had a flat tire and couldn't wait."

"A flat tire?" Danny shook his head. "That's why she was late," he muttered.

"Yes, sir. She said she'd go use the neighbor's phone and then she said thanks and she left."

Danny shook his head and rubbed a hand over his face. This was what he had wanted; he had wanted her to leave. But now that she had left, he felt guilty. He wished he had known about the flat tire, but when she had arrived late, he hadn't given her a chance to explain. His hand moved from his face to the back of his neck. "All right. Well, it's almost bed time. Head upstairs and get ready for bed."

Josiah climbed from the chair. He was about to put the book on the shelf, but he hesitated. "Can I take the book?" he asked.

Danny glanced at the title on the jacket and nodded. "But only a half hour, hear?"

Josiah nodded with a smile and hurried past.

Danny stood for a moment. Josiah's pleased face, Arnie's information and Miss Edwards all clamoring for his attention. He sank into the chair Josiah had vacated. He had to sort a few things out and since the information from Arnie was much less emotional than the others that was what he was determined to sort through.

Chapter V

When Danny awoke in a foul mood on Saturday, he blamed it on Flags' escapade. Danny hadn't slept a single, solid hour all night for worry over what may have been deduced from Flags' drunken ramblings. The children sensed his mood relatively quickly and they ate their breakfast in silence. As soon as it was over, they quickly cleared the table without being asked and then rushed outside to play. Danny got a light bulb from the closet and went to the front porch. When he dropped and broke it before he had even gotten the old lightbulb unscrewed, he decided perhaps he needed to admit there was more than just Flags to blame for his mood. There was his annoyance at himself for being rude to Miss Edwards.

After their noon meal of hotdish and fresh green beans Danny loaded the children into the truck and drove to his sister Sharon's. She had offered to watch them while he ran an errand; the errand being to have a stern conversation with Flags.

There wasn't a soul in Arnie's Place except Arnie, who was whistling poorly but enthusiastically, as he wiped down tables.

"Afternoon," Danny greeted, purposefully leaving off the 'good' because he couldn't quite stomach that on a day as awful as this one.

Arnie looked up, "'Ello, Danny! I was sorry to bother you last night. It's all okay, isn't it?"

"Flags here?" Danny asked ignoring the man's question.

"No. It's early yet. He'll be around later," Arnie replied as he continued to wipe tables.

Danny stood watching him, lost in thought.

"Did the interview go well?" Arnie asked.

Danny glared at Arnie as if he suspected him of reading his thoughts. "What?"

"Josiah said you were interviewing Miss Edwards when I called last night."

"Yah, it went fine," Danny replied sarcastically. "Josiah was more of a gentleman than I was, and she left before anything was decided."

"Well, it didn't matter anyway, did it?" It was more of a statement than a question and Danny felt cornered. "You had already decided not to hire her."

"I didn't say that," Danny said cooling slightly, because he knew it to be true. "I just don't know a whole lot about her."

"But how will you know, if you don't give her a job?"

"How can I give her a job, if I don't know her?" Danny countered with what he thought was better logic.

Arnie shrugged. "She's just a good girl who's been dealt a rotten hand."

"You know Miss Edwards?"

Arnie shook his head. "I remember her father. He would come in now and again, before he...well anyway. I don't know *her*, but I live on the same side of town. People talk in this place."

Danny shook his head muttering, "She's crazy."

Arnie looked surprised. "Half of what people say about her isn't true. She just needs a chance to get back on her feet."

Arnie obviously knew more about her than Danny did, or at least more gossip. Danny had only meant she was crazy for thinking of taking a live-in nanny job for a man she didn't even know. But he wasn't going to let Arnie know that he didn't know what he was talking about. "Great," Danny said though he obviously meant the opposite. "So the girl's been dealt a rotten hand. And you want me to ask this same young lady, whose been dealt a rotten hand, to come live with us…in our house. That would go over very well, I'm sure. Think people are gossiping now?"

Arnie shrugged. "People gossip. Never stopped you from doing what you thought was the right thing to do before now. Are you gonna let them determine what you do or don't do out of fear of what they might say? That's not the Danny I know. All I'm saying is, she needs a job. You need a nanny. Maybe it's not the best set-up. But it would work for the time being."

"Yah, it probably would," Danny agreed in irritation. Flags came through the door and Danny left Arnie before that man could say anything further.

Flags had lodged himself into a booth before Danny reached him. Flags greeted him with his usual light-hearted tone, "You look like death."

"I didn't sleep well," Danny growled, dropping to the bench across from Flags.

"Really? Why not?" he was extremely upbeat and Danny had an urge to shake him by the shirt lapels.

"I kept waking up, thinking I heard Balestrini's hitmen storming my house," he hinted.

"I slept like a baby," Flags related, ignoring Danny's concerns.

"I doubt that. Don't you feel even a little remorse?"

"Remorse for what? Nothing happened."

"Nothing? Really?" Danny kept his voice lowered, although there was no one else in the Bar. "Arnie said you were spouting off about the brewery."

"I wasn't spouting off," Flags defended himself. "McDonald and I were only sharing about the good old days when McGrady's Brewery was first new and…"

Danny interrupted him, "I don't care, Flags. Don't talk about it at all. Don't talk about any of the places we go. Ever. Get me?"

"Which side of the bed did you get up on? Maybe you should go back there."

"Flags! This is serious. What the heck were you thinking last night?"

"Danny, cool down. I can't believe you are this upset about my drinking habits. We've both been living with them for ten years. What's really bothering you?"

Danny leaned across the table for emphasis. "When your drinking habits endanger your life, I care. But when they endanger the lives of my kids, I will stop you. Get me?"

Flags obviously got him. His face was ashen and he looked sheepish. It was a full minute before he spoke. "I'm sorry, Dan'l. I don't think I realized it was that bad. Okay? I'm sorry I drink too much. I'm sorry I made you nervous. I'm sorry I can't keep my big mouth shut. I'm sorry."

Danny watched his face. He saw true remorse there, and he wished he hadn't blown his top. He wished he could tell him that letting his temper go was really this situation compounded by the Miss Edwards situation. But he couldn't really drag her into the conversation. And he didn't want to talk about her anyway.

"I know you're sorry, Flags. You always are. But will you lighten up on the drink? It's gonna shorten your life…and possibly mine, under the circumstances."

"Suppose I should. That's a good Lenten resolution," he suggested wistfully.

Danny's brow furrowed. "Flags, its August. Lent is almost six months away."

Flags grinned. "It'll give me time to get used to the idea."

Danny shook his head. "I'm going home."

Flags caught his arm as he stood to leave. "You believe me, that everything's okay, right?"

"I suppose so."

"That's a vote of confidence, if I ever heard one," Flags replied sarcastically.

Danny shrugged, "I'll believe you when we both wake up on the far side of next Thursday."

After leaving the bar, Danny drove straight out of town. Nothing cleared his head more than driving out in the country, away from the city and onto gravel roads like the ones he grew up on. He could think. He could reason situations out without being distracted.

Balestrini was a wearisome adversary and Danny couldn't take that threat lightly. There was always that chance that somewhere one clue would lead to another and Balestrini would figure out their entire scheme. But for now, Danny was reassured.

But being reassured in that dilemma, only meant he had to face the other dilemma of where to find a nanny. Danny had pretty much shot a hole in the only chance he had of hiring Miss Edwards. He felt like an idiot that the previous night he had wanted nothing to do with her, and today he was sitting here ruminating over the fact that the one woman that would let boys climb trees and not coddle his daughter was now out of the running because of his own ungentlemanly attitude.

If he hadn't been driving he would have kicked himself. As it was he turned the truck around and headed back to town. When he stopped his truck on the street in front of Chuck and Sharon's house, he knew that if he was given the opportunity, he would ask Miss Edwards outright. It was the only thing that made sense for the benefit of his children. He didn't really have a solution to his resolve to do so, but he felt better already for having at least cracked the door for God to make a move if He so desired.

***

Toby stood at the backdoor, attempting to put on his Church shoes. He kept falling over every time he tried to balance on one foot to put the other shoe on. Danny was getting frustrated for him, but the boy kept trying. Danny advised, "Tobias, please just sit down and put your shoes on."

"I can do it like you do, Dad," Toby insisted, as he fell over once more. "I don't have to sit down."

Danny acquiesced, but had to turn away. He wasn't sure how the boy had that much perseverance to do it the way he wanted to do it, when an easier way was available. Picking up the hairbrush Janey had placed on the table, he turned toward his daughter sitting on the kitchen chair before him. Janey already had her hands covering her face, preparing for the pain of her father pulling the brush through her morning tangles. He prepared himself for the whimpering that would commence any moment.

Instead he heard a tentative, "Daddy?"

"Hmm?"

"Can't Miss Edwards come and be our nanny?"

Danny didn't stop brushing, and the girl didn't see the wrinkled brow that had gathered on her father's face. No one had mentioned the woman all day Saturday. The kids wouldn't see Debbie until Monday, so she couldn't have put her up to it. "Why do you want *her* to come?"

Her little legs began to swing from her perch on the kitchen chair and her hands moved excitedly as she said in hushed tones, "She told me a secret. And it made me happy, cause things are gonna be okay."

Danny stopped brushing and squatted down beside her chair, "What secret?"

Janey turned to look directly into her father's inquisitive face, but she only smiled widely.

And he asked again, "What secret, Janey?"

Her eyes were wide, "But it's a *secret*."

"It's okay. You can tell Daddy."

"Okay, but don't tell anyone else," she admonished. She leaned closer to him and whispered, "She's afraid of new people too. But she still goes and meets new people and its okay." A worried look fell over her face and she gasped, "But don't tell her I told, please, Daddy."

Danny studied his little girl's face for a moment.

"She's a new people, isn't she, daddy? And I'm not afraid of her."

Danny relented for the sake of Janey's smile, "Person," he corrected and added thoughtfully, "she was pretty nice, wasn't she?"

"Yes. And she never said poor deer and I bet she makes nummy cookies, too."

Danny smiled, "I'll bet she does."

"That's what Toby said…can she come live with us, like Debbie does?"

Danny stood up and went back to brushing the mess. "Well, it's not that easy of a situation…but I'll think it over."

Janey clapped her hands and giggled. Josiah came into the hallway, "Are we ready to go yet?"

"Well, that's nice. Finally a child who doesn't want to be late for Church."

Josiah shifted from one foot to the other. "When we're late the kids pick on me, because the priest is my uncle and they think I should be there earlier than anybody else."

Danny sighed, and murmured, "Well, it might not be a perfect intention, but at least it's something." He finished tying a lop-sided bow in

Janey's hair, kissed the top of her head and put the brush down on the table. "Alright, everybody got shoes on? Let's get to church before the neighborhood baseball team gets there."

They arrived ten minutes early which made Josiah ecstatic until he realized he had to spend that time praying…but he endured.

Danny, grateful for the time, asked God for special guidance. He promised that if God really wanted him to ask Miss Edwards to be nanny, he'd do it…but he wasn't doing any chasing…God would have to provide the opportunity to see her again, without Danny's having to crawl to Debbie and find out a telephone number or an address. Those were his conditions, he hoped the Good Lord wouldn't take him up on it…felt a little as if he were testing the Lord, but he wasn't in a mood to cave to his kid-sister or his brother…he'd cave to God's will and that was it…but it better be good and clear, he wasn't making a move on any mumbling on God's part.

By the end of Mass, a very calming sense of peace settled over Danny, and he had a sneaky suspicion that the Almighty was against him on this one, just like everybody else.

***

It was just about ten o'clock Monday morning when Danny leaned against the water cooler, taking a break and chugging down water. Though the second to last day of August, the month seemed determined to make an impression before giving up the ghost to September. Leonard's thermometer had broken years ago, but Danny guessed the temperature hovered over ninety degrees, with the humidity taking a close second. Pouring half his cup of water down the front of his shirt and under his coveralls, Danny shuddered at how good it felt.

About that moment, his coveralls nicely wetted, he heard a woman's voice, "Excuse me, I was just wondering about my car?"

He turned around to find Miss Edwards standing in the open garage door, silhouetted by the brilliant sunshine. He couldn't see her expression, but she could see his in the shaded garage. "Oh, it's you..." she was flustered.

Danny was just as flustered, not because of their past meeting, or even that he had poured water down his front, but primarily because of his petition in Church the day before. If ever he had felt like God didn't listen, he couldn't feel that way about this situation. God had provided her in the flesh at his doorstep. He was so surprised that he couldn't recover enough to help her out of the awkward meeting.

"I…I was just wondering about my car. The driver, they towed it and he said he would drop it here to be fixed…"

"Your car? Which is it?"

"It's blue…" she stuttered. And he continued to look at her for a further description. "It is," she assured him, with a smile. He started to shake his head and she gave a laugh. "I'm sorry. It's, well it's…"

"Is it that Chevy sedan over there?" he asked pointing out the back of the garage.

She leaned slightly to see around him. "Well it's the only blue one I see, so it must be," she said smiling. Then she assented, "Yes, that's my car."

"Well, it's not ready yet. The other mechanic is down with something, and hasn't been in for a few days. Guess I'm a little behind. Soon as I'm done with this Ford, I'll bring it in."

"Oh would you? I'd really appreciate it! I have an interview on the other side of town and it would save…" her voice petered out as she realized the awkwardness of speaking of interviews to him. "It would just be…much…appreciated…"

Danny figured God had held up His side of the prayer, he'd better get around to his own. "Miss, Edwards, I should apologize for the other night. I had a lot of other things on my mind."

Miss Edwards didn't meet his gaze. "It was no problem, Mr. Navarone. Sometimes interviews don't go well, sometimes they do. Nothing's wrong with that."

"Well, there was something wrong with that. I was rude. I didn't let you make your excuse. I walked out on you for an impolite amount of time and didn't even help you with your car trouble. I was rude and that's the only thing that we learned from that so-called interview. I missed an opportunity to find out who you are and I am sorry."

She looked up at him, shock at his apology written clearly on her face. She recovered gracefully, smiled and murmured, "All's forgiven, Mr. Navarone."

"…But I can't fix your car in time for your interview."

Her eyes widened at his abrupt change of subject. "Ohhhh-kay." She was unsure if that was the end of the conversation and placed a tentative foot behind her to pivot out of the garage when he added, "But if you don't think it's too awkward, and if you don't mind that the muffler has a hole and is rather loud, you can barrow my Chevy."

"That's kind of you, Mr. Navarone. It might be awkward, but I'm afraid I'm not really in a position to be choosy. You don't mind?"

Danny smiled, "Wouldn't have offered, if I minded." He was glad he could at least do something small to make up for his foot-in-mouth attitude Friday night.

He walked her over to his truck and opened the door for her. She put a foot on the running board and slid onto the seat. Danny slammed the door with force and Miss Edward's exclaimed in surprise. "Sorry," Danny explained, "You have to do that or it doesn't latch." She smiled with a laugh, "I'll remember that. Thank you."

His hands were still on the door and he paused momentarily before moving away. He had to say something. He had promised to ask her if the opportunity arose. "Miss Edwards, you wouldn't consider a second interview, would you?"

She seemed to be studying his hands on her door but she answered politely. "You don't have to offer that, Mr. Navarone. I don't think that's necessary…I…I've really got to run, or I'll be late for this one…"

He pulled away quickly, wishing he hadn't said anything. "Good luck, Miss Edwards."

She smiled—but not at him—and drove off. He watched his truck until it was out of sight. Well, Debbie couldn't blame him and neither could Father Clancy. And he pretty much cleared himself of his promise in Church too. He had tried. He had apologized, and even asked for a second chance. It was in her court and she hadn't wanted to play so he was free from any guilt.

Danny walked back into the garage. But the Ford Crestline seemed to be frowning at him and he was a little annoyed either at it or at her and he kicked the tire before he stuck his head back under the hood.

Leonard sauntered out of the office a little too nonchalantly. "You know her?"

Danny kept his head under the hood. "Sure. She's the girl who owns that blue Chevy Sedan with the flat tire and the bent rim."

Leonard glanced over his shoulder at the car, but wasn't about to get side-tracked from his original line of questioning. "Yah, but you just loaned her your truck. Do you know her personal-like?"

"Aren't we all about helping our customers, Leonard? Isn't that what you tell us, every time I don't get an automobile done on time?" Danny was hedging. He could tell Leonard had some information on the woman that he sorely wanted to share. And Danny sorely didn't want to hear it. Leonard was a good boss, a good businessman and a good man in many other respects…but the man gossiped like an old woman and Danny didn't have the stomach for it any day, and today in particular.

But Leonard was not going to relent. "So you don't know who she is?"

"I told you, she's Miss Edwards. She owns the blue Sedan."

"She's JoAnna Edwards. Old Andrew Edwards's daughter. They say she's crazy."

"Aren't we all," Danny muttered, trying to kill the conversation.

"No, I mean *crazy*. Her old man lost everything and she just…well she just went crazy. He ran out on her and the business. She had to declare bankruptcy. I guess the courts were lenient seeing as how she was the daughter and all, but she just wouldn't drop the case. She kept insisting there was foul play. That her old man didn't run out on her, that he was murdered. Only there was no body. Pretty soon the police even said she was crazy…"

"Not officially," Danny muttered. They wouldn't make a statement like that unless they had something to back it up and frustration or hearsay wasn't enough for that.

"What'd you say?"

"Did you say to check the right headlight or the left?" Danny asked. He remembered perfectly well it was the left, but he was trying to get Leonard off the track of the woman.

"Right," Leonard replied absently.

"It was the left," Danny argued.

"If you remembered why'd you ask me?" Leonard snapped.

"To get you to stop gossiping about a young woman who's trying to get her life back together." Danny exploded. He stood up, banged his head on the hood and swore under his breathe.

Leonard was getting testy, "Thought you said you didn't know her personal-like."

"I don't!" Danny snapped, rubbing his head and pretending to be more upset about it than the conversation, which truth be told was a toss-up.

Leonard turned back toward the office, muttering something about tempers and getting up on the wrong side of the bed.

***

Danny was just lifting the repaired tire back onto the centering pin of the Sedan when he heard his truck coming up the road. He stayed where he was on the far side of the Chevy where he could watch her, but she couldn't see him. He saw her as she climbed out of the Chevy truck and hesitated. She hadn't gotten the job; that was apparent. She looked as if she wasn't sure how to come back to give him the keys without confessing the fact to him. He wished he could make it a little easier for her and without hesitating he stood up and walked towards her, lug nuts still in his hand.

She looked up when she noticed his shadow coming towards her. She tried to smile, but it was quivering.

He gave a sympathetic smile back. *How did it go?* seemed a little too heartless to ask, even for the sake of politeness.

She opened her mouth to say something but nothing came out and she merely handed the key back to Danny. Danny spoke first to relieve her embarrassment. "What can they really know from one interview? They either ask all the wrong questions or you give all the wrong answers. But it's not really a judgement of how well you would do the job. It takes a second one to find out who the person is."

"Yah, except if there is no second one, they'll never know what they're missing."

"You're right." He studied the keys for a moment, pocketed them and then looked off towards the road for a short time before he looked back at her. "So how about it?"

"How about what?"

"A second interview?"

"A pity interview? For the crazy girl who can't get a job on her own."

He colored slightly, at the remembrance of the conversation Leonard had forced on him earlier. And without a doubt she noticed and knew that he knew what people said about her. He tried his best to cover the situation. "No. A second chance for a heel of a fella who doesn't recognize a break when he's given one."

She studied him, as if she were trying to figure something out. He didn't exactly appreciate being looked at in that way, at least not by those brown eyes.

"Do you like children?" he asked to end the silent study.

She smiled a more relaxed smile than the previous one. "Yes, I love them."

"Can you cook?"

"Yes."

"Can you do laundry?"

"Of course."

"You're hired."

She laughed and the sound of it made Danny smile. "That's it?" she asked, "That's the interview?"

"What more should I ask?"

She shrugged, "I don't know. But…"

"But what?"

She gave a laugh "If that's the interview, how did I fail it the first time?"

He joined her in the laughter, "I lowered my standards."

She raised an eyebrow and looked unsure whether she should be offended or not.

Danny continued, "I eliminated the question, can you play the accordion and sing Puccini….I seemed to be losing people on that one all the time."

"Really? I don't know why," she said sarcastically with a smile, and Danny began to think that with her sense of humor she would fit in nicely after all.

"So do you want the job?"

"Yes...but only on a trial basis."

"A trial…you're trying *us* out?"

"Well, both ways. I try the job out, you try the nanny out. Either of us can end it after two weeks if it's not working…sound fair?"

"Yes."

"That was tentative. Yes, it's a good idea? Or yes, she's crazy and I'll humor her?"

Danny couldn't help but smile. "You take this crazy thing very lightly, don't you?"

"It's been with me for a couple years, it's easier to roll with it than fight it. So what it's to be?"

"I'll roll with it. You're hired for a two week trial." He offered his hand.

She looked at it as if she weren't used to people offering her a hand. Then she reached out and took it. Danny found that her grasp was good and firm, as if she meant it as a handshake, not flimsy as if she expected him to kiss it instead of shake it. He appreciated that. But he didn't shake it too long because he knew Leonard would be watching from the office window. Danny didn't mind so much his interaction with Miss Edwards, as he did the thought of what Leonard would turn it into when he told his wife and anyone else who would listen.

"So you'll start tomorrow?" he asked.

"Sure. What time?"

"Seven too early?"

"If this is a test for that two week trial, then no, it's not too early."

Danny smiled, "Fine."

"And my car?"

"Oh, well…I'll tell you, Miss Edwards, the next time you have a flat, stop driving right away and it won't take so long to fix. The rim looked like a dinosaur was using it for a chew toy." She made an apologetic face and Danny continued, "Give me ten minutes and I'll be finished. You can settle with Leonard in the office while you wait."

Chapter VI

The razor felt cold against his face, or maybe it was the water. Either way, Danny contemplated not shaving at all. It was probably more his mood than the razor or the water. The thought of Miss Edwards coming that morning was not doing him any good. The previous evening, all he could think about was how nice her handshake felt and how much he didn't want her to be in his house every time he came home. But he knew he was doing the right thing for the kids.

Debbie had taken the news that she was officially out of a job with an excited, "Gee, Danny, that's swell!" She had danced and hummed all the rest of the way through supper.

Unfortunately, Danny could tell by her smile that his sister had much more on her mind than just a new nanny for the Navarone household. He decided he was rather sorry that he had learned so well in the army how to watch for and read peoples' signs and intentions. Sometimes it wasn't really that helpful of a habit to have acquired. He wished he could just be oblivious to the undercurrents. But he couldn't. He knew exactly what Debbie had planned and he was determined to find the kids a nanny, not a mother. Debbie had said that he couldn't replace a sister; why did she think he could replace Lilian any easier? He finished shaving and tossed the razor on the sink counter.

He went downstairs, and setup a pot of coffee. He pulled on his boots and laced them up as he waited for it to percolate. This would be his last week of enjoying his morning coffee alone. Next week Tuesday, school would start and the kids would be bustling around getting their own breakfasts and rushing to pack lunches.

He was finishing his second cup when he heard the knock at the front door.

He sighed, pushed his cup aside, stood and took his time walking to answer the door.

"Good morning," Miss Edwards greeted before he could.

He nodded, "Won't you come in." She came in, along with two medium sized suitcases. "I see you've brought your bags, already."

"Well, I…I told you I needed the job."

He didn't follow and said as much.

She looked down at her bags sheepishly. "If I went back tonight, I'd be locked out. I was behind in my rent."

"Ah," Danny understood. "Then this is definitely the job for you. Eat free, sleep free, live free, what could be better?"

"It'll be alright, won't it? I mean…" she blushed and didn't continue.

Danny understood and reached for her bag. "If you're worried about your reputation, Miss Edwards, don't be. They have nothing to gossip about; I am not in the least attracted to you," he lied to set the woman and himself at ease.

"Thank you?…I think," JoAnna replied sarcastically with wrinkled brow, but Danny ignored her reaction and she continued. "But then, people don't care about truths when it comes to gossip…that's why it's gossip."

"Point taken. But a wise man once told me; People gossip. But we shouldn't let them determine what we do or don't do out of fear of what they might say."

"A priest?" she asked.

"Bartender," Danny corrected and almost laughed at her look of surprise. He motioned toward the kitchen. And she followed him down the hall toward the kitchen. He walked around the table and set her suitcases beside a door. "That'll be your room," he explained. "Debbie should be all packed up and out of there by this afternoon. She only stays here weeknights, but she has accumulated quite a collection. Coffee?"

She nodded. Danny poured her a cup, motioned for her to sit and took up his own unfinished cup. "Debbie can show you around the house today, give you the lay of the land. According to the boys the only thing you really need to know is where the food is kept and how to prepare it."

She laughed and asked after the general schedule of the day.

Danny rambled through it but finished, "Of course that will change come next week. They start school on the Seventh."

She nodded and nodded again as he explained a few more things. "But we can talk more tonight. Debbie will be here with you today and after that anything you need to locate, just ask Josiah. You could ask Toby, but he probably wouldn't know anyway. And Janey, well we'll see how she does today, she might just hang around the house. Anything none of them can tell you, just open a door or cupboard. There aren't any secrets in this house, and if you find one let me know, it's probably been missing for a good number of years." He paused. "Okay?"

She nodded again.

Danny peered at her, "You've been doing a good deal of nodding. Are you okay? Or is our trial over already?"

She gave a half-laugh, "Its fine. I just hope I do all right. The children don't know me. I don't want to mess up."

Danny gave her an encouraging smile. "You can't mess up. Debbie will be here with you all day…I can't guarantee she'll be here tomorrow, but things will go smoothly." It was amazing to him how easily he could say these things to her, when he wasn't sure of any of them himself.

He stood up. "Debbie should be out here shortly. Hopefully she can show you your room before you have three leaches on you…But I've got to run."

He didn't really. He could have stayed a few minutes more, but he really wanted to be out of the house before Debbie came out. One just never knew what a conniving twenty year old brain would work up in a matter of seconds if the situation looked ripe, and the one sitting at the kitchen table was prim picking. He excused himself and left Miss Edwards alone.

***

By the time Danny came home Tuesday evening Debbie was already gone. He walked in through the back door and found everyone washed and seated at the table, waiting. He looked around, a little confused.

"Debbie said you liked supper when you got home," Miss Edwards said as she brought a pot from the stove.

He nodded slowly as he took off his hat and hung it on the hook by the door. "I'm pretty sure she didn't mean that quite so literally," he explained, slightly surprised.

She paused, still holding the pot and said a thoughtful, "Oh…I wanted to do things right."

He nodded and because she was still stationary, he took the pot from her hands and placed it on the table. "It's fine. We can eat now. But I don't mind waiting. I've even waited up to two and a half minutes before I've blown my top…"

The children all started to laugh and Miss Edwards caught on to the teasing. "I'm sorry Mr. Navarone…"

"Would you call me Danny, please? You make this sound like the children are living in a reform school."

"All right. If that's all right? And you'll call me JoAnna?"

"If that's what you want."

She smiled. "Fine. And from now on I'll have supper ready for you three minutes after you get home…I'd like to see you blow your top."

Danny smiled and decided it might work out better than he thought. She was easy to talk to, she took teasing rather well and could give it back too. He took his seat, "Shall we pray?"

They made the sign of the cross, and said the blessing in unison. However, before the Amen, Janey piped up, "And please let Miss JoAnna stay forever. She's the nicest lady ever."

"Amen," the boys erupted.

Danny looked up from bowing his head in prayer. "I take it, it was a good first day."

JoAnna smiled winningly. “I guess so,” she agreed.

“We had a picnic!” Janey explained.

“And then we went on a wagon train!” Toby announced, as he grabbed a piece of bread.

Danny’s eyebrows rose at this bit of information but he continued to spoon out the stew, patient enough for an explanation.

“It wasn’t really a wagon train,” Josiah explained. “We just went for a walk and pretended we were on a wagon train.”

“And I was the scout,” Toby went on excitedly.

“Until he led us straight into a dessert with no watering holes,” Janey said sadly, as if they had actually been there, without water for days, possibly weeks.

So continued the conversation for the duration of supper.

***

The following days went as well as Tuesday. Joanna learned quickly and on Wednesday Debbie left by midafternoon. Thursday JoAnna nannied on her own and Danny was pleased with how well things had transitioned for the household. He was confident enough to leave for bowling without any worries.

Once again, Friday morning came much too early. But Danny rolled out of bed at the last minute, skipped shaving, and made it to work with a minute to spare.

Danny leaned over the engine of Mr. Cooper’s brand new ’54 Eldorado. He muttered something depreciating about new Cadillacs and grabbed his ratchet to loosen the two bolts that attached the fuel pump to the engine block. His fingers were like thumbs and he dropped the ratchet twice—it clattered loudly against the engine—before he realized he had a 3/8” socket instead of the 9/16” that he needed. This time he muttered something about Mr. Cooper and hoped Greg wouldn’t notice the unusual amount of commotion he was making just to remove a fuel pump. He wiped his hands across the front of his coveralls to remove some of the grease.

“Well, he’s done it again.” Leonard announced coming out of the office.

Danny didn’t look up from the fuel pump but asked with only half interest, “Who’s done what again?”

"*Le Saint*. Brought the payment Madeira's Grocery needed just before Balestrini's mug showed up to collect."

Danny didn't respond, and was grateful when Greg piped up from beneath the hood of the Bel Air on which he was changing the oil. "Madeira? Is that the guy with the kid with Polio?"

"Yah. The Grocer on 7th and Grafton Street."

"*Le Saint*, eh? Is that what the papers call the guy?"

"Papers?" Leonard scoffed. "The papers don't call him anything. They don't mention any of this. Where has your head been buried, Greg? Don't you know, the papers are owned by Balestrini? If the papers mentioned anything, about any of this, it would be to paint *le saint* as if he were the devil himself."

"Maybe he is," Danny muttered as he disconnected the fuel lines.

"What are yah saying, man? He keeps the mob off these people's backs."

"Yah. One month at a time. And each time he steps in to help some poor duff who's about to stumble deeper under Balestrini's thumb, he just makes Balestrini a little bit more irritated. And sooner or later Balestrini is gonna take revenge against this guy, or on the very people he's supposedly helping." Danny shook his head, "If this guy were really a saint he'd have gone after Balestrini and his whole operation and shut it down."

"And just how would you suggest doing that?" Leonard taunted.

Danny stood up, detached fuel pump in hand, and replied almost absently as he moved the broken lever on the fuel pump up and down. "If I knew that, I'd be *le Saint*, and do the job right."

Greg was following the conversation at a slower pace than the conversation was moving and interjected, "Tell me something. Nine out of ten people here-abouts is German descent, with a random Pole and Swede stuck in for good measure. How in the Sam-hill did he end up with a name like *le Saint*? That's Italian, ain't it?"

"French," Leonard corrected irritably. "So you'd do it right, would you?" he addressed Danny. "That's rich, considering you had your chance at fighting the bad guys once, didn't you?"

Danny shot him a look, surprised that the man had spoken almost vindictively.

"And you chose to walk away so I guess you can't be too

judgmental now, can you?"

"No, I guess I can't." Danny agreed, letting the comment slid. He supposed Leonard had heard that the Edwards woman was now Danny's nanny and was probably upset that he hadn't been the first to know. He focused on the job at hand, hoping the conversation would die off for lack of participation.

"Well, when it comes down to it," Greg interposed finally catching up, "how does anybody figure to do any good, when Balestrini's got everybody on his payroll. You never know who you can trust. Heck, I don't even known if you guys might be stoolies for Balestrini. Ferreting out info."

Leonard looked insulted, but Danny laughed. "Yes, Greg, because key in Balestrini's mind every minute is 'what is that mechanic Greg up to now?'" he joked.

Greg grinned, happy that at least one of his listeners had got his rare joking. "Still," he continued, "It's kinda scary when everybody knows that most of our lovely men in blue, seem to be doing alright. And if they are doing alright, they are on the take, 'cause no salaried officer makes that much money. I know there are the good ones. You know, like that Officer Carter, older fella, you know him? Writes a mean ticket, boy, don't speed through his beat, but as straight as an arrow. But then there's Chief of Police Hartley, lives high on the hog, and doesn't seem to raise an irate finger at Balestrini's shenanigan's much less send any of his squad out to investigate. I don't think he knows how straight an arrow is supposed to be."

"Hartley doesn't have a backbone to straighten. Much less lead a squad of men," Danny muttered. He didn't care much for Hartley, now or when they had been partners on the police force. Partners was a loose term—they had been assigned together—but Danny had a hard time trusting his back to him, which made the partnership all but impossible.

Leonard had taken up the conversation again, getting over being offended, and his words interrupted Danny's thoughts on Hartley. "You fella's talk as if us guys payin' our dues are the bad guys. We don't really have a choice," Leonard was saying. "This is the way it is, you pay or you leave…one way or the other. Most of us, we'd just as soon go of natural causes than unnatural ones. So we all pay. To most of us it's just a bill, like any other bill. You pay your 'lectric, your gas, your building rent and you pay Balestrini his protection fee. And there's no shame in that."

"No shame in paying dues to a man who'd kill you just as soon as not?" Danny looked up and met Leonard's gaze for the first time in the conversation. "You may tell yourself that, but I don't think that's how you feel. I don't think that's how any of them feels,"

"You better be darn glad I do pay my dues. Your job is dependent on my paying those dues."

"I know. That's why I know there's shame in it. You make enough in this shop to hire two mechanics, Leonard, but you can't even take your wife to visit her aunt down in Rochester. You may fork out the money, but who pays your dues, Leonard?"

The old man was taken aback momentarily.

"Greg and I are as much in this as the owners." Danny shook his head. "Doesn't matter what this *le Saint* does, we're all still under Balestrini's thumb. No matter who this guy saves for one more month, it all comes back around again, doesn't it? When's it gonna end?"

Leonard didn't have an answer. And he was modest enough at the moment to state as much. Nobody had an answer and he supposed that was the whole trouble. "All the same," Leonard tried to finish, "this guy, whoever he is, he's a good man, doing what he can to help. Takin' down Balestrini? That'd take the National Guard or an act of God."

Danny laughed good-naturedly at the man's two offered options, as if—to Leonard's way of thinking—they were close to being the same thing. "I suppose it would," he agreed.

Leonard headed back toward his office, and Greg aligned the funnel to start pouring oil back into the Bel Air. "Too bad a fella couldn't find out who the fella was. Maybe he could help him…somehow…"

Danny glanced over at him, did a double take, and stuck his head back under the hood saying nonchalantly, "Greg, don't you think it would be a good idea to put the drain plug back in, before you start pouring oil in the top?"

Greg swore, nearly dropped the gallon of oil and proceeded to scoot himself beneath the car. Danny could hear Greg just fine as he continued his conversation, but Danny listened warily. He knew who *le Saint* was, but no one else did. He felt as if they were fishing him out, but they couldn't know. "Yah think?" Greg asked, coming back out from under the car.

"I don't know." He hadn't really been listening, but he tried to fake it. "Maybe keeping it a small operation is why it lasts. Maybe not letting too many people help is what makes it work."

"Maybe. I donno." Greg was back to pouring oil in the top. "Or maybe he just doesn't trust anybody to help him. Or maybe he's trying to prove something."

"Maybe he is," Danny agreed. "Maybe he's trying to do something right, to make up for all the things he's done wrong."

He didn't see Greg shoot him an inquisitive glance. And any further conversation was interrupted by Leonard coming back into the Garage. "Are you two gonna stay here all night?"

"Just about done with the Bel Air," Greg growled.

"What about you?" Leonard demanded.

"What does Cooper *do* to his cars?" Danny muttered, still studying the pump. "This thing is brand new and it needs a new fuel pump."

"Fine. You can give it one tomorrow. I wanna lock up. My wife's making lasagna and I don't like soggy noodles. Come on, close it up. It's not milk, it'll keep until Monday."

Danny shook his head at the pump and then dropped it on his work bench. "Okay, but I've got the Olsen's Ford to fix on Monday, and that thing looks like a job and a half."

"Then I'll give you a day and a half to do it. Just go home."

"See you tomorrow, boss man," Greg growled as he slammed the hood on the Bel Air.

"Yah, cut the crap, Greg. Just go home. You too Danny. You guys do remember you have families, right?"

"Sure." Danny wiped most of the grease from his hands and tossed the rag on top the fuel pump. He snatched his hat from the peg and headed out the door just ahead of Leonard. Climbing into his Chevy, he tried twice to start it. Leonard looked over from where he was climbing into his Coup. "You know for being the ace mechanic you keep claiming to be, you sure drive a heap of junk."

Danny laughed, "I'm just so busy fixing your junk, mine gets put on hold." He shrugged, "It gets me here."

"Yah, but can it get you home?"

Danny tried again and she fired up. "Of course she can." He grinned and pulled onto the street. He was glad to be gone. The conversation had hit too close to home. It made him uneasy. Had he said too much? He shouldn't have entered into the conversation. He should have remained silent. But that would have been just as incriminating. Why had they gone into that topic of conversation anyway? It made him suspect Leonard. It made him suspect Greg. And he didn't like the feeling. He didn't like suspecting people that he trusted.

He wanted to trust more people, but he was finding himself trusting fewer and fewer. If only Lilian were there when he got home. Danny had always been able to talk anything over with her and she always helped him make sense of conundrums. But, when it came right down to it, that was the whole point…Lilian wasn't there.

Chapter VII

Danny woke with a start. Again. Though this wakefulness was the blessed wakefulness after a nightmarish dream. The wakefulness that is more of a savior than a curse; a wakefulness that one clings to rather than fights off.

Danny clung to it by reaching over and pulling the beaded chain on his bedside lamp, illuminating his room with a brilliance that peppered his sight with purple and green spots in the corners of his cringing eyes. Yet he continued to stare at the lamp as if it might disappear if he turned his gaze from it. He could have gotten out of bed, but he had had this dream and others like it often enough to know that his legs would be too shaky to hold himself upright. He brushed a trembling hand over his stubbled face, and wiped the salty sweat from his eyes.

Danny studied the ceiling, fighting to keep his eyes open. Someone had once told him in passing that dreams were the cause of stress. Someone else said that they varied according to what one had eaten the night before. Once, he had overheard a conversation in which it was said that all dreams were premonitions.

But he knew the truth. His dreams were not stress or food induced.

They were not of things to come. His dreams were caused by what had happened in the past. And what had happened he could not undo; he could not stop it then, and he couldn't go back in time to stop it now.

Now, he had to live with memories, the guilt and the nightmares.

The early morning hours passed in complete silence. Danny reached for the Bible on his nightstand. He would not allow himself go back to sleep. He never could sleep after such dreams; as he closed his eyes, he'd see the events play out again as if the inside of his eyelids were movie screens. But he couldn't seem to focus his eyes enough to read, so the Bible did him no good. He held it open, looking blankly at the page. During the War he had carried a small pocket prayer book throughout his tour in Italy, but he had memorized Psalm 91 and it was that which he prayed now: "You shall not fear the terror of the night nor the arrow that flies by day…All who call upon me I will answer; I will be with them in distress…" Again and again he recited the words, but he couldn't think beyond it, even to the meaning of the words.

At last, footsteps sounded in the hallway. He breathed a sigh of relief and laid back on the bed, exhausted. He heard giggles and he closed his eyes calmly. A chair scraped along the kitchen floor downstairs but he didn't hear anything else as blessed, peaceful sleep overcame him.

Almost two hours later, Danny came down the stairs, somewhat rested, but more irritated.

Josiah looked up from retrieving his ball from under the table. "Hi, Dad! Can I go to the soda fountain with the fellas this afternoon?"

Danny's head ached from lack of sleep. "I don't care," he said, with a little too much emphasis.

But Josiah only knew he had permission and the tone didn't affect him. "Gee, thanks, Dad!" and burst through the back door.

JoAnna caught the door on her way in. "Goodness, a tornado just left the house…did you see that?" she asked of no one in particular. Then on seeing Danny, "Oh, good, you're up…the kitchen sink is plugged…or something," she greeted with a smile.

"Good morning to you too," Danny muttered walking passed her to the coffee pot.

She noted his mood with concern and quietly retrieved a platter of warm muffins from the back of the stove, which she set on the table in front of him after he sat down.

"What's this?"

JoAnna glanced at him to see if he were joking. "Muffins."

"What am I supposed to do with them?"

"It's called breakfast."

He made an annoyed face. "I don't really eat breakfast," he fibbed.

"You should."

He turned to look at her in surprise. "What?"

"I said you should. You work hard every day, your body needs some nourishment, more than coffee to hold you until dinnertime."

"Miss Edwards…"

"JoAnna. I thought we agreed on a first name basis so that your house wouldn't be so cold and formal for the children."

He didn't like the way she was so confident at interrupting him. He began again, avoiding any name whatsoever. "My children need a nanny; I do not. If I choose not to eat breakfast that's my choice. And if I decide to eat breakfast, you certainly don't have to make it for me. I got along perfectly well before you came."

JoAnna placed her hands on her hips. "No one is forcing you to eat it, Daniel. If you don't want it, don't eat it. There's no need to lecture me…Janey, don't eat the butter by itself." She pushed the butter tray to the opposite side of the table. In protest Janey jumped off her chair and ran to the opposite side of the table beside the butter and her father.

She crawled onto Danny's unresisting lap. He didn't say anything to the little girl, and when she gave him her usual kiss, he was slower to respond and slightly distracted. But the corner of his mouth turned up almost involuntarily, even if his eyes didn't smile back at her.

JoAnna crossed the room to the ironing board she had left earlier.

"Why don't you go play?" Danny asked Janey quietly.

"Can I go play with Dory?" she asked excitedly.

Danny started to nod but saw JoAnna shaking her head. "No, her mother said she's contagious."

Danny dropped the girl off his lap. "Why don't you go play with Toby?"

Janey shook her head, "He doesn't want to play with any girls. We have cooties."

"Cooties aren't contagious. Go play with Toby."

Janey wasn't finished, "Do all girls have cooties?"

"I suppose so," JoAnna agreed when Danny didn't respond.

"Why?"

JoAnna thought for a moment as she draped one of the boy's dress shirts on the ironing board. "I guess, it keeps the boys away until you're old enough to get married."

"Then what happens to them?" Janey asked. Danny wished they would stop talking.

"They just disappear by themselves, I guess."

"You don't have to take medicine?"

JoAnna smiled, "No, you don't have to take medicine."

"Okay…do you have cooties, Miss JoAnna?"

JoAnna glanced discreetly at her left hand. "I guess so," she laughed. "Now go outside and play."

"Okay. But Toby won't let me play with him," Janey warned as she started for the door.

JoAnna advised with a smile, "Tell him I put your cooties in a box for today."

The house devoid of children, fell into silence. JoAnna turned back to her ironing, wishing she could lighten Danny's mood. If there were anything to the getting up on the wrong side of the bed theory, Danny had just proved it.

"Did you hear about Mr. Madeira?" she asked, searching for a topic not involving the house or kitchen sink.

Danny started. Even JoAnna? This was impossible. "How do you know Madeira?" he demanded, looking up from his now nearly empty plate.

She looked surprised at his demand. "He owns the grocery store, Danny. I do have to buy food to feed you guys…I even bought food before I knew you."

Danny looked down at the table repentantly, "Sorry." There was a long silent moment and then Danny made his half-hearted excuse, "I didn't sleep well. Guess I'm irritable."

"Really? I couldn't tell," she said lightly, with teasing sarcasm.

He pushed his plate back and stood up. "I'll fix the sink."

He opened the cupboard door beneath the sink.

"All I was going to say was that Madeira got the money he needed so that his little girl can have the treatment for her polio."

"That's good," Danny agreed, hoping if he wasn't too talkative, she'd give up on the conversation.

"Not that the Sisters at the hospital would have turned her away, even if they couldn't pay, but it all worked out." She was excited, and not even his mood was going to dissuade her story. "Mrs. Madeira told Mrs. Jansky that it was *le Saint*. Imagine, if it really was *le Saint* who helped them? They didn't see him though. I don't know how the guy gets the money to people with nobody ever seeing him. It's as if people are excited to tell what happened, but I don't think they really tell everything. I think they know something more about *le Saint* or at least who helps *le Saint*..."

"*Le Saint*," Danny muttered, as he tried to loosen the pipe.

"You sound like you don't like the man," JoAnna accused, pulling another shirt from the pile.

"Maybe I don't."

"Do you know him?"

Danny didn't answer that one. "Just get tired of hearing about him...*Le Saint*, this. *Le Saint*, that. What kind of a name is that anyway? Think he never did anything wrong..."

"Even saints were sinners, Danny. But he does a good job of helping people. Like a modern day Robin Hood, or Don Diego or..."

"Thought nobody knew who the guy was."

"They don't."

"But you do?"

"No. I just think whoever he is, he's amazing. I mean he keeps stepping in and paying people's amount just in the nick of time."

Danny was getting tired of having this conversation. "That's not amazing. That's calling it dang close. What if he were late? I mean, calling it that close, a flat tire could mean the difference between life and death for somebody." Danny reached out for a pipe wrench.

He fumbled for it and she picked it up and handed it to him. "You're such an idiot!" she said the word almost endearingly, with a laugh, "He's noble."

Danny balked at her teasing, "I may be an idiot, but you're being unrealistically romantic. You think this whole thing is just an episode out of *The Scarlet Pimpernel*. Blakeney rushes in at the right moment and snatches the aristo out from under the knife of La Guillotine."

She contemplated his accusation, and replied thoughtfully, "But, he does."

"Well, it's not helpful. The guy is just playing into the Underworld's hands. They don't care who pays it, they just want the money. If they have some guy that's simple-minded enough to bust his butt paying everybody else's fines and loans, they are sitting pretty and he's not defeating any enemy. He's just feeding a ravenous beast. He just enables them to grow bigger and bigger. A real hero…a real hero, would hit them where it hurts." He finally broke the coupling loose from its rust. "He'd take 'em down…somehow. He'd go to the core and rip the guts out of this machine that's taken over the whole south side of this city…the whole town, really." He shot a glance up at JoAnna who was still standing close to the sink, watching him in interest and a bit of surprise. "He's not a hero," Danny concluded abruptly, and refocused his full attention on the pipes.

"At least he hasn't run from responsibility. He hasn't given up trying to be a better person. At least he's trying to change something in this town." She turned and walked back across the kitchen to her ironing.

Danny pretended not to notice her retreat, but he watched from under the sink as she picked up the iron and—with her back to him—resumed her ironing. If she knew all that he knew, she would have agreed with him. And for that reason, he felt more at peace having her angry that he had snubbed her hero, than having her know that her hero was the man under the sink. And the man under the sink…wasn't much of a hero at all.

***

It was nearly ten o'clock that night when Danny closed the door on his study and walked to the coat rack. He usually never left the house late at night, but everyone had been asleep for over an hour. No one would miss his going out, and JoAnna was there if anyone should awaken. He lifted his overcoat off the hook by the door and shrugged into it.

"Where are you going?"

Danny turned sharply; he hadn't heard her movements behind him, which startled him for more reasons than wanting to get out of the house unnoticed.

"Out," he replied, shortly.

"It's ten o'clock at night."

"Thank you, JoAnna," he replied with a tinge of sarcasm, "But I can tell time, too." He turned toward the door.

"Danny!" she called. He turned but she obviously thought he wouldn't wait and had rushed uncomfortably close to him. He caught his breath, but he didn't respond.

"I'm sorry," she insisted bluntly.

"For what?"

"This morning. I…I said hurtful things, about men not…about people giving up and …I'm sorry. I think it came out sounding like I was condemning you for not fixing things and it was out of place and none of my business…and I have no idea what you have gone through. I'm sorry."

"That's not why I'm going out."

"It doesn't matter why you're going out. I just came out here to apologize…I…I was about to knock on your study door when you came out and then I got scared and then I wasn't going to…and then you were leaving and I just had a bad feeling that…I figured I better say something…if something happened to you and I hadn't…"

She was rambling and his only conscious thought was to pull her close and smother the embarrassed excuse on her lips with a kiss. He had to distract himself. "I've got to go…" he interrupted, placing his hat on his head.

"I know, and now I'm just rambling again…sorry. It's just that…"

He had to remove the temptation completely, however rude it may seem to her. "Good night, Miss Edwards," he said abruptly and opened the door.

She took a step back from him, and he noticed hurt in her dark eyes. He opened his mouth to apologize, but before he could make a half-hearted apology she replied, "Good night, Mr. Navarone" and fled down the hallway towards her back bedroom.

Danny slammed the front door behind him on his way out.

***

Danny wandered through the front door of Arnie's Place. Saturdays were a good deal busier than Thursday nights, which meant the smoke was a little thicker, the lights were a little dimmer and the music, of which there had been none before, was loud enough to prevent anyone from hearing his neighbor's conversation whether he wanted to or not.

Danny only nodded a 'hello' to Arnie and made his way to Flags' table. Flags was in the company of a man who was trying to tell a story which was almost unintelligible to Danny, because his lisp was so slurred. Flags, however, kept nodding and laughing, seemingly understanding everything the man said.

Danny shook his head in disbelief, but didn't interrupt as he stood beside their booth. Both men noticed him, but neither seemed bent on providing a moment for him to interrupt. Finally, the story apparently over, the second man leaned back and folded his arms with a final guffaw. Flags looked up, blinking several times, for the brightness of the dim lights that Danny was standing under. He squinted, "'Ello, Joe."

"It's Navarone, Flags," Danny corrected.

"Lieut? Naw. Tisn't Thursday," he looked across at his table partner, "Is it?"

The other man shrugged as if he didn't care one way or the other, picked up his drink and downed what was left.

"Flags, can I see you for a moment?"

"Well, that depends. Are you buying me a drink?" He was lisping nearly as badly as the other man.

"Sure. Black coffee or ginger ale? You choose."

Flags looked disappointed. "I've had better, eh, es-coose me, better offers. But beggars can't be, can't be…I forgot what I was saying…no matter…" He turned to the other man. "You have to es-coose me, MacDonal'. I'm going to have a very dry conversation with my frien' here."

MacDonald took his time comprehending Flags' intimation, but he finally caught the drift and rose to leave. He patted Danny kindly on the back as he wandered away, but Danny had a feeling it was more to steady himself than give Danny any comfort.

Danny sank onto the bench across from Flags.

"'Ello, Dan'l," he greeted, as if he only now believed him not to be Joe.

Danny shook his head and demanded irritably, "Why do you drink so much, Flags?"

"To make up for what you don't drink."

"I'm drinking tonight," Danny said. He pulled the bottle across the table.

Flags watched him. "What happened?"

"Nothing." He poured three fingers of whiskey in the glass and downed it.

Flags raised his eyebrows at the lie and the action and said, "Dan'l, you just drank more in one swallow than I've seen you drink in the last three years. What happened?"

Danny looked at the glass, slightly ashamed that he had even thought about trying to get drunk. He scooted farther into the booth and turned himself sideways so that he could stretch out his legs on the bench. He crossed his arms and legs, and looked out at the bar scene rather than at Flags. "How do you get over something that happened so long ago?"

Flags pulled the bottle back across the table to himself. "This is how I get past it. But that's not your way. Even if you want it to be, you'd be more miserable doing this to yourself than living with whatever ghosts you live with."

Danny met his gaze for a moment and then studied the empty glass. He was right, dang it. "So what is my way?"

"I don't know. I thought Bowling was taking care of that."

Danny scoffed, "That's a farce."

"Well *I* know that. But nobody else does. Isn't that the point?"

"I don't mean *that's* a farce. I mean the idea that what we do is actually helping anyone is a farce."

Flags folded his arms around the bottle and rested his chin on the top. "Really? You think so?'

"Cut the crap, Flags. Who cares what we do? Balestrini surely doesn't give a crap. We're like a little mouse that keeps stealing the cheese from his trap, while Balestrini goes on feasting on the banquet, barely noticing."

"Maybe. Maybe that is what we are to him. But you know the other mice in the house don't feel that way. They know they are surviving because the one guy, that one elusive mouse, is what's keeping them from sticking *their* neck in the trap and being caught."

"Is that helpful?"

Flags looked at him, "You may not think so, but I could name one or two who care."

Danny was already shaking his head, not wanting to listen.

Flags continued, "Like Benson's Hardware; Artimus over on 7th; Hemminger who need to replace his busted hoist appreciated it; and Siegmann; and heck, what about Madeira…if he knew who you were, you'd have free groceries for a lifetime…"

"That's not why we do it!" Danny snapped shortly, quietly.

"How about Halverson? Remember him?" Flags retorted, just as irritably.

Danny sank into silence. Of course he remembered Halverson. Wasn't Danny the officer who had seen him gunned down needlessly in the alley? Wasn't he the guy that had held Halverson in his arms when he lay dying? Wasn't he the guy who knew that Hartley needn't have pulled his trigger? Wasn't he the guy who hadn't said anything to his Chief of Police because he knew Wiley, his own Chief, was on Balestrini's payroll? Danny gritted his teeth. Halverson had been going to give up his gun to him, he knew it for a fact. Halverson wouldn't have shot him. Sometimes he had a fear that Hartley had known that too and had pulled his trigger anyway.

Finally he spoke, "Yah, I remember Halverson."

"Then you remember why we do this," Flags stated. When Danny didn't answer he poured himself another glass, drank half of it and studied his friend. He said in a low voice that became somewhat gravely with emotion. "Dan'l, stop beating yourself up because you can't change the entire world and see what you *have* changed. You may not save *everyone*, but you saved *somebody*. Why isn't that enough for you?"

"Why is it enough for you?"

Flags looked at him with sudden understanding. He paused a respectful moment before he murmured, "We can't go back, Dan'l. We can't change the past. You can't save Lilian."

Danny leaned his head back and closed his eyes. It was silent in the booth except for the clink of glass as Flags poured himself another drink. Danny didn't open his eyes but finally he murmured, "I know…that's clincher, isn't it?"

Flags sighed loudly, "That's the clincher for most of us…from Salerno to the Liri Valley to Monte Cassino and Anzio…"

Danny looked over at his friend. They had been over it a hundred times, it wouldn't do to say it again. He wondered why he could move past their time in the War and Flags couldn't; yet he couldn't move past what had happened to Lilian. "Another drink?" Flags offered.

Danny shook his head. "Nah…that one didn't sit well with my stomach," he admitted.

Flags gave a grin, "You never could hold it, could you?"

Danny laughed softly, "Not really."

Flags made a motion to the bartender and he brought over a bowl of pretzels. "See if that helps…plans for Thursday?"

"Got an idea. You?"

Flags shook his head, "Nah. Figured I came up with the last one. Try to top that?"

Danny smiled again, "Can't top that, can I? How about a game of Bowling?"

"You want to actually go bowling, on bowling night?"

"It'd be novel."

"It'd be boring."

"Alright, we'll go with my first plan. Seven o'clock?"

"Course."

"I'm going home," Danny stated as he pulled his legs to the floor. Glancing at the bottle on the table, he looked at Flags. "Don't drink any more tonight, hmm?"

"Why not?"

"Cause I asked you."

"You've been asking for the last seven years."

Danny relented, "See yah in a few days, Flags."

Chapter VIII

Home alone for the first time since she had moved into the Navarone house, JoAnna turned the burner out and placed the kettle of hot water on a trivet on the counter. Danny had had the children up and out of the house in time for early Mass. There was to be a farewell gathering for Debbie at his folks' place and what with all his siblings and cousins it would be an all-day affair. What a long day it had been so far without little feet pattering about and little voices asking questions. How quickly she had grown accustomed to them startled her. But it had been easy, almost unconscious. As a girl she had lived with only her father, and then she had been alone for three years. Three years…she hated the loneliness. She loved the ring of this house; whether it be shouting or crying or laughter, the noise all sounded glorious to her.

The doorbell rang, startling the silence. JoAnna hesitated. The front door was closed and the family vehicle was gone. She could pretend no one was home. The temptation to turn, take her tea and book into her room and pretend she hadn't heard it tugged strongly. She felt too new and timid to open the door when none of the family was home. What if the person visiting didn't know that there was a new resident and she had to explain…oh it was just too awkward, she couldn't do it. But then the visitor began knocking persistently and JoAnna had a sudden fear that something had happened to one of the children, so she put down her mug and hurried to the door. When she opened it, she found Debbie standing there smiling.

"Hello, Debbie. Aren't…aren't you supposed to be at your folk's place? There's a party there for you…Or was it a surprise? Did I just blow it?!" JoAnna covered her mouth in dismay at her blunder.

"Calm down, JoAnna. I know all about the party…may I come in?" she asked, and without waiting for a reply, opened the screen door and came in herself. "Don't worry about the party. It's customary for Navarone women to be late to any party given in their honor…Sharon was even late to her own wedding…are you busy? Can we chat?" Debbie led the way down the hall, leaving JoAnna no choice but to follow. Debbie kept up a steady flow of speech as JoAnna prepared another cup of tea. They seated themselves at the table.

Sipping her tea, Debbie sighed, "Ah, nothing better than tea in the morning…unless its coffee, I actually prefer coffee."

She was suddenly silent and JoAnna felt awkward, unsure if she should hurriedly make some coffee, or just try to save the conversation which from the get-go had been singlehandedly handled by Debbie.

"I wanted to chat with you before I left for school."

JoAnna smiled and murmured something about it being kind of her, and then took a sip of her tea as an excuse for not having anything else to say.

"You know when we first met after Mass that weekday…well, I can admit now that I was being purely selfish. See, I've had plans to go to nursing school since I was fourteen. But things happened you know…you see Danny's wife was killed a year before I graduated high school and well, Barbara took care of them for the first year, but the spring I graduated she had her first baby and Danny tried a couple nannies but wasn't very happy with that route and…well, you can't just up and follow your own plans when your brother's in a jam. So I stayed and have been taking care of the kiddos for two years. And I admit I was feeling a bit sorry for myself, this summer, as I knew more girls were preparing to start this fall with the nursing program. And I was just in Church listing my complaints to God when low and behold you walk in and kneel down right in front of me. What are the odds?" She put her chin in her hand, "Well, you'd have to figure out the number of people who could fit in one pew and multiply by the number of pews in Saint Francis and then…well anyway I don't need to know the numbers, I know that it was a miracle pure and simple. I mean you never sat in that spot before! I've never even seen you in St. Francis before and I go there a lot…have to, yah know, my brother is the associate pastor." She laughed. "So I just have to thank you, thank you for taking the job. I know that you will be fabulous!

"It hasn't even been a week," JoAnna reminded the girl. "Your brother may not be very happy with me either."

"I know, it hasn't even been a week and things are great! Trust me you're doing much better than the others!"

JoAnna didn't think Danny was quite as enthusiastic as his sister, but she admitted, "I hope it does work out. I enjoy the children so much."

"And what about my brother?" Debbie asked, her question dripping with inflection.

JoAnna colored, knowing what the young woman implied. She would answer carefully. "Well, I think he is a wonderful father to his children."

Debbie raised an eyebrow. "That's it?"

JoAnna studied her tea. "What would you have me say, Debbie? He is my employer."

"But as a man, don't you think anything…"

"Debbie," JoAnna stopped her. "Nothing that you could possibly be plotting is going to happen. He doesn't like me. I haven't been here a week, and do you know how many times we have argued?"

"About what?" Debbie insisted.

JoAnna shook her head and shrugged, "Everything. Breakfast, supper, *le Saint*, we even argue when I try to apologize for arguing. There isn't going to be anything more than just my being the nanny." Debbie had such a romantic heart, it was best to set the whole thing straight before she went off to school and imagined them married before she came home for Christmas.

Debbie pushed her mug aside. "Don't write him off so easily, JoAnna. You don't know him. Let me tell you about him…"

JoAnna's warning signal went off and she put up a hand, "Wait a minute. If you have come to gossip about your brother, I protest. He would not like that."

"Alright then."

She acquiesced a little too quickly, JoAnna thought.

Debbie continued, "I will just share a little about the family. You know, it would be helpful in knowing why the kids do certain things, to better understand the family."

Before JoAnna could protest, Debbie launched into a mini history of the Navarone family. After nearly an hour, Debbie finally stood and stretched. "Oh dear, now I'll be late…I mean later than even *they* make allowances for. If I am much later, they'll send out the Navarone Posse looking for me," Debbie laughed.

And as quickly as she had breezed into the house, she took her leave. JoAnna sat at the table, a cup of now cold tea before her. She hadn't fully understood all that Debbie had told her. Half of it she wished she hadn't heard, being a little afraid that Danny would be angry that she knew. That she knew so much more about his life than he probably ever would have thought it necessary to tell someone working as the nanny.

Still, some of the information she was glad she knew. Perhaps, as Debbie suggested, it would be helpful knowing a little history to better understand the moods of the children, or her employer.

Debbie had insisted on giving a full family history, starting with the very beginning: that Danny and Lillian had met and married during the War, and Josiah had been born before Danny returned in '45. When he did come back to Gilmore, with all his Army training he had been hired fairly quickly at the Police Department. Debbie had been very young then, only eleven when the War had ended, and she didn't really remember much of what went on in Gilmore in the years that followed only that Tobias had come along in '48 and Janey in '49. What she did remember was that when Lilian was killed, murdered actually, there had been some bad politics and scandals. Within six months, Danny had walked away from the Department and had taken a job as an auto mechanic. She hadn't known why, and nobody really talked about the decision, and she had never been brave enough to ask.

But they did still talk about Lilian. Danny wanted the kids to hear stories about their mother, but he wasn't always very good about talking about her himself, and he never talked about the night she was murdered.

Debbie seemed particularly insistent that she inform JoAnna—despite JoAnna's hesitation—that as to the post of nanny being replaced by a wife Debbie feared that would not happen. There were plenty of girls interested in Danny, but he never made a move on any of them.

Debbie had wrapped up the conversation—monologue, really—with a concise closing statement, that Danny was the best brother ever—besides Paul…and Thomas…and Clancy, well, Debbie couldn't honestly say who was the best, it depended on the day—but Danny was special, and he needed someone who could help him be the man he used to be. JoAnna feared Debbie was again hinting towards the wish of her romantic heart, but she decided to take the information as nanny and nothing more.

After giving herself some time to think, JoAnna stood and cleared the dishes from the table. Best to erase any evidence of her visitor. She felt guilty, as if she had learned too much. And the secrecy with which Debbie had obviously come made JoAnna wary to let anyone know that she had. She could envision Danny being angry; although she wasn't sure if he would be angry that she knew that his wife hadn't just passed away but had been murdered, or angry that his sister had been over there gossiping about him. She decided she was grateful for the information, but she was scared it might change the way she reacted to Danny…and that might make him suspicious. She was a girl with a secret, and that was a dangerous thing in the house of a man who was an ex-cop. Perhaps it was best to confess all…what a predicament to be in!

***

For Danny the day was long and restful. He was able to distract himself from Balestrini and JoAnna with the concerns and jobs of his siblings' lives and a game of family-style baseball. Josiah was ecstatic when he threw a ball that got Father Clancy out at third, and a little mortified that Uncle Richard caught what he thought was sure to be a homerun. But all in all it was a good day and Danny had a feeling if he didn't drive fast enough he would have to carry all three of them into the house and directly to bed.

He needn't have worried as they were much too excited to fall asleep.

JoAnna sat on the front porch with a skein of yarn and needles when they arrived home. Janey raced up the steps and threw her arms around her. "We missed you!" she exclaimed. "I ate a bug on accident and Debbie gave me her old paper dolls…they aren't even cut-ted out yet!"

JoAnna marveled at this bit of unconnected information and then asked the group, "Did you have a nice time?"

They answered with a variety of unconnected information, recounting baseball games and cookies and cousin Eddie's crutch "on account of he fell off the roof of the grainery where his brother Jeffy had thrown his slingshot."

Danny decided it was time to relieve her of the variegated conversation as he himself was getting lost in it and he had been with them the whole day. He ordered goodnights all around and warned he'd be up in ten, so they had better not dillydally. They rushed into the house, leaving Danny sorry he had said it, because it left him alone on the porch with JoAnna.

"Did you have a relaxing day off?" he asked, at the same time thinking he sounded like a fool for asking.

"It was very nice, although it's amazing how fast one gets used to all their excitement and how lonely it is when the house is quiet."

He looked at the house as if it were the house she were commenting on and not the children. "Suppose so," he agreed.

She didn't offer anything further about her day and Danny certainly didn't think it was his place to ask. So he stood and she sat in silence except for the click and scrap of her knitting needles.

"Did everyone get to see Debbie before she leaves?"

"Yes, almost everyone made it out to my folks. We didn't think Debbie was going to make it, but she showed up, late as usual."

"Oh?" JoAnna replied and something in her voice made it sound put-on and fake, as if it were old news.

He did a double take at her. "Yes," he replied a little hesitant because of her response. "She showed up finally…hope she gets over that quickly, I don't think the Sisters will be very forgiving if she's late to class or clinicals as often as she is late to family gatherings."

JoAnna laughed at the idea, "No, I don't suppose they would. I suppose she just had some friends to see before she leaves."

"I suppose she did…" he murmured thoughtfully, watching her.

JoAnna tried her best to fill the incriminating silence. "She is so excited. I'm glad she finally gets to go…" her voice trailed off. She was rambling and probably saying too much. He would guess what had kept Debbie.

"JoAnna…"

"Yes?" she smiled brilliantly, trying to act nonchalant, her heart pounding, for fear her secret visitor would be found out.

Her smile made him hesitate but he decided to ask anyway, "How well do you know Debbie?"

If it had been a little brighter on the porch he would have sworn she was blushing, but it was too dark to be sure. "Well, not very long, to be sure. But Debbie is very…gregarious…and I don't think the number of days matters as much as the intensity of the conversations she has with you…"

Danny couldn't help but laugh at her choice of words and description. "That's one way to sum up the girl, isn't it?"

JoAnna was grateful for the sound of his laughter, but wouldn't give him a chance to redirect the conversation. She collected her knitting, stood up and walked to the door. He stood in front of the door, as he had been throughout their conversation, on the pretense of following his children into the house to tuck them in. He didn't move out of her way, as she approached the door, and she feared he would question her more about her day and that she would have to divulge the secrets of her visitor.

"Would you like me to put the children to bed?" she asked, her heart pounding, but this time for his nearness.

He shook his head, "I'll finish the day out."

"Very well."

He still didn't move, he seemed lost in thought, as he looked at her. JoAnna flushed and forced a flustered, "Goodnight, Mr. Navarone."

Her salutation prompted him and he opened the door for her, and then corrected softly as she walked passed, "Daniel."

She was on the threshold and looked back over her shoulder, her face framed by her waves of wheat-colored hair, "Good night, *Daniel*."

Chapter IX

Monday dawned bright and early. Being Labor Day and the children's last day of summer vacation, they intended not to miss any of it. Tomorrow, Danny warned JoAnna, the kids would have to be dragged from their beds; but today they were up before anyone else and ready to spend the free day with gusto.

The night before, JoAnna had been determined Danny shouldn't know that she knew anything. But as she lay awake last night, pieces of her life began falling together, in a way she never thought possible. This morning, she could only ponder in awe and gratitude how God had put her in a place where something could finally be solved. She had waited three years to have an answer to a painful, life altering event, and now, it seemed as if God had placed her in a situation that could possibly produce some answers, and some long-desired closure.

Danny was working in his garage before JoAnna was up, she could hear him clanking on his car. The children finished their eggs and grabbed dish towels before JoAnna had finished buttering her toast. She took the towel from Toby. "Go on, all of you. I'll finish these up."

They didn't argue and remembered to throw *thank you's* over their shoulder as they clamored out the backdoor and into the yard.

After JoAnna had dried the last breakfast dish, she untied her apron and hung it over a kitchen chair. She walked out the back door and surveyed the children in the tree fort. Josiah was building an extension onto the tree fort and as JoAnna watched his perilous hovering and hanging and pounding, she decided it would be best to stop watching, rather than tell him to stop the addition. She walked toward the garage and through the backdoor.

Danny looked up from the new piece of gas line he held in his hand. "Good morning," he greeted, with a smile. The day had him in as good a mood as his children.

"Morning," she said, wandering slowly into the garage.

"Did you have a good sleep?" he asked looking back down at the piece.

"Not really," she admitted. She was distracted by the subject she wanted to broach and only realized afterward how stinted and rude her reply sounded. She added quickly, "But thank you for asking."

Danny laughed at her delayed pleasantry. "You're welcome. Why didn't you sleep well?"

"I couldn't stop thinking about stuff," she said unable to look at him and toyed with a greasy rag on a stack of crates.

Danny watched her with curiosity. JoAnna didn't usually avoid meeting his gaze when she spoke. "What kind of stuff, or shouldn't I ask?"

He saw her take a deep breath and then she looked up and stated abruptly, "You're a cop."

Danny raised one eyebrow in surprise at the announcement, however his surprise faded fairly quickly. "Ah-ha. So now we know why Debbie was so late yesterday."

His accurate guess threw her off her mission and gave him time to lay down on the creeper and roll beneath the dusty blue '49 Plymouth.

Regaining her composure, JoAnna insisted, "That's beside the point…you *are* a cop."

"No. I'm a mechanic," he said flatly, his annoyance more for his sister than for JoAnna. Silence descended in the garage except for the clicking sounds of Danny's ratchet as he loosened the bolt. He wondered what else Debbie had told her, and in the same instant decided he really didn't want to know.

A full minute passed, and two more bolts were loosened before he finally glanced over to see her ankles in her scuffed black flats. He heard uncertainty in her voice as she rephrased her question, "But you *were* a cop?"

"I *were* a lot of things," he replied calmly. "Now I'm just a guy with three kids. I work at a garage, bowl on Thursdays, usher on Sundays, would like to have a new car and a dog, but I've got neither."

"I knew all that before…except about the dog," JoAnna admitted. "But I didn't know you were a cop."

"You writing a book?" he asked sarcastically.

"No," she assured him, as if it had been a legitimate question. Then she knelt down on the garage floor so that she could peer at him beneath the car. He scooted farther along to the next bolt. "I need help finding a murderer."

Her words stopped his actions. Then he looked over at her to see if she were joking. But she was staring at him quite seriously. He rolled out from under his Plymouth and leaned up on one elbow, so that he could almost look her straight in the eye in her sitting position.

The nearness of his face to her own caught her off guard and she didn't say anything more. It had to be the sunshine, his good mood, and her blonde hair escaping from beneath her bright blue scarf, because he was enjoying her closeness and could have studied her blushing face at close proximity for some time. Instead, he murmured, "You're getting oil on your skirt," because he hadn't really taken her declaration seriously.

She glanced down. "It's fine. It's old anyway, I only wear it when I'm gardening…Will you help me?"

He leaned away from her slightly, "Maybe I *should* have gotten references before I hired you…? What does a nanny want with a murderer?"

JoAnna smiled at his teasing, but she wouldn't be put off now that she had finally gotten the conversation started. "I'm serious, Danny. Someone I loved very much was murdered three years ago."

She was looking down and didn't see how her words drained every drop of blood from his face. The humor and lightness that had been in his demeanor since she walked through the door was instantly gone. "Someone I love very much was murdered three years ago," he said the words as if he were repeating her statement, but he wasn't, he was saying it for himself, telling her. Only she didn't realize that he was saying them to her, and it frightened him that a big part of him wished she did.

She shook her head at his words, as if he had repeated them to mock her. "My father, Andrew Edwards was killed by Balestrini's men. But no one was ever convicted."

He regained his composure, but his good humor was gone for good. "Sounds like Balestrini's usual procedure," Danny muttered.

"What did you say?"

"I said, I'm sorry about your father. But what has that to do with my being a cop?"

"I thought perhaps you could help me find some evidence."

"Evidence? After three years? There's not going to be anything that would convict a man for a murder. And even if there was, no judge in this County would stand against Balestrini to convict the murderer."

He rolled back under the car to end the conversation. How it stung to say the words, knowing that the same held true for Lilian's murderer as well.

"So you won't help me?"

He tried to keep his voice steady and even devoid of any emotion, rather than let the pain reveal itself in his voice. "I don't know what you want me to do. I told you I am not a cop anymore." He tried to find some way to lessen his refusal. "Didn't the police have a suspect at the time? They may not have a tie to Balestrini, but they could at least try to get one of his henchmen off the streets."

"Well, no…" it was a drawn out negative response.

"No, as in no there was no suspect. Or no, as in no one you care to tell me about?"

JoAnna was silent.

"End of conversation?" Danny peered out from under the car.

"Well…there was no body."

Now Danny didn't respond. He waited for her to continue if she cared to explain.

"They killed him, but no one knows what they did with the body."

"JoAnna…"

"Let me explain. Please."

"Very well." He almost had the entire gas line off the car, he kept at the job as she spoke.

She began hurriedly as if she were afraid that Danny would suddenly leave the garage in boredom. "My father owned a Tailor shop on Grossmann Ave. I was a seamstress. He taught me the trade well, but all the books, the records, he took care of himself. Daddy never let me know much about the business side of the Tailor shop. But I do know that there was some kind of extortion that he was mixed up in. I can't tell you exactly what was going on. But every week, this guy would come and Daddy would pay him. Then one day, they had a heated argument. When they left together, Daddy said he had to see another man to settle a business deal. That was his only explanation.

"Only he never came back. The following day, I called the police to report him missing. They said they didn't investigate until someone was missing several days, as missing men invariably showed up with a hangover a couple days later. When they finally came, they took one look at our records…" she shook her head. "In the end, the investigating officer told me that if his books looked like our books, he'd disappear too. According to father's business records, we were so far in debt the only option was to declare bankruptcy. The Officer supposed that my father had decided to let the whole business fall in on itself and go on the lam so he didn't have to take the blame."

She looked beneath the car and met his gaze. His expression must have looked dubious to her because she hurried on, "But that's not what happened. Truly, that is not who my father was. Even if we were in debt, he wouldn't have left. He wouldn't have left his creditors…he certainly wouldn't have left me holding the bag! He was a good man. The only explanation is that he was killed."

She was silent and Danny wished she would continue; say something, anything. The silence was unnerving even though the job gave him the excuse to focus on the car instead of looking at her again.

"Do you believe me?"

"Yes, I believe you," he stated. He believed that Mr. Edwards had been killed, he didn't necessarily believe that he had been in the right while alive. He hoped they wouldn't go beyond the one fact to discuss the other.

"You don't sound like it."

He grimaced. "The truth of it is, JoAnna, they wouldn't have killed him if he refused to pay."

"What are you saying?"

"What I am saying is that it would do them no good to kill a man because he wouldn't pay. He also doesn't pay if he's dead. They would have used other tactics. They would have threatened to hurt you. Destroy his machines or store front to get him to see they were serious. But to step in and just bump him off does Balestrini no good."

She watched as he loosened the last bracket that held the gas line to the frame of the car. It clattered to the floor.

"You don't believe me? Just like everyone else, you think my father just left? And that I am crazy for not giving up on him."

"I didn't say that." How could he look her in those brown eyes and tell her that probably her father had been a conspirator and had used up his usefulness. That he was no longer needed in the Racket and had been eliminated as others before him and others after him. He couldn't say that, he would have to take a different approach. He scooted out from beneath the car and sat upright. "Look, JoAnna. You know the old saying, where there's smoke there's fire? Well it works both ways. Where there's a fire, there is going to be smoke."

"What's that got to do with murder?"

"What I mean is, where there is *murder*, there is always a *body*. Not just *some* of the time. *Always*. Understand?"

Her mouth opened as if she were going to object. But she dropped her gaze and looked disheartened. For a moment, Danny wished he hadn't been so hard, had dissuaded her interest in another way. He could feel himself caving and wanting to reach out and touch her in comfort, and to avoid anything of the kind, he stood up and studied the old gas line, fingering the two holes he had found. He picked up the new gas line when JoAnna slowly stood.

"JoAnna, I'm not saying that your father wasn't murdered. He could very well have been. I'm only saying that without the body as proof there's nothing else we can do."

"I can't believe that, Danny. I can't believe that if you knew a man had been murdered and his body destroyed that you would stand for that. I can't believe that of you. I may very well be crazy for thinking that my father couldn't do anything so despicable, but my father's disappearance is a fact. No one can prove it one way or the other. So I'm asking you, Danny, to please help me. I just want to know. To have an answer. You've lost a loved one. Doesn't knowing make it easier?"

Danny set down the gas line and wiped his hands on a rag, "Sometimes it's easier not knowing." Would he say that if he didn't know what had happened to Lillian? Or was he only saying that because he knew, in every detail he knew.

"Maybe so," she relented. "But I want to know. I need to have some kind of answer, Danny, some kind of closure."

"What if the answer is he's out there on the lam?"

"He's not," she said with conviction.

"What if the answer is he was working for Balestrini?"

There was a spark in her dark brown eyes and she challenged, "Then you can prove it to me."

The line between Daniel Navarone and *le Saint* was getting awfully thin and it was making him extremely nervous. He would have liked to do whatever she asked of him and as le Saint he could go down that road. But there was always that chance that one of these days, le Saint was going to blow the town wider open than Daniel Navarone could handle. And the fear lay in the uncertainty of who would be hurt in the process. He tossed the rag onto a crate at the side of the garage, and shook his head. "Believe me, you don't want to go digging up something in Balestrini's past. You came to the wrong guy. I can't help you. I can't give you the answers you want."

"Danny…"

"Dang it, JoAnna! I'm not a cop anymore. I'm a mechanic." he couldn't keep this peaceful discussion up anymore. He drew a deep breath and added more calmly, "I walked away from the Department for a reason, JoAnna. Can you understand that? I left. And I don't want anything to do with what I left behind. Any ties you think I have with those guys, are null and void. I barely know any of them even as friends any more. I have no intelligent ties with the Department."

She placed her hands on her hips, looked up at him, she even took a step closer. "You have instinct, Danny. What made you a great cop, is still part of who you are…"

"Stop it. Right now, stop it! If you believe your father is dead and gone than leave him dead and gone. I am not getting into this. That part of my life is over. I'm a different man today than I was three years ago. Do you understand? And I don't want to have this conversation again." He lowered his voice—conscious of how upset he was becoming—and repeated sternly, "I said, do you understand?"

JoAnna studied at him. She didn't just rest her eyes on a person who was speaking before her, she literally looked at him and Danny felt as if he had to put up guards to protect himself from her look. Her look wasn't harsh or judgmental, it was extremely gentle, as if she could read every line of worry and fear and love on his soul. She relented and gave a small honest smile. "I'm sorry, Danny. I do understand. I don't think I fully believe you, but I understand what you are saying." And as contradictory as her words sounded, Danny believed her.

She gave him a smile and walked towards the garage door. But at the door she paused and turned back, "And I think you should," she said.

"Should what?" Danny demanded, his frustration still piqued.

"Get a dog," JoAnna replied. "It would be good for you...and the children would love it…I heard Father Larson has puppies to give away." Her smile was gentle as she walked away as if all were settled. And Danny didn't know if the dog subject was settled or if he was going to prove her father had been murdered. Either way he knew he had lost the argument and he wanted to hit something. Instead he slammed down the hood of his still-not-running '49 Mayflower.

Chapter X

The following evening, after tucking in the children, Danny came down the stairs hoping to find JoAnna. He glanced in the living room but she wasn't there. She never sat in the living room in the evening; he supposed she didn't feel at home enough to do so. Danny walked toward the kitchen; if she was still there he'd talk to her, but he wouldn't disturb her in her room.

As Danny approached the kitchen, he heard JoAnna humming. For a split second, he thought about turning back. But he continued forward, and there she was, washing quart jars by the dozens.

"Are you canning again?" he asked, as he entered the kitchen. It was a stupid question as there was no other reason to wash so many quart jars, but he asked it anyway.

"Yes, tomatoes tomorrow," she made a face as she scrubbed. "Or Thursday. I forgot I told your sister Sharon I would help her fit a dress tomorrow. It's difficult to fit yourself…."

She was rambling again and he changed the subject and he leaned against the counter beside the sink. "What you told Janey seems to have worked. School was not as tragic as she imagined."

"Yes, I think she is really excited about it!" JoAnna agreed, then looked up at him surprised. "What did I tell Janey?"

"I don't know. Something about being scared of new people."

"Oh, that." She smiled and went back to washing the jars. "I was just trying to help her…I don't know…face her fears?" She shrugged and kept scrubbing the jars in the sink, continuing. "Sometimes we make nothing out of children's fears. We think that if we act as if there's nothing to be afraid of, they will follow suit. Like being scared of the dark. In reality there is nothing to be afraid of. It's the truth and they should just believe it. But fears," she shook her head, "fears don't always make sense. They can't always be reasoned away. Sometimes it's better to acknowledge them then to pretend they don't exist. Isn't it better to give them the nightlight, than tell them the dark isn't scary? Because for them it is frightening, and it is very real." She glanced up and found him, to her surprise, still listening to her.

"So you told her you were scared of new people too?"

Blushing, JoAnna looked back at her suds and jars, and said frankly, "I am. Until I get to know someone very well, I am usually very nervous every time I have to meet people in a new situation….it's probably very silly to you. But it's a very real fear. I don't know what to say, how to start a conversation. I…I'm not very good at small talk and I just feel awkward. Until I know someone well enough to know that I *don't have to* say anything at all, then it's easy to say *any*thing at all."

Danny nodded slowly. "Makes sense, I guess."

"What about you, Danny?" she asked, looking into his eyes with piercing honesty. "What are you afraid of?"

Danny quickly dropped his gaze, picked up a jar from the counter and dumped a dead bug and some dust out of it. "Me?" he replied sarcastically, "I'm the dad in the house, I'm not allowed to be afraid of anything." He grinned at her and handed her the jar.

JoAnna met his gaze and laughed. "Oh okay," she agreed. "I'll remember that."

She leaned over the sink to find another jar in the suds. Her hair was escaping from beneath her scarf and between the smell of her and the soap Danny knew exactly what he was afraid of, and he wasn't going to pretend it didn't exist. He was going to avoid it at all costs.

He dropped a second jar in her sink with suddenness and said abruptly, “I’ll be back late.”

JoAnna looked up, startled by the unexpectedness of his words and action. But he didn’t look at her. He turned without a backward glance and walked out of the kitchen.

***

Danny crawled into his truck and drove. He didn’t really care where he drove, he just drove to get out of the house. The smell of JoAnna was still in his nostrils. And his longing for her was still crowding his chest.

JoAnna hadn’t brought up the subject of her father again; she wasn’t the kind to ask for help after being turned down. And she certainly didn’t show any animosity toward him in her words or actions. But Danny thought about the mystery; he had thought about it a lot in the last twenty-four hours. He wanted to know the answer for her as well. But, as he had tried to tell her, she was asking the wrong person. She wanted him to find her father’s murderer, but he couldn’t even find Lilian’s murderer.

His frustration with himself had only grown in those same twenty-four hours. What was he supposed to do? Murders weren’t solved in Gilmore. People were either too scared or too highly paid to be witnesses. The evidence that may have been left at any crime scene was systematically destroyed by the investigating officer and if he wasn’t on the take, it invariably was thrown out by the Judge as circumstantial evidence. Danny had done the only thing he could grasp at in the moment. He had basically lied to her. Told her there was nothing he could do, when in reality, he and Flags could have at least tried.

And he knew exactly why he had lied to her.

After Lilian’s murder he had refused to be pushed by Balestrini, to fall under his intimidation tactics. He kept on the job because he thought he could somehow make a difference despite Chief Wiley’s misplaced loyalties. But when Halverson was killed, he suddenly realized that by staying on the Force, he wasn’t really *doing* anything that did any good. The only way he *could* do any good was to walk away. Walk away and do something that would stop the continuous monotony of Balestrini’s rule. Perhaps one man couldn’t bring down an operation the size Balestrini ran, but Danny could at least help men like Halverson.

He rubbed a hand over his face, trying to make sense of all his scattered thoughts. What was he even trying to solve? He was thinking about Balestrini when the issue was his nanny.

He had been right about JoAnna. He should have listened to his instincts. He had known living this closely with a woman would be a bad idea. Something inside him asked, *a woman? Or this woman?* He ignored his own question.

He couldn't do this much longer. He would have to find someone else. Clancy had initially suggested an employment agency. Danny would find another, older woman to be nanny and Clancy would help JoAnna find another job. *Isn't that just avoiding the situation?*

"There is no situation," he argued aloud. His voice sounded odd in the silence of the truck. The argument that JoAnna was great with the kids, couldn't be silenced as easily. How could he be so selfish as to overlook that?

And why couldn't he just admit that he was falling for her. There was nothing wrong with that. Lilian had been his love, but she was gone. He still loved her, but it was different now. And there was nothing wrong with loving JoAnna.

But again, wasn't his love for her also selfish? If he truly loved her, he should send her away; because having her close would be putting JoAnna in the same spot he had put Lilian? Across a line; with Balestrini on one side and the woman he loved on the other. He would be endangering her just as he had endangered Lilian.

You were supposed to learn from the past, not repeat it. But the situation was still the same. Balestrini was still running the town, Danny was still at odds with him. Only now Danny's actions were more veiled. Currently the veil protected him. What happened when the veil fell? Danny had to make sure it never did. And if it did fall, that it revealed only Danny on the other side and no one else. And that meant never letting anyone get close to him again.

He turned the truck around on a field road and headed back to town. His drive was plunging him farther into the confusion. Never getting close to anyone didn't seem to be a good answer. Father Clancy always said that man was created for community. Well, Danny was trying to do his best to serve that community, to make the city better. Keep people safe. But he also felt, as he had told JoAnna, that *le Saint* wasn't really doing anything but prolonging the tyranny.

How many people were he and Flags already endangering by their ventures? Could he morally accept getting anyone else involved, even as a fringe acquaintance?

A picture of Lilian's body flashed through his thoughts and he shuttered. Clancy had warned him against blaming himself for another's sin. But was her murder someone else's fault, or his own? What about the sin of omission? Or of commission? He should have been there. Lilian had been on that street corner, waiting for him, when they had taken her.

Danny stopped the truck and looked up at the church he had parked in front of. He had to stop going over and over the same situations. He had to trust that God was watching out for him. He walked into the church and sat down in the back pew. The Church was very dark, but he was grateful for the darkness. Only candles illuminated the sanctuary and he studied the red one suspended above the High Altar.

He remembered his feeling of peace about offering JoAnna the job and how smoothly the opportunity had presented itself. How could he doubt that she was supposed to be there? But Danny didn't trust himself. He had proved that he hadn't been trustworthy with Lilian, and when it came right down to it, he did not want a second chance to prove himself trustworthy. It wasn't worth the consequences if he failed again.

And on top of his own mistrust, there was the nightmare.

He hadn't had the nightmare for over a year, he felt sure. And now with JoAnna's arrival it was all there again. He couldn't help but tie her engaging smile—which reminded him of Lilian's—as the link between the past and the present. Between reality and the dream that had resurfaced. Only now in the dream, Lillian was there, but so was JoAnna. And then she wasn't and he couldn't tell…anything…dream, from history, from reality.

How was he supposed to move forward in life, when JoAnna's presence had brought him straight back to the beginning? And this after not even the full two week trial had passed.

How was he supposed to heal the past with anyone, let alone JoAnna, if she was the very thing that brought him back?

But he knew he had to go back. That was the only answer. He had to go back and tear it open to heal it. Like a wound that is partially healed but infected; he would have to reopen the wound to clear it of infection. But he wasn't sure he was ready. He wasn't sure he could do it. He was afraid of who would be hurt in the process.

Danny stood up to leave. He wasn't sure it had done any good to come. JoAnna and the nightmare and the situation with *le Saint* seemed only to be spiraling deeper into Balestrini's clutches, and Danny didn't want to bring in any more variables to the lives of those he loved and those he could not love.

He wanted to declare defiantly, "I'm not going back…and she's not staying." But when he looked back at the crucifix, he couldn't get the words out. And instead he murmured with resignation, and more trust than he actually felt, "Then you're gonna have to do this, because I can't."

Chapter XI

Danny woke early the next morning and left the house before anyone even had an inkling of stirring. He had slept well, dreams of JoAnna and his children had entertained him half the night, but they had turned sour by early morning and he had awaken in a deep sweat. And once again he decided she would have to leave.

But, by the time he arrived home from work that evening, he had resolved to do his best to put up with JoAnna's company for the sake of the children. The children talked and laughed as they shared stories of the day. JoAnna laughed just as freely as usual, although every now and then Danny saw her give him a sideways glance as if she knew he were off his game but had no idea what was wrong. When she gave him those curious, guarded looks, he jumped into the conversation with the children so that she couldn't guess she was right…but he had an aggravating feeling she still knew.

After putting the kids to bed, Danny found JoAnna sitting in the living room, knitting. He had insisted she use the whole house as her own, but now he was somewhat annoyed by her presence. He wanted to sit in the living room, but he wanted to sit there without her company. His resolve to endure the situation for the children but not himself was becoming very difficult. He would withdraw to his study, after settling a few matters.

"Oh, before I forget," he began from the doorway. "The kids mentioned something about a school picnic on Sunday."

"Oh, yes. The picnic for the beginning of the school year. They are so excited, even Janey."

He was annoyed at being interrupted, but then in his mood he probably would have been annoyed at not being interrupted. "I know Sunday is your day off, but would you mind taking them?"

JoAnna's brow wrinkled and she wrapped her yarn ends around her needles and said, "But it's for families, Danny. For families to get to know other families who will be at the school. Don't you think you should take them?"

"I would, only I really need to get the Plymouth running. I work all week at fixing other people's cars, and never get my own in running order," he said, trying to lighten the excuse.

Unconvinced, she stood and walked toward him so that they were both in the hall. He wished she had stayed in the living room.

"That's your excuse?" She asked, peering up at him with playful laughter in her eyes. "You can't take the kids on a picnic because you need to change your oil?"

"I didn't say change the oil." Danny shifted, uncomfortable with her nearness in the dim hallway.

She gave a small laugh, apparently unaware how annoyed he was. "No. But it sounded about as pathetic an excuse as that. Besides if you're still working on that car, how are we supposed to go to the picnic?"

Her apparent disregard for his wishes only increased his annoyance. "You can take the truck, or take them in your car. It's not that big a deal."

"Yes, it is, Danny." She was becoming more serious on the matter. "It's a *family* picnic. *You* should be taking them."

"I haven't had time to finish the car. I need to get it done this weekend."

"You don't have to work on Saturday. You can finish it Saturday."

Why did she need to make a court case out of everything? He took a deep breathe to try to calm his voice. "JoAnna, the *kids* want to go to the picnic. *I* think it would be good for them. *You're* better at arranging outings where there's food involved. So are you taking them or not?"

JoAnna placed her hands on her hips, "Are you asking or telling?"

"Asking," Danny thundered. "Didn't you hear the inflection in my voice?"

"Yes, Danny, I did. But you had the same inflection when you *asked* Josiah if he wanted to take the trash out…there didn't seem to be a debatable element in it."

"Are you gonna take the kids or not? I'm not asking again."

"Yes, I'll take them," she fired back.

"Fine!"

He started to turn away from her but she continued, "But I still think you should come as well."

He stormed around and faced her, his face livid. "JoAnna…"

She folded arms stubbornly across her chest. Before Danny could say anything further she insisted, "Daniel, the kids want to go to a *family* picnic to be a family and be with their father. They don't want to go to a picnic to be with their nanny!"

Her formal use of his name only made him a little more aware of how much he liked his name coming off her lips. Consequently he exploded, "Miss Edwards, I'm asking you to take them to a picnic, not adopt them. If you don't want to do it, just say so."

"I would *love* to go. But you should *want* to go! Your children love and adore you so much! And you must remember how it felt to show off your own father to your classmates? Kids like to show off their parents just as much as parents want to show off their children. They lost their mother three years ago, don't let them feel fatherless too."

Danny froze. The look on his face—or rather the mask that he had let fall suddenly, so that not even his frustration was visible anymore—was powerful. JoAnna blushed scarlet and he could only guess it was in regret at what she had said or that she was suddenly afraid of him. In any case she moved quickly away from him and hurried down the hallway toward the kitchen.

Danny stood for some moments in the entryway, still frustrated and at the same time wishing she hadn't been so right. He wondered how on earth she had just walked away, once again, the victor of an argument that he was pretty sure he had won.

***

Thursday rolled around again, and Danny parked his truck and made his usual roundabout way to Arnie's. As he stepped into the kitchen, Mrs. Arnie slid a batch of cookies off a cookie sheet. The smell wafted sweet and Danny groaned appreciatively. She looked up and smiled her toothy grin, "Daniel Francis, are you eyeing my cookies?"

"Maybe," he acknowledged.

She laughed and motioned towards the cookies. "Take one…but only one."

"Ah, Mrs. Arnie, you know with your cookies that is never a possibility."

She loved being loved for her cookies and laughed as Danny took two for starters and wandered out into the bar.

He scooted onto the bench at Flags' usual booth and waited for him to return from the bar where he leaned, swapping stories with another regular.

Eventually Flags sauntered back to the booth with a drink in each hand. "How's my drinking buddy?" he asked good-naturedly.

Danny raised an eyebrow and grinned. "No need to rub it in…besides with these I need coffee," he said indicating the cookies.

"With a stomach like yours you should drink milk."

"I would, but the cow dried up. If you felt that way, why'd you bring me a drink?" he asked, looking at the second glass.

"That's not for you. That's so's I don't have to get up again…Are we going to bicker like this all night, or are we gonna bowl?"

"It's early yet; you start bowling now, and you'll get caught. Let's talk shop for a moment…What can you tell me about a murder from three years ago?"

Flags looked surprised and Danny realized his first thoughts were probably about Lillian. Looking down at the table, Danny tried to clarify, "What would you say about a case where no body was found and everything pointed to a guy on the run…except one person very close to the guy disagreed?"

"I'd say Andrew Edwards."

Danny looked at him with utter surprise, "You know him?"

"Who?"

"Andrew Edwards?"

"Is that who we're talking about?"

"Yah."

"No I didn't know him. I just remember the case. Edwards Tailoring, the fella ran off and left his daughter to take the rap, but she wasn't buying what the cops said…It was all over the papers. Must have been about the time you were out with Lillian."

"What?"

"Three years ago, wasn't it?"

Danny nodded slowly, "I guess so, about that."

"Three years ago. I don't remember exactly when, but if you don't remember it, it must have been about the same time or shortly thereafter." Flags' brow wrinkled. "Edwards? Wait a minute…Miss JoAnna Edwards," he finished with a light-bulb effect.

"What?"

"That's the Edwards that's got your kids."

"Flags…"

"Arnie said you found a lady to take the kids, I didn't know it was Edwards's daughter."

Danny didn't want to be distracted. "Think there's a tie-in?"

"Tie-in to what?"

"I mean a correlation between Lilian's murder and Edwards?"

"Don't know. I mean, I don't know what you're talking about. All you said to me so far tonight was Andrew Edwards, and then the conversation broke into three separate trains and I haven't exactly followed any one of them completely."

Danny refrained from pointing out that he wasn't the one who kept jumping track. "But you remember the Edwards case?"

"Yah, he ran off and left the daughter," Flags started saying again.

"I got that part, Flags. But what about him? Was he clean? Did he just tank the business or was he involved in some racket?"

"Racket? What do you mean? You think he was gambling behind

the manikin?"

"I don't know, Flags. I'm asking. This must have been after my time, I've got nothing."

"Me neither. I'd have to look into it. There was another murder I was more interested in finding out about…must've been just a couple months after Lilian…"

"Yah, I guess so…don't you remember anything? Did they look for a body? Anything?"

"Well, I think there were a couple theories. Some said he tanked the business and went off and killed his-self. Some said he just made off…"

"I don't think he would've…"

"You knew 'im?"

"No. I just don't think a guy who could do that, could raise a daughter like Jo-…" Flags leaned across the table, his brows raised and the smell of liquor poignant on his breath. "Miss Edwards," Danny finished.

"Just won-ering," Flags sat back and finished his drink. "So you think this guy's too good to kill his-self or leave his daughter holding the bag; but he's not above being involved in some underworld racket, right?"

Danny shook his head, "I don't know what to think. I need to know more about the man; things that—as close as they may have been—not even his daughter knew about him."

"And you want me to do the leg work on this one?"

"Well, you do have a knack for getting people to share things with you."

"That's because I talk," Flags stated categorically. "You have to talk to get people to talk back at you…difficult concept for you, I know, but you should try it."

"I'll keep that in mind. In the mean time?"

"My drinks are gone," Flags informed him.

Danny took that to be an affirmative answer. "Good. Maybe tonight won't be a wash after all."

"When have I ever let you down, Lieut?"

"Let me see. Just last month there was the fifth of August; and before that there was June the twenty-fourth, and July the first …that was two Thursdays in a row…"

"All right, point taken. I'm not reliable. Wonder is you even keep me on the payroll. I suppose another of your partners in crime is better suited for this job?"

Danny shook his head, "Now you know why I keep you on the payroll."

"Yah. Gonna dock my pay?"

Danny nodded, "Probably. But don't worry. Half of nothing, is nothing."

"That's encouraging," Flags agreed and followed Danny toward the kitchen for a discreet exit through Arnie's back door.

***

Danny arrived home very late that night. The evening had gone well, but they hadn't found much for funds. But they also had left no trail and as Flags said, "It was a good dry run to keep them on their toes." Still, it always worried Danny to get home so late. Their escapades never worried him when he was on them. But as he made his way home, he always worried that somehow someone had identified them and that the henchmen would be quicker than he and would make it to his home. He worried that Balestrini would suddenly realize who the vigilante was who hit his random spots. And that he would send some wiseguy to Danny's home.

Tonight was no different and when he pulled into the yard his anxiety heightened. Lights lit the downstairs' windows. It was near enough to midnight, and every house on the street was pitch black, except a forgotten porch light three houses down. Danny didn't waste time putting the truck in the garage. He took the porch steps two at a time and opened the screen door. The storm door wasn't closed and he looked about the entry. "JoAnna?" he called softly; care for those who might be sleeping and partially for those who might be lurking. There was no answer and he didn't know whether to be thankful or in dread.

He poked his head into the deserted living room and moved down the hall to the kitchen. He stopped abruptly in the rounded kitchen doorway and breathed a sigh of relief.

JoAnna lay slumped at the kitchen table, sleeping. Her head lay across her arms, her hair falling over her shoulders and partly across her face; the blue scarf, that usually covered her hair while she worked, rested in her limp hand.

Danny looked about the kitchen; quart jars littered the counter tops. The last batch of tomatoes was still in the canner. He walked over to the stove, twisted the lid and lifted it off. No steam rose, so it must have cooled down some time ago. He set the lid to the side and then turned back to the table. JoAnna hadn't moved.

He walked closer, leaned over the back of another chair and watched her. He enjoyed the view. "I could get used to this, JoAnna," he murmured. "Having you to come home to."

He squatted down and leaned on the table and watched her peacefully pretty face. Reaching over, he brushed a bit of hair away from her face. "Did you hear what I said?" he whispered. Knowing that she hadn't was the only reason he spoke. If he had the courage to say that to her when she was awake, it might not be so stressful being around her. But as soon as those big brown eyes were open and looking up at him with any of their many expressions, he felt speechless; pulled between wanting to draw her close and wanting to push her farther away.

But she was safe company now. Safe because he didn't have to worry and wonder what her reaction to his advances would be. Safe because he didn't have to pretend he wasn't attracted to her. But only for this moment. He wouldn't let himself get used to her. She was just here for the children, he reminded himself.

Danny stood up and leaned over her. "Time for bed, Sleeping Beauty," he murmured. He scooped her up, and trembled slightly at how nicely she fit into his arms. Her head on his shoulder, she roused slightly to put one arm around his neck and to mumble sleepily, "Put me down, Danny, I can walk."

"I don't believe you," he replied, walking around the table toward her bedroom.

"I wouldn't tell a lie," she murmured her other arm going about his neck.

"Of course you wouldn't." He fumbled with the doorknob and opened the door.

She must have fallen back to sleep because she didn't say anything else. He laid her gently on the bed and pulled an afghan from the back of her bed to cover her. Without a word he crossed the room to the door and was just pulling it closed behind him when he heard her murmur, "Goodnight, Danny."

He paused in the doorway. "Good night, JoAnna," he replied and then hurriedly pulled the door shut behind him, aware how easily "I love you," was ready to roll off his lips.

Chapter XII

Josiah and Toby were in a mood. There had already been one near fist fight in the bathroom while brushing teeth and an incident in the kitchen that had only been settled by Danny's raised voice. Rain poured down outside which never boded well for a Saturday, particularly the first Saturday after school was back in session. JoAnna stood in the hall, hands on her hips, watching Toby as he made a meditated assent up the stairs to retrieve the pair of trousers that needed mending. "If he moves any slower, he'll be going backwards," she muttered to Danny as he walked by.

Danny glanced up the stairs, ready to add his own authority to the command at the slightest deference, but his son still displayed a forward motion, however slight, so Danny decided further commanding seemed futile. Still, hoping to increase his son's speed Danny advised, "Tobias, pick up the pace. At that rate, you'll outgrow the trousers before you get them."

Toby glanced back at his father and started to move a little faster, but not by much.

"That wasn't very helpful, but at least I tried," he muttered toward JoAnna who smiled in thanksgiving. "I'm heading over to Sharon and Chuck's," Danny continued. "His car won't start. I won't be back until this afternoon…" he glanced up at his disappearing son… "Do you want me to take them all with me? They're not exactly in good moods, are they?"

"Well, who can blame them? A down pour on your first free day is really not fair."

"Life isn't fair. But maybe a day inside with their cousins, won't be as painful as a day inside with their nanny…"

"Funny," she said, and rolled her eyes humorously at his joke.

"Josiah, Toby! Janey! Who wants to go to Aunt Sharon's with me?"

Feet thundered above, before the kids stampeded down the stairs.

"That's not exactly how you are supposed to come down those steps, is it?" Danny asked, adding in mock surprise, "And low and behold, who should be the first one down the steps but slow-poke Toby. Did you remember the trousers for JoAnna?"

Toby held the torn trousers up with pride, and then asked. "Can we go now?"

Danny said yes, to get their shoes…Janey held back a little. "What's the matter, Sunshine?"

Her eyes were wide and slightly disappointed. She held up her book, "JoAnna said she would help me cut out my dolls," she said sadly.

"You can do it another time," Danny insisted.

The little girl nodded slowly and was turning to go back up the stairs when JoAnna spoke. "It's okay, Danny. She can stay. I did tell her…"

"Don't you want some time off?" Danny muttered to the side.

"What for?" she asked him back in a whisper, and then said a little louder as she faced Janey, "I'd rather cut out paper dolls."

Janey's eyes grew twice as big and she looked about two inches taller. "I have two scissors," she announced proudly, held them up to be surveyed and then promptly dropped them with a clatter on the staircase.

JoAnna moved forward to help her and didn't see Danny's look of admiration.

"Alright, well you two girls have fun with your paper dolls. And we'll see you this evening."

***

When Danny and the boys arrived at their destination, Chuck opened the door and stepped aside as the kids burst into the house. They had polite greetings on their lips but Chuck only shook his head and pointed to the staircase. "My rebels are upstairs if you care to join forces…but let's have no destruction of the premises today. We'd like to leave the house standing, if you please."

Laughter ensued as the two families of children met mid-stairs and then raced up to the top. "Why does everything have to be like a cavalry charge?"

Danny shrugged, "They're a third of the weight of an adult and make three times the noise. Amazing the way that works, isn't it?"

Chuck shrugged into his coat. "I'll bring you to the garage. But I've got to make a few phone calls to the hospital while you work…"

"No offense, Chuck, but I don't think I could use your help out there, anyway. But if I'm ever bleeding you'll be the first one I call."

"Will I?" Chuck asked. He didn't look around at him, and Danny thought it odd the way he asked, but he ignored the imagined inflection.

Chuck opened the garage door and stepped inside. Danny followed but stopped short when he saw Flags on the far side of Chuck's Chrysler. "What the devil are you doing here?" he demanded.

Flags looked guilty and then pointed at Chuck, "He's my doctor."

Chuck looked slightly flabbergasted. "Don't say that! People hear that and I'll lose all my patients."

Danny wasn't calm about the situation and reiterated, "Flags, what are you doing here?"

"You told me to get back to you when I found things out."

"So you stalk me to my sisters? Thought you knew better than that."

"We thought it would be less conspicuous, your brother-in-law being my doctor and all…"

"Is there even anything wrong with your car?" Danny accused.

"Of course! Flags is a friend but I wouldn't lie for him."

"Calm down, Danny. Everything's fine. You fix the car, I'll tell you what I found out, you can leave and Chuck can give me a prescription, and we'll all leave with our legitimate alibis."

"A prescription for what?"

"I don't know. What sounds convincing to you?"

Danny shook his head and opened the car door. "Try to turn it over."

Chuck tried, but like the man had said, it wouldn't start. As Danny lifted the hood, Chuck handed Flags a flashlight and then without a word he left the garage.

Danny leaned over the engine; he flipped the two snaps on the distributor and lifted the cap.

Flags leaned under the hood with him, although he couldn't tell a distributor from a spark plug. "Ever hear of a man called Windy?" he asked.

"No. Should I have?" Danny asked checking the seal for moisture.

Flags shrugged. "You've been out of the loop for a while. It's excusable."

"Thanks for the reprieve. Is Windy a witness, an accomplice or the guilty man?"

"He's one of Balestrini's best wiseguys."

"Flags, you're shinning the light in my eyes, not on the engine."

Flags shifted the light and continued: "Windy Garnelli. Favorite weapon, his hands. Likes to see how close to death he can bring a man with his bare hands before he finishes him off with a .38. Unless the Boss says a quick job, then he's a dead shot at 60 ft. Scrawny, wiry fella, strong as an ox but moves like a panther. In short, not the sort of man you would want to meet in a dark alley."

"Doesn't sound like the sort of man I'd want to meet, period. But I asked you about Andrew Edwards. What's Garnelli got to do with Edwards?"

"I've found a witness that puts Garnelli outside Edwards' Shop the night of. And no question of doubt."

"So he's the guy that left with Edwards?"

"No. He's the guy that was waiting when Edwards came back home."

"Edwards didn't come back home. He left with the man and

JoAnna never saw him again."

"So she never saw him. Does she spy all around the place, watching every move? Edwards came home, all right, but when he did Garnelli was waiting for him."

"Flags you're getting ahead of me. What was going on? What's the tie between Edwards and any of these guys? Just a protection setup or what?"

Flags shrugged, "Maybe—not sure—but seems like the talk is that the tailor shop was doing more than altering clothes; they were altering books."

Danny looked at him, trying to register what he was saying. "You're saying…"

"They didn't just sew they also laundered."

"Stop with the puns, Flags, and get to the point. You think Edwards was laundering money for Balestrini?"

He shrugged, "Why not? Pretty easy to make the books work out in that kinda business. There isn't actually too much overhead coming in and out. Mostly manual labor and talent. And how would anybody gauge that, except by the books…and how do you prove that wrong?"

Danny walked to a small toolbox at the side of the garage and dug through it with more of a vengeance than necessary for a simple piece of sandpaper. Finally he came back, folded the paper in half and carefully slipped it between the contact points to file them flat again.

"Are you gonna say something or just fix the car?"

"Fix the car," Danny muttered. "That's what I came here for."

Flags made a face, walked over to the side of the garage and sat on a stack of crates.

After a couple minutes, Danny asked, "Do you have a match book?" Flags tossed him a tattered one and Danny proceeded to adjust the points. He pocketed the matchbook and picked up the cap. Wiping the inside to be sure it was free of moisture, he set it back down and snapped the clips back in place. Finally, he spoke, "So Edwards laundered money…but what happened to him?"

"Well—near as I can figure by different people's versions of a three-year old story and given the fact that people like to embellish an already good tale—the guy that came every week, was tall, intimidating guy…kinda like you…"

"Thanks…sounds like Duncan."

"Yah!" Flags said surprised. "That's the guy. How do you know him?"

"Unlike Garnelli, Duncan's been around a while. I remember him. Testified and sent him up…twice…not that it kept him there long."

"Hmmm…protection kinda guy or cooking the books?"

Danny shook his head, "Think he's done both for Balestrini. Jack of all trades. I knew him more in the protection racket. Like you said, he's intimidating. Good trait for the job."

Flags nodded, "Balestrini ever offer you a job?"

"Funny man." Danny stepped into the car and turned the key. The Chrysler turned over and started up immediately. He let it run a minute more, listening to the engine. Then he shut it off, got out and closed the car door. "Finish the story. What else?"

"In a roundabout way, that's it. It's all hearsay. Whatever happened between Edwards and Duncan while they were away mustn't have gone well. Garnelli was sent to kill Edwards. If he had done the job outside his Shop we would probably have a witness. Guess Garnelli is kinda bashful. Likes to work in private."

Danny's brow was furrowed. Flags already had Edwards killed off and Danny was still trying to understand the set-up. "So you think it wasn't protection being paid. You think Duncan was meeting to fix Edwards books; that Edwards was laundering money *for* Balestrini?"

"Maybe."

Danny didn't like how convincingly Flags spoke his '*maybe*.' He turned and moved the hood prop to close the hood. "But if he was working for Balestrini, why would he have him killed?"

"Edwards could have become a problem. Wanted too much money in return. Maybe he wanted out. He could have threatened to turn States Evidence against Balestrini for any number of reasons. Heck, knowing Balestrini, maybe Edwards just wore the wrong suit that day. I don't know."

Danny didn't realize how desperately he was trying to think of another excuse for Andrew Edwards, and barely heard Flags' numerous suggestions. "Still it could have been protection…or payment on a loan.

Maybe, like they said, Edwards ran his business in the ground, only instead of running he got a loan from Balestrini and when he couldn't pay, Balestrini collected."

"Lots a fellas owe Balestrini money. If he went around bumping' 'em all off he wouldn't come out very far ahead, now would he?"

Danny agreed, "Maybe Edwards refused to pay it back, or at least the outrageous interest."

"Danny, you're talking like a guy who doesn't know this world inside and out. If you've got a guy who won't pay his loan, you don't bump him off. Then how big a payment will he make?"

Danny shook his head. He knew it was only because he didn't want to go back and tell JoAnna that her father had been on the wrong side of a racket. There had to be another option as to why Balestrini would consider it important to send a hitman after a tailor. "Edwards could have had something on him? Balestrini, I mean. Maybe Edwards was trying to blackmail him?"

Flags was getting frustrated. "Maybe, maybe, maybe. We could throw out a hundred maybes, Danny. No matter which way you cut it, Edwards is dead and there isn't a body to prove it? End of story. Isn't that what you wanted? The end of the story?"

Danny shook his head. "Maybe that is all I wanted," Danny murmured. "I'll have to talk to JoAnna again." That wouldn't be a fun conversation.

But Flags was distracted, "Ah, JoAnna, is it? Lovely name for a lovely girl, I am sure."

"You want to meet my *nanny*?" Danny asked sarcastically.

"No. I want to meet JoAnna Edwards," he said with a glint in his slightly red eyes.

Danny walked toward the garage door, ignoring the comment and the insinuation, "See if you can dig anything else up. Can you meet me at Arnie's tomorrow night?"

"You think I don't have a life? Tomorrow's Sunday," he reminded him.

"So you want to meet at Church?" There was a hint of irony in his question.

Flags colored. "Make it Monday, if you please."

"Alright, Monday."

***

Arriving home, early that evening, Josiah and Toby burst into the kitchen from the back porch full of news about their cousins and Aunt Sharon. Danny was a few short and more leisurely paces behind them.

"Quiet down," Danny demanded of the children. "You can tell all about your day at supper. Go get cleaned up. You look like a couple street urchins… and don't drag your muddy shoes through the whole house…" Danny scooped up Janey, "How was your day, Sunshine?" he asked.

She pecked his cheek. "JoAnna cut her hand," she informed him, by way of an answer.

"Oh dear, nothing is sacred here, is it?" JoAnna moaned and he saw just a little pink coming to her face.

"You took the job, nobody forced you," he said dryly but with a smile. "Was it a bad cut?"

"That's a relative question," she hedged.

Danny raised an eyebrow, "Give me a relative answer."

"Well," she hesitated, "if you were asking me and Captain Hook at the same time…mine was not bad at all."

Suspicious, Danny held up his own hand; the knuckles were scrapped and not bent on healing any time soon, as he had banged them again that afternoon. "Compared to this, how bad a cut was it?"

JoAnna looked a little guiltier than before and pulled her bandaged hand out from under her apron.

"It's not bad," she insisted. "I just couldn't stop the bleeding."

"Oh that's all. You just couldn't stop the bleeding. Nothing to worry about. How did you *do* that?"

She cradled her hand when he reached for it, and explained, "I was talking to your mom on the phone when I was cutting up the carrots."

"Why didn't you stop?"

"Well, I couldn't just hang up on your mother. She wanted to know how the children were…"

"I meant stop cutting up the carrots, while you were on the phone."

"Oh." She looked confused and then admitted, "I didn't think of that."

Danny shook his head in amazement. "Are you sure you don't

need stitches?"

"Pretty sure," she said without conviction. When he looked at her for further explanation, she admitted, "I didn't really look at the cut, it kinda makes me sick when it's my own flesh."

Danny set Janey back on the chair she had been standing on, turned back to JoAnna, and ordered, "Take the bandage off."

"Danny…its fine."

"Take the bandage off," Danny reiterated more slowly.

A snicker drifted in from behind them and Danny turned to see the boys still standing in the doorway dripping trousers forgotten.

JoAnna smiled at them, somewhat mockingly, "You think this is funny?"

Josiah nodded, "Yah! You'll never win against Daddy. He's stubborn."

Danny wrinkled his eyebrows and defended lightly, "I'm not stubborn."

"Grandma says you're stubborn."

"Where does she think I get it?" Danny muttered under his breath. He took a step closer to JoAnna. "You're not gonna distract me, JoAnna. I want to see your hand."

JoAnna slowly held her hand out to Danny, who gently unwrapped it. He washed her hand over the kitchen sink, decided it wasn't in need of stitches, and then re-bandaged it in a much better fashion which made her hand still usable.

Supper was a loud affair, with the boys sharing their adventures and the girls trying to outdo them with their own. Neither caved and neither needed to; they were all laughing and joking so that they almost forgot dessert. Almost, but not quite.

Danny came down the stairs after tucking the children in. He wandered back down the hall and would have turned into his study, but he made himself cover the last few steps to the kitchen. He stopped in the doorway and watched JoAnna who was standing at the back door, staring outside as she distractedly pulled pins from her hair and let it fall to her shoulders.

She turned from the door, shaking all her hair loose with her hands, before stopping short on seeing Danny. "Oh!...I thought you'd gone to bed," She said, looking embarrassed and trying to pull her hair together again.

Danny wanted to tell her she looked fine…better than fine. But he shook off the temptation, well aware that his resolve to endure her presence for the sake of the children was crumbling. Instead he replied, "Thought about it. But we need to talk."

She looked surprised and said almost defensively, "My two weeks aren't up yet."

It was Danny's turn to look surprised, but he ignored the introduction to an entirely different conversation, one that he disliked more than this one. "Will you sit down, JoAnna?"

She shook her head, and replied nervously, as she half braided her hair over her shoulder, "I don't need to sit. You can just tell me whatever it is."

He relented, "It's about your dad."

JoAnna sat down.

"I've been trying to find things out…don't ask how," he ordered when he saw her mouth open. "You were right. He's not out there. He's dead."

She looked down, studied her bandaged hand for a moment, and then asked calmly, "Did you find out why? Who? Anything?"

"Garnelli," he replied because the *who* was simpler than the *why*. "But we've no witnesses to the actual murder. Just what the circumstances imply…your father was last seen with Garnelli and Garnelli is one of Balestrini's hitmen."

"What else?"

Danny shook his head slightly, murmured, "Nothing."

JoAnna stood and walked slowly to his side of the table. Danny could feel his heartrate increase the closer she came. She would get the whole truth out of him, she was capable of it with her large searching brown eyes. But how could he look her in the eye and tell her that her father quite possibly was on the take.

"What did you find out, Danny? You have to be honest with me."

He tried to avoid eye contact but she drew it from him. "There is talk that Balestrini used your father's tailor shop to launder his money from other…less dignified incomes."

"No." she said flatly.

"JoAnna, listen…"

"No. I'm not listening," she objected, turning around and covering her ears with her hands as she spoke. "You didn't know my father. You didn't know what he was like, Danny. He was principled. Determined. He would never have allowed something like that. He would never have agreed to it! He…he would have rather let his business fail than be a part of that. No, you're wrong Danny."

He took the suggestion in stride, "*Was* his business failing?"

JoAnna looked so wounded at his question, that he wished he could stop questioning her, but she had asked for the help. "I don't know," she finally admitted. "I told you, he never let me look at the books. But we were busy; we were always busy. We had plenty of customers…you can even ask around the neighborhood. People knew my father's work; they knew my father and he was a good man…he would never…I'm not crazy," she said, resorting to her usual defense.

"I never said that."

"You didn't have to," she stormed, tears threatening her eyes. "They all say it. The people you get your information from. The girl who thinks her father's a saint, when actually he ran out and left her…no wonder he left her."

"I already told you, I *know* your father was murdered."

"But how can I ever prove to you that he wasn't crooked before he was murdered?"

"You don't need to."

"Yes, I do, Danny," she stated emphatically. "Or you will never believe me."

"Why is that important? Why can't we just drop this whole thing? You know for certain he was murdered, he's gone. Just let it go?"

"Can you?"

"What?" he demanded, his face suddenly ashen.

"Can you let Lilian's murder go?"

He stared at her in shock. Turning away abruptly, he gripped the back of the chair, fighting down the anger welling up inside him.

JoAnna moved closer to him, contrite and compassionate, "I'm sorry, Danny…I didn't mean…I just meant…How can you ask me to let it go? If we know for certain my father was murdered than his murderer is at large…free to murder again. If you knew that about Lilian's murderer, wouldn't you want him caught? Stopped? I'm not after vengeance, but there is nothing wrong with justice. Don't you care that this same man, because he hasn't been caught, could be creating more victims?"

"You think I don't care!?" Danny exploded. He walked away from her, but it was never far enough. "You think I've enjoyed sitting here watching my town being killed, used and corrupted from the inside out? I lost good cop friends to bullets on the wrong side of town and they'd chalk it up to a gang incident, when the cop wasn't even assigned to that area. We lost good lawyers in random hit and runs or cut brake lines. And I lost *my wife* to murder and they said it was a kidnapping gone bad...And every day I watch judges turn a blind eye to blackmailers and murderers and an accusing eye on hard working grocers, mechanics and cops…"

"If you care so much about it," she interrupted her anger rising to almost meet his own, "then why don't you do something about it and stop believing the lies people create to avoid the repercussions of the truth!"

He stared at her. Her sudden accusation cut him deeper than he wanted to admit, not even so much what she said but that *she* had said it. It deflated his anger like a knife to a tire and he sighed and sank down onto one of the kitchen chairs. Slowly, his voice softened as he explained, "Those lies they create; they protect them from the reality of Balestrini."

Her own voice faltered as if she were unsure of what she was saying or what she had said. "I know…but for how long?"

Danny didn't respond; she was right. That was exactly what he had been saying for so long. How long? How long would he and Flags be able to keep playing the part of Robin Hood and Little John? How long would the town endure the kind of sins that went on in their streets before it caved in on its own depravity? How long before someone would rise up and defeat the man that Danny had been trying to bring to his knees since he came back from the War? The words JoAnna had spoken when she had praised *le Saint* came back to him: *At least he hasn't run from responsibility. He hasn't given up trying to be better person. At least he's trying.* But was he trying? Was he really, or was he avoiding what he knew he had to do on the pretense that he was doing something? He wished he could ask her, but he couldn't be straight to the point. Somehow he wanted to test her, to find out. "What would you have me do?" He asked quietly, sincerely, "Go help *le Saint*?"

She sat down across from him and shook her head. "No. I don't know. Maybe you're right. Maybe he isn't doing much good either. Maybe nobody can break this town out from under Balestrini's thumb. Maybe there's no such thing as a hero anymore."

"Life has a habit of making it easier to be a bad guy than a good guy. A good guy has to work four times harder at being good than the bad guys work at being bad. You can start feeling as if you're the only guy working that hard and it's difficult to keep going alone."

"But you're not alone, Danny."

"I know. But before…before, there was always Lilian, encouraging me; somebody I could fight *for* but also lean *on*. When I lost her, even then I wanted to set the whole town straight…I wasn't gonna stop until I did. But things…situations have a way of changing our minds. Things happen and things change…and I had to walk away. So I could…So I took up bowling." He finished abruptly. In a way, he wanted to continue the conversation, but he had said too much, or was getting there, and needed to stop. For her, bowling wasn't enough because she didn't know what bowling was. For him, it wasn't enough because he knew what bowling was and what little it did. But he had nothing else he could say.

"Maybe you're a little crazy too," she murmured and he glanced up to see her giving him a small encouraging smile.

He gave a short laugh, "The *maybe* is unnecessary."

She smiled a little broader, "I thought so too, but you are still my boss and I didn't want to say so."

Her smile caught him off guard and he smiled back enjoying the sudden joyful light in her eyes. They sat in silence for a long time, each lost in their own thoughts.

Finally, JoAnna pushed back her chair. "I should go to bed. There's Mass in the morning and then a picnic to get ready for…" her sentence trailed off, remembering their last heated argument. But he wasn't thinking about the picnic or their conversation.

Danny was still deep in thought and only replied with a distracted, "Sure, good night, JoAnna."

Chapter XIII

The dreary skies cleared late in the night, and when the sun arose on Sunday there wasn't a single cloud visible to threaten its shining. Danny parked JoAnna's Chevy on the street and whistled at the amount of vehicles lining both sides of the road. "I don't think you brought enough food, Miss JoAnna."

"You haven't seen the trunk, Daddy," Toby exclaimed leaning over the back seat. "Josiah and I carried baskets and baskets of food out this morning."

JoAnna laughed, "It was only three baskets and a small container, Toby." Both boys had already vacated the car, and didn't hear her amendment.

Josiah opened JoAnna's door for her, and headed toward the ballfield. "Hold up there, pilgrim," Danny called. "If you're going in that direction, don't you think you should help carry some of the food? And take your sister with you."

The boys hurried back and found Janey climbing out of the car.

She wasn't in nearly as good a mood as her brothers. She pulled at her dress, after sliding off the backseat. "Why did I have to wear a dress today? Why couldn't I wear Toby's old trousers? Now I can't climb trees or do cartwheels or anything!"

"Because little ladies…" Toby started to recite.

Janey interrupted, "I was a little lady at church. Do I have to be one here too?"

JoAnna laughed. "Yes, you do," she stated, with no room for discussion in her voice. She handed Janey a small container full of butter.

Each child laden with an item to carry, they headed back towards the school yard, Janey between them.

"We'll be lucky if it's still eatable by the time they get there," Danny muttered into the trunk as he reached for another item.

"It was just fresh bread," JoAnna explained. "If anything, it will just be a little flatter than intended. They are so excited!"

Danny smiled as he found the fresh apple pie JoAnna had baked. He held it up to give it an appreciative look and then handed it to JoAnna. "Who isn't? After a rainy Saturday, it's a perfect day for a picnic."

Her eyes were laughing as she looked up at him and teased, "That's not what you said on Wednesday. You weren't excited at all. What changed your mind?"

Reaching into the trunk for the picnic blanket and the last basket of food, Danny shrugged. "Had an argument with my nanny about that. I lost."

"I find it hard to believe you ever lose an argument."

"Well, you can't win 'em all. But just for the record books…my Plymouth still isn't running."

"You should find a mechanic who could fix that for you," she taunted, her expression belying the laughter in her eyes.

She stood very close to him, waiting for him to hand her the picnic blanket. But he hesitated, enjoying her nearness, his usual safeguard somehow diminished in the brilliant sunlight. "In any case," he replied, "whatever comes of my being here…you can't blame me."

"What do you mean?" she asked, this time innocently.

He gave her a look which implied she should know exactly what he meant, and closed the trunk. "Come on, half the food will be gone before we get there."

The green expanse between the church and the school was crowded with people of all ages walking, running and milling about.

JoAnna wandered about, helping to arrange the food on tables and visiting with the Sisters, many of whom she knew from her own school days. She met several of the extended Navarone family; not counting Danny there were ten Navarone siblings, and over half of them and their families were present. This one was his brother Mark; that one his brother Paul; there was his sister Sharon; and oodles of nieces and nephews who ran up at random points, in random conversations, with random people, to inquire bits of random information from parents.

It was a day filled with more simple fun than she could have imagined. She ran into people for whom she and her father used to do alterations; people that she knew from the parish; and people she knew from other shops. She hadn't realized how much she had withdrawn with all that had happened and how much she missed being part of the Parish

After her father had died, she had struggled to partake in activities without him. For a long time there had been a certain Howard, but he hadn't stuck around after the incident and she found it difficult to go to social events, even the Church socials that she used to attend with either Howard or her father. But today, suddenly the people she felt had been judging and accusing her, were gracious and welcoming. Of course not all—she noticed a few who avoided her—but she was so overwhelmed by those that welcomed her, that she chose not to spend any time thinking about the others.

JoAnna—slightly overwhelmed by more visiting in one day than she usually did in a month—wandered into the shade of a tree, shook out the picnic blanket and tried to spread it on the ground. The breeze had picked up slightly and was not cooperating with her attempts. "Having difficulties?" a man greeted from behind her.

JoAnna turned, and gave a timid smile to the good-looking—and slightly familiar—man studying her. "A little."

"I'm Joshua," he said as if it explained everything, and he started to straighten the far corner of the blanket. "Navarone," he added when he noticed JoAnna's confused look. He sat down on the corner of the blanket he had straightened.

"Oh!"

"That sounded, depreciating."

She laughed, "No, I meant it kindly. You looked familiar, but I wasn't sure why."

He held up a restraining hand, "Don't say it. I look like my brothers…only I'm the best looking of the lot, right? I knew it," he added hurriedly, before she could answer.

JoAnna laughed, "Well, you're as modest as your brothers, anyway." She sat down on the opposite corner of the blanket to help anchor it.

"Have you met our folks yet?" Joshua asked.

"No. Well not formally. But I've spoken to your mother on the phone. She seems a very easy person to talk to."

Joshua motioned toward JoAnna's hand and said, "Yes, I heard."

JoAnna laughed, "How on earth?"

"Janey can't keep a secret…everybody knows that…by the time this picnic is over, even the Bishop will know how you cut your hand…and he's not even here."

"Josh, are you terrorizing our guest?" Danny demanded as he and Clancy sauntered up to the blanket.

"No. I just wanted to meet the famous JoAnna everyone is talking about."

"Everyone?" JoAnna asked a little frightened.

Danny shook his head, and warned, "Anything Joshua says should be taken with a grain of salt."

"Pound," Father Clarence corrected calmly.

"Okay. Not everyone," Joshua amended. "But mom's bragging you up as if you were the best thing since the wheel was invented. And the way Debbie talks, I wouldn't be surprised if you're sure to be the next First Lady."

JoAnna wasn't sure how to react to those compliments, so she laughed and admitted that she hadn't even met the gentlemen's mother. She had only talked on the phone. "Remember?" she asked holding up her bandaged hand.

The men laughed. Joshua said, "Well, anyway, my brother has the prettiest nanny in Gilmore."

JoAnna smiled, "I'll take that with a pound of salt as well."

Danny wanted to say there was no salt needed for that compliment, but with two of his brothers there, he only unfolded the corner of the blanket with the toe of his boot.

"Do you have children here, Joshua?" JoAnna broke the silence.

"Me? No. Can't seem to find a woman who will put up with me."

"Then why are you here?" JoAnna asked and then clapped a hand over her mouth. "I didn't mean it that way…I meant, this is a *school* picnic…you know, for families of the…oh dear…"

Danny gave a small smile at her usual rambling. "He teaches boys Phy-Ed at the School," he explained.

Joshua continued, "And I kinda do the maintenance of the school…"

"And the pluming…" Father Clarence added.

"And the electric…" Danny supplied.

"But he refuses to paint the rectory," Father Clancy finished.

Joshua threw up his hands, "I never refused. I just said I thought that was more of a parishioner volunteer job, rather than a teacher's job."

"Oh, you have a job description now, do you? That's handy."

"You know, technically, the rectory is not part of the school," Joshua defended himself.

"So, you want us to put Father's housekeeper on a ladder and have her paint it?"

"No. But I know a guy named Daniel Navarone who's pretty handy with a paint brush."

"You're just afraid of ladders," Danny put in.

"Hey! I would rather discuss the issue at hand here, than suffer any more ad hominem attacks, if you please."

"Now, now, Joshua, no need to be hoity toity and throw Latin in our faces," Father Clancy admonished.

"Sorry, if I spoke over your head, it means…"

"I *am* the priest in the family, Joshua. I think I know what that means."

"Are you sure, *Father* Clancy? If you will recall, I did get better grades than you did in Latin, all through High School."

"Oh, don't remind me," Father Clarence put a hand over his face.

"Sister Mary Joseph still won't let me forget that. Seems like every time I go to the school, she introduces me to some mischievous boy with a black eye or a fat lip with a comment like 'You see, Jimmy, there's hope for you yet.'"

At first, JoAnna couldn't tell if they were having a good time or an argument, but soon she leaned back and watched the interaction between the brothers with pleasure. By the time the conversation ended they had already planned a Saturday to paint the rectory and Joshua promised to bring a ladder…although, he never did promise to use it.

Mother Mary Rose rang her old cow bell, the one she used to call the children in from recess, and the families gathered for the before meal prayer. Then they went through the lines of tables laden with food, and meandered out to the many blankets to eat and talk and enjoy the afternoon.

People talked and mingled and moved on to the next group to talk and mingle; and JoAnna met so many Navarones she was sure they made up half the school. Danny assured her, it was only about a third, but then laughed and said he was kidding…but JoAnna wasn't so sure.

Three-legged races, sack races and other races were played between children, then between children and adults and then children verses adults. The children continued long after the adults petered out.

Danny made his way to the picnic blanket under the tree. JoAnna sat alone, her light blue floral dress spread about her. Her wheat colored hair shone in the rays of sunlight that streamed precariously through the moving leaves of the elm above them. Danny regretted coming back to the blanket, but he could hardly turn around and walk away now. He sat down and stretched his long longs out before himself and sighed.

"One too many three-legged races?" JoAnna asked with a smile that lit her eyes.

Danny leaned back against the tree and tipped his hat down half over his face so he could politely avoid meeting her dark brown gaze. "It wouldn't be so difficult, if my partners weren't so short."

"You and Josiah did pretty well."

"He did, didn't he?" Danny asked, not a little pride in his voice. "He's got a good long stride, I was surprised." Danny drew a deep breath, grateful for the breeze and the peace.

JoAnna watched the crowds of children laughing and running. "Days like this are good for the soul. Just look at them."

Danny lifted his hat. But instead of watching the crowd he watched JoAnna watching the crowd.

"I'm glad I came today," JoAnna announced. "Events like this remind me that there are so many good people, and suddenly the scary things in the world aren't scary anymore."

"Balestrini's still there out there. There are still unsolved murders," Danny murmured.

She didn't look back at him, only gave a small shrug. "I know. I'm not denying the bad things are all still there. But the chaos and the uncertainties are suddenly smaller than they seemed. Perhaps that's as it should be. They are put in perspective. Suddenly you realize that this is real life and the other is just bits and pieces. All at once you know that things are going to be okay, even when the world seems overwhelmingly evil."

Danny studied her, unsure of her words. It wasn't that way for him. This day, this afternoon, was like a dream sequence and very soon he would wake up and have to go back to real life and all the pain and the uncertainties. Even the parts of this day that went with him wouldn't make the evil and the guilt any less to bear.

JoAnna continued, "It's a reminder for me that, He has already won the War, you know? We are just fighting the last battle."

"Sometimes the last battle is the toughest."

"For those of us fighting it, of course. But we have a good General." She turned to look at him over her shoulder unexpectedly "And if we surround ourselves with trustworthy fellow soldiers, we won't lose."

Danny didn't respond. How could he reply to a statement about being trustworthy, when he felt he hadn't been worthy of Lilian's trust, and so didn't deserve or want JoAnna's. He pulled his eyes from hers and watched the adults milling about. JoAnna returned to watching them as well and they were silent for some minutes.

He focused his thoughts away from the worry she reawakened in him and observed the crowd. He smiled slightly at what he saw there and he tipped his hat back down over his face and gave a small laugh.

JoAnna looked back at him again, "Why are you laughing?"

"You and that crowd."

"What about it?" she asked.

"Look at that crowd, *Miss* JoAnna." She was looking and he went on, "We're sitting here looking at them and discussing the problems of the world. They're standing there looking at us and assuming we are talking about very different things. Once again I say that if the rumors start now, it's nobody's fault but yours."

"What are you talking about?"

Danny gave another muffled laugh. "You, my lady, are a single woman working as a nanny for a widower. That in itself will feed gossiping tongues for a good long while. And now we have added a school picnic to the list. As you said yourself, family school picnics are for families."

JoAnna considered the myriads of people around the green school yard and noticed for the first time several of the people watching the couple beneath the tree. They turned quickly when she met their gaze. The full impact of her attempt to get Danny to be there for the school picnic finally dawned on her. And she breathed out, "Oh dear," with not a little anxiety.

From beneath the hat came a slightly facetious, "Yes, darling?"

Then she saw his chest start to shake with silent laughter and she burst into laughter herself, which caused him to laugh out loud as well. He was glad she could laugh about it. It put him more at ease and moved him lightly past their deeper, darker conversation. He pushed his hat back to reveal his face, he blue eyes shining. "The next time I ask you to take the children to an event without me, will you do it?"

She looked back at him thoughtfully, contemplating the day, before she answered. "Maybe," she agreed, but her tone said otherwise.

"Stubborn to the last." He shook his head in resignation and then stood with purpose. "Think I'll cause some more commotion in the little old ladies of Gilmore and leave you now…probably we had a fight. I'll go see how the boys are getting on at that ball game over there. Excuse me, please."

Chapter XIV

JoAnna watched him walk away. She wished he hadn't said anything. She had been enjoying the day, but now she felt acutely the eyes focused on her, in addition to eyes she simply imagined. She couldn't sit here all afternoon and at the moment, she could not walk up to anyone and calmly start a conversation, what with rumors lurking in the back of her mind. So JoAnna stood and walked along the tree line that separated the school yard from the church yard until she came to Fischer's orchard, which ran the length of the back of the school yard. She wandered into the grove of trees; it would be a relief to get away from spying eyes. She should have thought of the consequences before she pestered Danny into coming. Of course, she had meant for him to take the children by himself, not for her to go along. Still, she could hardly object when he had finally given in and agreed to come.

It wasn't that she was completely opposed to the idea of being interested in Danny; it was only being gossiped about, that she had an aversion to. She had had enough of that with her father's disappearance; dealing with the many ways one little truth turned into so many little lies when wielded on the tongue of a very capable gossip. Suddenly, something innocent and true became embarrassing and hurtful, and the victim—wishing to defend herself, could not even begin because the gossip had grown so out of proportion. She hoped this current gossip remained clean and innocent; JoAnna didn't want Danny's good name besmirched.

As she walked and thought, JoAnna smiled for the first time at the thought of what everyone else might be thinking. She wouldn't mind if Danny were actually interested in her; he was a great man. Lilian had been a very lucky woman. The children were wonderful as well. Whatever woman did manage to finally win Danny's heart would be very blessed. *I wouldn't mind winning his heart myself,* JoAnna thought lightly, pulling a leaf from a branch and studying the veins in it as she wandered. A nagging feeling churned in the pit of her stomach, warning her to steer clear of these thoughts. But as she walked a little farther and ignored that nagging feeling, she realized with suddenness that she really didn't want to think about any other woman being in Danny's life. She didn't mind Lilian; JoAnna thought of her as a friend, someone she was helping because she couldn't be there any more to care for her family. But the thought of anyone else standing beside Danny caused a grip on her heart so tight that JoAnna stopped and caught her breath.

"Oh dear," she sighed aloud. Was she in love with him? She hadn't meant for that to happen. Not at all. She couldn't be in love with him. She couldn't. That hadn't been the plan. No, no, no. She was just working for him. She was just the nanny. She leaned against the tree. Now how was she going to go back and face the crowds? Just minutes before, she could look back at them and smile innocently; but now, now that the truth had dawned on her that she *was* in love with Danny, she wouldn't be able to meet their stares without blushing. She touched her cheeks now. Just the thought had raised her temperature and she was sure she was scarlet.

She'd walk; she'd just have to walk this off. It was just a preposterous idea that she had imagined too far. She would be fine if she could just get the thought out of her head and think of something else for a time before she went back to the picnic.

So JoAnna walked. She was thinking of everything from the red apples ripening around her to the way the sun trickled through the leaves and danced on the ground. She was doing a pretty fair job of pretending not to think about Danny. Lost in her own thoughts, she didn't notice the sound of voices growing louder. Suddenly, she stumbled upon two men who were talking just ahead. The man facing her wore a white Panama hat and nodded in her direction. She saw the man with his back to her stiffen and then turn to face her as the first man walked away, farther into the trees.

JoAnna smiled, "Hello."

He stared at her for a moment and then greeted, "Good afternoon."

"Are you Mr. Fischer?"

"Fischer?"

"Yes. I thought this was Mr. Fischer's orchard. It's very beautiful."

"No, I'm Hartley. Lloyd Hartley."

"Oh, Mr. Hartley, it's nice meet you," she responded offering her hand, "I'm JoAnna Edwards. I…I'm sorry if I interrupted anything, I didn't mean to. I was so distracted, I didn't even realize where I was walking."

"It was nothing, Miss Edwards," Mr. Hartley insisted quickly. "Miss Edwards," he said the name again, slowly. "Aren't you Daniel Navarone's nanny?"

All the thoughts of possible rumors flooded back into JoAnna's mind, and she hoped sheer will power was enough to keep the color from rushing to her face. She smiled innocently, "Yes, I am. Do you know Mr. Navarone?"

His brow wrinkled slightly. "I'm Lloyd Hartley," he repeated and when she only looked slightly confused he explained. "Chief of Police. I used to work with Navarone."

"Oh, yes. Chief of Police. I suppose I should know that, shouldn't I?" She blushed.

"Navarone and I had a beat together when he was still a police officer," Hartley continued. "Doesn't he talk about me?"

JoAnna could feel the color fighting to rise, but she gave a small laugh, "No. That is to say, Mr. Hartley, I am just the nanny after all."

He nodded, "Yes, of course. Well, we were partners, at the time…I mean when his wife died." JoAnna felt as if she were under scrutiny.

"Oh. I…I don't really know much about it. It's hard sometimes to figure things out but I never know how to go about asking, without sounding coldly curious. But it would be nice to understand at least for the children's sake, you know?" She was rambling again, and to a complete stranger. Why must she always be so nervous?

But he was obliging, perhaps too much for a stranger. "I don't know how they made it through. How *he* made it through. Seeing your wife murdered before your eyes…" he stopped abruptly, realizing that maybe he was rambling too. She nodded, trying to encourage, not wanting him to feel as awkward as she felt at the moment. But he fidgeted and shook his head, "Rough times. Rough for him, rough for the kids. Guess I don't blame him for resigning."

The laughter from the school yard seemed to be coming closer through the trees and Hartley switched nervously from one foot to the other. Janey burst around the last group of trees into the clearing, followed closely by her father who scooped her up at her squealing before he saw JoAnna and Hartley.

He set Janey down at his side without a word, but Janey, oblivious to the sudden tension in the air, ran to throw her arms around JoAnna.

"Hello, Navarone," Hartley greeted.

Danny was still staring at him, though the look was one of contempt more than surprise. "Hartley," he greeted simply.

"How've you been?" Silence was the only answer. "Haven't seen you in a long while."

Danny's answer was slow in coming and JoAnna thought the Gettysburg Address could have been recited in the length of the silence but finally he said, "I'm fine, Hartley." But he didn't reciprocate the cordialities.

Hartley stood awkwardly, not having been invited to say anything more and unsure how to spontaneously interject it. He gave JoAnna a forced smiled. "Well, I guess I'll head back to the picnic," he said to her. Then to Danny he addressed, "I was just chasing some of those fun-loving boys from the orchard. They always seem to wander in here when there are school events going on. Mr. Fischer doesn't like it."

"We must keep those boys in hand, mustn't we, Hartley? Wouldn't want them to turn into hoodlums later in life. By then they are impossible to catch, aren't they?" Danny replied sarcastically.

Hartley's lips tightened. He met Danny's glare with one of his own, but he dropped his first. He then looked apologetically at JoAnna. "Miss Edwards," he stated graciously and tipped his hat.

He began to walk past them back toward the schoolyard, but paused when he came abreast with Danny. "Look here, Navarone. I know you still blame me for Halverson's death, but I couldn't see what you think you saw. I was protecting my partner. You hesitated, after all. I thought you were done for."

"Forget it," Danny interrupted forcefully, not bothering to look at him. "Forget it, Hartley. It doesn't matter."

"Navarone..." he said again. Danny met his gaze and waited, but Hartley saw something there that made him change his mind and he turned and walked back to the picnic.

Danny watched him go, his jaw set so rigidly that it could have been chiseled from granite.

JoAnna watched Danny watch Hartley. Her conversation with Hartley hadn't lasted more than a few minutes, but the difference between the atmosphere before and after Danny arrived was as if a cold front had moved in on a late October day. She nearly shuddered from the chill.

She was grateful when Janey tugged at her skirt. "What's the matter, Miss JoAnna?"

JoAnna looked down at her and clasped her small hand. "Nothing. Nothing at all," she assured the child. "Now tell me, what were you and your father doing out here in the orchard. Looking for apples?"

"No! Not apples! Ice cream!"

"Ice cream?! In an apple orchard?"

"No, silly goose!" the little girl laughed. "Father Clarence is *making* ice-cream. If we don't hurry, it'll be gone!"

Danny, pulled from his thoughts by his little girl's giggles, turned and faced JoAnna. "We came looking for you. She didn't want you to miss out," he explained and although he said it lightly, JoAnna could see that the laughter that had been in his eyes earlier that afternoon had vanished. "Do you know Hartley?" he added suddenly.

JoAnna's eyes widened at the question. "No. I mean I just met him, but I didn't...I don't know him..." she trailed off, wondering why he had asked and why the tone of his voice made her answer so defensively.

"Come on!" Janey insisted, taking both of her hands and pulling.

"If we don't hurry Toby and Josiah will eat it all!"

JoAnna turned to the girl and laughed, "I'm sure they can't eat it all that fast! But I'm coming!" She was a little worried that Danny wouldn't follow, that he would wander the other way and find Hartley. She didn't know why it worried her, but it did. She reached over and slipped her arm through his. "Come on, Danny. You don't want to miss this. Ice cream is your favorite."

He allowed a smile to pull up the corner of one side of his mouth and walked along with them. But he raised one eyebrow in protest, "I always thought chocolate cake was my favorite."

JoAnna laughed, and teased in a patronizing manner, "Oh. Well, don't tell Father Clarence that and I'll bake you a chocolate cake tomorrow."

He walked closely beside her, her arm still looped through his and her other hand still clasped by Janey. He was definitely the wrong man to be falling in love with and if she had known anything about falling in love or not falling in love she would have stopped herself right there. But she didn't know, so she couldn't stop herself.

As they neared the edge of the orchard, JoAnna could see the crowds of people and the sudden thought of all they were saying about her and Danny made her color, so she discreetly let go of Danny's arm and hurried ahead with Janey.

Chapter XV

Danny paced the study floor, a cigarette clenched between two fingers. The pleasant effects of yesterday's picnic had worn off long ago. Now there was only the sour memory of Hartley and the certain knowledge that everything Danny wanted from JoAnna he could never ask of her.

Flags hadn't been at Arnie's as they had agreed on Saturday. Danny had left word for Arnie to call when Flags finally came, but it was nearly nine and he had still received no phone call. He worried that he had sent Flags on a suicide mission. He had told him to find out more about Edwards. What if asking more questions had gotten Flags into some kind of trouble. And what if digging up that trouble caused a chain reaction that led back to JoAnna, back to his family.

Danny put the cigarette to his lips, realized he had forgotten to light it, and tossed it onto the desk. Why hadn't Flags at least called him? Danny leaned on his desk, knuckles white. He wanted to go for a drive, but then he wouldn't be home to get Flags' call. He had to have some other distraction. He spied the old mantle clock in a box on the bookcase. He had taken it apart months ago to fix it and never got it together again.

With somewhat of a fevered mission, he snatched up the box and walked out to the kitchen. The children were already in bed, but JoAnna was folding laundry at the kitchen table.

"Mind some company?" he asked.

"No, of course not," she replied, though she looked down quickly and he thought she blushed slightly.

Danny sat down and scattered his own pieces of the clock over the other half of the table. "Can't seem to get this thing together again," he said by way of an explanation.

"A little like humpty dumpty, hmmm?" she asked still intent on the towel she was folding.

"Don't say that," he muttered. "They never succeeded with him."

JoAnna didn't respond. Danny watched her as he sifted through the clock pieces. She was in a worse mood than he was, if that was at all possible.

She looked up and met his gaze and asked, "Is something the matter?"

"I was about to ask you the same question," he murmured and for the first time she dropped her gaze before he could even think of dropping his. "Did Josiah…"

"No," she interrupted. "The kids are fine. They haven't done anything wrong."

"Well, I don't know if I believe that," Danny replied.

JoAnna gave only a small smile at his comment.

Danny thought of how beautiful she had looked the day before. Dressed in her blue floral dress, laughing and talking, eyes glowing, hair shining; she had been radiant. Tonight she was like a timid mouse. When she did meet his gaze, there wasn't the usual laughter in her eyes, only sadness.

"Are you lonely?" he asked feeling as if he were pulling the question out of nowhere.

She replied with a look of surprise at his question. And after some stuttering, stated, "In a house with three children?"

"I didn't ask if you were bored, I asked if you were lonely." She didn't reply to that clarification and he continued, "What I mean is, well, you can have an evening off. I mean, if there is someone…that is, if you want to…well, I mean if you have…"

"There isn't anyone to invite over, Mr. Navarone," she said curtly.

Danny flinched at her sharpness. He had hurt her by his offer and he regretted coming out to relieve his own anxieties only to cause her pain. "I'm sorry, JoAnna," he replied sincerely. "I guess I just stuck my foot in my mouth."

"It doesn't matter," she said but she didn't look up and instead searched desperately for the second sock to the pair.

"Of course it matters. Is that why you are sad tonight?"

She looked up in surprise, blushing beautifully. He wished he had caused it, and not just by his impudent question. Pulling a matching sock from the pile she replied, "I told you, there isn't anyone."

"But there was," Danny corrected.

She looked confused as to how he knew.

"What happened?" he asked.

JoAnna shrugged and didn't answer for some moments as she focused on her basket of socks. Danny thought perhaps she wouldn't at all. But finally she confessed, "I'm not really sure. His name was Howard. And I thought he was pretty perfect at the time. We enjoyed each other's company. We enjoyed doing a lot of the same things together. We..." She paused and then went on as diplomatically as possible, "Well, anyway, it just didn't work out. With my father's death or *disappearance*," she corrected, "Howard decided there was just too much turmoil to try to also work on a relationship. So we called it off."

"Called what off?" She gave him a look, and he continued almost stupidly, "A wedding? You were engaged?"

"Yes," she replied dully, clutched another matching pair of socks and busied herself with the folding to avoid seeing the look on his face.

When her silence continued, Danny stated, "He left you."

Eyes wide, she insisted, "We weren't married yet." Danny only took that as a defense of her good name rather than any defense of Howard.

"That's a good thing," he said passionately, his brows furrowed. "It's best to find out a guy's a jerk before you marry him. What was his problem? The situation too delicate for his ego or too touchy for his climb up the boss's ladder?"

Danny took her growing color to be an affirmation of his supposition. How a woman whom a man supposedly loved could be less important to him than his own ego or job was a conundrum for Danny; how JoAnna herself could draw that into question for anyone was a completely foreign concept. The thought occurred to Danny—a little too late, he realized as her silence grew—that perhaps JoAnna still loved the man.

JoAnna finished the basket of socks and felt obliged to somehow end the horrible silence. "I'm okay with it; it's over and I know now it was actually a good thing to break it off…but it's still awkward…I feel like a failure when I think about it. I just thought things like that were supposed to be forever."

"When it's the right thing it will be forever." She didn't look at him, and his concern for her sadness deepened. He had a few choice words he would have liked to have voiced to Howard. The harder thing to do was speak consoling words to JoAnna without letting too much of his heart be visible. He insisted, "JoAnna, listen to me. Don't believe the lie that you failed. You would make a perfect wife and mother. If Howard was too much of an idiot to know that; if he had his chance and blew it; more fool him."

JoAnna met his gaze, her dark eyes searching his face for something; something that he had walled up and wouldn't let out in her presence again. He wanted to break her gaze, but he didn't want to hurt her more than she had been.

"Are you still in love with him?" he asked suddenly.

She smiled in surprise, "No. No, not at all."

"Good," he said. "Because you deserve much better than any Howard." Satisfied by her smile that she was no longer in such a gloomy mood, Danny refocused his attention on the clock.

JoAnna shook out a sheet to fold. "What about you, Danny? Why haven't you remarried? I noticed several young woman helping at the picnic who were trying to catch your eye."

Danny colored, "Don't. I've been trying to avoid Katrina Gottwald for seven years…"

"Seven years…but…"

"My point exactly."

"Is Miss Gottwald the only reason you haven't remarried?"

Danny squinted as he used a tweezers to place a spring back into the clockworks. "No. It's just a hard thing to think about doing." He could hardly add that he didn't feel safe having a wife with his pastime.

JoAnna was definitely cured of her moodiness. Her usual bantering was reappearing and Danny was almost sorry he had tried to cheer her. "They say, that those who have had a wonderful marriage the first time, marry again. Those who have had a difficult one, are very wary of stepping into it again. Which are you?"

"I'd say I am the first. Marriage isn't easy, mind you. But I wouldn't trade a moment, even of the tense arguments, for any of it not to have happened. Still the re-marrying thing isn't as easy as some would assume."

"What's the hardest part?"

"I guess it's just hard contemplating it with three kids in the picture. I can't just look at, *do I like the girl*? I have to figure out if she likes them; if they like her; if all of us are a good fit together. Finding that one person that fits, is hard. But when you throw three other variables into the picture is gets complicated and I'm not that complicated of a guy."

"So you've taken women out?"

"Sure. But…I don't know. The women I've taken out…half of them want me to pretend Lilian never existed, but she did, and she was a very real part of my life…we had three kids together. The other half seem to be interested *only* in my kids. They want to talk about them and only them."

"Isn't that a good thing? I mean, you just said you had to take into consideration that you have three kids."

"Yes, but if that's all they're interested in, what happens to the two of us after the three kids are grown and gone? Just doing things together doesn't mean you're perfect for each other. Interests change, people change…but having a common goal, a purpose together, that makes it last. I'm not trying to be that complicated. I just really don't know how to find that happy medium of someone who cares about all of us."

"That is difficult," JoAnna admitted, and reached for another sheet.

Danny didn't want to explain or answer any more or her questions. He changed the subject quickly, "Apparently, not as difficult as getting all these pieces back into the clock. It's never a good thing to have left over pieces when you're done fixing things."

He ignored her look of surprise. And she only replied with a non-committal, "You think so?"

"Well, Leonard always frowns upon it."

She laughed, "I feel the same way when I have left over socks after laundry is done."

***

Danny sat at the table, leaning over Josiah's math book, trying to explain the problem to the boy who had informed him that his teacher "didn't know nothing". Danny corrected "anything" and then tried to decipher the problem himself. But the problem of JoAnna was more worrisome than Josiah's math problem.

It was Tuesday—two weeks since she had first come—and the agreed upon trial period was at an end. Danny supposed that meant the situation was either over or they were committed to the arrangement. He wasn't sure he was content with it either way. He certainly didn't want her here, but he wasn't ready to let her go, either. Last night, when he had felt the nightmare returning he had called to mind JoAnna in her blue floral dress laughing up at him at the picnic and had fallen asleep on that blessed memory. He had slept well. But he wasn't okay with that, because she was also the one that had brought back the nightmare.

"Don't cha think, Dad?" Josiah asked, pulling Danny from his reverie.

Danny scowled at the problem in reply and shoved JoAnna from his mind though she stood just behind them at the kitchen sink. Danny read the problem over again, and finally grasped it enough to explain it to Josiah. Still, the boy didn't understand. Danny tried again when the doorbell sounded.

JoAnna murmured, "I'll answer it."

Danny was wondering how many different ways there were to explain a single problem, because he knew he was running out of options to make it clear to Josiah.

JoAnna returned. "Danny. It's Father Clarence. He wants to see you in your study."

Just as Danny began to rise, Josiah exclaimed, "I get it!"

Danny grinned. “Good. Do the next two and have JoAnna check your work before you do the entire page.”

Danny’s smile to JoAnna as he left the kitchen revealed his pride in his son, and maybe a little pride that he had been able to help as well. JoAnna smiled up at him as if she were just as proud.

Danny walked to the study, confused that Clancy hadn’t come the few feet more to greet his nephew whom he surely had heard exclaiming over his math. But when he saw the look on his brother’s face, only the idea of Flags’ unresponsiveness was on his mind. “What’s happened, Clancy?”

“Close the door,” Clancy ordered.

Danny did so. “Is it about Flags?”

Clancy’s brow furrowed, but he shook his head. “I have something to tell you…it’s not going to be easy…I confessed a young woman, early this morning, a girl really. I gave her the Last Rites…she was only fifteen…”

Clancy stopped midsentence and the silence made Danny uneasy. He didn’t want to stay in the room to hear the rest, and he had to walk to the far side of the room to make the door a less tempting escape. Then he prodded gently, “What happened, Clancy?”

His brother covered his eyes with a hand for a moment, and when he took them away Danny realized he had tried to wipe away a tear but the remnants lingered at the corners of his eyes.

“Clancy…”

“Don’t stop me, Dan’l. I’ll never get this out and you need to know. What I’m telling you her parents told me after the Sacrament…after she passed away.” He turned away, unable to face his brother as he spoke. “They had taken a loan from Balestrini, as you might guess. When the time came to pay, they didn’t have enough to pay back the amount plus the outrageous interest. The guy Balestrini sent to collect told them they would have to make the payment another way. He suggested their daughter could serve as payment,” Clancy clapped a hand over his mouth as if to stop himself from saying anymore. But finally he continued, “They tried to stop him,” he shook his head, “when he brought her back he told them, the next time he knew they would pay on time…and so would all their friends.”

"Who did it?" Danny demanded. His face, taunt and cold as if it had been carved from granite, held eyes that were sparks of flint, frightening.

Father Clancy shook his head and wiped a hand over his face, "I don't know his name. They said he came with Duncan, but they hadn't seen this man before. He was short and wiry and mean…I don't know."

Danny stood there, unable to move and paradoxically being unable to think and unable to slow his racing thoughts all at the same time. He didn't know the man's name either. But he knew the work of his hands. He realized suddenly that Clancy was watching him. He looked up. "I'm sorry, Dan'l…maybe I shouldn't have come."

"Why did you come?"

"I don't know," Clancy looked away and then admitted, "I guess like everyone else in this town I was hoping *le Saint* could set it all right…that's not true. I wanted my big brother to come and fix things…But I don't know *how* I expected you to fix them. Perhaps it wasn't even worth telling you. The next time anybody sees the man, they will probably be dragging him from a river." Danny raised eyebrows in surprise but Clancy finished, "Not by me. Pray God, not by me. But the girl's father…there was nothing I could say…nothing convincing I could even think of to say to try to persuade him otherwise…" the priest buried his face in his hands, "Not when I felt the same way he did, God forgive me."

"If all it took was wanting to, there'd be a few more bodies in the river…her family will never find him. And if they do, it will be the innocent that's dragged from the river." Danny thought his own voice sounded very calm for all the rage inside that was attempting to drown his common sense. He stood stationary, but only because every muscle of his body was taunt and to have moved would have been to move with a vengeance and he couldn't trust himself. The intense anger he felt somehow quelled the nauseating feeling in his stomach at Father's story. He could see, the girl, though he didn't know her, and he could see Lilian's broken body and he wanted to kill; in a way he had never wanted to kill before, even throughout the War. That a man like Balestrini could walk the streets free and good people lived in fear for their families was so enraging he could hardly contain himself.

Finally, Danny opened his desk drawer and pulled out his shoulder holster. He checked the magazine of his pistol and then re-holstered it.

Father Clancy watched him and asked tentatively, "What are you gonna do?"

"Something I should have done a long time ago." Danny slammed the drawer shut.

"Dan'l…"

Danny turned and raised a fisted hand, shaking a finger in Clancy's direction. "I'm gonna break the back of Balestrini's ring if it's the last thing I do."

"Dan'l, you can't take the law into your own hands."

Danny looked at him with surprise. "What do you think I've been doing these last three years, Clancy? Bowling? You know as well as I that Hartley and half the Department are on the take. You said yourself you wanted *le Saint* to do something…well don't stop me now that I actually am. It's taken me three years to work up enough anger to do this. Are you gonna be the one to stop me?"

"I don't want to stop you, I want to help you. But setting yourself blatantly against the law, especially the law in this town, is asking for a bullet in the back."

"What would you suggest?"

"Something legal."

Danny looked at him as if he had clearly lost his mind. "What?"

"Something legal," Clancy reiterated. "We need legal evidence. If we just start bumping off his guys for every one of ours, we'll turn this town into a bigger blood bath than it already is. We need papers, evidence, something to prove his crimes. Something to tie him to…anything. But something we can bring before the DA and have a lawsuit against him."

"Because that's never been tried before," Danny countered sarcastically. "Do you know how many times I put some of those thugs behind bars, only to have them released on a trumped up technicality?"

"It has to be this way, Dan'l. No other way will break his back. They never nailed Al Capone with any crime, until they went after him for tax evasion. Well, even if that's the best we can do, at least it's something, and it could be held up in court. So maybe we don't go to the County DA. Balestrini's territory is bigger than that anyway. If we get the right kind of evidence we can take this to the Minnesota Attorney General."

"Burnquist?" Danny nodded slowly, thoughtfully. Clancy's half-a-plan was helping his own common sense win out over the rage that had been pulsing through his veins. He liked the sound of Clancy's idea. The logic of it. If they could get far enough away from their own city and county law there might be a chance.

Clancy watched his brother for a very long moment, grateful to see Danny's rigid stance softening somewhat, wondering what he was thinking. Finally Clancy ventured, "Now what are you gonna do?"

Slipping his holster back into the desk drawer, Danny amended, "Think I'll wait until Thursday and then see how Mister Guiseppe Andreadi feels about bowling."

Chapter XVI

"You're late," Danny admonished. He had been sitting in Flags' booth for the better part of an hour and that man had only just come into the bar.

Flags gave a non-committal response.

"Where have you been?"

"I was at Big Lake," Flags informed him, dropping to the bench opposite Danny.

"Oh? Fishing?"

"No. Drinking," Flags replied honestly.

Danny pushed a mug towards him and poured coffee. "You should have been fishing."

"You shouldn't have asked."

"I needed you Monday."

"We always meet here on Thursdays. It's Thursday. Why should I be here on Monday?"

"Because we agreed on Saturday that we had to meet on Monday to…talk things over."

"Oh."

"Oh?" Danny didn't look up, but he could feel his shoulders stiffen at Flags' one word reply. He trusted the man with his life, but it was hard to trust that he could stay away from the bottle.

"Lighten up, Lieut. I'm here now. Sober just like you like me. Well, sober enough. Let's go now."

"What's the hurry? Andreadi doesn't lock up his office until eight."

Flags looked up slowly from the cup of coffee he was studying with unwarranted disdain. "Guiseppe Andreadi?"

"Sure. What other Andreadi did you want to visit?"

Flags raised his eyebrows. "I didn't really want to visit any Andreadi. Why did you choose this particular place?"

"Why not?" Danny threw off the question lightly.

"Danny, you do remember that Andreadi handles just about all of Balestrini's legal affairs. And that his office is guarded and probably mined."

"So-called."

"What?"

"Balestrini's *so-called* legal affairs. If Balestrini has any *legal* affairs he keeps them pretty well hidden."

Flags took a drink. "We're going to raid Andreadi's office and the strongest you've got for me is coffee?"

"It's black and thick enough to float a horseshoe, as Josiah likes to say. Are you in?"

"Just why this particular place, Danny? You get a sudden death wish?"

"Last week was a bust. I told you we needed a big catch this time. But now I want to hit them where it hurts. I want to do something more than just annoy them."

"Yah, but Danny, Andreadi's office? That's like…"

"Like the big bones. That's hitting them where it hurts. We get in *there*...well, Flags, you know as well as I that that office is where all the big bucks change hands. You want to raise the hair on their necks? We show them they don't have a safe haven. You want to come away with the loot that will pay off half the markers out there? We hit Andreadi's office."

"Yah, but after we're done raising the hair on their necks, they're gonna raise the hair off our scalps and who's gonna pay our funeral bills?"

Danny studied his own mug of coffee and replied in an inaudible whisper, "I'm sure Father Clancy will ask for a special collection."

"Danny, come on. This isn't just a summer picnic. This is…this is…"

"I'll tell you what this is," Danny interrupted, fire in his eyes. "This is the last straw. I'm tired of laying low. Of playing tidily-winks, while Balestrini runs this whole city, and Garnelli abuses the innocent. This isn't revenge, this is defense on the offense. Its time somebody stood up and did something more than just paid off a few loans.

Flags watched him. "What's going on, Danny? What happened?"

Danny squirmed. "Nothing. Nothing happened…At least nothing should have happened. We should have done this long ago and maybe nothing more would have happened. Are you with me on this job or no?"

Flags studied him for a moment, unsure whether his former lieutenant, whom he had followed unquestioningly in Italy, suddenly had a severe bout of despondency that Flags should talk him out of, or if he should go along to keep the man from doing anything stupid. "I'm with you, Danny. You know, I'm always with you in this."

"Alright then, have another cup of coffee, order some pie and talk about something else for a while."

"Sure. Sure, Danny." Flags studied him. "Everything alright? I mean, you and JoAnna…"

"What about JoAnna?"

"Nothing. You just seem…"

"I *seem*? And you bring up JoAnna?"

"Why are you snapping at me? She's a good kid."

"She's not a kid."

"Glad you noticed."

"I'm not blind, Flags."

Flags muttered something into his mug of coffee as he took a drink and the conversation switched to the Milwaukee Braves and the New York Giants, although for Flags the World Series was almost as depressing as the Balestrini situation.

Danny glanced at his watch, "It's about nine. You ready?"

"Ready as I'll ever be, I guess."

"That'll have to be good enough."

The men made their way inconspicuously to the office building of Giuseppe Andreadi. As expected, a guard stood duty; a plainclothesman who didn't seem to think anyone would ever attempt to break into Andreadi's office building, or perhaps he thought no one would try to get past him. Either way, Danny and Flags left him with that illusion, knocked out and tied up behind the garbage can in the alley.

They made their now uninhibited way into the building and then up two flights of stairs to Andreadi's office, making sure to close things up tight behind them, so as not to give cause for alarm to anyone who would happen by. Andreadi's office door was solid oak, with an upper half of frosted glass and two locks. Danny stood watch as Flags' expertly picked first one lock and then the other and opened the door. When they entered Andreadi's office, Flags pulled the blinds before Danny turned on the lights, and any lingering caution disappeared as they headed to opposite sides of the room and began digging. All the caution in the world wouldn't give them more time before somebody figured out they were missing a man. Now they had to work fast, caution be hanged. The guy in the alley wouldn't sleep forever.

Working on a safe behind a lovely portrait of someone's mother—he was pretty sure it wasn't Andreadi's—Flags glanced in Danny's direction. "What the devil are you doing in a filing cabinet? I thought we were gonna pay off all those markers…"

"I'm after Balestrini. I need proof…"

"Balestrini! Hold on there, partner. When did that enter the picture?"

"You just get the money, I'll find the evidence."

Flags grumbled but went back to the safe. "Ho-ho!" Danny heard him exclaim a very short moment later.

"What'd you find?"

"Papers."

"What kinda papers?"

"Like somebody's papers on a good idea for what to do with Edwards Tailor shop."

"Let me see that." Danny took the paper and read over the garbled notes. A smile touched his lips. "Flags, I might just buy you a drink for this."

"That'll be the day."

"What else is in that box?"

"You can search it. No money. I'm taking a crack at that portable safe by that potted sequoia. We *are* still looking for money, right?"

"I don't give a darn about money any more. I want something big to bust Balestrini's guts wide open."

"And if you get your head blown off, trying to gut shot Balestrini?"

"At least my kids won't be living under the same thumb when they grow up."

"What about if your kids grow up without a dad?"

"Shut up, Flags. How do you expect to open a safe, while you're talking so much?"

Flags fell silent and Danny found a few desk drawers of paperwork to explore. Not that Andreadi would have too much that would be traceable lying about in an unlocked desk drawer, but it was worth a quick glance.

In the silence, Danny thought he heard something downstairs. He paused in his rifling. "We gotta go, Flags," he ordered, shoving a few more papers into his pockets.

"This thing has got to be loaded," Flags insisted, although he hadn't managed to open the safe yet.

"Yah but with what? Come on," Danny insisted.

"Who cares? We'll find out later."

"You're gonna bring that whole thing with…"

"Heck yah!" Flags exclaimed. "We can just take it with us. I'll pick the lock when there's no one breathing down my neck."

"Fine, then. Pick it up and let's get out of here."

"Quiet, I hear something."

There were footsteps outside the office door. There was no need to stop moving, whoever was outside the door knew very well that they were there. Danny pulled the lamp cord to make it just as dark in the office as it was in the hall. He swore under his breath.

"Now, now, Lieut," Flags hissed. "You know how your mother

hates swearing."

Danny ignored him and pictured the lay-out of the building in his mind, trying to figure out the best option for a successful escape.

Flags moved toward the office window and opened it. The fellow in the hall must have been of a jumpy nature, because through the frosted glass Flags' movements could not have been more than an abstract shadow. The bullet smashed through the glass of the office door and splintered the filing cabinet Danny had been searching through.

Flags and Danny both backed farther from the door. Their only other escape was a door on the far side of the office; but they would have to cross the door with the shattered glass to get to that door.

"What are we gonna do?" Flags asked shoving his pockets full of items that he thought could be potentially damaging…or maybe he was just giving himself padding from shrapnel, Danny wasn't sure. Flags still hadn't opened the safe so it wasn't that. Another bullet hit the door jamb.

"I'll try throwing a few bullets his way and you run for it," Danny ordered in hushed tones.

"Me? What about you?"

"Well, if I throw them accurately enough, we won't have to worry about that, will we? Come on. You ready or are you putting those papers in alphabetical order?"

"Start throwing," Flags agreed.

Danny didn't bother to look first, he just shot a couple times down the hall to make the other guy duck and Flags got to the far side of the room without a hitch. "Okay, come on."

The wise guy threw his own bullets down the hall, and by the direction they were hitting, there was more than one guy. "God help me," Danny muttered. He waited for the shooting to stop, trying to calculate what the other guys were planning, wondering if they had others coming up the alley to block their only escape. About now, the shooter was probably wondering if he had hit his target, probably getting antsy to check. Danny took his chance, lunged, fired three shots waist high down the hall and dove to the far side of the office. He only briefly saw the man that was coming toward him, but he heard him cry out and fall as Danny's bullet tore into him.

When Danny reached the last opened doorway he found Flags

peering out another open window. "Come on, dang it. You can't fly!"

He shoved Flags down the steps ahead of him. More bullets followed—obviously able to do stairs quicker than the men the lead devils were tailing.

Danny and Flags burst from the back door into the alleyway, a good staircase and a half ahead of the pursuing henchmen. Flags caught Danny's lunging figure and kept him upright. "Come on, Lieut, no time to lay down on the job."

Danny grabbed at him, thankful for the support but vaguely curious why Flags thought he needed it.

They made it around the corner of the building and dove into an alley and to the back street where Flags' rusty old Ford was parked.

"We've got to get you to the hospital," Flags said as he spun away from the curb and back onto the main drag.

"Hospital! What are you talking about?"

"You're bleeding like a stuck pig, that's what I'm talking about!"

Danny looked down at his arm for the first time, as if it was only now dawning on him that he had been shot. Blood stained the front of his shirt, ran down his arm, and dripped from his fingers. "How did that happen?" he muttered, distractedly. Then to Flags, "No, not the hospital. If they suspect they hit one of us, they'll look there."

"Oh, fine. So you just want me to save a stop and go directly to the cemetery."

"Stop it, Flags. Just drop me off at the Bowling Alley."

"Are you kidding me?"

"Do I look like I'm kidding?" Danny demanded. "The bowling alley."

Flags decided he didn't look like he was kidding, he looked like death; the blood had washed from his face and Flags had a bad feeling it had all run right out the hole in his arm. "Lieut…"

"Dagnabbit, Flags. I'm serious. The Bowling Alley. Then meet me at my house. But take a roundabout way. Don't come directly there, get me?"

"Sure, I get you," Flags replied irritably.

Pulling up to the curb just before the bowling alley, Flags asked, "You're gonna drive yourself home?"

“I have to, Flags.” Danny got out without another word of explanation and climbed into his own truck. He would have to shift left handed which would be a feat in itself, but he wasn’t causing any scene and he was gonna play the part if it killed him…he had to think of a new phrase, that one was not very comforting.

Chapter XVII

JoAnna lay awake in bed. Danny was on her mind. She wished she could stop herself from thinking about him when she didn't need to. But it always started with a legitimate thought, such as, she should tell him about Josiah's run in with Bobby down the street, when suddenly without warning, she would be thinking about how she could tell him, how he would react, that she wished it would be a dialogue about what to do, instead of his usual monologue of, "I'll take care of it." She knew he would, but she wanted to be part of it. She wanted to help; she wanted so much to be involved in the solutions as well as the problems. But she knew it never would go further. How could it? She could feel herself becoming one of the two types of women he avoided. Standing there loving him, children or no, and wanting, wishing he would notice her, children or no. And the next day—who was she kidding—the next hour, she was fawning over the children and wishing she were their mother, not their nanny….but he would only see the woman who wanted him alone, or the woman who wanted his children. His wouldn't see her, JoAnna, the woman who—at least according to herself—would be a perfect fit into Danny's world.

She wanted to tell him that she loved them all…but the idea of the words forming on her lips made her almost sick to her stomach at how pathetic it would sound. How very improbable it would seem. She would be saying to him exactly what he wanted to hear from a woman, and although it was exactly what she felt, it would come across as if scripted just to make the situation perfect. Which it was, but…Ahhh! It was too confusing. Everything fit so perfectly, and yet, because it was perfect, it couldn't work and she was getting a headache just trying to reason the straightforward, logical chaos of it all…

She threw the quilts back and stood up. It was ridiculous. She couldn't sleep. She had prayed, but somehow no matter how hard she tried to remain in the Thy-will-be-done mode, she could feel her heart, begging God to let Danny notice her, just give her a chance. And that didn't seem very non-committal on her part. So she decided she couldn't pray right now. Praying was the only out, but it only made her think of him, and she really, really needed to stop thinking about him.

She reached for her robe and pulled the lightweight blueness around her, buttoning it at the waist. She walked into the kitchen. Supper. What was she going to make for supper tomorrow? That was a good thing to think about. She turned on the light and looked about. He eyes found the clock on the wall above the refrigerator. Eleven-thirty. Not even midnight yet. Not exactly a normal time to think of supper. But one never knew, Friday could be filled with hectic activities…like, getting the children off to school, and digging the onions and hanging out laundry…who was she kidding? She could plan supper through all that, she had done it before.

Wandering into the hall, she stopped at the small table that seemed to collect everything. She noticed the mail which she had forgotten the evening before and picked it up. She walked down the hall, opened the study door and, without really looking, walked in. She stopped abruptly in the doorway, the envelopes falling from her hands one at a time as she stared ahead of her.

At the large oak desk over which she so often found Josiah bent, sat Daniel. Only the lamp lit the room, illuminating his washed out face. He had unbuttoned his shirt and had slipped it off his right side. The fact that he was half undressed didn't shock JoAnna; it was the fact that he was wiping blood from his arm and trying unsuccessfully to stop more from flowing down that startled her.

"I'm sorry…" JoAnna stuttered. "I was just bringing the mail…or I would have knocked…"

It was a ridiculous thing to say under the circumstances, however she had no other words. Danny took a moment before replying, "Close the door, JoAnna."

Forgetting the dropped mail, JoAnna backed out quickly, pulling the door with her. She stood there, staring at the closed door, when it was yanked open. Danny stopped abruptly, not expecting her still to be standing there. He took a breath, which seemed to pain his shoulder. "I meant with you on the inside," he stated.

She said 'oh' and followed him back into the study, closing the door behind her.

He went back to his position behind the desk. "Don't look at me like that," he commanded.

"Like what?" she asked regaining her composure.

"Like I just murdered someone in a back alley." He picked up a cloth and began dabbing at the blood again. "The accusation in your eyes makes it difficult to ask you…"

"…To help you stop the bleeding," she finished as she took the cloth from his hand, folded it twice and laid it on the wound. She applied pressure, and he took a deep, sharp breath, leaning back in the chair slightly.

"Actually, no. I was going to ask you to not say anything to anyone about this."

"Is the bullet still in there?" she asked peering closely at his wound.

"Of course it is," Danny growled. "Otherwise you'd have to plug the hole on the other side too!"

"Good point. Does bowling often end like this?" she asked sarcastically.

Danny wasn't in the mood to be put on the spot. "Can I help it if the other guy is a sore loser?"

"Suppose not. Are we just leaving the piece of lead in your arm as a souvenir or are we going to dig it out ourselves?"

"It's like a big sliver," Danny replied, calmly. "Can't you get a tweezers and..."

"Sure why not?" she rejoined his sarcasm, "and I'll let you have a popsicle while I dig for it."

"Thanks."

"No trouble at all, Daniel."

Danny looked up at the use of his full name. "Are you mad at me for something?"

"You said you weren't a cop anymore. Why are you coming home shot up, like an episode of Gunsmoke?"

"I'm not a cop. I didn't know the guy was gonna shoot at me or I would have ducked. And I'm not sure if you're mad because I came home or because I'm shot."

"I'm not sure either. But if you didn't know you were going to be shot at, why did you take your gun with you?"

He looked up at her, but she was intent on her bandaging. "Are you spying on me?"

Her dark eyes darted a glance at him. "No....no!"

He gave her a look that said he wasn't believing her.

She pushed his coat off his left side and tugged at his shoulder holster. "You obviously had your gun with you."

"You're here for the kids, not to take care of me."

"*You're* here for the kids...maybe you should remember *that* the next time you go *bowling*. They already lost one parent. They don't need to be left orphans."

"If you're done," he began.

"No, I'm not. You're still bleeding and we either need a doctor or I need that set of tweezers..."

"I meant with the lecture; the doctor's on the way."

"Oh."

The study door opened with a small squeak. JoAnna jumped, but Danny looked up expectantly. "What took you?"

Flags entered the room. "You said to make sure I wasn't followed. I wasn't followed."

"Coulda bled to death waiting."

"Naw. Figured you'd have a nice nurse waitin' up fur yah."

"Oh you did, did you?"

"Sure…and I was right, wasn't I?"

"You?" JoAnna gasped. She eyed Flags' disheveled appearance. "You're a doctor?"

"When I need to be. I was a medic during the War."

"A medic?"

"Sure. Nobody seems to trust me with a scalpel anymore," he admitted, as he pulled a scalpel from his bag. "But then beggars can't be choosers…can they?"

"Danny!" JoAnna looked at him desperately. "You're not going to let him…"

"He's sober tonight."

"Sober? Danny!"

"Would you rather get your tweezers?"

"No need," Flags interrupted. "I have my own. Only mine are called forceps. You see? Same principle really, just a fancier name…and well, supposedly more sterile."

"Supposedly?"

"Well, if it wasn't for the fact that I keep my bag in the back seat of the car, where I, um, sorta keep everything else… anyway, it'll all be fine. I've a bottle of whiskey here too…for sterilization," he explained, when both parties looked at him suspiciously.

"See, JoAnna. Everything will be fine." But Danny's voice had lost a little of his conviction.

***

Danny came down the stairs slowly. Any sudden movement jarred him all the way up to his shoulder and then the pain shot all the way back down to his feet. Flags had told him a sling would alleviate some of the pressure, but he couldn't risk being seen by someone while wearing a sling. So he just cradled his arm and made his way to the kitchen.

JoAnna stood at the kitchen stove. She turned toward him as he came into the room, though he didn't think he had made any noise. She looked at him with one of those all-encompassing looks of hers and he wished any one of the kids were there to distract her. But it was Friday and they were surely already at school.

"You're *le Saint*, aren't you?" she said without preamble.

He glanced over at her in surprise. But he didn't answer and took a seat at the table.

She didn't prod for an answer, but filled a plate with food and brought it to the table. Any other morning she would have walked away and returned to her task at hand. But this morning, she sat down beside him. "How's your shoulder?"

"Hurts like…" she raised her eyebrows and he finished, "the dickens."

She smiled at his correction and then asked again, "Are you?"

He ignored the question. "Why didn't you wake me? I'll be late for work and Leonard will never let that die."

"You called in sick," she said as she reached over and pulled his shirt off his shoulder to check the bandaging.

He pulled his shirt back over his shoulder as if he were embarrassed. "I did?"

"Well, I did. You have the flu."

"I have the flu?"

She looked at him. "Are you going to repeat everything I say today? You have the flu. You're staying home with the flu. I told Leonard. I told the children. So there is no reason why you can't just stay home and stay in bed and rest all day without anyone being the wiser. I need to check the wound."

Danny lifted his arm and rested it on the table, cradling it so that she couldn't touch it. "What about Balestrini? Did you tell him too?"

JoAnna sighed and relented, "Eat some breakfast, Danny. You need nourishment. Flags said you should have had a blood transfusion. I don't think you should even be out of bed." She stood and returned to her dishes.

He ate slowly. Somehow the plate seemed very far away. He felt very hungry but too tired, as if eating were just too much work. He pushed his plate back. "Think I will go back to bed."

He stood up and swayed slightly, but JoAnna was there almost instantly and put an arm about him to steady him. "You're a good leaning post," he murmured and walked toward the stairs with her help.

"Thanks," she smiled, "At least you think I'm good for something."

"You're good for a lot of things," he said. "You always make me smile." He shouldn't have said that. He should just shut up, but he was so exhausted and queasy, he figured talking was the only thing to keep him from passing out before he had reached the top of the staircase. "You're good at doing laundry," he murmured, trying focus his blurred thoughts to remember her good qualities that did not involve her smile or her eyes. Joanna laughed at that and he muttered, "Well, that didn't come out right." He faltered on the step and JoAnna gasped, certain they were both going to fall backwards down the stairs. But he caught himself with her help and the railing and he continued upward. "You are very good at arguing," he continued.

"Is that supposed to be a compliment?"

"You do it so well, I figured you were trying to perfect the art," Danny said and laughed in spite of himself.

She laughed too. "I only argue when I firmly believe in the thing I am arguing for," JoAnna argued logically, as she pushed open his bedroom door with one hand.

Danny lowered himself onto the bed. "It could be the loss of blood, but are you arguing about arguing?"

"Just lie down, Danny. You've got to rest."

The slight pressure of her hand on his good shoulder felt as if it held the weight of an anvil and he sank back onto the bed. "Well you can't argue with the truth. You're the best thing that's happened around here in a long time. After all, there aren't too many nannies that would dress a fella's gunshot wound."

She pulled the quilts up over him. "How many fellas come home from bowling gunshot?"

"It was your fault," he murmured.

"My fault! How did you arrive at that one, Mr. Navarone?"

"I told you if I were *le Saint* I'd go rip the guts out of the Balestrini machine. Hit him where it hurts. You told me I couldn't run from responsibility, that *le Saint* was at least trying to do good in this town." Between the medicine Flags had given him and his loss of blood he would probably regret, or forget, everything that he was saying. He hoped it would be the latter. "You were right. But it was only because I was afraid. Afraid of endangering you, just as I endangered Lilian. But I have to finish this. I've left it undone for too long. Somebody's got to put these guys behind bars."

"Maybe you should have just left it for *le Saint* to finish," he heard her reply slyly.

"I told you the guy wasn't doing the job right."

"He was a hero to a lot of people."

"Yah, even to you," he murmured as he closed his eyes. "Brought him down to earth for you, didn't I? Made you see what I see. That he's just a mortal, man. Bleeds red blood…all over the desk…" his voice was trailing off, even he could hear that. But it took entirely too much energy to speak any louder.

"You made him more real," she corrected. "He's more of a hero to me now than he ever was before…but I'll never be able to tell him that."

"He probably wouldn't listen even if you did," Danny murmured.

She smiled and tucked the quilts closer around him, "No, he probably wouldn't."

"It's cold in here," he said. The bedding felt heavy but he couldn't feel the warmth yet.

"I know," she agreed, although she didn't think it was. "You'll warm up. Just rest, Danny." She retrieved another quilt from the closet and spread it over him.

Chapter XVIII

The week passed with little chaos. Danny called in sick again on Monday but Tuesday he wouldn't be convinced to stay home. By the end of the day, Greg's growling told him he hadn't been a whole lot of help. He went to bed early.

Wednesday he felt much better, but JoAnna deflated it by reminding him that that was what he had said Tuesday morning. He went to work anyway.

Thursday morning he didn't tell anyone he was feeling much better, but he really was and when he got home from work Thursday evening, JoAnna offered the information herself. "You seem to be doing much better."

He wanted to be just a little sarcastic and ask if she really thought so. But he didn't. Instead, he asked after supper. "It will be ready in a half hour or so."

Danny made a face. "It's Thursday. I'm going bowling."

She turned around, hands on her hips. "Daniel Navarone, you cannot go bowling. Your arm is not healed."

He raised an eyebrow at her and murmured so no one could

overhear, “It’s not really bowling, remember? I’m not going to tear anything open.”

“Oh. Because what you *actually* do is so much less strenuous than bowling?” She shook her head and was probably rolling her eyes at him, but he had turned away to avoid further discussion. She wasn’t finished, “After the children are in bed, I need to change your bandaging.” She said it without any question in her voice and he wanted to object.

“Are you a nurse?”

“No. But I’m the best you’ve got. So you might as well cooperate.”

Before he could make a reply of any kind, Josiah leaned his face against the screen door and said, “Daddy, a man outside said he needs to talk to you.”

“What?” Danny demanded. The constant thought of Balestrini, and the thought of a man approaching his son in the dark, collided together in his mind and he responded with more anger than alarm.

“A man outside said he needs to talk to you,” Josiah repeated.

“I heard you,” he snapped. “Get in here.”

Josiah came in unsure why he was in trouble when he had merely delivered a message, and he had only repeated it because Danny had asked him to.

“Where is he?”

“Outside. By the trash can in the alley.”

Danny shot a quick look out the screen door, but it was dark and he could only see the illuminated back porch. “Stay in the house,” he ordered and shot a glance at JoAnna.

She put a restraining hand on Josiah’s shoulder as he objected, “But, Toby and I…”

“I said stay in the house,” Danny ordered and let the screen door slam at he left.

He walked toward the alley, his heart pummeling the inside of his chest, ready to attack the man who had approached Josiah. He slowed as he saw the man’s form on the far side of the garbage can. “You wanted to see me?”

“Not in the mood you’re in,” Flags growled back.

Danny could have slugged him he was so happy to hear his voice. “Dang it, Flags you scared the heck out of me.”

"There's a greeting for you."

"I thought we agreed, you'd never come here."

"You didn't seem that upset to see me last week."

"That was different. Hold on, I'll turn some lights off and you can come in and we can talk. It's safer that way."

Danny went back to the house. He was grateful when he found JoAnna had taken all the children upstairs. He switched off the back porch light and the kitchen light, then retreated to his study where he waited for Flags to follow.

When Flags came into the study, Danny didn't start with any pleasantries, "What's up?"

"I wanted to see how you were."

"That's it?! You wanted to see how I was?"

"Well, come off it, Lieut, you looked like death the last time I saw you. How was I gonna know if you were still alive? And she," he motioned to JoAnna whom they could hear as the children played jax on the hallway floor upstairs, "played the Nazi nurse and wouldn't let me near you."

"Good for her. You're not exactly supposed to come to the house, remember?"

"I'm getting the hint. Yah know, for a guy who is supposedly a friend, you're not very friendly." It was difficult to say whose anger was more piqued, the two men matched each other tone for tone.

"Pardon my bad manners. I like to keep myself *and* my friends alive."

"Thanks. I just figured you wouldn't be coming to *Arnie's*…"

"I was just on my way…"

"Really? The Nazi nurse was gonna let you go?"

"Stop calling her that! Her name's JoAnna," Danny's temper subsided quickly and he finished almost sotto voce, "and between the two of you, you saved my life."

"Well, let's not get mushy about it," Flags replied with annoyance. "But Danny you did lose somewhere around a quart of blood last week. I don't think bowling or drinking would be such a good idea."

Danny sighed and sat down at his desk. He cradled his arm. "Alright. You're right. You're both right. Are you happy? No bowling…no drinking."

"I didn't lose a quart of blood," Flags corrected. He pulled a flask from his coat pocket. "Mind?"

"I guess not. Have a seat." He motioned towards a chair.

Flags seated himself, took a quick drink and replaced the flask before beginning, "I found out more about Edwards."

Danny met his gaze, but waited for him to continue.

Flags continued, rubbing a hand over his stubbly beard. "Some of those papers we took from Andreadi's office were very telling. I don't know if they would be the kind of evidence that you were looking for but it gave me some leads about Andrew Edwards. Seems Balestrini was getting fixed up with a new venue for money laundering. Something happened and the plans had been cancelled or at least drastically postponed."

"Edwards' place? Like we talked about?"

"Figure so. Edwards Tailoring. It would have been a good front. Good, honest family business, run by hard, working-class people. Trustworthy, right? Balestrini held a loan on them and all he needed to do was call in their marker and it was sink or swim. They either paid up right then and there, which would have been impossible and he knew it. Or they would lose everything…or they would play the game his way."

"So they weren't paying protection. They were paying a loan. Only Balestrini didn't count on Edwards character balking at his changing the rules of the game."

"I thought you didn't know him."

"I didn't. Not personally. But I'm beginning to. If Edwards had half the moral character JoAnna's got he probably would have spit in Balestrini's eye at the suggestion of any such racket."

"Balestrini doesn't take too kindly to being told no," Flags observed.

"And so we can safely assume that after the meeting letting Edwards know how he could save himself and his business, Edwards would have known too much for Balestrini to let him live if he wasn't going to play ball. And with Edwards out of the picture it would have left it open for Balestrini to work on JoAnna."

"But he didn't," Flags corrected. "He let the whole thing go, and destroyed it by faking the books into bankruptcy instead." Flags scratched his head. "Think he found another venue? A safer bet, a more obliging partner?"

"Maybe."

Flags rubbed a hand across his mouth, obviously dryer than he liked, but he didn't reach for the flask again. "Now what?"

"What about the safe you carried out of Andreadi's office?"

Flags grinned. "I pitched that out the window in the stairwell, remember? I don't think they've found it yet."

"You don't think?"

"Well, I didn't want to go back there too soon after the raid…might be suspicious."

"Might be," Danny agreed.

"Thought I'd go scope out the alley later. There's so much junk in that alley, I don't think they'd find it even if they would think to look there. But, you know as well as I that they're thinking if somebody had enough gall to go in and steal it, they sure as heck wouldn't leave it right outside the place they stole it from."

"I was thinking that too."

Flags sputtered, "Well, it was you or the safe, Lieut. I could only carry one."

"Alright, alright. Don't get uptight. I can wait. Waited this long, another couple days will just make Balestrini sweat a little more."

Flags hesitated and then looked at the floor as he spoke. "You sure you want to do this? We keep going, we're gonna blow this thing wide open."

Danny thought for a long moment before answering. "These past years we've been fighting from the trenches, but sometimes you have to climb out of the trench and advance toward the enemy, instead of waiting for him to come to you."

"What about your family?"

"My family," Danny repeated. "My family is without Lilian because of Balestrini. My family is the reason I need to go forward, so that other families don't end up like mine, like Halverson's." Danny hesitated. He thought of the parents of the young girl Father Clancy had told him about. "It's because of the families of all those other people continually being threatened, bullied and blackmailed that I think we need to keep going. Don't you agree?"

Flags was silent and Danny felt uneasy, as if something he had said made Flags nervous. Flags was rarely at a loss for words. "What else, Flags? What aren't you telling me?"

Flags still wouldn't meet his gaze. "You start asking questions, you learn things."

"What kind of things, Flags?"

"Three years ago April…"

Danny could feel his heart beating faster but he tried to keep his breathing calm.

Flags continued, "There was a guy that night. You said you saw him, but you didn't know his face. You looked though all the profiles, you described him to me many times…and I couldn't help either…"

His voice trailed off, and Danny knew that the night still confused his friend. Flags still wondered but never asked for more details, only took what Danny had offered. And Danny had only told him a couple facts. That Lilian was dead and the description of the man…

"What about him, Flags?" Danny demanded.

"Never found out who he was." He was stating the same facts over. "Nobody knew where he went…people started thinking he was a phantom you made up. "

"Flags, what about him?"

"He wasn't a phantom. I found out who he was." Finally Flags looked Danny in the eye, and stated flatly, "Tony Limbardi."

***

Danny left the house without his supper. He left with a curt, "I'm going out," and no more explanation than that, though JoAnna and the children were gathered at the foot of the stairs looking at him expectantly. He drove around for nearly an hour and finally stopped in front of the church. He sat for some minutes, debating whether he to go to the rectory or the church. He didn't want to face either his brother or his God at the moment but this was the only place he could go. By the anger that was mounting inside him, Danny knew that any of the other places that he wanted to go would have placed him in danger, both physical and spiritual.

Danny walked slowly into the church and even more slowly up the center aisle. The light of the waning moon gave very little light through the stained glass windows. Danny could feel his anger boiling over and he wanted to hit something, destroy something. He stood stationary before the altar, his fists clenched, his teeth clenched, and his body rigid with anger.

Finally he had a name. Finally he had proof. Finally there was a tie to reality for a night that still seamed steeped in fantastic horror. Tony Limbardi. His wife's murderer had a name. The man that he pictured, the man that he remembered, the man that came back again and again in his nightmares to haunt him. Tony Limbardi. The man who was his arch-nemesis, who had taken everything from him, had a name.

Danny's body ached with its rigidity, but still he stood, the suppressed anger of three years locking his movements. "Tony Limbardi," he breathed the name aloud through clenched teeth. Then he looked up at the Tabernacle, and his eyes slowly traveling upward to the Man on the Cross above.

He began to pace the length of the aisle in front of the sanctuary. "Forgive him?" he said aloud as if the words commanded in his heart had been a verbal communication. "How can I forgive him, Lord? For a man who steals to feed his family, I have forgiveness. For a man who lies about his criminal past so that he can get a good job and start over, I can have forgiveness. But for a man who cheats and steals so that he can get ahead at the expense of his neighbor? Who deliberately desecrates life and…and innocence…that I cannot forgive."

He turned away as if he didn't want to give the Man on the Cross the chance to reply. But He did reply and in Danny's heart he heard a small voice, "We don't justify the sin, but we must forgive the man."

"Don't quote me 'hate the sin, love the sinner,'" Danny said forcefully, facing the altar in a swift movement. "They're too difficult to separate when innocent lives are being torn apart."

He wanted to fight with someone, anyone, but the Man on the Cross only responded with a look of love and compassion. Danny saw the blood on His face from His crown of thorns and he knew he was going to lose this argument. And he knew how much he wanted to lose it, but he didn't know how to retreat.

The Man on the Cross had more to say and slowly Danny felt his body relaxing, he felt his muscles releasing and finally, mind over matter, he could consciously force his body to its knees at the altar rail. *God forgive me*, he prayed. *Help me to forgive. I can't forgive him, help me to forgive him*. He repeated the prayer over and over, not knowing what else to pray. The way he felt, he didn't think there was any other prayer to pray. The intensity of the hatred he suddenly felt for Limbardi terrified him. Suddenly the phantom was real. The phantom had a name. He had become a real person to be hated, instead of the phantom that only haunted Danny. Limbardi was a real person who had taken someone real away from him.

Danny didn't know how long he remained on his knees. When he finally felt calm enough to stand, his knees were stiff and his shoulder throbbed. Danny looked up at the tabernacle, grateful for the peace that had come to subside the intensity of his anger. He made a fist with one hand, placed it over his heart, then moved it away, opening his fist as if to physically drop his anger, his hurt, his pain in front of the tabernacle. That's all he could do. He didn't know how to forgive the man. So he felt the best he could do was give it to Jesus and let Jesus forgive and teach him how to forgive. Then Danny stood and left the church, a tiny bit of fear that he actually would forgive taunting him in the corner of his mind.

Chapter XIX

Friday dawned as usual, but Danny wasn't in a mood for sunshine or birds chirping. He hadn't slept and between the pain in his shoulder and the pain in his head he wasn't sure he would be any good at work. For a change he growled at Greg more than Greg growled. Once, Greg even asked him what was up. But Danny ignored the question.

Danny called JoAnna to tell her not to wait supper as he was staying late to finish the Cadillac that he should have been able to finish by five. She sounded concerned and he had a suspicion she didn't believe his reason, even though it was the honest truth. Greg had left a little after five and Leonard had left an hour after that, and as they each left, Danny felt the distraction and alarm and anger slowly creeping up with no one else to distract him. It was nearly a quarter to eight before Danny dropped the hood on the Caddy and locked up the Garage.

Danny's drive home after work continued in this distracted tone, but the truck almost knew the way by itself, like an old pony making for the barn. But when Danny saw the lights flashing in his rear view mirror he knew it wasn't quite the same. He glanced at the speedometer and knew he couldn't have been going over the speed limit. He pulled his truck to the side of the road. His heartrate slowly rising as thoughts of last Thursday's events flooded his mind. He wondered who Flags may have unearthed to get the name that he had given him. He gripped the steering wheel and took a deep breath to steady his racing heart. He hoped the pounding in his shoulder would subside so the officer wouldn't see the pain reflected in his eyes. The man behind him couldn't know any of the things Danny was thinking; not about Limbardi, or Andreadi, or his throbbing shoulder…but what if he did know something. Danny said a silent prayer for the throbbing in his shoulder to lessen so he could think straight.

He watched the officer in his rearview mirror as the cop got out of his car and took note of Danny's license plate. Walking up to the side of the truck, he spoke clearly, "License and registration."

Danny looked up abruptly at the sound of the voice. It was Sergeant Carter, an older cop who had trained Danny on the job when he was just out of the Service. "Good to see you, Navarone," he muttered almost under his breath.

Danny handed him the two forms. "I'd like to say the same, only under different circumstances it would be easier."

"Well, under these circumstances, I figured this would be the best way to speak to you."

Danny was glad Carter was looking at the papers so he couldn't see him grimace for the pain in his shoulder. "I wasn't speeding," he defended only for something to say.

Carter was still looking at the license. But spoke, "I wanted to offer my help. Only there isn't a way to do that without *not* being able to help."

"I'm not sure I follow you," Danny said cautiously. He knew very well what the man meant, but he wasn't at all sure if he was safe in acknowledging it.

"What I mean is, Navarone, there are still a few of us with a backbone in this department even if your old partner hasn't one. I tried to see you earlier this week. Brought the squad car by to check a tire while on my route, but you were out sick."

"Yah, the flu, you know."

"Sure, that's what they said," Carter agreed.

Danny had a horrid feeling that Carter was playing along with him, or that he was playing along with Carter and he didn't know which one was playing and which was real.

"Anyway, things are getting hot around town. Somebody's getting testy and somethings gonna blow. Before they do, just wanted you to know where I'm at. I'm here to help, if you trust me. I don't know how I can but I assume you would know that better than I."

Danny took back the license and registration. He was still unsure how to respond. It could be a set up. He didn't feel comfortable saying anything at all. "How are you going to explain pulling me over? I wasn't speeding."

"Your taillights burnt out. I won't write you a ticket this time. Just a warning." He patted the door and when Danny met his gaze, Carter taunted with a glint, "Best see if you can't find a good mechanic to fix that for you." He turned without another word and walked back to his squad car.

Danny watched him in his rearview mirror once again. Carter had been a good cop. Danny hoped he still was. He hoped it really was just a warning. He would have to be careful. He and Flags would have to lay low. He pulled away from the curb, careful not to be too suspicious in waiting too long. His mind was racing, trying to go over everything that had happened the night he had been shot. But half of it was so hazy he couldn't place some of the details.

One more stop before he went home. He'd see Flags once more. He had to know if they had done anything that could have put Carter on to them. Or was Carter just putting out his own feelers? Maybe he was on the level. Maybe he just knew Danny well enough from their years on the Department together to know what he was doing. After he had left the job and started bowling, Danny had distanced himself from everyone in the Police Department. He knew that most would see it as weakness; that Lilian's death had been too much for him to handle. He had been okay with that. Even for those whose friendship he had truly enjoyed, he knew that it would be better to be almost alone than to risk putting any of them in danger or to endanger himself and Flags because too many people had too many clues to put all the pieces together.

But Carter had put enough together to know. How many others had put two and two together to arrive at four? He made a turn, it was out of the way, but he would stop in at *Arnie's* on his way home from work. He had to see Flags right away and tell him to lay low, lay very low. He didn't know how to respond to Carter's warning. But he knew enough to lay low until he had figured out how to read the man. Flags wouldn't know enough. He was brash and overoptimistic, so he had to be warned.

Danny parked his truck in front of *Arnie's Place* and walked in the front door. Flags wasn't in his usual booth. Danny ducked behind the bar and into Mrs. Arnie's kitchen. The smell of beer bottles soaking in lie soap stung his eyes, but Mrs. Arnie wasn't tending to her bottle washing. She stood at the table wrapping a chunk of ice in a towel. She turned to the side as Danny entered and he saw Flags sitting at the table holding his head in his hands.

"Don't you think black coffee would do the trick better than ice?"

Flags removed his hands to reveal the beginnings of what would very soon be a very nasty looking black eye. "Since when do you treat a black eye with coffee?"

Danny relented, "I'm sorry, Flags, I thought…"

"I know what you thought," Flags replied peevishly.

"Don't you be treatin' him as if he didn't have the perfect right to be thinking' what he was thinking, Peter Anthony," Mrs. Arnie accused as she placed the towel of ice gently, although not too gently, over Flags' eye.

She turned and walked past Danny touching him lightly on his arm, Danny tried to hide his grimace until she had left the room. "You run into a door?" Danny asked to cover his wince.

"No, I didn't run into a door. This wasn't no accident," Flags replied peevishly, removing the towel for a viewing.

"I suppose I was the cause," Danny asked.

"Aren't you usually?"

"You're in quite the mood. Would you rather have a slug in your shoulder?"

"You've got nothing to complain about. I pulled that out."

"Dug more properly defines what you did," Danny muttered, supporting his arm gingerly. "Where'd you get the black eye?" Danny asked, attempting a realistic sympathetic note.

"In an alley between Hanson's and Madison's," Flags replied

sarcastically.

"I meant, who gave it to you and why?"

"Remember the guy I told you I never wanted to meet in a dark alley? Well, I met him."

"Garnelli?" Danny's concern was a little more genuine. "What happened?"

"I told you, I've been asking questions…Balestrini doesn't like it."

Danny pulled a chair closer and mounted it backwards. "Doesn't like the questions. Just the questions, right?"

"Sure. What else?"

"Well, we aren't exactly picking daisies on Thursday nights. You're sure he's not objecting to…"

"Our bowling habit?" Flags shook his head. "Garnelli thinks I'm a wino with a big mouth for gossip and an infatuation for digging up old skeletons. He couldn't tie us to anything else."

"Maybe," Danny got up and began to pace the floor. The condition of Flags' face made him nervous. "I got pulled over before I got here."

Flags touched his eye, "I'm supposed to feel sorry for you? I got a black eye and a head ache and you got a ticket?"

Danny ignored him, "It was Sergeant Carter. Only it wasn't just the taillight that made him pull me over. He offered help."

"Did you take it?"

"I wasn't sure what to do with it."

"From Carter? You must be joking."

Danny eyed Flags' face. "Things seem to be getting a little hot all the way around."

"You're really shook up if you think Carter is hinky. You think I got a black eye for stealing Andreadi's papers? Believe me, Garnelli would have done much worse if Balestrini suspected us of anything. Garnelli was just trying to teach me to mind my own business. And stop asking questions. If he thought I had gotten any answers I probably wouldn't be here. As to Carter, they couldn't turn that man if they put him on a dizzy dollar."

Flags removed the towel once again, this time to feel the extent of the damage.

There was a knock at the curtained doorway. Danny walked over and pulled the curtain to one side. Mrs. Arnie smiled, "Are yah expecting any visitors, Daniel Francis?"

"Like who?"

"Like Clarence Michael," Father Clarence interrupted from just behind Mrs. Arnie.

"Definitely not!" Flags called from his seat at the table.

Father Clarence laughed and stepped into the kitchen. "Well, Peter, I haven't seen you in ages. Still the gracious, welcoming brute I remember hanging around all my older brothers."

"I wasn't *that* much older." Then pretending his pride was greatly wounded he continued, "Did you come here just to pick on me or is there a reason you've graced us with your presence?"

Clancy eyed Flags' black eye and replied, "It looks as if someone else has done enough picking on you for one day. In any case, I came to deliver a message for your friend, Danny."

"What's the message?" Danny asked.

"How'd you know where to find him?" Flags wanted to know.

"I called the house and JoAnna said she didn't know for sure, but thought maybe he'd gone bowling again…I don't think she approves of the sport."

Danny shrugged, "Just not the way I play."

"Ah, so you've met JoAnna too?"

"Who's JoAnna?" Mrs. Arnie asked, pausing in her retreat to her living quarters and becoming much more interested in the men's conversation.

"Ah, guys. Can we get back to the matter at hand?" Danny asked desperately, because he desperately didn't want to discuss JoAnna.

"JoAnna is Danny's nanny."

"Nanny?" Mrs. Arnie exclaimed. "Oh!" with much more inflection than befitted a one syllable word.

"Nanny, housekeeper, secretary…" Flags began and finished, "nurse."

Danny groaned and all eyes seemed to study him, "Yes, Joanna is the nanny. She lives in the house and takes care of Josiah, Tobias and Janey and if she had it her way we would have a dog and I wouldn't go bowling on Thursday nights. Can we get back to our conversation, please?"

"You know, Barney Johnston got a nanny for his two kids after his wife passed," Mrs. Arnie began. "Sure enough if two years later they weren't married. No foolin'."

Danny could see he wasn't going to have his way, so he threw in his chips with mock surprise, "Two years? What took him so long?"

"He didn't have a sister and kind brother to help prod the proceedings," Father Clarence murmured.

Danny would have rolled his eyes, but he was too concerned with the reddening of his neck when Flags said, "She's a regular she-bear. Protects her wounded cub like no other?"

"Clancy!" Danny pleaded desperately, "What was the message?"

"It's a note. I only read the beginning. A man stopped me on the street and gave it to me, I guess he thought I was you."

"First time that's ever happened," Flags muttered from behind his ice pack.

Danny opened the note and read it as Father Clancy and Mrs. Arnie continued the conversation about JoAnna.

Danny's face drained of color as his eyes scanned the short scawled note.

"What is it?" Mrs. Arnie gasped. The tone of her gasp scared Flags so that he stood up and dropped his ice. Father Clancy held his breath and looked expectantly at his brother.

But Danny didn't say anything. He snatched up his hat and without any farewells, headed for Mrs. Arnie's backdoor.

Mrs. Arnie and Flags exchanged worried glances but only Father Clarence moved after Danny. His stride was just as long as Danny's but he had to stretch it to catch up with him before they reached Danny's truck. "Danny, hold up."

"No time," Danny snapped, opening the driver's door.

"Then I'm coming with you." Danny didn't respond and Clancy made it around the truck and into the seat as Danny began pulling out of the parking space. "Let me see the note."

Danny passed it to him as he drove up to Main Street. *"Little boys can't play baseball with broken legs."*

It was unsigned.

"Ricardo Balestrini," Danny muttered as Clancy folded the letter.

Father Clarence crossed himself.

Danny shifted harshly and ground some gears.

They turned onto Main Street and drove several blocks when break lights began illuminating the street. "What's up?"

"Looks as if there must have been an accident up ahead."

Danny muttered something under his breath and Father Clarence refrained from asking what. They slowed down and Danny slammed the palm of his hand on the steering wheel, "I'm not waiting around for this."

"What are you going to do?" Clancy asked glancing at the flood of cars around them.

"Get home the fastest way I know how," Danny answered, putting the truck in neutral and getting out.

"You can't just leave your truck in the middle of a traffic jam."

"Watch me."

"Danny!" Clancy called, trying to get out as fast as his brother but Danny was already two cars ahead by the time Clancy got his door closed. There was nothing to do but lift his cassock and catch up with his brother. Cars began honking all around and a couple of drivers leaned out their windows to yell various impolite epitaphs at the man and the priest following him.

Father Clarence made a mental sign of the cross hoping the Bishop wouldn't hear about this little episode and wondering vaguely what these motorists could possibly be thinking about the scene.

Danny's thoughts were concerned with one thing and one thing only, getting home. He dodged in and out of cars and trucks and finally reached the sidewalk, now only a step ahead of his brother. Father Clarence knew better than to say anything to his brother and besides that, he was out of breath, so he kept his thoughts occupied with prayers of petition.

The brothers charged up the front steps, making no attempt to muffle the sound of their entry. Danny burst through the front door, heading for the staircase, when the view in the living room caught his eye. Both men stopped dead in their tracks.

Chapter XX

The dying embers of a fire glowed in the fireplace and the red glow cast eerie shadows on the form lying on the rug beside the couch. Danny moved toward JoAnna's form. He wanted to rush but it was as if his body were held captive in a surreal dream, or reenactment of the past and he couldn't break himself away. JoAnna's hair covered her face and he saw no signs of life. Finally he reached her and he drew her light body up into his arms and brushed her soft, wheat-colored hair to the side.

Stirring, she opened her eyes halfway. "Danny," she murmured, then her eyes flew open and she sat up. "Oh, dear! Danny. I'm sorry, I didn't mean to fall asleep. I…"

Her voice broke Danny's dream-like trance and he rose like a towering tornado. "Damn Balestrini," he swore, with no care for priest or lady. He stormed to the staircase.

"Dan'l!" Father Clancy called after him. But he had reached the top of the stairs and entered the boys' room.

JoAnna rose slowly and stood, confused, fear rising inside her. "Father Clarence?"

The priest turned and looked at her, obvious relief still written across his face at her well-being. "Come on, JoAnna, we'd best help him."

"Help him with what?"

"With whatever he needs," Father Clarence replied abstractedly. He led JoAnna up the stairs to the children's room. They found Josiah and Toby both sitting on the edge of their bed slightly dazed at being awakened so suddenly from a sound sleep. Danny was just coming back into the boys' room, a sleeping Janey draped over his shoulder.

"Danny, what are you doing?" Father Clarence asked calmly, though he was tense for action at any moment.

"*You* are taking my children to safety." He laid Janey on the bed. "Get her dressed," he ordered and although he didn't say her name or even look at her, JoAnna knew he was speaking to her. She moved deftly to the child and did his bidding, trying to make sense of the two men's conversation.

"Safety? Where can you send them to be safe from Balestrini, Danny?"

Danny hadn't stopped moving. He was pulling out suitcases and clothes, but he paused long enough to face Father Clarence. "I don't know. But they're not going to stay here waiting to be murdered in their beds."

"Danny!" JoAnna gasped, horrified that he had said it in front of the children. But luckily, the children were still too groggy to pay attention to the activity around them.

He met JoAnna's gaze for the first time since he had found her downstairs and he turned to Clancy, "Do you know what that was downstairs? That was three years ago. And Balestrini hasn't even moved a muscle yet. Can you understand?"

"I know, Danny. I know. But running doesn't work. Not from men like Balestrini. It never has and it never will."

"Well, I can't just sit here and wait. Coming home every night wondering if I'm coming home to a family or a morgue."

"Danny, listen to me. The police…"

"Don't talk to me about the police. Don't you think I know the system? You know I've tried to work with the system." He paused. "If it was just me I'd stay and fight no matter what the cost, but I can't risk the children's lives…I can't lose them, Clancy. You have to take them away for me."

Father Clarence looked about the room at the three sleepy children and the calm, but definitely frightened, woman. "Danny, *you* have to take them. I can't do it. It wouldn't be safe. If I take them and they follow me…you'd be better at protecting them."

Danny was becoming irritated. "If I take them, they are sure to follow. Balestrini is after me, or he wouldn't have threatened my children. You have to take them, so that maybe these guys will stay here to keep an eye on me and won't bother to follow."

"Danny, listen to me. I'm not as agile as I was. I haven't been in the army for 10 years. I…I wouldn't be trustworthy in a fight. Please, Danny, don't make me do this."

"It's the only way, Clancy. You have to do this. I have to stay and you have to go, there's no other way."

Clancy stopped arguing as they gathered the children and sparse supplies and brought it down stairs. Danny left them all at the foot of the stairs and headed toward his study. Father Clancy watching his brother, ordered, "Get the kids in your car, JoAnna," before following his brother.

JoAnna did as she was told. She picked up Janey, Josiah obediently took his brother's hand and they made their way to the driveway. The boys crawled into the backseat without a word, but Josiah's look said so much more that JoAnna didn't know how to respond. "It's okay. We're going to be fine. We're just going on a little trip together. We'll all stay together…it will be like a vacation." She kept up the light trivial banter for Josiah's sake…Janey was sound asleep again and Toby pulled his coat up over his ears as if he were too tired to listen to anyone.

JoAnna watched the two brothers as they came out of the house. They were speaking, but even as they approached the garage, she could not make out their parting words.

Father Clancy climbed into the driver's seat beside her, his cassock catching on his knees so that he pulled it up over them, revealing his black trousers underneath. He backed the car out of the driveway in silence and JoAnna wondered if he were angry at his brother or just scared. She waved a hand to Danny who stood on the sidewalk in the dark hours of the night, watching them drive away. She wouldn't have told Father Clarence, but she would have felt better if Danny were driving. It wasn't that she didn't trust Father Clarence, but she had a feeling he was right; he looked just like his brother but in a fight, Danny was the better pick.

She didn't really know what was going on or what to expect or where they were going and the man beside her didn't seem too anxious to share any of the details with her either. He was very tense. In her limited experience with Father Clancy, he was either offering encouraging advice, or teasing his brother incessantly. But now he just sat beside her, gripping the steering wheel and focused on the road ahead illuminated by the headlights.

"Where do we go from here?" she asked quietly.

He didn't respond. JoAnna took a deep breath. Perhaps he hadn't heard her.

She said a little louder, though rather unsure of herself, "Father Clarence, you told Danny it wasn't possible to run from Balestrini…so where do we go from here?"

The man beside her turned and glanced at her and then back at the road. She wasn't sure of the look he had given her; in the darkness she could only make out the whites of his eyes and half his expression. It made her uneasy.

But he glanced over at her again and a small smile began to pull at the corner of his mouth and then, his shoulders seemed to relax slightly. "I guess Clancy's plan worked," Danny said and then he gave a relieved laugh. "If we fooled you, we may fool a few of Balestrini's men too."

***

The relief that Danny sat beside her in the driver's seat distracted JoAnna from her question, and it was some time and distance before she mustered the courage to ask again.

Danny was doing a pretty good job of just driving and not thinking. He didn't want to think about what had happened, what could have happened, what could still happen. He just wanted to drive.

"Danny?"

He acknowledged she had spoken by a sideways glance, hoping she would take the hint that he didn't want to talk.

She didn't take it. "Where are we going?"

"Does it matter?"

"Yes." He did a double take at her confident answer. "Father

Clarence said it wasn't possible to run from them. Is it?"

Again he didn't answer and saw her bite her lip in a worrisome fashion and then turn and gaze out the side window. Nearly ten minutes passed before he finally murmured, "It has to be possible."

She turned at his words, slid across the bench seat and—before she could stop her impetuous action—she leaned over and buried her face in his shoulder with a murmured, "Oh, Danny."

Danny wished he could wrap his arm around her to hold her as he drove, but his shoulder was throbbing mercilessly. He didn't want her to move—he wanted her to stay close beside him—but he couldn't endure the pain more than a few minutes. "JoAnna, my arm," he whispered.

She gasped and drew back quickly with a mortified apology. "Does it hurt much?"

Danny shot her a look from the corner of his eye and then smiled to relieve her anxiety. "As a lady once said to me, that's a relative question."

She didn't respond in kind, but retrieved a scarf from the pocket of her coat. She slipped it around his forearm and reached up to tie it around his neck. "It will take the weight off your shoulder while you drive," she explained, her lips close to his ear. He nodded his thanks.

She finished tying the scarf but didn't move away from his side. Finally, he took a brief glance at her. She was watching his face. "I can't even pray," he confessed.

Her understanding look was filled with compassion. "That's okay," she assured him. "I've been praying since we left the house."

His relief that she was praying the words he couldn't say was beyond measure. But he couldn't say as much, and only said his profound thanks with his glance.

Seven o'clock came and so did the sun. It didn't take long for the children to awaken and proclaim themselves famished. Danny pulled off the road at a tiny little town which spread itself on either side of the highway. But it didn't spread itself too far; in point of fact, a church sat on one side of the road and a small establishment—which was a grocery store, with a gas pump out front and a bar out back—were the only two buildings of public use to be seen. The other buildings, some fifteen in number, were all residential. Hurriedly, Danny discarded the make-shift sling and began unbuttoning the cassock. "Help me with this," he muttered as he tried to shrug out of it while still sitting behind the wheel. JoAnna pulled at the sleeve here and tugged at the sleeve there until they finally removed it just as the gas attendant came up to the window of the car. "Fill 'er up, Mister?"

"Please. And check the oil, will you?"

"Sure, Mister."

Danny opened the car door. "Everybody out. It's the only pit stop you get."

The children filed out and the attendant at the pump said, "Ladies' Room is around back, if you'd like to freshen up."

JoAnna said her thanks and took Janey's hand as they all made their way in the direction the attendant indicated. "Do I look that bad?" JoAnna muttered to Danny.

Danny looked her up and down and decided he couldn't see a single thing that he'd change, but he could admit to himself that his opinion was slightly biased. Aloud he could only admit, "We don't exactly smell like daisies, I suppose."

A reply which made JoAnna wish she hadn't asked.

"I'm going into the store here to get some grub for these famished street urchins," Danny said. He handed JoAnna the crushed up cassock. "Keep that, will you? Clancy will want it back.

She shook out the crumbled ball and began to fold it. "Tell me, Danny, which one of you really is the little brother," she asked, as the children used the restroom one at a time.

"We both are."

"You can't both be the little brother. You told me you weren't twins, and even if you were, one had to be born first. But you were born eleven months apart, so which one came first?"

"Oh that. Well, I am the *older* brother, but he's taller…by half an inch. So he's my *little* brother, but I'm his *little* brother. Get it?"

JoAnna laughed, "Yes, I get it."

He grinned at her. "Meet you back at the car."

When he had paid for the gas and groceries and arrived back at the car, JoAnna had the children running laps around the car and pump. "We're running off energy," JoAnna explained, although she was only standing and timing them with her watch.

Danny nodded, a little mystified by the odd site. “They look a little like dogs chasing their tails,” he acknowledged.

“Well I didn’t want them to get too far away…and they…”

He handed her the bag of groceries so that she couldn’t continue in a ramble, and ordered everyone back in the car. They pulled away from the gas pump and back onto the road. “Nice little town,” Danny observed when they were out of it. “I like it.”

“It’s certainly not Gilmore.”

“That’s probably why I like it,” Danny muttered.

***

They drove the better part of the day, stopping only when someone insisted it was that or there would be an accident and they didn’t mean one with dents. When the sun set, they took turns telling stories. Josiah’s usually dealt with a young boy managing to avoid attending school, but doing other great things; Toby’s were always very short and usually ended with fits of laughter so that no one could actually understand what had happened, but they laughed all the more; Janey’s always involved a princess but went on for so long that the boys groaned and begged someone to put them out of their misery.

Interrupting the dramatic moaning, Danny suggested, “I say its JoAnna’s turn to tell a story. And you had better be respectful and quiet and listen.”

JoAnna tilted her head at the sternness in his voice. “You make it sound as if my story is bound to be boring. And as punishment for being troublesome they have to listen to the bitter end,” she accused, feigning offense.

Danny laughed. “Well you do ramble…”

JoAnna acquiesced with a slight blush. “Let’s sing!” she suggested.

And Danny laughed again at her scapegoat, but the children excitedly agreed.

They sang every song they knew from *Tom Dooley* to *Battle Hymn of the Republic* and even the ditty from the *Halo Shampoo* commercial. One by one, the voices dropped out of the travelling choir as one by one the children dropped off to sleep.

Danny nudged JoAnna when he saw Josiah nodding in the rear view mirror. "You can stop. You knocked the last one out."

"My singing is *not* that bad," JoAnna replied with mock defensiveness.

"I meant it as a compliment."

"If that was a compliment, you need practice," she laughed. Danny shifted in his seat, and JoAnna offered, "Do you want me to drive for a while?"

Danny frowned and shook his head.

"Aren't you tired?"

"Sure. But if you just stop singing, maybe I can stay awake."

"Okay. I won't sing you to sleep." JoAnna fell silent and Danny decided that was worse as he tried to stifle a yawn.

"Joanna."

"Yes?"

"Talk to me."

"What do you want me to talk about?"

"I don't care. I just need you to talk to me to keep me awake."

"If you don't give me a topic, I may start rambling. And you don't like it when I ramble."

"I never said I didn't like it."

"You always interrupt or walk away when I do."

Danny shrugged. "Sometimes you ramble because you're nervous and don't know what to say, so I interrupt so that you don't have to keep on feeling nervous, or worried no one understands what you are trying to say."

JoAnna stared at him, mentally remembering the times he had interrupted and recognizing that many of those times it was true. She smiled. "That's sweet, Danny," she admitted with not a little surprise.

"You don't think I can be sweet?"

"Well, I'd say yes, but then I remember all the other times you've walked away from me while I was rambling. I admit I am probably boring, but walking away is not very courteous."

"Those were the times you were rambling because you were so excited about something."

JoAnna stared at him. He knew her much better than she would have guessed and a little too well for her comfort at the moment. "I'm excited, so you just walk away? Thanks a lot."

"Walking away seemed like a better response than…" he stopped midsentence.

JoAnna raised her eyebrows. "Than what?"

Danny thought better of finishing his thought and shook his head, "Nothing."

"Nothing? Oh, that's helpful. Well, guess I should be happy we are stuck in a car so that when I start rambling you can't walk away and won't have to do *nothing*. We wouldn't want you to be tempted to do *nothing*."

Danny's eyes darted toward her face again, and he gave a half smile. "Thank you, it's appreciated." It was too dark for JoAnna to see the spark in his eye.

JoAnna smiled back but shook her head, "I still don't know what you're talking about, but I guess that doesn't matter."

"For now, no." He shifted in his seat. "Tell me about the kids' week," he prompted to save the dying conversation.

So she did. She talked about Mr. and Mrs. Jansky down the street who had a dog that always came over to use the Navarone's yard as a dumping ground and about Mr. Peterson's horrible taste in sweaters, and the time she had the other day trying to help Josiah with his arithmetic.

"I told you, I'll help the kids with their homework…"

"You were *bowling*." She said the word with the same sharpness ever since that late Thursday night.

He glanced at her, and found her smiling at him despite her jab. "Go to sleep, JoAnna."

"You told me to talk to you."

"I changed my mind. You're too distracting."

She surveyed the road ahead. "From the wide open road ahead? There hasn't even been a deer to swerve around."

"Good night, JoAnna."

JoAnna leaned back against the seat and closed her eyes.

Danny drove on.

Chapter XXI

Danny drove on. He was dog-tired. He knew that he should stop. But the fear of not being able to protect his loved ones still surged through his body such that he was aware only of a physical weariness, while his mind was so alert he wouldn't have been able to sleep anyway. Not until they were someplace safe. He was taking them to the only place he knew that should be safe.

Another two hours passed before he turned into a long, gravel driveway and followed its path for a quarter mile, before it brought them to a farm yard in a grove of trees. The headlights illuminated the white siding and blue shuttered windows of a large square farm house. He turned the car off and sat for a moment letting his eyes grow accustomed to the complete darkness. The moon was barely a sliver, but as the minutes ticked by, more and more of the yard morphed into tangible shapes out of the blackness.

Finally, Danny stepped out of the car and walked up to the house. He fumbled for the key in an empty flower pot on the steps, unlocked the door and walked in. He tried the light switch, and electric lights came on in the hallway. That would be enough to get everyone inside. Peeking into the living room and kitchen, he found that the house was mostly furnished. In the living room white sheets covered much of the furniture, and the kitchen had table and chairs, though he doubted there would be any dishes.

Removing his sling once more, Danny made his way back to the Chevy. He touched JoAnna's sleeping form lightly, "Come on," he urged. "Doesn't a warm, soft bed sound good?"

Without waiting for a reply, he opened the back car door and caught Josiah who had been leaning against it in sleep. Josiah woke in an instant and slid out of the car. "Where are we?"

"Just a farm place. Help me."

Josiah looked around for the first time. "Gee, this is swell," he enthused. Then the *why* they were here came back to him, "Isn't it?"

"Peachy," Danny agreed distracted. "Here take your sister's bag. JoAnna, can you take Janey? Is she too heavy for you?"

JoAnna was groggier than Josiah but she picked up the girl, still sound asleep on the back seat. Danny scooped up Toby, who muttered at his father that he really loved the dog. Danny smiled at the boy's dream and decided JoAnna was right, he really should get a dog…when this was all over…if he were still alive…

Josiah held the door open as everyone filed into the house. Danny laid Toby's limp body on the couch and JoAnna sat on the other corner holding Janey. She waited while Danny went upstairs to find beds and bedding. When he came down with heavy footsteps he shook his head. "Sorry. Guess there aren't any beds. We'll have to make do with one couch and the floor."

JoAnna was too tired to object. She let Danny take Janey from her arms and stood up to allow Josiah to curl up on the corner of the couch opposite his brother. Then Danny situated Janey in the middle. JoAnna covered them with random bits of clothing: Janey's nightgown, Danny's coat, Father Clancy's cassock and her own coat.

She turned and found Danny peering up the chimney. "Hope this thing isn't plugged up with any nests," he muttered under his breath as he started to situate a few pieces of wood in the fireplace.

"Has it been a long time since anyone lived here?" JoAnna asked.

"I don't know."

Her eyes widened, but Danny wasn't looking at her. "You don't know? Don't you know where we are?"

"Sure."

"But?"

"But I don't know how long it's been since anyone's lived here," he restated.

"Danny?" She wanted him to look at her and focus on the conversation.

"Yah?" He remained focused on his fire-building skills and avoided the conversation.

"Where are we?" JoAnna demanded.

"In a farmhouse somewhere in the Dakotas."

"But how did you know this place was here? Did you just drive up the first driveway we came to and decide to spend the night?"

"Course not. That wouldn't be safe. I heard about this place special. A friend of a friend…" he blew at the small flame he had created, "…of a friend…" he blew again, "…of a friend…"

"Of a friend of Flags?"

He stopped blowing and looked over his shoulder at her. "You catch on quick," he admitted with a crooked grin that looked decidedly like Toby.

Exhausted, JoAnna sat down on the hardwood floor and leaned against the couch. It wasn't the most comfortable position, but at this point her body would have been grateful for a dirt floor. But she couldn't close her eyes. She was wide awake now, alert, and well aware of all the danger they had run from and possibly brought with them.

Kneeling on one knee before the fire, Danny observed the kindling as it caught the flame and began to burn brightly. He was glad the kindling had been bone dry and had started easily, he didn't have the energy to work hard at lighting this fire. He listened attentively to the slow breathing of his children. They were all asleep again, even Josiah, and Danny was grateful.

Glancing over his shoulder he found JoAnna watching him. His nerves were tense and on edge but he didn't want her to know how worried he was, so he gave her a smile. She tried her best to smile back at him, but it was slow and unsure. He had no words to say to encourage her, so he turned back toward the fire. Unbuckling his shoulder holster, he pulled out his .45, checked the chamber and placed the gun on the floor. He rolled up the holster and placed it alongside the gun.

"Do you wish you could be a cop again?" JoAnna asked.

Her question surprised him, not so much that she had asked him, but that he had never asked himself the question before.

A few minutes passed as he poked at the wood and added a little more kindling, before he replied, "I don't know…I hadn't thought about ever having the chance. I don't know what I would do."

"You go out *bowling* every week and you hadn't thought of it?" JoAnna asked, her inflection implying disbelief.

Danny turned his head to look at her, and he could see the corner of her mouth curving up in tired laughter. He chuckled himself, "I couldn't go *bowling* if I were still a cop…it's against the law."

"Oh I get it," she said, pulling up her legs and resting her head on her knees, "You can break the law as a civilian but not as a cop. Is that it?"

Thoughtfully, Danny folded his arms across his knee and massaged his right shoulder with his left hand. "In Gilmore, I would say it's just the opposite."

"My point exactly," she murmured, her eyes closed now.

"Which is why it seems to make sense to me…doing the opposite of the norm in Gilmore."

"Crooked cops and saintly robbers…and you said this wasn't an episode of the Scarlet Pimpernel."

Danny shrugged and adjusted the fire with an iron fire poker. "It isn't; it's real life."

"Still, we have crooked cops, but that doesn't mean every cop is crooked."

"Sure, we have crooked cops, crooked politicians…I sometimes wonder if there is anyone in the town who isn't on the take." He grumbled the last words more to the fire than to JoAnna.

But she responded anyway. "You can't live life suspecting everyone."

"Why not?" he countered, still focused on the fire.

"Because you have to trust somebody. You can't live life behind a wall."

"You saw the note I received before we left?"

Her face paled slightly and she nodded, "Father Clarence showed it to me."

"Then you know why I suspect everyone."

"But…"

"I've got Clancy. I've got Flags. I don't need anyone else."

"What about me?" she asked timidly.

Danny glanced over his shoulder at her but looked away quickly, the pain in her face was acute. She was different. He had never suspected her of anything other than being able to reawaken his heart and for that reason he had built a wall. Not because he didn't trust her, but because he didn't want her to trust him. "Of course. I wouldn't have brought you here if I didn't think you were trustworthy."

They were both silent. JoAnna watched the fire and Danny intermittently before speaking softly, "Do you ever feel as if there are two Gilmores? There's the Gilmore that Father Clarence and the Sisters and Mrs. Jansky and all of those good people belong to and then there's the Gilmore that you talk about, that no one seems to acknowledge."

Sighing heavily, Danny sank to a sitting position, his back to the side of the mantle, his face finally meeting JoAnna's gaze. Her peaceful demeanor calmed so much in him, he could have just sat and studied her gaze. But that would have been uncomfortable for them both, considering. He dropped his gaze before he responded. "They know about it," he admitted. "It wasn't that long ago that life was very different in Gilmore. And those good people still remember those times. And they worry about the state of Gilmore now and what it will be like when their children are grown. But they don't talk about it. You talk about it and you end up like Madeira, struggling for a dime, a penny. You end up dead, like your father. You end up…"

"Like you," JoAnna finished.

Danny met her gaze and nodded, "Like me."

He didn't drop his gaze this time. The brilliance of the fire just behind him, threw most of his face into deep shadow, and in the safety of the shadow he studied her with such love that it had to be written clearly across his face.

But JoAnna couldn't see the expression on his face, she only knew he was looking at her. She wanted to crawl into his arms and stay there forever, but fear and prudence told her to remain where she was. Finally she closed her eyes so she didn't have to say anything else…so that she wouldn't say anything else…

The warmth of the flames against her face and the peaceful breathe of the children sleeping behind her, relaxed her. She wished it would stay like this. A little farmhouse far away from everything. Far away from Balestrini; far away from murder and deceit; far away from protection fees and bribes; far away from everything that they had left in Gilmore…just her and Danny and the kids. Just them, just like this. She squeezed her eyes tighter as if to preserve a dream that for a moment, one tiny little moment, was her reality. From her closed eyes, two tears trickled down her cheeks. She turned her head hoping Danny hadn't been looking at her and wouldn't see.

But a tiny voice asked with worry, "Why are you crying, Miss JoAnna?" Janey's eyes were wide in the firelight.

Danny looked over at the couch quickly; they hadn't known the girl was awake. He shushed her gently. "Everything's okay. Everybody's just tired. Go back to sleep, Sunshine."

Janey took in her father's words but looked at JoAnna once more and then asked "Do you need a hug?" JoAnna turned slightly and reached up to hug the little girl. Janey kissed her and said "You don't have to be scared, Miss JoAnna, 'cause you're not alone."

JoAnna smiled. She had told the little girl exactly that just a couple nights before when Janey had been afraid to go to sleep. JoAnna tucked the coat about her again. "See? All better," she assured her, though frankly the hug had made it a little worse; an obvious reminder that the family she was surrounded by was not her own. JoAnna kissed her forehead and Janey closed her eyes.

JoAnna sat back down and pulled her sweater snuggly about her shoulders. Danny watched her, but this time she didn't notice. The little girl's breathing changed to once more match her brothers' slow breaths of sleep. "Why are you crying, Miss JoAnna?" Danny whispered his daughter's question, with more feeling than she had ever heard him speak to her.

She took a breath, which came out sounding more like a sob, before begging, “Please don’t ask me.”

His lips parted as if he would say something more, but he changed his mind, and instead watched her with searching eyes in the firelight.

Avoiding his gaze, she studied the flickering flames of the now blazing fire.

After a few minutes of silence, Danny suggested, “Why don’t you lay down and get some rest.”

“Aren’t *you* tired?”

“Sure,” he admitted, “but I want to make sure the fire is going to keep burning before I sleep.” He motioned toward the rug they had pulled between the fire and the couch, “Stretch out here and get some sleep.”

JoAnna acquiesced and lay down, folding her arms across her chest to hold the warmth to herself. “Good night, Danny,”

“Sweet dreams, JoAnna.”

JoAnna placed a hand over her eyes as if to shade them from the light of the fire, but really she was hiding the wealth of tears that followed his simple good night wish. It wasn’t supposed to be like this. He was supposed to love her back…or she was supposed to be able to make herself stop loving him. At this point, she would have been content with either, if only the pain in her heart would stop.

Danny had said he needed to watch the fire, but he sat for the longest time watching the woman. She meant more to him than he cared to admit to himself let alone to her. How could he have let it happen? He hadn’t meant to fall for her. She was supposed to be there to help the kids; care for the kids. He knew as well as anybody that they needed a mother figure in their lives. But he did not need a new love. Yet there she was. Lying in front of him. Her body shivering slightly from the cold that the fire couldn’t totally diminish.

Distracting himself, Danny turned towards the fire. He added more wood, building it like a teepee so that the fire would burn longer into the night. He checked the kids on the couch and tucked the corners of the clothes around them once again. Then he lay down between the couch and the woman. He lay on his back for some time, hands cushioning his head as he watched the reflection of the flames dance on the ceiling. He thought he had been running from Balestrini, from Garnelli, from three years ago, but he finally realized that even before they piled into the sedan late Thursday night, he had been trying to run from something he had brought with him. And she was lying right there close to him.

He rolled to his side to face her. She had her back to Danny and he saw her shiver in the cold. He moved closer to her and brushed her hair behind her ear so that he could see her profile. She was asleep, and she slept soundly. Gently, he placed his arm over her, felt her back sink against his chest.

And he slept soundly, as he hadn't for a very, very long time.

Chapter XXII

Somewhere a light flickered. In trying to pull himself from sleep, Danny thought that the fire had flared up, but no intense heat accompanied the light. He commanded his body to move, to rouse himself from deep sleep. He felt the warmth of a body close to his, and upon opening his eyes, he found JoAnna nestled against his chest, his large arm still resting over her, encircling her, keeping her warm in the absence of the fire. She began to stir at his movement and he removed his arm quickly, though it was stiff and very sore. His senses were catching up to his consciousness and he sat up quickly, noting the light from the hallway.

"What's going on here?" a man's deep voice demanded. "Who the devil are you?"

Danny was on his feet in an instant, fully awake and berating himself for sleeping so soundly. He moved naturally to shield JoAnna and the children from the intruder.

"I should be demanding that of you," Danny declared. "This isn't your house."

The authority in his voice caught the large man off guard. "No…no, it's not. I'm a neighbor. This place had been empty for months. But that doesn't mean just anybody can crash in and steal from it."

"We're not just anybody," Danny said, authority still in his voice. "We just bought the place. Purchased it last week."

"Well, I'll be…no foolin'?"

Danny tried to lighten his demeanor, though his heart was in his throat. "No fooling," he agreed.

"Well I'll be…did you hear that Peggy? Neighbors!"

Peggy made her appearance from behind her large husband; she lowered the hoe she held grasped in her hand and smiled widely. "Ah, now isn't that sweet. Neighbors. Why we haven't had neighbors in this place for, well, I don't know, must be about two years now. Ain't that right, dear?"

The man agreed with a nod and offered Danny his hand. "My name's Tasche. Marcellus Tasche. This is my wife, Peggy."

Danny shook hands. "Daniel Navarone," he said, debating belatedly whether or not it was a good idea to say his own name. He motioned toward JoAnna who had risen and come up beside him. "JoAnna," he said, purposefully dropping the last name; they could infer whatever they liked.

Throughout the ensuing apologies, pleasantries, and fake explanations, Danny tried to reorient himself to where he was and what he needed to be doing. For the moment, he didn't even know what time it was, although the sun was shining in the doorway and the windows in the kitchen.

The talking woke the children, who proclaimed themselves hungry.

JoAnna tried to shush them politely, but Toby wasn't just hungry he was famished and said as much. "Well we'll get going so you can get these young'uns fed," Peggy offered.

"But where will we get the food?" Janey piped up innocently.

Danny picked her up to shush her. "We'll be fine," he assured her and the Tasche's.

Peggy sighed in sympathy. "Oh, of course. You only arrived late last night. You haven't made it to the store for food."

"We don't have any dishes for cooking either," Janey piped back up.

Danny patted her arm, trying to remind her not to interrupt, but she shrugged and said, "But Daddy, we don't. We don't even have beds."

"Our things were supposed to arrive before us…but I guess they didn't," JoAnna supplied quickly.

"No, nothing?" Marcellus asked.

"Nothing," Danny replied, avoiding the double negative.

"Well, we'll have to help you out there. Come on, children," he said heading toward the door without waiting for any assents or arguments. "We're going back to our house for a nice big breakfast. Well, it will almost be dinner by the time we get you there and fed. But what do you think of fresh eggs…"

"Do you have chickens?" Toby asked, snatching up his shoes and following the man to the porch. "My grandma and grandpa has chickens…they're mean?"

"You're grandparents?" Marcellus asked holding the door for his wife and the two boys.

"No! The chickens!" Toby corrected.

Danny put Janey down and she hurried ahead to catch up to her brothers.

Only Danny and JoAnna remained in the house. Danny took a deep breathe, the first he had allowed himself since being awakened.

"Now what?" JoAnna asked in a hushed tone.

Danny walked back to the fire place, shrugged into his shoulder holster and coat. "We have breakfast," he said re-holstering his .45.

"And then?"

He met her worried look. "You can't live life suspecting everyone," he replied to her look.

She gave a smile but argued, "That's unfair."

Danny relented, placed a hand on her elbow to escort her from the house to the porch. The children were already scrambling into the Tasche's automobile. Danny put on his hat and helped JoAnna into her coat, murmuring over her shoulder, "If Balestrini knew we were here, he would have sent his henchmen in after us." He motioned to the vast landscape around the farmyard. "They could have killed us in this house and no one would know for three years. He wouldn't bother sending a neighborhood farmer to fake us out."

She glanced around at the vast, open fields, with not a tree in sight. Then she turned around and looked up at him, “Thank you, Danny” she said.

Danny didn’t know if she was thanking him for helping her on with her coat, relieving her anxieties or maybe possibly keeping her warm the night before. He feared it was for all three and he dropped the smile and said, “Let’s go eat some eggs from some mean chickens.”

They spent the entire day with the Tasches. That generous, cheerful couple prepared enough food for them as if they suspected that the Navarone’s had two hollow legs each, which Danny admitted, the boys ate as if they did.

Then the Tasches showed them around their farm place, of which they were obviously very proud and well they should have been. It was a leisurely walk and they were all grateful to stretch their legs in a peaceful, safe place. The wind blew softly across the open fields and the children marveled at the wide countryside, with very few trees to block the great distances. Janey walked beside her father and slipped her little hand into his. Then she pulled forward until they came abreast with JoAnna and she slipped her other hand into JoAnna’s hand. “That’s better,” Janey declared.

Danny was inclined to agree but didn’t say as much.

The children took turns on the tire swing, and when Mr. Tasche offered an old tire that they could have for a swing of their own, Janey looked at the tire longingly and then inquisitively at his father. But Mr. Tasche thundered through that look with the proposition that they would come over the next day to help hang it.

Supper was offered and Danny tried to decline, but Peggy reminded them that they hadn’t any food at their house, so they had better stay to supper before they went home. So Danny relented and JoAnna was grateful. As they were preparing to finally head back to the farm place, Peggy insisted that they take quilts and mattresses with them.

“Just until your things arrive,” Peggy explained. “You can’t turn it down for the children.”

“But that isn’t really necessary…” Danny replied.

“Oh, stop it,” Marcellus ordered “Floors are for walking on, not for sleeping. Just use it and be grateful.”

Danny smiled and nodded. "Then I thank you."

"Don't thank me yet," Marcellus laughed. "You've got to help me get them from down stairs. Peggy seems to think they can fold up like paper and weigh just as much. I'm not as young as I used to be."

The men headed for the staircase to retrieve the mattresses and Danny heard JoAnna exclaim, "It's very kind of you both. You've been so good to us…"

"Oh of course dear, we're excited for you. We could use nice folks like you moving in the area. Such a sweet young couple, and a growing family." Danny didn't look back to see JoAnna's face. He wondered vaguely if Peggy had meant that the children were growing or that the family was going to be growing bigger with additions.

With the mattresses strapped to the roof and everyone and the quilts piled on top of each other inside the car, they waved good-bye to Peggy. "You just get settled for the night," she ordered in a motherly voice. "We'll be heading into church in the morning, if you'd like to come? We could pick you up or you could follow us? Marcellus will convince Jerry to open his Mercantile and let you pick up a few things though it will be Sunday. It's the Christian thing to do…"

"…Not to let your neighbors starve," Marcellus muttered in the driver's seat. "…that's how I'll have to put it, or he'll grumble about it till Kingdom come."

Danny smiled at the couples bantering and explanations. After Marcellus dropped them at the farm house, and they had finished carrying the mattresses into the house, Danny thanked Marcellus once again.

The children, pleasantly worn out by nightfall, went to their beds with little effort. Josiah got the couch to himself. Janey and JoAnna shared the smaller mattress and Toby and his father shared the large mattress closest to the door.

Danny checked the chamber of his gun and laid it on the floor close to the mattress. He sighed deeply. He was beat. To all outward appearances, it had been a restful day, free from any worry, but that which he had brought with him. And the worry he had brought with him had to be addressed soon. Soon, he would have to go back. Now that he knew his family was safe, he would have to go back to face what could possibly be already unfolding in Gilmore. Balestrini had figured out that Danny was a thorn in his side; there were other situations that would be rent open as well.

He thought about the night before, how restful it had been. But how frightening it had been to be awakened so abruptly. How dangerous it could have been that he hadn't heard the Tasche's drive up or enter the house. If it had been anyone else, who knew how deep their graves would already be.

His teeth clenched and his hand moved involuntarily for his gun, as if he wanted to be sure it was still there. He could already hear Toby's deep slow breathe of sleep. He allowed himself to relax a little, conscious that his movements might disturb his son. But if he relaxed too much he feared he would fall asleep, and he would not let himself do that tonight. He wanted to rest, but he feared sleeping. He thought of JoAnna, just a few feet from him. He had slept so well, with her on his mind, but that was dangerous. He wouldn't think of her tonight. He would think of Balestrini and only Balestrini and then maybe sleep wouldn't come. Then perhaps, he would be on the alert and no one would be hurt or endangered.

He closed his eyes, content with the prospect.

Very soon, he was asleep.

He awoke, sitting in a chair. Instantly he knew where he was. He was there again. In the room that he had sat in three years before. A room he had sat in again and again in dreams and nightmares ever since. It was a cold and barren room, but brilliantly lit. He knew it was a dream, but he couldn't stop what was happening. Sometimes he would tell the other people in the dream that it was a dream, but they only laughed. And then he began to doubt that it was a dream. Began to doubt that maybe this time, once more, it was reality.

So here he sat once more in that chair. Only in the dream he wasn't tied as he had been the first time. Then, they had tied him to the chair and there was nothing he could do but watch what happened. But in the dream, this maddening dream, he wasn't tied. Yet he still couldn't move. He was free, but he remained in the chair. He was free, but still, he could do nothing. Sitting there watching the scene over again. Wanting to fight to stop them, and being held by some invisible force that kept him there. Watching

Lilian being slowly murdered in front of him, one more time…only tonight…tonight it wasn't Lilian. Tonight it was JoAnna. JoAnna, her laughing eyes not laughing but pleading with him to help her, save her. Why didn't he save her? And he sat there unable to leave the chair to which he wasn't even tied.

Danny felt hands grasp him by the shoulders and finally his frozen state was shaken and he reached out and grabbed the person firmly by the arms. The dream fell away in a moment and he realized that he was sitting on the mattress, gripping JoAnna's arms, his fingers like claws into her arms. JoAnna gave a muffled cry as she sank to the floor beside the mattress.

He sat there for a lingering moment as his mind processed slowly what was dream and what was reality. In the dim light from the dying fire his eyes focused on Joanna's frightened face staring up at him. He let go of her arms, almost thrust her away from him and she fell backwards on the floor. He wiped a shaking hand down his perspiring face and over his chin.

He muttered what was half prayer and half apology as he stood up and left the living room with hurried steps. He was so intent on getting out of the house and away from everyone that he didn't bother to muffle the slam of the screen door.

The slam seemed to startle him into a conscious reality. It had been a dream, a nightmare, he assured himself. It wasn't reality, no matter how real it had seemed. He stood on the edge of the porch and took his first deep breath since he had been awakened. He wiped a hand across his chin and then held the hand away from himself, staring at it as it continued to shake. He clasped his hands together, trying to stop them from shaking, and when they didn't, he shoved them both into his trouser pockets in exasperation.

Looking up, Danny searched the starry sky for some distraction. But it only made the scenes of the nightmare come back to him. The ache in the pit of his stomach was so painful he felt as if he needed to be sick, but he hadn't eaten all that much that day, and had nothing with which to be sick. And now he stood out here, realizing that the dream was subsiding but the fear he had of losing JoAnna was so real and so forceful that he didn't know how to deal with it.

He lit a cigarette, angry at himself because whenever he had had these nightmares these past three years he had never allowed himself to think about them once he had awakened. Exhaling, Danny clenched his teeth. "God," he prayed in desperation, "Where's your mercy now?"

Danny heard a movement behind him, and watched as JoAnna came out of the house and slowly, silently closed the screen door. He remained where he was, dreading her words or her nearness.

She came up to him and reached out a hand to touch his arm. "Danny, are you alright?"

He withdrew his arm sharply.

But she continued despite his coldness, "I didn't mean to wake you. You were moaning in your sleep…I didn't know if you were sick or dreaming."

"Forget it," he snapped and flicked his cigarette over the railing. He folded his arms, leaned against the porch post and studied the starlit farmyard.

"Danny?"

He glanced down at her but didn't reply.

"I don't want to leave you alone out here. You're upset…"

"It was just a bad dream, JoAnna. I'm fine. Just go back to bed," he ordered.

"Don't you want some company?"

"Not particularly," he lied. "I'd rather be alone."

"Nobody likes to be alone after a nightmare," she argued, in her usual matter-of-fact manner. "Especially after one that seems so real."

"JoAnna!" his tone was the one he used when he was upset with the children.

But she countered calmly, "Yes?"

He set his jaw, but she couldn't see that in the shadow of the night, and only stood there looking up at him. He wanted to pull her into his arms and hold her. He wanted to know for certain she was real, she was safe; to chase the terrifying feeling of how real the nightmare felt as far away as possible. Instead he turned and walked down the length of the porch, hoping she would leave.

But JoAnna didn't leave. Without a word she sat on the top step of the porch and studied the multitude of stars as if it were the most logical thing in the world to do in the middle of the night. Danny remained in the darkness. He watched her and the site of her in the starlight calmed him, until the nightmare had dissipated enough for him to know what was real and what was imagination. He was peaceful again. He breathed easier. He could think straight.

Finally, Danny walked over and sat down beside her. Danny leaned his elbows on his thighs and proceeded to light another cigarette. He focused on the task, aware that JoAnna was studying his face in the glow of the match. It was haggard he felt sure, much more than she had ever seen it.

The match expired and the darkness gave her the confidence to speak. "You need sleep, Danny."

"Yah," he agreed. "Tried that, didn't I? Wasn't very restful."

"What did you dream about?" she asked tentatively.

Danny didn't answer at first. He smoked almost half the cigarette before he knew his voice was strong enough to murmur without cracking, "Lilian." And then he added with more truth than he had intended to share, "and you."

He knew she was looking at him but he only studied the end of his cigarette. He couldn't face her now, he couldn't look at her, knowing how much he cared for her, and how much was still so unsettled, how much Lilian was still there.

The silence lengthened. If she didn't say something soon, the conversation would be over for sheer length of nothing being said. Too far gone to revive. He had nothing to add, but he wished she would say something, anything, even her rambling would have been appreciated.

Finally she began to speak with words soft and soothing. "I dream about my Dad sometimes. I dream that he's still here. That we're working together, or taking a walk. It's such a wonderful dream that it hurts so much to wake up. And as real as the dream is, and so soothing to the hurt, it would almost be better not to have dreamt it at all, so that I wouldn't feel the pain of losing him again when I wake up. Do you know what I mean?"

He was watching her in the dim light of the almost moonless night sky. "Maybe," he replied, because he had only half been listening to her words, mostly he had been watching her expressions and listening to the rising and falling of her voice. He wished he could bottle the sound of her voice and just play it over and over, it was so gentle on his ears and easy on his heart. But he was grateful for a subject other than his dream and asked, "What do you miss most about him?"

JoAnna thought for a long moment, her face turned up to the night sky. "I think," she murmured slowly, "I think I miss his gentleness the most. He was always so calm, and patient. Even when I was little and got into trouble, he never raised his voice. And if he did, I knew that I had really messed up." She gave a small smile at some unspoken memory. "It was just me and him for as long as I can remember. I miss him every day." She looked over at Danny. "Do you dream of Lilian often?"

Danny looked away at the question. "It wasn't a dream. It was a nightmare. About the night she was murdered."

"Oh."

He realized he was making this a very difficult conversation for her to attribute to, so he continued. "It's always the same nightmare. Every time I have it…only tonight it was different."

"How?"

He looked at her—her inquisitive face, her brown eyes—and quickly looked away. "Doesn't matter," he murmured. "Can't change the past, and history always repeats itself."

"That's silly," JoAnna countered. "You might as well say we're stuck in a world where we have no say in the outcome. That things are ordered and we are merely players of the part."

"Maybe we are," he muttered, thoughtfully watching the ashes fall from the end of his cigarette.

"You don't believe that," she laughed.

"Why not?" Danny asked, purely for the sake of argument and to see the fire in her eyes at a worthy dispute. "If we're good people doing good things, then why did we both lose someone good to murder?"

"If that's what you believe, then why do you go *bowling*?" His eyes widened with surprise. But she insisted, "I mean it, Danny. It's the same principle. If you think it doesn't matter, than why do you try to do so much good by helping those people?"

"We've been through this conversation before, haven't we? Didn't we determine it doesn't really help anyone? Gilmore is still stuck in the same cycle. But you changed the subject."

"Why do bad things happen to good people? Isn't that the same question man has been asking since the time of Job?"

"So? What's the answer?"

"I don't think even Job figured that out. Except…" she hesitated.

"Except?"

"Everything happens for a reason," she murmured a little softer.

"Does it?" he prompted because he didn't want her to give up on the conversation.

"Of course," she insisted. When he met her gaze she looked away quickly and continued a little hurriedly and he knew she was nervous. "Well, that is to say, I don't mean that murder happened for a good reason. Murder happens because, I don't know, because men are selfish and want something they think they can get only by killing someone. It's not that I think it happens for a reason, but God can bring good out of that evil. The only thing is, we have to trust Him and open our eyes to see when He *has* turned a curse into a blessing…sometimes we miss it…"

"Trust. That's your answer?"

"It's not *my* answer. I think it's *the* answer."

Danny fell silent. What had begun as a way to keep her talking had ended with a knife in his heart. Hadn't Lilian trusted him to protect, to save her? He drew on his cigarette once more and then tossed it onto the gravel. "Sometimes trust is misplaced."

"It's never a bad idea to trust God."

"I wasn't talking about God," Danny stated.

JoAnna looked over at him pointedly, as if she could read his thoughts. "I trust you, Danny." She said it so simply, so matter-of-factly, that he believed her.

And because he believed her, he stood abruptly. "I wish you wouldn't," he said the words almost angrily. "I've already endangered you far more than I ever had a right to. Can you understand that? Balestrini's not playing tiddlywinks. You play against him and you either lose or you're dead, there is no winning option. I've been playing against him since the War, JoAnna, and I lost. I lost Lilian. Do you understand what I'm saying? Lilian's death was my fault. The night she was taken and killed, she was standing on that corner waiting for me. If I had been there as I said I would be, they couldn't have taken her. I should have been there, JoAnna, and I wasn't. I didn't protect her." He rubbed a hand over his face, muttering, "And that's what I dream…every…dang…time."

JoAnna sat still for a long moment, his tall form over her, seeming even bigger in the looming darkness. Yet she mustered up her courage and replied softly, "I still trust you, Danny. I don't believe that it was your fault even if you were late. And I trust you."

Danny looked down at her, almost caving to the desire to pull her into his arms. Finally, he murmured, "I don't want you to trust me, JoAnna. I care too much about you."

They stood there for a long moment, Danny towering over her, hating Balestrini for creating this fear of loving in his life. And her looking up at him, wishing he knew how trustworthy he was despite the odds, and wishing that she could make all his doubts go away. But nothing could be solved on that farm in the Dakotas. They would have to go back to Gilmore. Both Danny and JoAnna knew it and both feared the consequences.

JoAnna touched Danny's arm gently, "Come back in the house, Danny. Get some rest."

He followed her up the steps, but changed his mind, "It's almost sunrise. Think I'll just sit up."

The tone of his voice held no room for dispute. He opened the door for her and as JoAnna walked past him she looked up, "You're a good man, Daniel Navarone. You're brave, and you're kind, and you *are* trustworthy…"

"Sort of like a Boy Scout," he offered with a crooked grin.

She smiled up at him, "Sort of," she agreed. He was still holding the door and waiting, and she stood up on tiptoe kissed him on the cheek and fled into the house.

Chapter XXIII

The sun rose more slowly than Danny had anticipated. He had to distract himself from the night and the dream and JoAnna, so he contemplated what he had to do in order to leave. He would have to head back to Gilmore. But he wasn't okay with leaving JoAnna and the children alone. He had no fear that Balestrini had any idea where they were. But he was taking no chances that Balestrini's wiseguys might stumble upon them on an off chance and find them unprotected.

A little after 5 a.m., Danny called Flags and found that man in an uncharacteristically cheerful mood despite being aroused before the sun. Danny related his plans and his need for help. He barely had to ask for what he needed; Flags, being sober, filled in the blanks.

"I'll put Carter on the road as soon as I get ahold of him."

Danny hesitated.

Flags insisted, "Are you kidding me, Lieut? A man who saved your rookie hide how many times? You think he could turn?"

Flags' teasing affirmation was enough to convince Danny of Carter's trustworthiness. Flags told him Carter would break the speed limit to get there. Danny refrained from telling Flags that it would be the first time Carter ever had, if he actually did. The man took his job to the letter and even speeding for him was a capital offense. Danny figured Carter wouldn't be there until late that night. Danny could wait, though; he would have the afternoon to see that JoAnna and the children were well settled before he left them. Left them? For how long? Would he be back to collect them, or would someone else?

Flags interrupted his thoughts. "I said, how's your arm?"

"What arm?" Danny asked unthinkingly.

Flags laughed. "Hopefully you still have two. But I'm inquiring about the one that I had the pleasure of digging a bullet out of."

Danny changed the receiver to his left hand and tried to move his arm in a full circle. He only made it half way around before he grimaced and had to catch his breath to keep from moaning. "It's fine," he replied.

"I can tell," Flags agreed sarcastically on the other end of the line. "What good are you gonna be to me when you get back here?"

"I'll be fine. You just keep out of the limelight until I get there, hear?"

He wrapped up his conversation with Flags, who informed him proudly that he had retrieved the safe from the alley. Danny was a little afraid of what Flags would try to do alone, before Danny could get back. But he would wait for Carter.

When Sunday finally did dawn, the Tasche's came by to escort them to church. After church, they cornered Jerry to open his Merchantile, which he obligingly did. JoAnna invited the Tasche's to brunch at the farm, insisting on repaying a small portion of their continued generosity.

After the meal, JoAnna and Peggy set about cleaning up the brunch dishes, for there was little left of the brunch itself to clean up. Marcellus and Josiah busied themselves hanging the tire swing much to Janey and Toby's delight.

Danny wandered off alone. His thoughts were lost in what had to be done when he returned to Gilmore and how they could legally trap Balestrini. That somewhere in the things they had confiscated from Andreadi's office there had to be evidence, some scrap of something that would help put Balestrini behind bars. He wandered into the empty barn and folded his arms across the top rail of a stall.

The barn light flickered on and Danny turned his head to see

JoAnna hesitate in the doorway. “Everything okay?” he asked.

She nodded her head and walked toward him. “The Tasche’s are playing the part of grandparents. They’re very good at it. Their own grandchildren live nearly six hours from here, so I think they’re enjoying the opportunity.”

She was too short to lean on the top rail, so she turned and leaned her back against the stall. He had gone back to contemplating Balestrini long before she came up beside him and she asked, “What are you thinking about?”

“Leaving,” he said bluntly, still not really paying any attention to her.

JoAnna didn’t respond for a moment. “Right now?”

He finally looked down at her, one eyebrow raised. He gave a half smile, “No…but soon.”

“When?” she asked pointedly. Her eyes reflected worry and he thought they look instantly moist.

“Later tonight, I guess. Flags is sending Carter to stay with you and the children. He should be here by then.”

She looked away and sighed, “Do you have to go?”

Her words made the smile fade from his face and he seemed to withdraw although he didn’t move any farther away. “Can’t stay here forever.”

“Couldn’t we try?” she tried to joke, but she did a lousy job and her voice caught on the end of the question.

“Try to forget what we left back in Gilmore? Good luck on that one. We’d have a real swell life here, with that at the back of our minds.”

“I didn’t really mean it,” she admitted. “So you’re leaving?”

He didn’t think it was worth answering, and she went on before he could think up a proper response anyway.

“Before you go, I have to say something.” Tears started rolling down her cheeks. Danny caught his breath, but she brushed the tears away impatiently, “No, don’t stop me. I just want to tell you how sorry I am that you lost Lilian. I wanted to say it last night, and didn’t…I just wish…I don’t know…if I could have taken her place, then we’d both be better off, wouldn’t we?”

“JoAnna, stop! Don’t ever say that.”

"But it's true. No one would be missing me. My dad is gone and then I'd be gone and you and the kids would have Lilian…and…"

"JoAnna!"

"Why? Why did it have to happen this way? Doesn't He know that it doesn't make any sense? That it would have been less painful for us all?"

"JoAnna, stop it! What's the matter with you? Just last night, you said…remember, what you said? Everything happens for a reason…"

"Oh don't worry," she cried, brushing more tears away. "I'm just making a fool of myself now. I guess I just wanted to let you know how, how absolutely sorry I am that you had to endure seeing your wife murdered and losing her so tragically. I wanted you to know…and I...I just wasn't brave enough before and now that you're leaving…"

Danny stood frozen before her. Staring at her as if he had never seen her before. "What did you say?" he demanded.

She stumbled over her words and they petered out until she just stood looking at him and his incredibly stern and paling face.

"I…I said, I'm sorry for your losing Lilian…"

"No. What did you just say about Lilian?"

More tears rolled down her cheeks, but his instant sternness made her forget them. "I don't know what you mean, Danny. What's wrong?"

"You said, about Lilian, about my *seeing* her. Isn't that what you said? That I saw her murdered? Is *that* what you said?" he demanded.

JoAnna cowered, though she had no real fear of him, "Yes…I guess…I…didn't you?"

"*Who* told you?"

"Danny, you're frightening me? What are you talking about? Didn't you?"

"Yes. I did. But *who* told you?"

"I…" she faltered and fell silent.

"Listen to me, JoAnna. I saw them kill Lilian. But no one knows that I saw them except *them*. After she was dead, they took me and dumped me in a ditch outside of town. They left her where they killed her, where the police found her. Do you understand what I'm saying? No one knew I was there. And I told only one person. And it's a pretty safe bet that he never breathed a word? So who told you?"

JoAnna shook her head. "I…I don't know. I don't…"

"JoAnna, you have to remember. Whoever told you, knows something about that night. Whoever told you knows what went on that night. I need to know who told you."

"I don't know," she insisted.

"Think!" he persisted almost ruthlessly.

She put her hands to her face, trying to remember. "I am. I'm trying to remember."

"JoAnna," he pleaded.

"Please, Danny. I'm trying…It was…it was at the picnic, I think…" She hashed it around in her head, over and over, trying to pinpoint who had spoken the words. It hadn't been a big deal at the time. It had been spoken out of turn, as if anyone who knew Danny knew the fact. She hadn't thought much of who was telling her the information, only of the information itself, of how much more Danny had been hurt than she had realized. "Hartley," she suddenly said without hesitation.

Danny turned slowly around and stared at her. "Who did you say?" he demanded incredulously.

She looked up and met his gaze, more confident in her answer now that she had heard it spoken aloud. "Mr. Hartley," she said again.

"No," Danny said sharply. "Not Hartley."

"But it was, Danny. I remember I ran into him…don't you remember, when you found me in the orchard. We were just talking and he mentioned it in passing, I don't even know how it worked itself into the conversation. He said he always thought you were one of the best cops in the Department…that it was a shame what had happened, and he supposed seeing the woman you loved murdered would do that to the best of men…Couldn't he have known?"

Danny began to pace. His shoulders were rigid and set and he was trying to hold back the anger that had been inside for so many days.

"Danny, what's wrong? You just gave me the third degree, as if I were keeping something from you and now when I remember, you don't believe me."

"I believe you," he replied heavily, "But I don't want to believe you."

"Danny, please! Tell me what's going on? Isn't he the one you told?"

"No. I told Clancy…and no one else. I haven't told another soul that I sat in front of them while they slowly murdered my wife. They tied me to a chair and killed her right in front of me…" his voice drifted off and then he said flatly, "If Hartley knows…Hartley was there."

***

Danny walked out of the barn into the brilliance of the afternoon sunshine. He stood for a moment, allowing his eyes to adjust to the light after the cool shade of the barn. He was looking for Tasche.

Marcellus was giving Janey a push on the swing and Peggy stood close by telling Toby he would have to wait his turn. Danny walked over purposefully and asked of the man, "Want to see the farm?"

Marcellus looked up. And as odd and abrupt as the question sounded, he took it in stride, "Surely do."

The children were excited to follow, but Danny ordered them to stay with Mrs. Tasche and JoAnna who had followed from the barn.

He didn't meet JoAnna's gaze as he walked away with Marcellus. They walked to the far side of the barn until they came to the cow yard. The fence was in need of repair and had clearly not been in use for some time.

"Can I ask for your help?" Danny asked.

Marcellus surveyed the cow yard. "Fence needs mending."

"That's not the kind of help I need. How are you at handling trouble?" Danny asked without preamble.

Marcellus met his look without surprise. "I can hold my own. But I probably haven't faced the kind of trouble you're talking about."

Danny's brow furrowed, curious how he knew.

Marcellus leaned toward him and spoke softly, as if there was someone who might over hear, "Not too many farmers carry a sidearm in these parts." Danny's hand went instinctively to feel his .45 in its holster and he smiled when Marcellus continued, "Don't worry. The missus didn't notice, and your's doesn't seem to mind."

"Have you got a gun?"

"Do I need one?"

Danny sighed. "I don't know. I hope not. I have a friend coming to help out. But I need to head back to Gilmore, sooner than I thought. I won't leave JoAnna and the kids without protection. You'll help?"

"You trust me?"

"I do," Danny replied a little surprised himself. JoAnna should be proud of him.

"Must be quite a mess you're in if I need to go get my gun. How'd a nice couple like you get in a mess like this?" Marcellus asked in surprise.

Danny sighed. He'd skip the long "couple" explanation. "It's a long story."

"Well before I go home to get that gun you think I'll need, don't you think you could tell me the short version. I'd hate to find out too late I was defending the wrong side."

Tasche was right, of course. Danny couldn't ask him to possibly risk his life without some kind of explanation.

Danny drew a deep breath before he began. "Sometimes I don't think I know," he admitted. "There were bad politics creeping into Gilmore before the War. But not like this. And there were those trying to fight it, to bring it out in the open. But like most in the '30's, we were hit hard on all sides, like a lot of towns around here. There were the devastating blizzards in November of '40 and again in March of '41. Then the War came." Danny shrugged. "People were distracted. Distracted by the suffering of families here, by the danger to their boys over there. I suppose it kinda makes a fella over look things that should be obvious. When Balestrini came around in '42, nobody really took notice. They were watching out for Hilter and Hirohito more than for any dictator in their own backyard. And Balestrini found a ripe place to fence a lot of funds he was making illegally.

"By the time things were over over there, they were over over here too. Balestrini had taken over by default. When all us soldiers finally made it back home, it was too late to prevent the takeover, Gilmore was already in the thick of it. Some held out longer than others. The Police Department still had a lot of good men when I signed up. Some we lost to 'accidents,' some caved and some were crushed out." He met Tasche's eyes. "Now it's time to crush Balestrini out."

"And that's what you're headin' back to Gilmore to do?"

"Hope to."

Marcellus studied him for a long moment. "Reckon I'll get my gun for that," he said, then turned and walked away.

Danny smiled with relief. He followed the man back to the farmyard.

It wasn't ten minutes before Marcellus was back and Danny had made his goodbyes to the children. Luckily they hadn't a premonition of what was up, although Josiah seemed reluctant to let Danny leave alone.

"Don't you think I should go with you, Dad?" he asked

Danny shook his head, "Need you to stay here and take care of our ladies, Josiah. Will you do that?"

Josiah nodded.

Danny offered Marcellus a hand as a silent thank you, then walked toward the car.

He hadn't yet reached the car when he heard the screen door open and close.

"Danny!" JoAnna rushed off the porch without care for who in the yard saw or heard her. She stopped short only a foot from him. "You're leaving."

It sounded more like an announcement than a question and he would have liked to ignore it altogether. "I told you this morning that I would be."

She accused, "No good-byes?"

"JoAnna," he said it pleadingly, begging her not to argue with him, just this once.

She looked up at him, her eyes wide and inquisitive. How he wished her could tell her things. Not things about what he and Flags did, not things about anything. He just wished he could tell her…anything. He wished when he came home, he was coming home to her. And yet, everything that was looming over them all, it was as if it wasn't over them it was between them. And mostly it was on him, a million bits of conversation they had had together flooded his mind, accusations, since apologized for, and demands and questions and inadequacies…and there was no way he could ever be what she had thought of *le Saint*.

She stood there facing him, watching him, waiting for him to finish, she was so close yet he felt as if he was so far from being able to touch her. He finally said, "I'm no saint."

Her eyes were wide, "Maybe not. But then no saint ever canonized himself."

"JoAnna," he began again.

But she interrupted, "Danny, I know you're not a saint. And you're not a savior…but that doesn't mean you aren't a hero. To all those people you help, you save from Balestrini, you *are* a hero, to your children, who idolize you…"

"What about to you?"

"To me?" she seemed slightly taken back. But as long as he had finally found the courage he might as well proceed.

"Yes, JoAnna. What am I to you? *Le Saint*? A hero? Or…" He saw the color slowly rising in her cheeks.

"My boss?" she proposed with a small smile.

He gave a smile back. "Is that it?"

She looked down. "That's an unfair question to ask your employee."

"Alright…you're fired," he said flippantly. "Now, what am I to you?"

She raised her head, little affected by being fired, actually slightly emboldened by it. "What am *I* to *you*?" she asked reversing the question with emphasis.

He looked at her, finally with enough confidence not to let her return look scare away his gaze. But the words wouldn't come. He wished he could tell her that she was what he wanted to come back to, when everything was over. She was what he breathed, what he needed; what he wanted. How could he say that to her knowing that he had to leave and what he had to do? But he knew his eyes spoke volumes that he refused to allow his lips to say and for once he didn't mask them.

Her lips parted in surprise at his gaze and her breath quickened, but she didn't say anything.

Finally, he reached out and took her arms gently and started to pull her closer, when he saw her grimace. He let go of her, embarrassed that his touch had produced such a reaction, at the same time noticing a dark bruises on her arms. "What happened here?" he demanded.

She wouldn't meet his gaze and didn't respond. Danny gave a look of disgust as he realized what the bruises were. He dropped his hands from her arms and JoAnna thought by the look on his face that he was going to be sick. "*I* happened," he moaned. "Last night when I had the nightmare, isn't that right?" She didn't respond. "Why didn't you say something?"

"It doesn't matter," she insisted.

"It does too matter. Look what I did to you."

She covered the bruises on both arms with both hands. "Danny, they don't really hurt that much," she fibbed. They were quite tender, but it hurt worse to see him in agony over them.

Danny turned away from her. How he longed to draw her so close to him, he had hardly ever even touched her and now when he had actually got close enough to touch her, he hurt her. He had to leave this place. Leave her. He would go and finish what he had left undone for too many years. She was better off without him, and the children would be safe here with Marcellus and Carter and JoAnna. He started toward the car.

"Danny, wait!" she insisted. She was coming after him. "You asked me a question. Don't you want to know the answer?" She walked in front of him, blocking his passage to the car.

She was very close to him, and he wanted to back away but he only stated, "I changed my mind. I don't think I want to know…what you think of me."

Her mouth parted twice before she could make herself speak. "Everything," she finally announced.

"What?"

"You're everything to me, Danny. Maybe it's not my place to say so, but…you did fire me…and…Oh, Danny, I love you so! I don't ever want to lose you…" She put her arms up and leaned against his chest and cried into the lapel of his jacket.

Danny slowly encompassed her in his strong arms and held her close as she continued to cry. He wished he could say it back to her. But he didn't. He only held her. And prayed for the strength to walk away.

They stood together for several moments. Danny needed to go, but somehow he couldn't be the one to separate them. He couldn't walk away with her standing there, clinging to him.

Finally, JoAnna pushed gently away from him. "I'm sorry. I'm okay now. I…You can leave, Danny. I…I just needed you to know, before you left. I needed to tell you…I couldn't bear your leaving not knowing that."

She stepped back one pace, and Danny let her out of the circle of his arms. He couldn't say what he wanted to say to her, but with a thumb he wiped a large tear from her cheek. "Take care of the children for me?" he asked.

"I will."

"I'll be back," he assured her.

"I know."

"Carter's a good guy. You'll be safe here."

"I know," she assured him.

He still hesitated.

"Go on," she encouraged him. "We'll be fine."

Danny climbed into the car and drove away from the farmyard without a backward glance.

Chapter XXIV

Danny parked Joanna's car in the alley behind his house. It was as dark as when he had left it how many days ago. But not all was as he had left it. He walked up the back porch and opened the screen door. The storm door swung open from just a light touch of his hand, because the strike plate had been torn from the jamb. Danny glanced at the door to find that the knob was half torn from the wood.

He reached for the light switch, and pushed it, then pushed it again. He wondered if Balestrini's men had cut the power before they stormed the house or if they had done so much damage that the fuse had blown. His eyes were accustomed to the darkness outside, but the night sky had afforded some light and so he waited a moment for his eyes to adjust to the complete darkness of the interior of the house. Before he moved in any direction he wanted to know what was out of place. Shapes were becoming clearer and he moved to the right and fumbled for the kitchen drawer, where there would be a flashlight. But there was no kitchen drawer, just a hole where it belonged. He knelt cautiously and found the drawer on the floor, its various contents half scattered about it.

Pencils. Screwdriver. Ruler. The flashlight! Sliding the switch, the beam of light illuminated the floor. He moved the beam cautiously about the lower portion of the kitchen. Chairs lay overturned, cupboard doors hung open, and kitchen utensils and other items littered the floor.

They had obviously had been looking for something. Somewhere between when he and Flags raided Andreadi's office and when Balestrini figured out that it was Daniel, something important had gone missing. Danny took that as a good sign. There was something in the safe Flags had pilfered that Balestrini did not want discovered.

Danny kept the beam low and moved deftly up the staircase and into the master bedroom. He took little notice of the many items that had been destroyed or overturned throughout the house. He was on a mission and no broken frames or torn curtains would deter him. By the glow of the flashlight he changed into a clean suit of clothes with determination. He found his extra .45 in the bottom of a disheveled dresser drawer. He loaded it, tucked it into his back waist band and stuffed a handful of shells into his pocket. Dropping the top of a long, narrow tie box off the dresser, he paused a moment to consider the small note inscribed inside: "To my loving husband, all my love, Lily." Then he scooped up the muted red tie and in a few swift motions had tied a perfect double Windsor about his neck.

As Danny stood before the mirror, adjusting his shoulder holster, his eyes weren't seeing his own reflection. They were seeing the face of a young wife he had lost three years before, and of a few good cops he had lost over the years. Only when he saw the innocent faces of his children and JoAnna did he meet his own gaze in the mirror. The others were in the past, there was nothing more that could be done for any of them. But JoAnna, Josiah, Toby, Janey…they were full of life and joy for that life. He intended to keep them that way, no matter the cost to himself. Leaning on the dresser, he studied his face as if he hadn't seen it in a long time. He thought of all the faceless men, unknown to him even now, men under the thumb of Balestrini whom he and Flags had helped, and the many more who had had their lives as tragically affected by Balestrini as Danny himself. Danny looked away sharply and pulled his suit coat over his holster. He crossed himself as he headed down the stairs. "God forgive me. I should have done this three years ago."

He left the house on foot and walked several blocks until he came to a telephone booth and called for a taxi. There was no sense giving Balestrini an easier time tracking him than he already had in a town the man ran like clockwork. He asked the taxi driver to drop him off at Arnie's Place.

Danny didn't bother to knock on Arnie's backdoor. He just opened it and went in. Arnie was out in the bar. Danny nodded at Mrs. Arnie and continued across the room.

"Powers out at my house. May I use your phone? Is Flags out front?" he asked, not giving time for Mrs. Arnie to respond. He picked up the receiver and began dialing the number.

"Is Father Navarone there?" A pause on the line. Mrs. Arnie tugged at his sleeve. "Hello, Clancy. It's Danny."

"Praised be Jesus Christ! Are you alright?"

"I'm fine."

"Where are you?"

"*Arnie's Place*. Can you meet me here? I haven't a car and after I meet up with Flags I'm gonna need..."

"Didn't Arnie tell you?" Clancy interrupted.

Danny stopped short, the sound of Clancy's voice and the look on Mrs. Arnie's sorrowful face frightened him. "Tell me what?" he asked tentatively.

"Dan'l...Flags is in the hospital."

Danny closed his eyes, wishing he could block the words he was hearing, and then asked much too calmly, "What happened?"

"Balestrini happened. Or rather, Balestrini sent Garnelli again, and this time Garnelli didn't hold back."

"God have mercy," Danny breathed.

Clancy replied hurriedly, "Dan'l, stay there, I'll be over to pick you up."

"No," Danny ordered, "Just meet me at the hospital."

"The hospital? Dan'l, no. Balestrini's looking for you. Why do you think Flags is in the shape he's in? Balestrini will find you for sure."

"Good. I hope he does." Danny slammed the receiver into the cradle with no offense intended toward his brother.

On his end, Father Clancy replaced the receiver slowly. He was quite still for a moment as he prayed, "God, let Flags live…please, God…If he dies…" He shook his head and didn't finish the thought aloud.

***

Danny stood outside for a moment, letting his eyes grow accustomed to the darkness. But before he could take a step in the direction of Arnie's proffered car, a broad-shouldered man stepped from the shadow of the building and stood in front of Danny. He took his own sweet time blocking Danny's way as he lit his cigarette. Danny watched him patiently, knowing exactly who the man worked for.

The man finally looked up. He took the cigarette from his lips and breathed out smoke, "Come here often?"

"You oughta know," Danny replied without expression.

"Once, sometimes twice a week. But haven't seen you in a while."

"Miss me?" The man didn't answer and Danny was growing severely impatient. "Am I making Balestrini nervous?"

"What's he got to be nervous about?" the man hedged.

"You tell me."

"He's got nothing to be nervous about," the man replied casually, drawing another breath on his cigarette.

"Then my drinking habits shouldn't worry him either." Danny pushed past the man, partially hoping the man would try to stop him, but knowing he wouldn't. If he had been sent to stop Danny, Danny would have been gunned down as he came out the door. The man had been sent to watch Danny and report back to Balestrini. Danny knew he wouldn't make a move until it was preapproved by Balestrini. Danny made his way to Arnie's car without a backward glaze.

At the hospital, Danny didn't bother checking for tails or hoodlums lurking in darkened corners. He charged up the steps, inviting anyone with a notion to follow him. The night nurse said something about it not being visiting hours, but Danny ignored her and headed for the elevator anyway.

When he reached second floor, he met Father Larson leaving the room. "Flags in there?" Danny demanded.

"Yes. But Mr. Navarone…"

"I'm in no mood to talk."

"I think you should listen," Father Larson advised.

Danny stopped, his hand on Flags' door.

"I just finished administering Extreme Unction."

Danny's eyes closed. "Is he…is he dead?"

"No. But it won't be long, I'd afraid."

Danny nodded and wiped a hand across his eyes. "Clancy is on his way, will you see he gets in here as soon as he gets here. He'd want to see Flags before…"

"Sure," Father Larson interrupted kindly.

Danny closed the door behind himself and his gaze traveled down the length of bandages shrouding the man on the hospital bed before him. Only Flags' left hand and his face were visible, and even they were badly bruised. Danny couldn't move any closer for a moment. The nurse saw him hesitating at the door. She hung Flags' chart on the foot of the bed and moved to the door. "I'm sorry," she murmured, as she moved past him. "I'm so sorry."

Danny walked to the bed almost in slow motion. Flags didn't move a muscle and Danny feared that he had arrived too late, but he greeted aloud anyway, "Flags?" He saw Flags' eyes move beneath their lids and he continued, "What's going on? Just cause I leave town for a few days, doesn't mean you get to lie around on the job. I expect you to carry on as usual."

Flags opened one eye partially; it was still a greenish color from last week's black eye. The other was surrounded by bruised swollen flesh. "Lieut," he murmured in a raspy, pain-filled voice. "You sure are an ornery son of a something…don't you know this is a hospital. You're supposed to be quiet."

"Pardon me," Danny replied in a hushed voice, though he left a bit of sarcasm in it so Flags wouldn't be upset that he really was sorry.

Flags' face did some contorting in pain and he made a noise, so Danny knew he was trying to say something through the pain. He wanted to tell him to stop trying to talk but he knew Flags wouldn't want any pity. "I keep telling you not to mumble, Flags," he ordered with a half laugh, but he was silently kicking himself on the inside.

He was grateful when Flags laughed, but the laugh turned into a cough and Danny tried to calm him. "Shhh. Don't talk, Flags, just rest."

Flags found his voice this time. "Rest? What the devil for? You think I hung on just to see your ugly mug one last time?" He coughed again and then wiped blood away from his mouth with a towel he had clutched in his good hand. "Got important stuff to say." His voice faltered and Danny leaned over the bed. "Lieut, Murdock's abandoned warehouse by the train yard? It's not abandoned. Remember, just like you thought all those years ago…You should take a tour of that place. You'd like it."

Danny nodded, "I'll do that. Is that where you met up with Garnelli?"

Flags moved his head a bit from side to side. "Nah. You didn't know it, Lieut, but I'm a popular guy…Garnelli came *looking* for me."

"They say it's nice to be popular?"

Flags squinted at him through his one good eye. "You can have it. I'd rather be invisible. Garnelli followed me on my way home from Arnie's. Seems like they were having trouble figuring how they lost your trail and wanted a few answers. I told him you weren't worth finding—you couldn't throw a strike if your life depended on it—and I was the real bowler of the duo…watch Garnelli, Lieut. I knew he was a good man with his fists but I never figured him for a man with a knife."

"How is he against a .45?"

Flags eyed Danny for a moment, a little worry creeping into his eye. Danny didn't want to cause any last stress, so he tried to change the subject, "Flags…"

"Don't go sappy on me…I've got something else…Don't go after Balestrini, he's not man enough to meet you one on one. He's a wolf and wolves always travel in packs."

"You want me to back down after this?"

Flags closed his eyes, and Danny could see pain riddling his face. "I left you a present, Lieut. Go back to your old familiar bowling locker, you'll find some nice treats. Balestrini raided it after you were gone, but I waited until after he had scoped it out, then stored the good stuff there. Should be safe as a safe."

Danny gave a smile. "You know, for someone who's been hit on the head as hard as you have, as many times as you have, you're still pretty quick."

"That's because I haven't had a drink in three days."

"How does it feel?" Danny asked casually.

"Wonderful," Flags replied sarcastically. "Feel like I've been hit by a train. They tell me I look it too. I told you giving up the drink wouldn't do for me."

"First couple days are bound to be the worst," Danny offered trying to sound as light as possible.

The door opened and Father Clancy came in. "If that's Chuck," Flags growled, "tell him if he starts poking and prodding me again, I'll flatten him."

"It's Clancy," Clancy greeted.

"Well, Clarence Michael," Flags coughed out. "I thought I got rid of you earlier this evening."

"You did but I came back, Flags. I thought maybe there'd be something…"

"No way. I'm not confessing no sins to you, Clancy. Don't look at me like that. You don't have to worry none. Father Larson took care of all that stuff. But I told you a long time ago, I couldn't confess to a guy that I served with in the Army…it'd be like confessing to the Lieut."

"Not quite," Danny offered.

"Says you," Flags muttered back, but his laugh turned into a cough. He tried to keep the conversation going, but his voice was getting weaker and his cough was getting stronger.

Finally, the nurse insisted that they had to leave. Flags needed to rest. Danny said he wasn't leaving him and she left in a huff to find Dr. Kendris; but Chuck was on their side. Some twenty minutes later, Flags died, a Navarone brother on either side of him, each praying and each trying to let go of a friend who had been a brother in two wars; one on foreign soil and one in their home town.

Danny left the room with slow measured steps, Clancy on his heels. "Where are you going?" Clancy whispered.

"To see a friend," Danny muttered as he put on his hat.

"Balestrini?" Clancy's voice was tinged with worry.

Danny shook his head. "Lloyd Hartley."

"Hartley? What does he have to do with…"

"Don't try to stop me, Clancy. I have to do this. This isn't just about Flags…or Lilian…or any one person."

"I'm not gonna stop you, Danny. I'm on your side, remember?"

"Don't be. I don't want anybody on my side. You're on my side you'll get the same thing Flags got and I don't want that on my conscience."

He began to walk away and Clancy stopped him. "Dan'l, you can't fight this alone."

"I'm not alone."

"Let me come with you."

"No, Clarence. It doesn't work that way this time."

"I wanna help you…"

"You're good at praying…that would help."

"Don't do anything you couldn't tell your mother," Clancy tried to caution lightly.

Danny turned to meet his brother's gaze. "Look, Clancy, I'm not proud of what I have to do, I wish I didn't have to do it. But Balestrini has to be stopped. One way or the other, he has to be stopped."

Clancy nodded and Danny started to leave once more, but hesitated. "Clancy, if I don't make it…will you...the kids…"

"You'll come back," Clancy insisted, offering his brother his hand.

Danny shook his hand gratefully and left the hospital.

Chapter XXV

Danny left Arnie's car in the hospital parking lot and took another taxi to the business section on the east side of town. Quite possibly the cabbie wouldn't notice the tail that was following them and maybe he'd be able to lose the tail without even knowing it was there. Danny didn't care. There wasn't time to care. Balestrini would be out in force to get him. By the way his house and Flags had looked, Balestrini wasn't playing for pennies. The cabbie dropped Danny off outside the large brick police headquarters, a building he hadn't been inside for three years.

Danny hurried up the front steps; he didn't want to be gunned down on the steps this close to completing an overdue job.

It was nearing midnight and only a few people populated the foyer. The desk sergeant was occupied with a distraught, middle-aged woman ranting before him. Danny made his way uninhibited up the stairs and then down the hallway to the etched glass door painted "Hartley-Chief of Police."

He unbuttoned his coat to make his gun easily accessible and opened the door. Hartley sat at his desk, writing diligently on a stack of papers. "Keeping busy, I see," Danny greeted.

"It's polite to knock," Hartley stated without looking up.

Danny didn't respond. Closing the door, he locked it, causing Hartley to look up quickly at the sound.

"Navarone," he breathed.

"Navarone," Danny acknowledged.

"I…I didn't know you were back in town," he faltered.

"I didn't know you knew I was gone," Danny baited.

"I…well, I had heard…something like that…"

Danny let it go. "Working late, I see. Nice to know our Chief of Police is such a conscientious, diligent protector of the city's people."

Hartley regained his composure and leaned back in his chair, obviously remembering that this was still his office, his department, and his men outside that door, locked or not. "What do you what, Navarone?"

"I want some answers, Hartley." Reaching beneath his coat, Danny pulled his .45 from its holster with one smooth unhurried movement. He didn't point it at Hartley, he just held it casually in his hand. "Just some answers."

Hartley started forward at the sight of the gun.

"And for you can keep your hands away from any drawers or buttons that could call for help," Danny continued. "Better yet, Hartley, why don't you just get up and go sit in that chair over there. I'm sure you'll be more comfortable…I know I will."

Hartley rose and walked slowly around the desk to the chair Danny had indicated. "One second," Danny stopped him. He came up behind him and did a quick frisk. He pulled Hartley's duty Smith and Weston from its holster and pocketed it.

Hartley sat down, straightening his suit jacket and crossing his legs as if it were an interview and not an interrogation. Despite Danny's gun and his lack of one, he still considered himself in control of the situation. Or at least he hoped to be giving that impression. "Now that we're both comfortable, what can I do for you, Navarone?"

"Like I said. I just want some answers."

Hartley looked at him blankly.

Danny stared back until Hartley dropped his gaze. Danny asked, "Remember Flags?"

"Flags? That old drunk you used to get information from when we were looking for a stoolie?"

Danny nodded.

"Haven't seen him in years. Never was very helpful to me after you left. What about him?"

"He died tonight."

"In a gutter no doubt."

"In a hospital bed."

"Okay? You want me to send flowers?"

"No. I want answers."

"Quit the run around, Navarone. What do you want me to answer?"

"After all those years on the Force together, you knew as well as I what your men were dealing with. And I've been wondering, after you were made chief, why you didn't do anything to help them clean up this city? I wondered why, now that you were in a position to make changes to Wiley's dirty cop structure, why you didn't make those changes?"

"Navarone, listen to me..."

"No, Hartley, you listen to me," Danny exploded. "How many of those same spots are still going un-surveyed. The same spots you and I cased and watched for signs. The same places we knew stuff was happening, but Chief Wiley never let us make a move on. I wanted you to get your act together and follow through. You had the authority. But what did you do with it? You sold it to the highest bidder. Just like Wiley." Danny shook his head in disgust. "So much for honor."

"Navarone, it's not that easy. You know what it's like. Balestrini has men everywhere. And when he has a job done, it's done right."

"Right? Is that what you call it?"

Hartley backwatered, "I didn't mean right as in 'the right thing' I meant "do it right," without any loose strings, untidy messes, yah know?"

"You mean unlike the Tetley incident last May here in town?" Danny baited.

Hartley's eyes widened; for a man who hadn't been on the Force for over three years, Danny knew more than was comfortable.

"All that nasty evidence left lying around for the police to pick up and dispose of themselves," Danny continued.

Hartley threw up his hands. "Navarone, what do you want of me?"

"I *wanted* you to do the job the city had entrusted to you! I wanted you to go full bore and rat out all the slime in the dark of this city. I wanted you to help make the streets safe for a decent woman to walk down, so children can play in a neighborhood without their parents fearing for their safety. That's what I wanted a week ago, but it's not anymore. Because I'd be coming to the wrong guy, wouldn't I?" Danny asked, taking a menacing step forward.

Hartley glanced from Danny's face to his gun and then back nervously. Then he said as calmly as his shaking voice allowed, "I'm sorry, Navarone, I think I missed the beginning of the argument you seem to have with me."

"Really?" Danny asked. "Because I just found out that you *didn't* miss the beginning of this argument. I just found out that you were there…at the very beginning…

"Beginning of what?"

"Let's talk about April 5th, 1951. Remember that date, Hartley? Because I do."

The color drained from Hartley's face, and he sank deeper into his chair. "Navarone…come on, I'm your friend…"

"No, Hartley. I had my doubts before, but it finally all started falling together and it's making more sense than I care to admit. Now I want the rest of the answers."

The stillness of the .45 in Danny's hand sobered Hartley but he tried to remain cool and collected. "Come on, Navarone. What are you going to do? Shoot me in cold blood? Times really have changed you."

"I came back to bust this town wide open…and you're gonna help me do it."

Hartley studied him for a moment before he finally answered flatly, "They'll kill you."

"You mean, they'll kill *you*," Danny corrected and he saw a little more color drain from Hartley's face. Danny moved around to the far side of the desk and began opening drawers one after another.

"You think you're gonna find evidence in my desk drawers?" he asked contemptuously.

"No. I'm looking for something to *make* evidence," Danny corrected. He found the dictation machine on a small table behind the desk and pulled it roughly closer to his prisoner. "This will work fine…Start talking," he ordered, as he sat down on the corner of the desk and pushed down the record button.

"You're crazy."

"Come on, Hartley. Something more original than that." Danny's eyes were chips of blue steel and Hartley squirmed at the way the gun rested so easily in his hand. "I'll help you," Danny prompted. "Let's start with a guy named Tony Limbardi…you tell the story."

All pretense of playing dumb fell from Hartley's face. He could see Danny was determined and consequently he was desperate. "Navarone, you've got to believe me. It wasn't my fault. I…I didn't know what they were gonna do. I didn't know."

"You were there, weren't you?"

"Yes. Yes, damn it, I was there. But I didn't know. You've got to believe me. They told me you were getting too hot. You were closing in too fast. They had to stop you…"

"Then stop *me*! Why did you go after Lilian?"

Hartley, noticing that his explanation seemed to be increasing Danny's anger rather than pacifying it, was getting worried. "When we were out on the beat together, I'd try to dissuade you from certain things. Sometimes we wouldn't go ahead with things you suggested. Like the Murdock Warehouse and that time by the river…But you weren't listening to me as much, you were getting suspicious of me. I told them that…but they didn't want to stop you cold. They were afraid that if you were killed, there would be an investigation and that would tear the thing open wider than if they just dissuaded you. So they wanted to threaten you with Lilian…"

"Threaten me?" Danny towered over Hartley, and the Chief's tall stature suddenly seemed puny and insignificant.

"You've got to believe me, Navarone. Balestrini thought if she were scared badly enough she'd convince you to let up, or you'd be scared enough for her sake to let up. Limbardi got a little carried away. I didn't know what Limbardi was gonna do…what he did! I kept you late…I thought he was just gonna…"

"Gonna what? Break her arm? Rape her? You make me sick, Lloyd Hartley. Sitting there trying to justify…if I didn't have a conscience, I'd kill you right now." Danny took a step back from the chair as if to physically remove the temptation to do so. He prompted as calmly as he could, "So you delayed me and they kidnapped her. Then what?"

"You know."

"I want *you* to tell it," Danny demanded, motioning toward the dictation machine on the desk, its spools still spinning.

Hartley shook his head and buried his face in his hands. "Tony Limbardi was a damn fool."

"So are you."

"If only you hadn't followed."

"She'd still be dead."

"But I followed you, and then they made *me* watch." Hartley swore vehemently. "How many nights have I seen that over and over. How many times have I wished I were dead so I don't have to relive what I did…wishing I could stop it."

Danny stared at him. Then—to temper the anger that suddenly surged within him—he murmured, "But you could have. *You* weren't tied to a chair."

Hartley's eyes brimmed with such remorse that Danny looked away and asked, "Where's Limbardi?"

Hartley looked confused for a moment. "Limbardi?" He shook his head. "Balestrini didn't like his style. He made too big a mess and he left too many witnesses. Sooner or later somebody was gonna trace a hit back to Limbardi and Limbardi wasn't exactly a loyal henchman, just an efficient one. If they traced it to Limbardi, they'd have had Balestrini for the promise of an acquittal. And anybody would have given that to get Balestrini. But it wasn't after Lilian; it was probably a good year and a half later. If you'll look back in the police files, you'll find an unidentified body was pulled from the East dam." Hartley leaned back in his chair, as if relieved. "That's justice, I suppose," he finished, "though not the kind you were looking for."

"And Halverson. Was that justice too?"

Hartley glared at him, the remorse receding and his anger regaining control. "Yes, I killed Halverson. There's no new news in that. He was crazy. Trying to hold up Davidson's. Who did he think he was? Did he think he'd get away with burglary?"

"You made sure he didn't," Danny corrected. "Why, Hartley? Why'd you shoot him? He was giving himself up."

"I told you I couldn't see that from where I was. You hesitated and I saved your life."

"I don't believe you."

Hartley told Danny where he could go.

"I told you once, Hartley," Danny advised as he overtly eyed the .45 in his hand, "This is your story, I'm not gonna tell it for you. Why'd you kill Halverson?"

"I had to," Hartley breathed between clenched teeth. "There was someone else in the Apothecary that night. He needed to make a clean get away. If we had arrested Halverson, we would have gone into the Apothecary to see what was taken, stolen, destroyed. But Duncan…" he grimaced as if he hadn't meant to say the name, but continued, "Duncan had too long of a rap sheet to get caught, and Balestrini needed him. So I caused a disturbance in the alley to give him the time he needed to get away."

"Halverson was the disturbance," Danny stated. The coolness with which Hartley referred to Halverson's death as a distraction made Danny's blood boil. He clenched his teeth to calm himself.

"Yes. That's all. Halverson was the disturbance," Hartley conceded.

Almost a minute passed before Danny could steady himself and his voice enough to prompt, "Andrew Edwards."

Hartley tensed once more, and almost bolted from his chair in his anxiety. "My gosh, man! Do we have to go through them one at a time, detail by detail?"

"It's your life; I just want a record of it."

"Damn you, Navarone."

"Come, come, Hartley. You're the one who sold your soul for thirty pieces of silver. Now you have to face the hangman's noose."

"Hangman's noose, my foot! You have no right to do any of this. You're not Homicide. You haven't got a warrant. You…you're not even a cop. You'll go to jail for this."

"Well, it's good to see you want to put *someone* in jail. I thought maybe you gave up the habit. Still, and I may very well go there, but I look at it this way, Hartley. If I have to serve time to see that *you're* put behind bars, I'd gladly do it…maybe we'll be cellmates. Beginning to get the picture?"

Hartley set his jaw but before Danny could reiterate the question of Andrew Edwards someone tried the office door. The visitor seemed agitated as they heard a keychain jingle, fall to the floor and then be picked up again. Danny gave Hartley a threatening look and then stepped silently behind the door. It opened and a middle aged, middle weight, middle height man entered, speaking hurriedly to Hartley, "Duncan said I should come tell you right away; Navarone's back. I saw him at the hospital."

"And how'd *you* come? By Pony Express?" Hartley snapped.

Closing the door, the man turned and saw Danny leaning against the filing cabinet, gun in hand. He started to push his coat back and Danny stepped forward waving his gun a bit. "You go ahead, reach for your rod…and Hartley will be the one lying on the floor full of lead."

"Put your hands down, Gimpy. For pity's sake, he's mad enough to kill us both, and have the whole Department in here."

Gimpy lowered his hands slowly and muttered to Hartley, "Angry mad, or crazy mad?"

"You said it, Gimpy," Danny answered and collected the gun Gimpy had been too slow or too smart to draw. "Take a seat, Gimpy. You look tuckered out."

Gimpy scowled and sank onto the small office couch. Leaning back on the desk again, Danny resumed his interrogation. "Well, seeing as how two heads are better than one, maybe you'll be able to give me better answers to my questions. Tell me about the Edwards set-up."

"Who's Edwards?"

"No more games, Hartley." Danny raised his gun.

"For gosh sake, man, I don't know everything. Can't you see, I am just one guy against a mob? I just do what I'm told to survive."

"I can name a lot of men who do what they need to survive. Halverson was one. But you are one of the guys who does whatever he can to thrive…and that's not the same. Tell me, Hartley, how many innocent men have you thrown under the bus, so that you can have a posh job? How many innocent men have you denied Police protection to because you were scared for your own hide? You make me sick, Hartley, sitting there in a uniform, living a lie that you protect people. The only thing you've ever protected is your own life, and from where I'm sitting it wasn't worth it. You damned your soul to save your mortal life. Do you think it was it worth it?"

Hartley eyed him for a long moment and then littered the air with a few choice curse words, before he replied, "There was no Edwards set-up."

"Then why kill him?"

"How'd he know Garnelli shot him?" Gimpy asked.

"Thank you, Gimpy." Danny smiled a mocking half grin and Hartley glared at them both. Danny motioned toward the dictation machine, "Now that that fact is settled for prosperity I wanna know what was involved in the Edwards set-up."

Hartley leaned forward. The more questions Danny asked the more anxious Hartley became. Danny wondered vaguely if it was in fear of the Mob or the Law, but he kept pushing for answers.

"There's nothing to tell."

"Go ahead and bore me. I'd like to hear it anyway," Danny insisted, calmly.

Hartley looked from Danny to Gimpy. A madman and a stoolie; he didn't have a chance. One would kill him if he didn't talk and the other would squeal that he had talked. He relented. "Balestrini had a few too many unaccounted for funds and he needed a fresh place to launder them. Edwards' Tailor Shop was prime picking. Honorable folk like the Edwards—even a man as diligent at his job as you had been wouldn't have suspected them. Edwards was doing just fine. He made a living, and he paid his protection fee to Balestrini, like everybody else on Grossmann Street. Whenever Duncan came for the fee, Edwards paid up front, in cash. He did everything in cash, never trusted banks.

"So Duncan raised the price just enough so that Edwards started coming up short every other month or so. Duncan let it slide to lure him in and when the time was right, he told Edwards he had to allow Balestrini to use his place as a front. Edwards refused. Balestrini didn't think he'd hold out. Thought he'd cave under pressure. Balestrini was wrong."

"That's not the end of the story."

Gimpy had had enough, "He's crazy, Hartley. What's the matter with you?"

"Shut up," Hartley hissed under his breath. "He's crazy and if you had any sense you'd beware of the man now more than ever."

"That's right, Gimpy. Before I kept my wits about me. But now, you never know what I'll do. Now, tell me, how did you finish off the Edwards setup?"

Shaking his head, Hartley defended, "It wasn't me, Navarone. I was still just a beat cop then. Balestrini managed that one alone. Not even Wiley was needed."

Danny wasn't convinced and his face reflected as much.

Hartley continued, "When Duncan couldn't convince Edwards, he brought Edwards to Balestrini; figuring facing the Boss himself, Edwards would kowtow. But Edwards still wouldn't play along and Balestrini figured no other form of threats would convince him. So he sent Edwards home, but then sent Garnelli after him. When Garnelli took Edwards for a ride to do the deed, Duncan snuck in the place and fixed the books good, so it looked like Edwards had run his business into the ground. When the police went to investigate—a legitimate investigation, Navarone—there was nothing that looked out of place. It looked like a clear-cut case of a man going bankrupt and then going on the lam. The case was closed as such."

Danny stood, watching Hartley as if he expected him to continue.

"I swear, Navarone," Hartley insisted. "There was no dirty work by the police department on this one. Balestrini did it all, I only learned what went down much later, when Balestrini made me Chief."

Danny pushed the stop button at Hartley's admission of being given the position by Balestrini. He had gotten much more than he had hoped on those little spools. If he lived long enough to share them with Burnquist, it would be a miracle. But right now, he had to move, and move fast. Chances were Duncan hadn't been very far behind Gimpy when he sent him ahead to warn Hartley. "Stand up, both of you. We're going for a ride."

"A ride?" Hartley stood, but Danny could see he was a little shaky.

"Call it a field trip," he explained. Before he could insist that Gimpy follow suit the telephone rang. Perhaps he had waited a minute too long. Three sets of eyes starred at the telephone for a long moment before anyone spoke.

"Now what, Navarone?" Gimpy needled.

"Answer it," Danny ordered, as if that were obvious.

Hartley walked tentatively toward the desk, as if he were afraid Danny would suddenly change his mind and stop him with a bullet. He reached for the receiver and Danny laid the barrel of his gun against his neck, "Just don't forget who'll be the first one to die if anything happens."

Hartley cleared his dry throat, "Hello?…Duncan? What the devil are you doing calling me on this phone? What? Oh." He turned and held the receiver out to Danny, "He wants to talk to you."

Danny took the receiver and motioned Hartley back towards his chair.

"Navarone? This is Duncan," a familiar voice greeted. "Remember me from the old days?"

"I remember you. Do you remember me?"

"Sure. Why do you think I'm on the phone and not outside that office door?"

There was silence as if Duncan thought the question needed an answer. Danny didn't give him one.

Duncan continued, "We make a move toward you and Hartley's dead. Ain't that right? Even Hartley knows that and he was your partner."

"Are you just calling to chit chat? Or is there a point to this conversation?"

Duncan sputtered at being interrupted and then demanded, "You should come down to the Murdock Warehouse. There's a friend here and well, I just think you'd be interested in seeing the person."

"I don't think there's any friend of yours I want to see except Balestrini."

"Oh, he'll be here too. Believe you me. But ah…this fella, he ain't *my* friend. He's your's and well, you might miss him if you don't come…fact is, he kinda looks like you…only he wears a long black dress."

Other than the harsh set of his jaw, no emotion showed on Danny's face, and very little revealed itself in his voice. "Thanks for the invitation, Duncan. We were just on our way, anyway as I am very interested in seeing Murdock's old warehouse. Another friend of mine told me I'd find it very interesting...Only thing is…how do I know *I'll* make it out alive?"

"Come off it, Navarone. We all know how this thing works. Balestrini wants Hartley back and he wants him alive. It's a pretty safe bet you feel the same about your priest brother. I figure it's an even trade."

"I don't think that's even, but I'll take it, 'cause I'll be getting the better man," Danny responded and hung up before Duncan could say anything further.

Danny eyed the two men in front of him. "Well, Hartley, it appears you have friends who care about you. Shall we go meet them?"

Hartley didn't look entirely thrilled, but Gimpy stood and smiled smugly.

"I wouldn't feel too superior, Gimpy," Danny warned. "I don't think they even know you're here. But you'll still be the first one with lead in his guts if you try anything on the way."

"You're taking us both?" Hartley asked.

"Well, I'm not leaving Gimpy here alone," Danny explained, as he lifted the lid off the dictation machine and pocketed the two spools of recorded ribbon. "He might get lonely and do something I'd regret."

Hartley still hadn't moved, "I was only thinking one on one was better odds for your getting there alive."

"I enjoy risks. You oughta remember that Hartley," Danny replied. "Besides, if anyone's not making it there alive, it won't be me. Get up, Hartley. Balestrini wants to see you." Hartley stood up. Danny thought he faltered a little, and he had to quell a bit of compassion that he felt rising in him. Balestrini wanted Hartley back alive for only one reason—to personally ensure he wouldn't talk, by having him killed himself. But Danny couldn't help that now.

Chapter XXVI

The three men took a back staircase down to Hartley's car in the squad parking lot. Danny motioned for the two men to get in the front, telling Gimpy to drive. He didn't trust Hartley, but he trusted Gimpy less. The drive to the Murphy's Warehouse was uneventful but tense. By the time Gimpy turned onto the gravel driveway, the night was blacker than pitch.

Gimpy parked the car, its headlights illuminating the side of the warehouse. "Now what?" he demanded.

"Leave the headlights on," Danny ordered, as he got out of the back seat and motioned for his two hostages to follow. Danny surveyed the building for a moment. "Just like old times, isn't it, Hartley?"

Hartley looked at him, almost wild with fear. "For pity's sake, Navarone. Don't do this. They'll kill me. No matter what, they're gonna kill me. Please, Navarone…what about all those years on the Force together…"

Danny looked at him, "Yah, Hartley. What about those years together? And you just stood there and watched them kill my wife. What about all those years?"

"Don't you know what I have been trying to forget all these years? I've had to live with that!"

"*I've* had to live with that," Danny responded passionately.

Hartley took the point, but his fear erupted in pleading. "Danny, you've got to listen to me. I'll go to the DA with you. Anything. I'll tell him everything I know. I…I'll get you your job back…you can have my job…"

"You're in no position to bargain, Hartley. You lost that about three years ago. Move out." Hartley's offer was tempting, but there was more at stake now with Father Clancy somewhere inside the warehouse.

They walked to the door and Gimpy reached for the handle.

"You better hope things go down as planned, Gimpy," Danny cautioned. "'Cause I don't trust you, and I'd rather have you dead than where I can't see you."

They walked through the door and each of them stopped short at the bright lights inside. Danny blinked several times and glanced up at the row of windows lining the top of the warehouse, where the brilliance of the lights should have shown to the outside. Heavy blackout curtains hung over each of the windows.

After their eyes adjusted, the three men started forward, following a maze-like pattern through huge piles of boxes and stacks of furniture and even automobiles. Danny took it all in without much expression and murmured, "Planning a rummage sale, Hartley?"

"Not me. None of this is me, Navarone. I just…"

"Save it for the judge. I think I can get the picture." They kept walking. "Nice place for an ambush."

"They won't try anything," Gimpy insisted.

"You better be right."

"Up there's the office," Gimpy offered, pointing to a structure in the middle of the warehouse. The room on top had windows three quarters of the way around it and lights shown through the left half of them, nearest the door. A metal staircase led down to the main floor.

"Alright, let's get closer so they can hear us," Danny ordered. They walked to the edge of the stacks of merchandise and stopped both men with the barrel in Gimpy's back and a hand on Hartley's shoulder. "Duncan!" Danny called out.

"Yah?" a voice hollered back.

"It's Navarone."

"We see ya. Come on up."

"I don't think so. We'll talk down here. Tell your boss that he can come down."

They heard voices murmuring, and finally Balestrini stepped out of the office and onto the platform at the top of the stairs. He was tall; it was difficult to tell how tall as his position at the top of the stairs made him seem enormous. His full head of coal black hair, and his perfectly tailored suit made him look more like a politician than a mob boss. Even his smile was debonair. He stood there, hands on his hips, surveying the men below him as if they were mere rubbish. Danny didn't feel any fear, but he felt Hartley's shoulder tense up beneath his hand.

"Well, well. Daniel Navarone. Nice of you to drop in."

"Isn't it, though? I try to be obliging as much as I can, when I can."

Balestrini started his way down the metal staircase. "Kind of you," he said sardonically, "But then, you've been paying me visits all along haven't you?"

"If I had been doing it for the praise, I'd have left a calling card…no need to thank me."

Balestrini kept moving down the stairs, but Danny didn't move out from behind the crates. Balestrini halted. "Thought we were gonna talk?"

"I can talk from here. I'm not bringing out my target until you bring out your collateral."

Danny saw Balestrini's jaw set. "Still the over-cautious cop, aren't you? You think that everyone is here for you to command?"

"Well, for the moment, with Hartley in my hands, that's exactly what I think."

Balestrini relented and motioned to someone inside the office and they all watched the doorway as more figures emerged. Father Clancy walked out, his hands behind his back, looking slightly more perturbed than frightened. The man who followed looked much older than Danny remembered, but he couldn't mistake the angular jawline and old white Panama for anyone other than Duncan. A third man followed after Duncan and by his wiry frame, Danny could only guess that it was Garnelli, the henchman Flags had told him about and later faced.

Duncan had his pistol in the small of Father Clancy's back and kept it there as they descended the steps and assembled on the floor of the warehouse. When they reached the base of the staircase, Danny prodded his two hostages out into the open. He glanced at his brother and noted quickly that he looked to be unharmed. "You know, Balestrini, you ever want to confess, the church doors are open to all, you don't have to kidnap our priests."

"Don't try to be funny, Navarone. I want my man back…you want yours."

"Don't try to sound noble, Balestrini. It's really not your thing. You want Hartley dead before he says too much. That's what you want. You don't care if I kill him or one of your henchmen does it. You just want him dead."

"Don't you?" Balestrini baited. Danny wished he could have answered negatively, quickly and confidently, but he was still fighting the rage in himself. He couldn't fake it.

Balestrini smiled. "Everybody gets what he wants, Navarone. We trade up even-steven. I get Hartley before he talks…you get your brother, alive…everybody walks away happy. Get me?"

"Everybody, Balestrini? Now who's being funny? Tomorrow there'll be another Edwards and another Flags and another Lilian. Not everybody walks away. And it's about time somebody did something about it."

"Meaning you, grease monkey?"

"Meaning me."

Duncan took the gun he held at Father Clancy's back and placed it against Father's throat. "You gonna do it over your brother's dead body?"

Danny glanced at him depreciatingly, as if he weren't worth answering. He continued to address Balestrini when he spoke, "You killed Lilian three years ago and tonight Flags died. There were probably a hundred more between there. You think threatening to kill Clancy is gonna stop me now that I've finally got you all where I need you to blow this city open."

"He's a priest!" Hartley exclaimed. Danny wasn't sure if he was telling the information to him or his comrade. He seemed to be surprised at everyone's lack of knowledge.

The comment only propelled one man to speak, Father Clancy himself. “When it comes right down to it, we both want this organized mob disbanded and we’d both sacrifice our lives to see it happen. There’s enough Navarones around to follow through once one or the other of us is gone.”

“Well, Balestrini? What are we gonna do?” Danny asked, emboldened by his brother. “Before I had Hartley…now I’ve got Hartley and Balestrini…and after five years I’ve finally seen the inside of this *abandoned* warehouse. How long do think your house of cards stands after tonight.”

Balestrini wasn’t giving in, “You’re out numbered, Navarone.”

“Well, our dad always says the measure of men isn’t in the quantity it’s in the quality. Who’s the better man?”

“Better man be damned!” Garnelli piped up. “All I know is if you don’t care about the priest then our bargaining chip isn’t any use to us after all.” Before anyone could respond Garnelli had drawn a knife and hurled it directly at Father Clarence. Flags’ description and his wounds were proof enough that the throw would have hit home, except that Hartley jumped in front of the priest and caught the knife full in the chest. Danny, who had been moving to knock Clancy down, caught Hartley on his decent. Balestrini saw his chance and ran for the cover of a stack of crates while Gimpy grabbed the shocked priest’s arm and twisted it behind his back, forcing him back into the maze of boxes and crates.

Danny looked down at the dying man in his arms. A man with whom he had been acquainted for so many years, so many years ago. Hartley’s eyes were dimming quickly and Danny wished he hadn’t implied to him that he didn’t care whether he lived or died. He did care, he just couldn’t process the betrayal quickly enough.

Hartley breathed shallowly, “I…plea…forgive…”

“I forgive you,” Danny murmured quickly. Hartley grew limper and Danny feared he had spoken too late. He repeated a little louder, “I forgive you, Hartley.” He didn’t know if Hartley heard, the man’s expression didn’t change as he died. Danny heard a small chuckle nearby. He looked up knowing he was now covered by two guns; Garnelli’s and Duncan’s. “You just killed your own man,” he accused Garnelli.

Garnelli walked forward and pulled the knife out of Hartley with little compunction. "And now I'm gonna kill you, copper."

Danny didn't wait to try to dodge Garnelli's knife or Duncan's bullet. He lunged at Garnelli, knocking him backwards, sending the knife flying. Danny rolled off him, knowing Duncan would be preparing to defend his comrade with a bullet. True to character, a .44 slug hit the concrete just inches away from Danny's thigh. He fired back. His aim was good and Duncan stumbled back against the banister and fell to the floor.

Garnelli wasn't on his feet when Danny ran after Balestrini and Gimpy. He rounded the barricade of crates just as Garnelli started lodging lead in his footprints. Garnelli was almost as good a shot with his sidearm as with his knife, so it must have been an angel preventing Danny from taking lead.

Hurrying around several corners, Danny mentally weighed his odds. He had taken Gimpy's gun, so unless Balestrini had more than one firearm on him, Danny only had to worry about one man when he caught up to them. He paused to listen for any clues as to the direction the others took. He could hear Garnelli cursing several yards away and knew he had temporarily given him the slip. He heard muffled voices and followed the sound to an open section where Clancy stood between Balestrini and Gimpy. "I'll keep the priest with me," Balestrini was saying.

"I'll take him with me," Danny interrupted. Gimpy whirled to face Danny and when he did so, Clancy swung his arm and sent him sprawling, knocked out cold. Danny made it to Balestrini in time to knock his gun from his hand and pin him up against a machine. "I see you've still got a great back arm, Clancy," he complimented his brother.

Clancy shook his arm as if trying to shake off the pain. "Yah, only it's kinda rusty, so don't do that again." He walked toward Gimpy, "You want this one, too?"

"Nah, leave him. Let's get outta here before Garnelli calls for reinforcements."

"What about Hartley?"

"He's dead," Danny answered coldly, but only so his emotions wouldn't creep out. Balestrini smiled and Danny had a strong temptation to pistol whip him, but he quelled it. "Don't worry, Balestrini. He told some good stories before we even came down here."

"I'll bet he did. But can you tie any of them to me?" Danny didn't answer. “You’ve got nothing, Navarone,” Balestrini threatened, although the barrel of Danny’s .45 was biting into his neck.

Danny didn’t have time to think about whether Balestrini was right or not. He had to get out of the warehouse alive. He pushed his prisoner ahead of him and called over his shoulder, “Come on, Clancy.”

Clancy moved, but instead of toward the perimeter of the building where they were sure to find a door, he was inching back towards the staircase and the office. “You go on, Dan’l. I’ll catch up.”

Danny grabbed his shirt sleeve. “What, are you crazy? You can’t go back there.”

“I’ve got to,” Clancy pulled away.

“He’s dead, Clancy.”

Clancy grabbed his brother’s hand and tore his grasp from his arm. “I’ve got to get back up there. They took my overcoat when I first got here…”

“Your overcoat?” Danny exclaimed in disbelief. He didn’t let go of Father’s Clancy’s cassock.

The priest turned to him earnestly. “They got me here by telling me you were dying. I brought the Blessed Sacrament. It’s in a pix in my overcoat.”

Danny let go of his sleeve instantly and when Father Clancy moved away Danny was right behind him, Balestrini in tow. They moved quietly back through the maze. “Any idea of how many men are in this place?” Danny asked his brother in a whisper.

“As far as I know it was just this lug, Garnelli and Duncan.”

“Good. Then unless Gimpy wakes up, there’s just Garnelli.”

Clancy gave him a side-ways glance, “What about Duncan?”

“He’s dead, I think.”

“He’s dead, you think?”

“Well, I didn’t exactly have time to check his pulse.”

Father Clancy peered around the tower of boxes. “Think I should run as fast as I can or go slow and hope he won’t notice the movement?”

“Are you kidding?” Danny scoffed. “We all go together and hope he has enough sense not to chance a shot while Balestrini’s with us.”

“Okay, Little Brother,” Clancy agreed.

“On my word, you head out first and fast.” Danny grabbed

Balestrini's hand and twisted his arm behind his back. "You keep your feet moving like there's a fire on your tail or you'll have lead in your back."

The Navarone boys looked over the open area and with a momentary glance at each other started off for the stairs. Three men running up a set of stairs had never been choreographed as well as it turned out for them. And as luck would have it, or rather Providence, not a shot was fired.

Danny pushed Balestrini ahead of him across the room. He leaned against the wall and watched the warehouse floor below them. Father Clarence retrieved his overcoat from where Duncan had tossed it. He found the pix. He couldn't take the chance that they might not get out of there alive, so he knelt down and received the Blessed Sacrament. He stood slowly and nodded to Danny that he was ready to go.

Danny started to motion to Balestrini to move out ahead of him when a shot rang out from the warehouse below and the glass window shattered. A bullet caught Father Clarence just right of his center back. Moaning, he dropped to the floor. An exclamation was torn from Danny's lips and in one swift movement, he whirled, knocked Balestrini cold with the butt of his pistol and fell over Father Clarence. He turned his brother over in his arms. "Clancy. Clancy," he pleaded.

Father Clancy coughed and lifted a hand to stop Danny from opening his shirt. The bullet had come clear through him and left both his front and back bloody. "I don't think it will do any good, Dan'l."

"Clancy, don't you die on me too. You hear me?"

Father Clancy coughed again and blood trickled down his mouth and ran down his cheek. He wheezed and spoke, "I…thought I was bringing you Viaticum tonight. I guess it was for me." He smiled. "But it's better this way, Danny."

Danny clenched his teeth as he shoved his handkerchief into Father Clarence's cassock. "You're not dying, Little Brother. You hear me?" His voice shook with emotion.

Father Clancy nodded a weakening head, "Okay, Little Brother. Whatever you say," but he closed his eyes and fell limp in Danny's arms. Footsteps sounded on the metal staircase and Danny grabbed his .45 again and moved, crouching, away from the light of the doorway.

Garnelli's voice carried into the room as he climbed the stairs, "Well, well. That was some fancy shooting if I do say so myself. Don't you agree, Balestrini? I just got me a cop at long range, with a handgun. That's something to write home to mother about, don't you think?"

He just reached the top platform and was silhouetted perfectly in the frame of the door. Danny gave him a moment to spot Balestrini passed out on the floor and Father Clancy's body as well. "Depends on what kinda mother you've got, Garnelli," Danny said rising to his feet in the shadow of the room. He saw Garnelli's wiry frame taunt as a barbed wire fence before finishing, "You just shot the wrong Navarone."

Garnelli didn't try to correct his mistake; rather, he turned tail and hurried down the steps as fast as he could. Danny bolted after him and took one shot at Garnelli before he followed down the stairs. When Danny reached the bottom of the stairs Garnelli had escaped into the maze of the warehouse.

Danny pursued him like a lone wolf, steady and determined and slowly gaining ground. They exchanged shots at every opening of the chaotic maze and, at every encounter, Garnelli's shots seemed to be getting wilder. At one point, Danny spotted blood smeared on a crate Garnelli had leaned across. One of Danny's shots had hit home; hence the poor marksmanship on the part of a very skilled marksman. Finally, Garnelli ran out of room to run and he stood, pinned against a locked door, blood was coloring the side of his shirt, just above his hip.

Danny rounded the last turn in the maze, not expecting Garnelli to be facing him. Garnelli raised his gun to fire, but his hammer slammed down on an empty chamber. His arm dropped to his side and Danny advanced on him calmly, his own gun raised and aimed at Garnelli. Sweat ran down his face and he was breathing hard, as was Garnelli. Danny clenched his teeth and growled, "I oughta give you what you gave Flags."

"That old drunk! Why do you even give a damn?"

"I oughta give you what you gave, Clancy," Danny finished. "But I won't. God help me, I won't."

"Crazy copper," Garnelli muttered. In one slick motion he let the empty gun fall from his hand and he suddenly held his knife. He threw it and Danny had just enough time to duck, but the knife caught him in the right shoulder, a tender spot still not fully healed from his bowling wound.

Involuntarily, Danny dropped his own gun and reached for the knife. Garnelli lunged at him with his bare hands and wrenched the knife from Danny's shoulder.

Danny kicked and fought as hard as he could, but Garnelli's bear-like hands were always there, grabbing and ready to stab and slash with the knife. At last Danny's searching, fumbling hands were able to get his second gun from his back waistband. He brought it around and swung it up in his left hand, firing just as Garnelli was about to sink the blade into his chest. Danny tried to protect himself as Garnelli fell on top of him, but Garnelli was dead before he landed and the knife clattered to the cement beside him.

Danny let his own head fall back on the floor. He was breathing heavy, heavier still for the weight on his chest and the immense pain of his knife wound and other cuts. He heard hurried footsteps coming through the maze. He closed his eyes for a moment and prayed. If they were more of Balestrini's men, he didn't have much fight left in him. His whole body seemed to be throbbing from the knife wound and loss of blood from his shoulder. He could barely move with the weight of Garnelli's dead body on top of him. But as the steps grew closer he twisted his upper body enough to swing his left arm, now his gun hand, in the direction of the opening in the maze.

Three men rushed through into the clearing. The first one kicked the gun from Danny's hand before he could fire a shot. He moaned at the contact of the man's boot with the back of his hand. "Get this body off him," a voice ordered.

Danny looked up as one of the men pulled Garnelli off of him. The lights seemed brighter than they had been even when they first came into the warehouse. It was difficult to keep his eyes open. The first man crouched down beside him. Danny recognized the man's eight-pointed hat and his badge and he tried to breathe easier, though the pain over his whole body and especially his shoulder didn't really allow it. "State troopers? What are you doing here?" he asked unthinkingly.

"*Somebody*," the man began with pointed inflection, "kidnapped Gilmore's Chief of Police. What do you think we're doing here?"

"Never been so glad to hear somebody say they've come to arrest me," Danny murmured. He pulled his hand closer and rubbed it where the trooper's boot had made contact.

"Sorry about the hand. I didn't want to be shot."

"Can't blame you. I wouldn't want to be shot either…what took you so long?" His brain seemed to be swimming in an ocean and whatever came out of his mouth wasn't what he actually wanted to say.

"Well, pardon me," the trooper replied sarcastically. "Next time you want to get caught breaking the law, call us first, and we'll be happy to synchronize watches with you."

Danny tried to laugh and he tried to sit up, but did neither very well. The trooper offered a supporting arm, "You're hurt, Navarone. Let me take a look at that shoulder."

"Forget me, we need a stretcher."

The trooper glanced at Garnelli, "He don't need no stretcher."

"Not for him. For Clancy." Danny cradled his bleeding right arm with his bruised left hand, but continued, "Garnelli shot him. He's upstairs in the office. I don't know if…"

"Glencoe!" the trooper interrupted.

The second state trooper who had pulled Garnelli off Danny turned around, "Yes, sir?"

"Go see if that ambulance has gotten here yet. Be sure they head up there first. There's a guy who'll need medical attention right away."

Glencoe rushed off and Danny started to follow slowly after him, "You need a stretcher yourself, Navarone." Before Danny took another step, the third trooper took his left arm and drew it about his own shoulders. Danny looked down gratefully at him, "I think JoAnna might have to call me in sick again tomorrow," he murmured incoherently before he passed out. The two troopers lowered him gently to the floor and waited for another stretcher.

Chapter XXVII

Danny drifted in and out of consciousness; between the past and the present; between reality and imagination for the better part of a week. He'd awaken, or he would think that he had awakened, and would have an entire conversation with JoAnna who was sitting beside his bed, only to wake up a little later and have the nurse tell him her name was Beatrice, not JoAnna, but JoAnna was a pretty name, although if she had had her choice she would have picked Susan…

He closed his eyes again. When he awoke later he tried to ask after Clancy, but the room was dark and no one answered him.

When he closed his eyes again Balestrini came into his room, only this time he knew it was a dream and he told him to get lost, which Balestrini, obliging as he was in dreams, got lost. At which point Flags told Danny he should be more polite, which was definitely a dream because Flags would have told Balestrini much worse. Only thing was, Balestrini he knew was a dream, but Flags seemed as real as Beatrice.

By the time Danny awoke for real, Beatrice was gone and so was the month of September. Beatrice had been replaced with a woman who was stouter and sterner and grumpier than Beatrice had been in reality or his dreams. He was still trying to differentiate between what had been real and what had been dreams when he asked, "How's Clancy?"

"Clancy who?" the stouter Beatrice demanded, not waiting for a response before ordering, "Give me your arm."

Danny tried to oblige, but he didn't seem to have full control of his muscles so grumpier Beatrice sighed dramatically and reached for his arm herself.

"His heartrate is seventy-nine," sterner Beatrice muttered to someone on the other side of the room. Danny turned his head to see, although his neck was stiff and sore and pulled at his shoulder horribly.

Chuck was studying a chart on the other side of the bed. Relieved, Danny tried again, "Chuck, Clancy…"

"That will be all, Nurse Thomsen."

She nodded and muttered something else and left the room. Danny lost his nerve after the nurse left, so he inquired instead, "How are the kids? JoAnna?"

Chuck looked up from his chart and drew close to the bed, not to talk, but to poke and prod around the bandaged shoulder. Danny remembered what Flags had threatened when Chuck was poking at his wounds and thought he might do the same. "Chuck, what about Clancy?" he demanded through teeth clenched in pain.

Chuck avoided the question with his own protest, "Will you have a little respect? It's Father Navarone, or at least Father Clarence."

"How is he?"

Chuck wouldn't meet his gaze. "Next few days are critical. We'll see…"

"Chuck…"

"The doctor had to remove half his lung…"

"Half his lung!"

"Men have survived on less. He still has a lung and a half left…he's from strong stock. But he's not in the clear yet."

Danny closed his eyes again, then opened them to study the ceiling. "My family?"

"They're good and well, Danny. The kids are out at your folks, having a high old time."

Danny waited for Chuck to go on about JoAnna but he didn't. "And Miss Edwards?" he asked, his heartrate rising.

Chuck did a double take. "She's well, too. She's staying with Sharon and me. Put her in with Agnus and Bridgette. Not sure how she feels about it, but the girls think it's swell. Your house is still in chaos; nobody's staying there for a long time, including yourself. So don't think I'm signing you out for any rest and relaxation any time soon."

***

It took another two days before they let Danny get out of bed. More accurately, it was another two days before they couldn't stop Danny from getting out of bed. They wanted him there another four days. But whenever he asked after Clancy, no one would answer his questions, so Danny made his way down the hall to his brother's room.

Clancy lay asleep on the hospital bed. The cannula across his face made him look unnatural and startlingly vulnerable. Danny sat in the chair beside his bed and waited. He wished Clancy would open his eyes and say something, but Chuck had told him they were keeping Clancy sedated so that he could heal properly. Danny supposed it was for the best, but he didn't like it.

Danny remained in the hospital another two days, most of the time in Father Clancy's room. Nurse Beatrice assured him that if he spoke, Father Navarone would probably be able to hear him, even if he couldn't respond. Danny sat there studying his brother, knowing a hundred things he should say to him and only being able to talk about old memories from when they were kids, when they served in the War together with Flags. He talked about everything he wanted to remember and nothing he wanted to say. Danny wished he could look him in the eye and tell him how much he meant to him. He would probably never have the courage once Clancy woke, but it seemed more cowardly to say it while he slept.

Danny left the hospital two days later. His mother agreed with the hospital staff that he should spend the next week in bed. Her agreement was irrelevant. Danny spent the night in bed, but was up with the kids early the next day. Josiah stayed close to his father, always asking what he could do to help, extremely conscious of Danny's bandaged shoulder. Toby wasn't conscious of anything except that he had his father's complete attention and his grandmother's cookies at the same time. Janey practically hung on Danny for the better part of the next three days, and Danny only objected to her hanging on his right side. So she glued herself to his left side as they walked around their grandparents' farm and played games gathered around Grandma's kitchen table.

From Hartley's confession on the dictation tapes and further questioning of Gimpy, the authorities were able to find Andrew Edwards' remains. The coroner got what he needed and the body was finally, after three years, turned over to the church for proper Christian burial. Danny's mother insisted that Danny stay home and rest when he informed her that he was going to the wake. Still struggling with exhaustion and a lot of pain, Danny obeyed his mother. But nothing would stop him from attending the funeral the following day.

The funeral mass for Andrew Edwards was well attended; and the rumors of his dishonestly and shame of running out on his daughter seemed to have been forgotten by everyone. Danny suffered through the mass, distracted by thoughts of Flags' funeral—which had happened while he was unconscious—and that of Hartley, Duncan and Garnelli. He felt an overpowering burden of having caused so much death, he could hardly stand upright.

When everyone processed out of church following the priest and the coffin toward the parish cemetery, Danny merged into the crowd. After the burial, people gathered around JoAnna. She was dressed in black and the black veil she wore shielded her face from his view. He was glad, he couldn't have borne to see her after all this time with tears in her eyes.

He wandered away from the site and found Flags' grave. The fresh-turned ground was clay-like and littered with small rocks and one wilted bunch of flowers.

He knelt on one knee and said a silent prayer. After a few moments, he reached into his inside suitcoat pocket and pulled out a flask. "Brought you a drink," he murmured softly. He set the flask on the ground before the tombstone. He smiled at the thought of Flags' face alit at the prospect. "Don't worry, Flags. I still haven't caved. It's ginger ale." He wanted to say other things but he knew he couldn't and he fell silent.

It was some minutes before a shadow fell over the stone and he looked up to find JoAnna standing beside him. Danny wiped the beginning of a tear from his eye and stood as JoAnna bent down and placed fresh flowers on the mound of dirt.

She stood close to him, her black veil framing her pretty face, and looked up at him with brown eyes moist with tears. He wanted to pull her into his arms and console her, he wanted to be consoled by her. But he felt too that the hand he wanted to offer her, was stained with guilty blood and he couldn't reach out to her.

He glanced back toward her father's gave, where only the retreating backs of the crowd could be seen as they made their way to their automobiles. Only the graveyard men were left to fill in the grave. "You have my condolences," he said.

Compassion filling her eyes, she nodded. "And you have mine, Danny."

He tried to shift the conversation away from his loss, away from Flags. "Must be nice to have all those friends back, now that they know the truth."

JoAnna gave a fleeting glance to the diminishing crowd. "I suppose so," she murmured. Then she met his gaze directly and admitted, "But the only person that really matters, believed me before my father's body was found."

He looked down at his hand resting in the sling and made no reply.

Embarrassed by his silence at her confession, JoAnna searched for something else to say. "I know Flags was a very dear friend. I'm sorry I didn't get to know him better…"

Danny smiled at the thought. "The two of you would have gotten along fine. He enjoyed a good argument as well."

JoAnna smiled, and tears trickled down her face. "I've been putting fresh flowers on his grave every couple days…they don't last very long with the frost…I don't know if he would have cared, but I thought you would want him to be remembered."

Her compassion touched him so that he couldn't resist touching her and he reached out and clasped her hand in his good hand and gripped it comfortingly as he continued to study the tombstone.

They were silent for a long time, both lost in thoughts of the loved ones they had lost. Finally Danny murmured, "I'll walk you to your car."

JoAnna nodded, in a mixture of emotions; sadness for the loss of the men they were leaving behind them and happy that Danny hadn't relinquished her hand.

***

Danny climbed into his truck and drove. He drove away from the cemetery, away from the city and then back again, the thoughts in his head making as many U-turns as his truck.

At last, he stopped in front of the rectory. How many times had he parked there, and gone in to hash out problems with Clancy? Now he couldn't; Clancy was flat on his back in a hospital bed. Slowly, Danny walked into the nave of the church, illuminated only by the rays of the setting sun trickling through the stained glass windows, enfolding the interior in colorful and deepening shadows.

Danny stood for a long moment, remembering with what anger he had last approached this same altar. Hesitating, he moved slowly toward the sanctuary and knelt at the altar rail.

Kneeling there in His presence Danny felt so much guilt and shame he couldn't look up at the Man on the Cross. Bowing his head, he listened. Listened for words, a feeling, something that would help. It was a long time before he heard anything other than the words of condemnation that kept running back and forth in his mind. *You messed up big time. Clancy wouldn't be in critical condition if you hadn't gone vigilante. Hartley would still be alive. You wanted to stop Balestrini so that no one else would be hurt, but look at all the others you hurt in the process. You wished Hartley dead, and now he is dead.*

Danny saw everything that had happened in two lights. He saw it as he had actually seen it, and he saw it all as the newspapers had interpreted it. *Vengeance. Murder. Vigilante.* The words swam before his eyes, and made him doubt his own motives. He rested his head on his folded hands, uncertain of everything that had happened. He remembered his own thoughts, his temptations, when he had learned what Hartley had done…what he hadn't done…the drive back that night…If he had met up with Hartley sooner than he had, he feared what he might have done… But by the time it all unfolded…Flags being beaten…Hartley standing there shaking at the prospect of meeting up with Balestrini…Danny hadn't felt any anger, he didn't remember having time to feel anything. He had just been trying to survive. He hadn't wanted anyone to get out of that warehouse who would find his kids and JoAnna…he had wanted to get Clancy out of there. *He* had wanted to get out of there alive…

Finally, Danny looked up at the Man on the Cross, almost pleading with Him to condemn him, as he condemned himself.

But the Man on the Cross gazed down with no condemnation; He looked down with only compassion on the wounded man before him. Danny felt a huge weight slipping from his shoulders, as if the burden were even alleviating the physical pain of his injured shoulder. He lost his concerns and self-accusations in the overwhelming feeling of peace that swept over him, and he lost track of time as well.

Until suddenly, he heard footsteps behind him and his instincts stiffened his shoulders and he spun quickly to see who was coming up the aisle. He spotted Father Larson and sank to a sitting position in his relief, feeling slightly foolish for his initial fear.

Father Larson wasn't as relieved. "Daniel Navarone," he exclaimed. "What are you doing here? Is everything alright? Father Navarone…"

Danny smiled reassuringly. "Yes, Father, everything's fine. We're all fine."

"You gave me a fright. I thought perhaps…"

Danny didn't want to hear what he thought had happened. He had to believe that Clancy was going to be all right. He stood and assured the elderly priest, "He's fine. The doctors say he's healing quickly."

"And you?"

Danny looked at his arm in the sling. "Coming along. I just wear this to please my mother."

"I didn't mean your arm," Father Larson stated.

Danny glanced at the priest and then up at the Tabernacle. "I'm doing much better. We had a heart-to-heart." He motioned toward the altar.

Father Larson smiled. "That's good. He likes those. Anything I can help with?"

"Time for confession?"

The elderly priest met Danny's gaze. "Always."

Chapter XXVIII

After Edwards' funeral the situation in Gilmore went crazy. The Minnesota Attorney General heard that Danny was up and about and his men took charge of Danny as if he were a criminal, which technically, his brother Joshua admitted, he was…kidnapping the Chief of Police wasn't going to go unnoticed. Still, though he wasn't under arrest, Danny was prime witness to a great many things.

Balestrini was in jail and awaiting trial. Gimpy was in jail and waiting for his broken nose to heal. Father Clancy's back arm was stronger than he knew.

They had recovered the contents of the safe Flags had hidden in Danny's bowling locker, and found plenty of evidence to bring against Balestrini. Burnquist assigned a lawyer that Danny trusted implicitly and had full confidence that the man would persevere against all odds.

All through the drama, Danny longed for JoAnna, but he never saw her—unless dreaming counted, because he dreamt sweet dreams of her often and he thought of her more often than he dreamt of her. Clancy had awakened in the midst of all the court drama, and Danny also tried to get away to see his brother. But, every time he put on his hat to drive over to see JoAnna or Clancy, there was always a cop or lawyer or newspaper man standing outside his parents' door waiting to waylay him. Danny would have liked to use an old bowling tactic and just disappear for a while but he didn't want to obstruct the flow of justice in getting Balestrini or anyone else behind bars for good. So he tried to hold his temper and be patient. All the while, wanting to see Clancy for himself, and missing JoAnna's smile and her laughter so much it was beginning to put him in a sour mood.

When the month long court case finally wrapped up, Balestrini was convicted of multiple felonies and sent to a State Prison. Gimpy, and other of Balestrini's wiseguys, were in the midst of their own individual trials. The Attorney General's office had enough to get them well on their way to helping Gilmore clean out the gutters of their city. After Balestrini's conviction they sent Danny home because he was looking peaked and they feared they'd lose one of their primary witnesses. Danny took their advice and went home and slept for two days.

Waking up the next morning, Danny found it was nearly November. He was determined to visit Clancy and see JoAnna despite any odds that anyone placed in his way. He had a little bit of fear that by this time she had probably forgotten all about him. Still he was determined to see her and finally speak his piece.

Since the children were not allowed in the hospital, the adults had to take turns going up to see Father Clancy. After early mass, Danny settled his kids and his parents at Joshua's house and headed over to the hospital first. When he walked into the hospital room he found Clancy asleep. Settling into a chair, Danny waited patiently for Clancy to wake up, but he didn't and Danny closed his own eyes.

"Hey! Hey, Dan'l," a voice croaked.

Danny startled awake and sat up straight, a smile touching his face at the familiar voice. "You're awake."

"Yah," Clancy acknowledged, "What about you, why are you sleeping in a chair like an old woman? Mom and Dad kick you out?"

Danny folded his arms and crossed his legs. "I wasn't sleeping. I was praying."

Clancy chuckled, "Yah, I know a little about that kinda prayer myself."

"How do you feel?"

"Tired."

"Really? You've been in bed for a month now. How is that even possible?" Danny joked.

"I don't know. Try being shot in the chest sometime."

"No, thanks. I was stabbed and shot in the same shoulder. That was enough fun for me."

"You look good."

Danny raised an eyebrow. "Thanks. Sorry, I can't say the same about you."

Clancy gave a laugh and then hugged the pillow to his chest to alleviate the pain it caused. "That wasn't kind," he breathed out.

Danny looked genuinely concerned. "Sorry…how do you feel?"

"About as good as I look, apparently. But back to my earlier statement, you look good."

"Why do you keep saying that?"

"Believe me, it's not your charming good looks or lack thereof…I mean you, in your eyes, you look good. Much better than I've seen you in a while."

Danny smiled. "I am. I'm doing much better than I have in a long while."

Clancy asked pointedly, "Jesus or JoAnna?"

Danny scratched his head, and then grinned as the color rose on his neck. "Can I say both, as long as it's in that order?"

Clancy grinned. "Okay by me." He held up a hand to shake Danny's.

But Danny shook his head. "Don't congratulate me yet. I haven't asked her."

"Haven't asked her yet. What are you waiting for?"

"Don't get your dander up. I'm going there as soon as I'm done here."

"Well, you'd done. I'm still breathing, you're good to go."

Danny laughed. "All right, I'm going." Danny clapped his hat back on, grateful that his brother was sending him away, it had been a difficult decision on who to visit first. He walked around the bed but Clancy stopped him, "Dan'l?"

He paused. "Yah?"

"Thanks."

Danny raised one eyebrow. "For what?"

"For saving my life."

Danny offered him a hand. "Right back at 'cha, Little Brother," he said with sincerity.

Clancy shook the hand, and grinned at his brother. "Now go ask her," he ordered.

Unfortunately, Danny was waylaid once again. Before he could leave the room, Debbie made her entrance. She didn't greet either of her brothers but exclaimed, "Daniel Francis, where is your sling?"

Danny, annoyed at being held up once again, argued, "My shoulders good enough."

"*Good enough* is not *good enough*, Danny. When the doctors say you can stop using the sling, you can stop using the sling, and not before," she ordered. "Where is it?"

"Just because you are going to be a nurse, you think you can order every patient around this hospital."

"Just the ones I'm related to," Debbie said, pulling Danny's sling from his pocket. "Which lately seems to be a lot of them."

"You know, Debbie, we still have a mother, you don't have to play the part," Clancy stated.

"Apparently I do. I leave for just a couple months and look what happens! Both of you in trouble and bleeding and…you, Clarence, should lay back and rest."

Danny was losing his patience and headed for the door.

"If you ask me, you both need a keeper," Debbie informed them and busied herself picking up discarded coats and cards and wilting flower petals as she continued. "Speaking of people available for the job, Danny, how's JoAnna?"

Danny stopped, brow furrowed. If she would stop talking he could find out. "I wouldn't know," he replied irritably. "I haven't seen her since her father's funeral."

Debbie planted two fists on her hips. "I know I've missed out on a lot of what goes on here, but wasn't that a long while ago?"

"Yes, it was," he agreed, with frustration. "I've been trying to get over there for four weeks and every time I turn around they drag me here and drag me there…"

"So what are you doing here?"

Danny almost glared at his sister. "My *brother* almost died and I thought I should visit him, do you mind? Besides, I don't need my kid sister to set me up with anyone."

Debbie shrugged, "Well, *I* thought I did a pretty good job. Don't you agree?" She asked Father Clancy.

"I certainly do," Danny responded before Clancy could. Both brothers laughed out loud at the look of utter surprise Debbie gave Danny. She realized she had missed more than gunfights while she was away.

This time Danny wouldn't be stopped. He clapped on his hat and headed for the door. Debbie was sorry to be losing a chance to cross-examine her brother and called, "Will I see you for supper?"

Danny glanced back, a glint in his eye. "Only if she says yes."

***

The aroma of freshly baked cookies permeated Chuck and Sharon's kitchen. JoAnna pulled the last pan from the oven and touched one with the tip of her finger. She smiled at her accomplishment. Usually she burnt at least one pan of a batch of cookies and today she had succeeded without one overly-done cookie.

She walked to the table and began to move the cookies gently to the newspaper she had spread for cooling them. Children's laughter filtered in through the backdoor, although it was closed to keep out the chill.

Several Navarone cousins had congregated in the backyard as their parents went up to visit Father Clarence. After all Chuck and Sharon had done for her on her return, JoAnna was glad to help out by watching the children.

She wished Danny's kids were here; she missed Josiah's intelligent conversation, Toby's silliness and Janey's excitement over little things. Perhaps they would come later and she could at least say hello. JoAnna busied herself, rearranging the cookies and wishing she was visiting with the adult members of the family instead of being left at home with the children as if she were only the nanny…which she was, but that didn't stop her from wishing.

It had been so long since she had seen Danny she couldn't tell what she imagined in his voice and his looks and what she had actually seen. She prayed for him every day, and then worried about the trial and his injuries and if he would ever be able to get over Lilian's death.

Sometimes she worried that he thought her a silly girl, throwing herself at him the way she had the day he left the farm. She had confessed that she loved him! And he hadn't said a thing. Yet, at the funeral she had still been brave enough to tell him that his opinion was the only one that mattered. She blushed at the thought and turned to the dishes at hand.

As the sink filled with water she remembered his words at the farm when he had said that he cared for her. And at the funeral she thought she had seen a look…How could she possibly know what love looked like in a man, when all she had known was Howard. She should be grateful that Danny stayed away, to see him again was bound to be humiliatingly awkward.

Perhaps she should apologize for throwing herself at him, crying on his shoulder when he had much more important things to worry about. Or, maybe it was best to pretend it hadn't happened. Perhaps he didn't remember it at all. After all, there had been a lot going on. A lot had happened. He probably hadn't really even paid attention to it at the time, just a silly girl having a normal everyday nervous breakdown. If she didn't bring it up, he wouldn't remember…but if he did remember and she didn't apologize…Oh, this was all much too confusing. She would just hope that he continued to avoid her…if he was avoiding her…oh dear…

She piled dishes into the sudsy water. Whatever the case was, JoAnna knew she couldn't go back to being his nanny. In the last week she had investigated and found an evening shorthand class beginning in November. She had always found shorthand to be fascinating. Not that she had any desire to learn it, still the fascination would help with motivation she supposed. After the classes, assuming she could learn the concept, she could apply for a secretarial job and get a small apartment of her own. Not that she really wanted to be a secretary. As a matter of fact she didn't really want to live all alone in an apartment either.

She would rather have a house filled with a husband and a bunch of kids, a nice dog—no cats. A backyard, big enough for a fort to be built by the kids, or a giant tree for a tree house. JoAnna dropped a plate she was washing and heard it break against another in the sink. She frowned and searched cautiously for the pieces in her water. The daydream was really a waste of time, rambling in her thoughts as she so often did in her speech. Everything she was pretending to dream up already existed. Danny and his kids, the house. Josiah even had a treehouse half built in the backyard. The only thing that was missing was the dog…and the fact that she didn't belong in the picture. Who was she kidding anyway?

The doorbell rang and JoAnna instantly froze. It was too soon after the arrests for any of Balestrini's henchmen to do anything…at least she hoped it was. Still, she hesitated for a moment more, nervous with Chuck and Sharon out of the house and all the children in the backyard…she didn't want to go to the front of the house but decided she couldn't live behind locked doors forever. Drying her hands on her apron, she walked down the hall and opened the door, secretly hoping that she had taken enough time and no one would be waiting. But when she opened the door, she found Danny standing on the other side; his arm once again without the sling Debbie had insisted he use.

"Danny! I…" her surprise made her speechless. "Sharon's not here," she stumbled.

Danny smiled. "I didn't come to see Sharon. I came to see you." And the sight of her standing in the doorway, her beautiful brown eyes wide with surprise, the same blue bandana tied about her hair, a disheveled apron tied about her waist, made any doubt that may have lingered, vanish completely. He knew exactly what he wanted and how much he wanted her.

JoAnna only replied, "Oh." But didn't move to open the door.

Unsure how to read her reaction he asked, "May I come in? Or shall I say what I came to say from out here?"

"Yes, of course," she invited, he could see color rising in her cheeks but she still didn't move.

He smiled again as he took a step toward the screen door, and asked in a low voice, "Yes, I should say it from out here?"

"Oh, no. I mean, come in." She backed away from the door. "How's Father Clancy?" she asked hurriedly before he could say anything.

"He's doing pretty well, as well as can be expected for having lost half a lung, I suppose."

"That's good. That's great."

"How are you, JoAnna?" he asked and studied her so thoroughly she knew it wasn't asked out of politeness, but because he cared as deeply as he had said.

She caught her breath and could only whisper, "Fine." Danny took a step closer to her and she hurriedly changed the subject. "And the children, how are they? I've missed them so."

She thought she saw a glint of laughter in his eyes, but he responded patiently, "They're fine, too. They're here," he motioned to the outside. "They'll be excited to see you…but I guess cousins took precedence."

"As they should," she agreed.

She finally smiled and Danny almost pulled her into his arms right then, but he had waited this long, he could wait a little longer. Still, he closed the distance with one more step.

JoAnna asked, "Will you be able to move back to your house soon?"

Danny didn't really care about houses at the moment but he replied, "Well, the house is still in chaos; nobody's staying there for a long time. But I know a couple guys pretty handy with hammers. Should be able to get it patched up in time for…" he paused.

"For what?"

He ignored her question. "JoAnna, the day I left you at the farm…"

"That day?" she said hastily, "I thought you had forgotten all about it." She wished he had; she couldn't bear the hurt. All the things she had said, and he hadn't even bothered to respond. She wished he hadn't brought it up.

Her response made him hesitate briefly. But he took a breath and plunged forward anyway, "That night, I wanted to tell you something, but I…I couldn't. So let me say it now."

She looked up at him, her brown eyes wide and anxious for what he would say.

And then out of his mouth, the words he had stayed for so long fell easily, naturally, his voice deep and husky with emotion. "I love you, JoAnna."

Her heart pounded, the emotion in his eyes and his voice captivated her. But, unwelcomed though the image was, JoAnna immediately saw Howard in her mind's eye, and heard him say those same words to her. JoAnna dropped her gaze when she spoke, "Sometimes people say that, but they don't really mean it."

"Have I ever told you a lie?" he asked, his voice low.

She looked up and asked pointedly, "*Have* you ever told me a lie?"

"Once."

Her heart contracted. "What was it?"

He took the last step to close the distance between them and slipped a gentle hand on her waist so she couldn't back away. "I told you you shouldn't worry about the gossips, because I wasn't attracted to you."

Her heart was racing, but she asked playfully, "And now you think I should worry about gossips?"

A smile pulled at the corner of his mouth, "That wasn't the part that was the lie. Now you tell me, did you?" he asked tentatively.

She was getting confused and his hand on her waist wasn't helping her think straight. "Did I what?"

"Say it, but not really mean it?" he demanded, his other hand slipping about her.

"No," she admitted, but it was only a whisper.

His brow furrowed, and he hesitated in pulling her close. "No, you didn't mean it?"

JoAnna's eyes widened in worry. "No! I meant, no I didn't say it and not mean it…I mean I said it and I didn't meant it…Ah! I meant everything I said that night. I do love you…so much…I'm rambling…"

Danny smiled and murmured, "I love it when you do that."

She looked unsure or possibly annoyed. "But you're always *tempted*."

"Marry me and it won't matter."

"What won't matter?"

"That I'm tempted."

"To do *nothing*?" she demanded, her annoyance heightening.

He smiled, drawing her a bit closer to him, "Yes."

"Danny, that still doesn't make any sense," she murmured, her heartrate quickening. "How can you be tempted to do *nothing*?"

"I wasn't. I was tempted to do this." He bent down and kissed her lips. She kissed him back and although he liked it very much when her arms moved up and about his neck, he pulled back a bit. "Only that'd be better if we were married," he murmured.

"You're gonna marry Miss JoAnna?" an excited voice asked from the porch.

Danny and JoAnna both looked over to see Toby's face pressed against the screen door.

Danny smiled at the interruption. "I don't know," he looked back at JoAnna, "Will you marry me?"

Before JoAnna could respond, Toby exclaimed, "Gee, that would be swell! Then we'll have a mother! We can go on picnics and you could sew my patches on my Scout Uniform."

JoAnna laughed, "I did that before."

"I know. But gee, having it sewn on by your mother is better than by the nanny…even if she is the same person."

Danny interrupted, "One thing at a time, Tobias. She hasn't answered my question." Danny pulled JoAnna back toward him, his arms encircling her a little tighter. "How about it, Miss JoAnna? Are you gonna marry me?"

She looked up, her eyes sparkling. "Well, really, Daniel Navarone. I don't go around kissing men I don't intend to marry. What kind of a girl do you think I am?"

He met her gaze. "Crazy," he murmured. "But I like crazy."

She smiled up at him.

They heard Toby groan. "That's no answer."

She turned her head and smiled at the boy, "Yes, Toby. The answer is yes. I'm going to marry your father and yes I'm going to be your mother. And yes, I'll sew badges on your Cub Scout Uniform."

Toby grinned but didn't reply to the couple. Instead he turned and bolted from the porch and they heard him announce to his siblings and cousins outside, and consequently to the entire neighborhood, "Daddy's gonna marry Miss JoAnna!"